CHASING
STARLIGHT

ALSO BY TERI BAILEY BLACK

Girl at the Grave

CHASING STARLIGHT

TERI BAILEY BLACK

**TOR
TEEN**

A TOM DOHERTY ASSOCIATES BOOK
NEW YORK

CHASING STARLIGHT

Copyright © 2020 by Teri Bailey Black

A Tor Teen Book
Published by Tom Doherty Associates
120 Broadway
New York, NY 10271

www.tor-forge.com

Tor® is a registered trademark of Macmillan Publishing Group, LLC.

The Library of Congress Cataloging-in-Publication Data is available upon request.

ISBN 978-0-7653-9951-9 (hardcover)
ISBN 978-0-7653-9953-3 (ebook)

Our books may be purchased in bulk for promotional, educational, or business use. Please contact your local bookseller or the Macmillan Corporate and Premium Sales Department at 1-800-221-7945, extension 5442, or by email at MacmillanSpecialMarkets@macmillan.com.

First Edition: 2020

Printed in the United States of America

0 9 8 7 6 5 4 3 2 1

FOR MY GRANDFATHER JAMES ANDERSON, WHO WORKED AT THE MGM MOTION PICTURE STUDIO AS A PROPMAKER FOR THIRTY YEARS, THROUGH THE GREAT DEPRESSION AND THE GOLDEN AGE OF HOLLYWOOD

CHASING STARLIGHT

CHAPTER 1

1938 CALIFORNIA

When Kate Hildebrand had pictured stepping off the train in Hollywood, she'd imagined palm trees and sunshine, not this inky-black night and strange, warm wind. A loose sign banged in the restless air and leaves rustled.

She stood in the shaft of light spilling from the train, her heart thumping harder than it should have, wishing she'd taken an earlier train to arrive in daylight.

Kate hated the dark.

Behind her, the Santa Fe Super Chief screamed a warning whistle and chugged into motion, moving on to San Diego. In front of her, the other teenaged girl who'd disembarked was greeted by a large family, everyone hugging and talking at once, and the man who'd dozed most of the day dropped his suitcase to embrace a woman holding a baby. Farther away, a cluster of men in suits and hats shook hands.

No one approached Kate.

She lifted her chin to see better below the brim of her stylish blue fedora, but didn't find her grandfather.

Not that his face was all that familiar to her.

He'd come to San Francisco for Thanksgiving when Kate was eight—an attempt at reconciliation with her mother that hadn't gone so well—and he'd returned for her mother's funeral a few years after that, but Kate hadn't seen him because she hadn't attended. Since then, there'd been a few birthday cards and awkward phone calls, but Kate knew more about her grandfather from movie magazines than memories, and those magazines were a decade old, from his heyday in the 1920s.

No one had written about silent film star Oliver Banks in a very long time.

The station wasn't as grand as she'd expected, just a wide stretch of concrete with a stucco building and two lanterns casting more shadow than light. No movie stars arriving to swarms of fans, like she'd seen in magazines. But then, this wasn't actually Hollywood, just the neighboring town where her grandfather lived—Pasadena.

The other travelers drifted into the dark, taking their cheerful voices with them, leaving Kate alone with her luggage—two enormous trunks, a small suitcase, a cosmetic case, and three hat boxes. Her entire life packed into a few square feet of space.

"He's expecting you," Aunt Lorna had insisted yesterday as she'd packed for her own trip in another direction—which for Aunt Lorna meant tossing clothes on the bed for their housekeeper Hattie to pack. "I sent a telegram and it's all set. I hope you've finished packing."

"You know I have." Lists written. Tasks crossed off. Everything Kate owned neatly folded and organized, her telescope tucked between sweaters.

"Which outfit for boarding the ship?" Aunt Lorna had asked. "Something pretty?" She'd held up an apricot-colored dress. "Or the expected nautical?" In her other hand, she'd held up navy with gold buttons.

"Nautical," Kate had advised without much thought because Aunt Lorna looked chic in everything. She had the same lean figure as all the Hildebrands—including Kate—and the same red hair, cut chin length, carefully curled and tucked into place. Aunt Lorna's shade was bright copper, helped by a bottle; Kate's, auburn.

Aunt Lorna had held up a fox stole, the engagement ring on her left hand sparkling like a block of ice. "What does one wear in South America, do you think?"

"Safari hats, I should guess."

"How ghastly."

Kate had dropped to the sofa under the window, stretching out her long legs. "What if I despise Hollywood?"

"Oh, darling, how could you possibly despise Hollywood? All those movie stars and pool parties."

"I doubt my grandfather dines with Cary Grant. His friends will all be ancient." She'd hesitated before asking, "Can I come back if I hate it?"

Aunt Lorna had given her a sideways look. "You've burned that bridge, I'm afraid." Two weeks ago, her fiancé had found Kate's list of *Seven Reasons for Not Marrying Mr. Norton,* and his requirement that Kate not live with them after the wedding had become nonnegotiable. "Besides," Aunt Lorna said in a gentler tone. "You don't want to live with him any more than he wants to live with you."

No, Kate didn't want to live with Mr. Norton, who insisted on eating in silence to aid his digestion. But she didn't want to leave home either. "I'm the first girl to ever be president of the astronomy club, and I'm leaving before I even get started. I'm going to miss the yacht club dance next week. And Meg's birthday party. I just wish you'd waited until I was done with high school to get married."

"Sadly, wishes don't pay the butcher."

"Or the housekeeper," Hattie muttered, stuffing newspaper into the toes of glittering party shoes.

Uncle Harvey had died two years ago, but Aunt Lorna had never seemed to grasp the concept that continuing to spend lavishly without an income led to an empty bank account. She owed every dress shop in town, and poor Hattie hadn't been paid in months. Mr. Norton and his gold-mining fortune had come along just in time. They would be married by the ship's captain, and then spend a month in South America inspecting Mr. Norton's gold mines—his idea of a romantic honeymoon—before returning to Aunt Lorna's house in San Francisco. While they were away, the house would be gutted and remodeled, Kate's bedroom turned into an office for Mr. Norton.

"Hattie, I want all the jewelry in my cosmetic case so I can keep it close on the ship," Aunt Lorna said, holding up a strand of pearls. "And don't forget about the movers tomorrow, putting everything in storage while the house is remodeled. And Kate's car—"

"Yes, ma'am, picked up by the new owners." Tactful Hattie. She knew Kate's car was being repossessed by the bank—one debt Mr. Norton refused to pay.

Her darling little roadster gone. Her bedroom demolished. Even Aunt Lorna—the closest thing she'd had to a mother in four years—sailing away after a quick kiss at the train station that morning.

This was Kate's new life.

And no one to greet her.

She left her luggage on the platform and entered the small station, which was deserted except for an elderly man behind the counter. "If you're going to San Diego, you missed it."

"I just arrived. I was expecting someone to pick me up."

The man pointed to a pay phone in the corner.

Kate slid a coin into the slot, waited for the operator to pick up, and then said, "Oliver Banks in Pasadena."

"One moment, please."

The ticket agent looked at her more closely after hearing the name. Kate turned away, tugging at the brim of her hat.

"I'm sorry, but I don't have a listing."

"Can we try the address?" Kate reached into her purse for the worn envelope from an old birthday card she'd thought to grab as she was packing, and read aloud, "Thirteen fifty Starlight Circle."

"One moment, please." The line crackled with static. "I'm sorry, but I don't show an active line at that address."

An uneasy feeling crept through her. How could her grandfather not have a phone? "Are you sure?" She repeated the address.

"No active line, I'm sorry."

"Thank you." Kate hung up and turned slowly.

The elderly ticket agent squinted at her. "Say . . . you're not that granddaughter who—"

"I need a taxi," she said shortly.

His expression softened. "Sure, I'll call Ernie. Take him five minutes to get here." He reached for the phone behind the counter.

Her hands trembled as she returned the envelope to her purse.

Always the same when someone recognized her: initial excitement, followed by morbid curiosity, shifting into pity as they remembered the grim details of the newspaper story that had captivated the world four years ago. At least newspaper photos were black and white, so her red hair didn't give her away.

Ernie took fifteen minutes to arrive and looked so bent and frail, Kate feared he would snap as he carried her luggage to the taxi. He put one of the trunks on the back seat, which meant Kate had to sit up front with him.

They rolled through a downtown area that looked closed on a Sunday night—except for a nightclub called the Galaxy, with a couple in evening clothes arguing out front. Kate heard distant jazz music as they passed.

The taxi turned into a residential neighborhood, and the tension inside her settled a little. Even in the dark, she could see that the houses were grand, set back behind sweeping lawns. Her grandfather had quit acting a long time ago, and he'd probably lost a fortune in the stock market crash and depression, like everyone else, but it looked like he still managed to live well. Her gaze lingered on a particularly beautiful gray house as the taxi pulled up at the curb. "Is this it?" she asked, pleased.

"*That's* it," Ernie corrected, rolling the car forward to stop in front of an imposing stucco mansion with dark wood trim and a tile roof. Not as lovely as its neighbor, but still large and impressive.

Then Kate noticed the plywood over one of the upstairs windows. The broken railing on the balcony. Tall weeds covering the lawn. The front door gaped open for some reason, casting a golden light that was more eerie than welcoming, shadowed by overgrown trees.

Her hopes sank. "Are you sure?"

"If you're looking for Oliver Banks, this is the place. Lived here as long as I can remember."

Kate waited near the taxi as Ernie made several trips with her luggage, then had no choice but to pay the man and watch him drive away.

The trees rustled in the strange, warm wind.

She looked up at the full moon, glad she hadn't missed it in the chaos of traveling, and her nerves calmed a little. Jupiter's tenth and eleventh moons had been discovered at Mount Wilson Observatory, only a few miles from here—the world's largest telescope, one reason not to completely loathe the idea of living with her grandfather.

Kate made her way up the long front path, clutching her purse, stepping around gaps in the bricks. Ernie had placed her luggage just inside the open door, so she entered as well. She started to close the door but saw that it had been purposefully propped by a large bust of Beethoven, so she left it ajar.

She stood in a grand foyer with terra cotta tiles underfoot and a curving staircase hugging the left. A rectangular table dominated the space—a dining table by the look of it, oversized and out of place, covered in strange clutter. An empty fishbowl next to an ornate vase, next to a crate of soda bottles. She noticed a hulking figure in the corner and gasped, stepping back, before realizing it was only a stuffed bear on its hind legs, wearing a Three Musketeers hat.

Kate inhaled and straightened the front of her traveling suit. "Stop it," she hissed. This was her grandfather's house. Nothing dangerous here.

But then, why hadn't he come out to greet her? He must have heard Ernie bringing in the luggage.

Several arched openings led deeper into the house. The one on the right revealed a living room with lights on, as messy and strangely decorated as the foyer. Much of the room was out of view, so she called out, "Hello? Grand—"

The whine of a violin cut her off—one ominous note hanging in the air . . . stretching . . . making Kate hold her breath . . . before sliding into an eerie melody. More of a keening wail than a song, full of dark, jarring notes that made her skin crawl. Kate glanced over her shoulder at the staircase, half expecting to find a vampire lurking.

She hadn't known her grandfather was musical.

Cautiously, she made her way to the living room, each step bringing more of it into view. She stopped just past the archway.

At the far left, another wide opening led to what must have been the dining room, but without a table. In the empty space, a bald man played the violin, his body swaying with each sweep of the bow. Not her movie star grandfather. This man was short and stocky, with a face as angry as the music pouring out of him.

He seemed unaware of her, so she took a moment to inspect the living room. Two sofas faced each other: one, an Art Deco fan shape that belonged in a stylish city apartment; the other, tufted green velvet that would have looked at home in a manor house library. The gilded coffee table was cluttered with dirty dishes and newspapers. A tall bookcase was in the middle of the room, next to a wingback chair, its shelves overstuffed with books and yellow *National Geographic* magazines. And, absurdly, there was a rusty wheelbarrow near the front window, filled with hats.

The music stopped abruptly, leaving throbbing silence. Kate looked to the dining room and found the violinist glaring at her, the bow frozen on the strings.

She straightened. "Excuse me, I'm looking for Oliver Banks."

"Who are you?" he asked with narrow-eyed suspicion.

"I'm—" She stopped herself, not wanting to reward his rudeness. "This is his house, isn't it?"

"Sure, sweetie, but he doesn't want visitors." The stocky man turned to the side, putting her out of view, and started playing again.

Kate wavered, wanting to say something scathing but not wanting to shout over the music. Finally, she turned away.

Back in the foyer, another arched opening led toward the back of the house, where dim light leaked from a room on the distant left. The kitchen, she guessed, but she would have to walk down a dark hall to get there.

She wished she'd arranged to arrive in daylight, when she was capable of confidence and easy smiles. Her other self.

A haggard-looking dog padded from the back of the house, paused at the edge of the foyer, then whimpered and returned the way it had come.

Kate followed the dog, clutching her purse at her waist, angry at her own racing heart. She heard a masculine voice in the kitchen and tried to reassure herself that her grandfather would be delighted to see her. That he'd only lost track of time. But the sinister music had crept into her bones, and everything about this place seemed strangely off-kilter, like one of those funny houses at the carnival, where the floors tilted and walls leaned.

At the end of the hall, the back door was open, revealing a moonlit yard. Kate felt a tickle of fresh air and suddenly understood the propped front door, allowing a cross breeze on such a warm night. A sensible idea, which calmed her nerves. Kate liked sensible.

She entered the kitchen on the left.

And stopped short.

A teenaged boy with his hair slicked back lay on the floor, his head flopped to the side, his eyes staring lifelessly. Another teenaged boy glowered down at him, breathing hard, holding a butcher knife. "You put up a good fight," he said in a dark tone. "I like that." He turned to look at an old man in striped pajamas cowering against the kitchen counter. "Now you."

"Please," the old man whimpered, lifting his hands. "Take my money but leave me alone."

Her grandfather, Kate realized with a little yelp of horror, and the boy whirled to face her, gripping the knife.

Never had she seen such eyes—sizzling with hatred, accentuated by dark, arched eyebrows on fair skin. The overhead light cast his face into hollow shadows beneath stark cheekbones. The face of the devil's son. His eyes flickered surprise at seeing her.

"No," he growled, taking a step toward her.

Kate turned and ran, banging into the door frame. She straightened and ran on, down the hall, through the wailing music. She rounded the dining table in the foyer. Tripped over one of her hat boxes. Gasped and stumbled around the trunks—out the front door, into the dark night.

A gust of dry wind tossed leaves across the front path as she ran.

CHAPTER 2

One of Kate's heels caught in the uneven bricks, jolting her to a stop. She pulled her foot out of the pump and continued in a lopsided limp—then stopped with a cry of frustration, yanked off the other shoe, and tossed it. She continued down the front walkway, the bricks sharp on her stockinged feet, her skirt too tight for more than prancing steps.

She couldn't outrun him like this. Her only hope was to hide. She glanced back to make sure he hadn't appeared, then darted into the weedy grass on her left, aiming for the dark row of trees dividing her grandfather's property from the beautiful house next door. As she reached the cover of the low-hanging branches, she heard him in the doorway and stopped, whirling to look, hoping the shadows hid her.

The boy paused on the front stoop, silhouetted against the light, still gripping the knife. He turned his head to search the dark yard, giving her a glimpse of his evil smirk in the half-light. "Come out, come out," he called, sounding amused by the chase. "I'm not going to hurt you." He seemed to realize the knife proved otherwise and lowered it, pressing it against his thigh.

Kate's heart beat wildly enough to hear. She hoped her grandfather had escaped out the back door.

A car started on the road, and the boy trotted toward the curb, stopping with a growl of frustration as the car drove by. He stared after it, then turned back to the house, not looking so amused now that he thought she'd driven away for help.

Moonlight illuminated his face as he walked. Eighteen or nineteen, she guessed, wearing a sleeveless undershirt tucked into belted trousers. Dark hair, tousled by the wind, and those devilish eyes. He bent to pick up one of her shoes, then took a few steps and picked up the other. He held still for a moment, running his gaze over the dark yard, then continued to the house, taking her shoes with him. He pushed the bust of Beethoven out of the way, and the door swung shut, cutting off the light.

Kate exhaled a gasping breath. She had to call the police. She turned and pushed her way through the shrubbery, and then ran across the neighbor's enormous lawn, her silk stockings slipping on the grass. She banged on the door and pressed the doorbell several times.

A pretty, blond girl opened the door, looking annoyed. "We heard the first knock."

"Your phone—I need to call the police!" Kate pushed her way past the girl and spun in a circle in a gleaming foyer. "Where is it?"

"Bonnie, what's going on?" a feminine voice called from upstairs.

Kate tilted her head back and saw an elegant blond woman at the top of the staircase. "I need to call the police! There's a boy next door with a knife. He chased me, and I think he—" She didn't want to say it.

"Bonnie, lock the front door, and then show her the phone." The woman started down the staircase, adding in an undertone, "No need to guess which house."

Bonnie turned the lock and led the way into the living room, glancing back at Kate with wide eyes. "What happened?"

Kate spotted a white telephone on a side table and snatched up the receiver. "Hello?" She tapped the holder a few times. "Hello, are you there?"

"Central," a woman's voice answered with maddening calm.

"I need the police—and hurry!"

The blond woman entered the living room, dressed in a long gown, as if going out for the night. "Are you all right, dear? Has one of those dreadful people hurt you?"

"I'm fine. I ran outside when I saw."

"Saw *what*?" Bonnie asked, fascinated. She looked a little younger than Kate, maybe fifteen or sixteen.

"Pasadena Police Department," a man's voice said on the line.

"I need to report a murder. He had a—"

"What's the address?"

"Address?" Kate reached for the birthday card envelope and realized she no longer had her purse. She must have dropped it along the way.

The blond woman took the receiver. "Thirteen forty-eight Starlight Circle. That's my address, and I live next door. This is Dorothy Fairchild."

"*Murder,*" Bonnie breathed. "Was it a thief? They're always leaving that door open."

Her grandfather had begged the boy to take his money rather than hurt him. "I think so. They were in the kitchen, and I—"

"*They?*" Bonnie's blue eyes widened. "Was it gangsters from that club? Did they have Tommy guns?"

"No—no, nothing like that."

"Police are on their way." The blond woman hung up the phone and turned to Kate, her beautiful face tight with worry. "You say someone's been killed? I hope . . . I hope it wasn't Mr. Banks."

"No, a younger man."

Bonnie gasped. "Not the nice Mexican boy?"

"I don't know." Kate forced herself to remember the lifeless young man on the floor. "I don't think he was Mexican. And the one who did it—" The memory of the pale, shadowed face and menacing eyes sent a chill through her. "He wasn't either."

The woman touched Kate's arm. "I'm so glad you came to us. That house is nothing but trouble lately. I'm Mrs. Fairchild, and this is my daughter, Bonnie."

"I'm Kate Hil—" She stopped before giving the name that would link her to the house next door. "I'm so sorry for barging in."

"Don't be silly." The woman ran her gaze over Kate's stylish traveling suit and hat. "You don't look like the sort of girl who would be at that house. Are they friends of yours?"

Kate hesitated before saying, "No." She barely knew her grandfather.

"Well, it's a dreadful situation. A retired actor who takes in boarders. Unsavory people coming and going at all hours."

"One of them is a *communist*," Bonnie said. "But the Mexican boy seems nice."

Her mother cast her a sideways look. "How do you know so much about them?"

"Just what I overhear. The communist has a loud voice."

Kate looked at the dark front window. Aunt Lorna couldn't have known, or she wouldn't have sent her here. "Do you think the police will take long? I'm worried about . . . the other people in the house."

"The police station isn't far. I'll wait outside and show them which house it is."

"Mama, there's a killer on the loose!"

"I'm sure it was only one of those boarders, and he's run off by now. But you stay inside."

"If you're going, I'm going." Bonnie headed for the door.

Kate hesitated, and then followed the mother and daughter into the night. The trees blocked their view, so they made their way down to the street and walked cautiously to stand in front of her grandfather's house, remaining back in the shadows of the trees. Light glowed around the edges of the living room drapes, but Kate couldn't hear any violin music.

The strange, warm wind stirred the branches overhead.

Bonnie leaned closer. "I'm an actress. We were supposed to start filming tomorrow, but—"

"Not now, Bonnie," her mother said.

Kate hugged her waist, staring at the living room window. She hoped the violinist had escaped. He must be one of the boarders.

Bonnie whispered, "Do you know the boy named Aurelio?"

Kate shook her head. "No."

"He seems awfully nice. Sometimes he waves at me across the yard."

Mrs. Fairchild looked at Kate. "If you don't know any of them, why were you at the house?"

Kate was saved from answering by the arrival of two police cars. She quickly told the officers everything she'd seen, describing the boy with dark hair holding the knife, the old man in striped pajamas—without admitting her relationship—and the violinist. The policemen fanned out in the dark, two cautiously entering the front door, one going around to the back, and one staying behind on the driveway.

Mrs. Fairchild said, "I've seen that boy you described with the knife, and he does look like trouble. He's one of the boarders."

Maybe he hadn't paid his rent, and when her grandfather had tried to kick him out, he'd snapped.

Bonnie said, "Mr. Banks deserves to get murdered if he lets people like that live with him."

"No, dear," her mother said quietly. "He was a wonderful man before he fell on hard times."

Hard times. Kate stared at the hulking stucco mansion, wondering where she would sleep tonight. There might be a late train back to San Francisco, but where would she stay once she got there? The furniture had been moved into storage today and her car repossessed. Aunt Lorna was on a ship in the Pacific Ocean, and Hattie had gone to Sacramento to stay with her sister while the house was remodeled.

Bonnie leaned close to Kate's ear. "I can see into their house from my bedroom window. A new man moved in a few weeks ago. None of them like him very much, but he won't leave."

A gust of warm wind rattled the trees.

Voices drew Kate's attention to the front door. She caught her breath as the boy who'd had the knife came into view. But he wasn't wearing handcuffs, he was laughing with a policeman.

"What's going on?" she murmured, doubts churning.

The policeman left the house and came toward them. "No one dead in there, just a bunch of actors rehearsing a scene." He gave an easy laugh, his gaze settling on Kate. "Sorry for the fright, miss, but this is Oliver Banks's house. You've heard of him?"

Her gaze darted back to the boy in the doorway, who lifted a hand in distant greeting, looking amused. An actor. Her face warmed with embarrassment. "Yes. I've heard of him."

"So . . . no one's been murdered?" Bonnie asked.

"Not tonight. I'll get home in time to kiss the kids good night." The policeman chuckled as he turned away.

The boy disappeared into the house, leaving the door propped open with Beethoven, allowing Kate to hear the laughter and ringing voices inside. Shadows moved behind the living room drapes.

Her face burned.

"You mustn't blame yourself," Mrs. Fairchild said, touching her arm.

"I'm so sorry for disrupting your evening," Kate said stiffly.

"Don't be silly. We were happy to help."

"It was exciting," Bonnie said.

"Do you need a ride home?" Mrs. Fairchild asked. "I was about to go out and could drop you off. Do you live far?"

Everything Kate owned was inside her grandfather's house, but that didn't make it home. "No, not far." They would learn the truth eventually. "I live here now, with my grandfather, Oliver Banks."

"*Grandfather?*" Bonnie's eyes widened with new fascination. "But that means you're—" She didn't need to say the name. Everyone in the world knew about Oliver Banks's granddaughter.

Mrs. Fairchild studied Kate more closely in the moonlight, her expression softening. "I see it now. You dear girl."

Kate didn't want their pity. She'd had four years of suffocating pity. She turned and made her way up the brick path to the door.

CHAPTER 3

From the foyer, Kate saw four people gathered around the strange jumble of furniture in the living room.

Her grandfather stood near the fireplace, talking in an animated voice, older and grayer than she'd expected. When he'd come for Thanksgiving, nine years ago, he'd still looked like Captain Powell, the swashbuckling sea captain he'd played in silent films, fighting off pirates with clashing sword fights. Now, he wore striped pajamas with a food stain on the lapel—obviously not concerned about picking her up at the train station.

He noticed her in the foyer, and his face lifted in a welcoming smile. "Aha! Our brave heroine dares to return!" The charming dimples were still there, and the liveliness in his face that had made him the biggest movie star in the world for a decade. "Enter, good citizen, and allow us to prove we aren't quite as nefarious as we appear!"

Kate smoothed the front of her stylish traveling suit and entered the room with as much dignity as she could manage in her stocking feet. "I'm quite embarrassed for all the fuss I caused."

"Nonsense! Most fun we've had all week, wasn't it, boys? And

Lemmy is quite alive, as you can see." Her grandfather lifted an arm toward the fan-shaped sofa.

The young man she'd thought was dead gave her a smirking wink. "Scared you, didn't I? Guess you were wrong, Hugo—I *am* a good actor."

"At playing dead, sure, I'll give you that."

Kate's gaze shifted to the source of the voice.

The dark-haired boy who'd wielded a knife sat in the wing-back chair, the haggard dog at his feet. Handsome, in a rebellious sort of way. Sharp cheekbones and those frightening eyes, staring back with an amused tilt of his lips that struck a nerve in her.

She straightened her posture and looked away. She wanted her shoes back.

The last person in the room—the bald violinist—glared at her from the green velvet sofa. Up close, she saw that a scar ran from his mouth to his ear, as if his cheek had been sliced open and sewn back together.

"You must join our merry party!" her grandfather cried, lifting both arms. "A pretty girl like you is surely here for Aurelio, who's at work tonight, but you're welcome to join us while you wait. Come now, don't be shy—at least tell us your name."

The truth hit her. He didn't recognize her. She'd come all this way to live with him, with nowhere else to go, and he'd been too busy playing with his friends to remember her arrival. Which was as humiliating as it was infuriating.

Kate went with the fury. "You were expecting some other granddaughter to move in tonight?"

The room fell silent.

Her grandfather gaped. "*Kitty?* What are you doing here?"

"Aunt Lorna sent a telegram."

He shook his head, befuddled.

"I told you," snapped the violinist. "I put it on that junk pile of a desk of yours three days ago."

"Well, then, that explains it." Her grandfather's dimples returned. "And here you are—a lovely surprise. Just a lovely— wonderful—marvelous surprise." He crossed the room and pulled her into an awkward embrace that smelled of hair oil and stale laundry. He leaned back to see her better, clasping her shoulders. "I should have recognized that ginger hair. Goodness, look how big you are! You must be—what now? Fifteen?"

"Seventeen, Grandfather."

"Oh, call me Ollie, everyone does. Seventeen, of course, born in '21. I was never any good at math." He released her shoulders, his smile starting to look a bit forced. "So, tell me, my dear—to what do I owe this delightful visit?"

He really didn't know. "Aunt Lorna is getting married, and her new husband doesn't want—" Kate darted a look at the three strangers in the room; it was none of their business. "I'm supposed to live with you now until I leave for college next fall. She sent the telegram."

His alarm showed for a heartbeat before he schooled his face into the role of loving grandfather. "Well, that's marvelous, isn't it? Did you hear that, boys? Kitty has come to live with us."

"I go by Kate now."

"Kate, of course, that's how you sign your letters. All grown up and come to live with me. Marvelous."

"One big, happy family," drawled Lemmy, the young man she'd thought was dead.

"You must meet my boarders. Over here, we have Reuben." Her grandfather lifted a hand toward the green sofa.

The bald violinist gave her a scowling nod. His scarred cheek sagged slightly, giving him the gloomy look of a bulldog. About forty, she guessed.

Ollie added in an undertone, "You mustn't mind his grumpy nature. He can't help it."

"Born on a Monday," Reuben said darkly, as if that explained everything.

"And this is Lemmy—still breathing, I'm happy to say." But

her grandfather's smile faltered as he nodded toward the young man on the fan-shaped sofa. "Lemmy's only been with us for a few weeks, but we're enjoying getting to know him, aren't we, boys?"

The other two remained silent.

Lemmy snapped his chewing gum. "Can't beat the rent. I might never leave." He winked at the violinist, who glowered back.

"And lastly, but certainly not least—" Her grandfather's voice dropped to a dramatic low. "We have our murderous villain . . . *Hugo Quick.*"

Kate tried to feel indifferent as she looked at the boy in the wingback chair, but she hadn't forgotten the way he'd looked holding a knife. His eyes bored into her, the amusement gone now that he'd learned she was the girl from the headlines. "Welcome, Kate. Sorry I frightened you." His voice had an underlayer of rasp in it. "Ollie was showing me how to retain some dignity in the role of homicidal maniac. I'm in a play that lacks nuance, with an idiot for a director."

"Play," the violinist Reuben scoffed. "Back-alley horror show, more like it. Stabbing pretty girls while a bunch of perverts watch from the audience. Buckets of fake blood."

Hugo shrugged, still looking at Kate. "The role is less than ideal." His dark hair was overgrown, bangs falling across his forehead.

"But a worthy start," her grandfather declared. "A chance to practice your craft on a real stage. Some producer will be out for a night of debauchery and notice your excellent stabbing technique, and before you know it, your name will be on theater marquees across the country." Ollie swept a hand. *"Hugo Quick."*

A name as distinctive as his sinister features. Kate looked away. "You all live here?"

"Plus Aurelio," her grandfather said. "Who will steal your heart the moment he smiles at you. Don't say I didn't warn you."

Kate did a quick count. "Five of you living in this house?"

"Oh, plenty of space. Reuben and Lemmy share the big room upstairs, Aurelio has the small, and Hugo sleeps in the backyard."

"Pool house," Hugo elaborated in his low rasp. Whenever he spoke, the dog lifted its head.

Her grandfather spread his arms. "And that, my dear, is our cast of characters. I have more rooms than I need, and this sorry lot needs a roof over their heads, so it works out perfectly."

Except for me, Kate thought. If there *were* an extra room upstairs, she couldn't sleep mere feet away from a bunch of men. Couldn't share their bathroom.

All at once, she felt the weight of the day. Waking up before dawn to get to the train on time. Hugging Aunt Lorna goodbye. The long, rumbling train ride. Finally arriving, only to find this strange old mansion with a killer in the kitchen. Calling the police and making a fool of herself.

She felt light-headed. If she didn't sit soon, she would collapse. Or worse—burst into tears.

"Give her Aurelio's room," Lemmy said, working his chewing gum. "He can sleep on the sofa."

"Oh, no—my room, of course," her grandfather said quickly.

Kate's good manners snapped. "I can't sleep in this house. Surely you see that. I'll have to stay in a hotel until I can reach Aunt Lorna."

"Oh, yes, a hotel—of course. The Huntington is nearby. Lovely establishment."

"You kidding me?" the bald violinist said. "You can't afford the Huntington. Or any hotel." He looked at Kate. "Can you?"

She opened her mouth . . . and closed it. She had some money in her purse, but it would disappear fast at a nice hotel, and she needed it for a train ticket out of here. "Not at the moment."

Hugo rose from the wingback chair, the dog rising with him. "Take the pool house. It's private."

The fact that he was only half-dressed suddenly seemed more obvious, his sleeveless undershirt tight across his chest. His bare shoulders were nice, carved with lean muscle, with a splash of sunburn as if he'd been outside without a shirt today.

Heat rose in her face, and she looked away. She couldn't sleep in his bed. "No, I'll . . . I'll sleep on the sofa. Tomorrow, I'll figure something out. I have friends in San Francisco."

But none she could live with. After Mr. Norton had insisted she move out, she'd made a list of friends who might take her in for a year—only three names, and the awkward rejections had stung. Aunt Lorna had finally made arrangements for Kate to live with old Mrs. Foster next door. Then, three days ago, Mrs. Foster had died, leaving only one option. A telegram had been sent, and Aunt Lorna had said everything was set.

Now, she saw that if her grandfather *had* seen the telegram, his answer would have been no. He wasn't going to turn out four boarders—four friends—to accommodate a granddaughter who was a stranger.

"The old housekeeper's room!" her grandfather cried, his face brightening.

"It's full of junk," Reuben said.

"Oh, it's perfect. Come, come—everybody come!" Ollie led the way toward the back of the house, calling out as they filed after him, "Dear Mrs. Pace! How I miss her roast chicken and apple pie!"

Reuben muttered, "If you'd paid her, she might have stuck around."

They entered the kitchen where Lemmy had lain dead an hour ago—a large room with a black-and-white checkered floor and a long table in the center. Her grandfather continued into a hallway in the back corner, but it was too dark for Kate, so she lingered in the well-lit kitchen.

"You eaten recently?" a low voice asked behind her shoulder.

She whirled to see Hugo standing in nearly the same spot he'd stood an hour ago, leering over a dead body. She stepped back, pressing a hand to her stomach. "No, but I don't think I can eat much."

"That's good, because we don't have much." He smiled and pulled out a chair at the table. "How about eggs and toast?"

Kate hesitated, then cautiously sat. "Just eggs, thank you." She saw a couple of sticky patches on the table and kept her hands on her lap. The sink overflowed with dishes. The floor needed mopping. The boxy appliances looked ancient.

What a fool she'd been, coming to live with an old bachelor, expecting anything different.

Hugo heated a pan and cracked eggs into a bowl, cooking with ease, knowing where to find a whisk.

Reuben carried out a couple of old paint cans from the housekeeper's room, Lemmy walked out with empty wooden crates, and her grandfather dumped a stack of fat phone books in the corner of the kitchen.

"I should help," Kate murmured without really meaning it.

Hugo set a plate of perfectly scrambled eggs in front of her, followed by a cup of warmed milk sprinkled with cinnamon. Kate only sipped the milk to be polite, but its warmth was so comforting, she kept drinking.

Hugo disappeared for a few minutes, then returned with her shoes. "I think these are yours."

She avoided looking at him as she slipped the pumps onto her feet. "I don't suppose you found my purse? I dropped it somewhere."

"I'll look for it after I bring back your luggage. I was thinking I'd put the trunks in the laundry room since your room is so small."

Your room, as if she planned to stay.

"Very well." With shoes on her feet, she felt more like herself.

Reuben walked by with an armload of pillows and bedsheets, then returned a few minutes later to tell her the housekeeper's room was "clean enough." Kate doubted that but stood, tugging her jacket straight.

The short hallway didn't have a light, only the glow from the kitchen. She passed the laundry room and a small bathroom, then paused in the threshold to the housekeeper's room, her gaze skimming a sagging bed and nightstand. Ollie and Lemmy stood near the dresser, arguing over the straightness of a picture on the wall.

Better than the sofa, at least, but too dark. The kitchen light barely reached this far. Kate leaned through the doorway, searching for the switch.

"No electricity back here," Reuben said.

Kate straightened, her heart skittering into a faster beat. "Then I can't sleep here. I don't sleep in the dark."

Ollie and Lemmy turned to look. "What are you talking about?" Lemmy asked. "Everybody sleeps in the dark."

"Well, I don't," she said coolly.

She saw the subtle shift in their faces as they remembered and understood. She glowered back, hating that everyone knew. Hating that she would always be that weak, pitiable thirteen-year-old girl in the headlines.

For seven days, her photo had been on the front page of newspapers, captivating the world. But for Kate, the seven days had been a timeless hell of darkness and silence. An immeasurable black void.

She glared at the ugly housekeeper's room, hating the clammy fear that had taken hold of her. The heavy beats in her chest. The queasy knot in her stomach.

Ollie cleared his throat. "I'll see if I can find an old kerosene lantern somewhere." He shuffled from the room and the others followed, murmuring excuses.

Only Reuben remained, his scarred, bulldog face unexpectedly sympathetic. "How about we keep the door open? That enough light for you?"

Kate considered it. The faint glow from the kitchen seemed sufficient. She picked up the wooden chair by the bed and set it in front of the door, propping it open, and her panic started to subside. "No one must close this door or turn off the kitchen light."

"I'll make sure everyone knows." Reuben started to leave, then turned back. "You want me to sleep on the kitchen floor? I don't mind."

Kate filled her lungs, embarrassed. "No, but thank you. I'll be fine as long as the light stays on."

Reuben left, giving her a final, worried look over his stocky shoulder.

She entered the laundry room, where Hugo had placed her luggage, and was relieved to find a lightbulb with a chain. She opened her smaller suitcase, pulled out a silky nightgown, picked up her cosmetics case, and crossed the short hall.

The bathroom was no more than functional, intended for servants, with a stained pedestal sink and rusty fixtures. No counter space for lining up her things the way she liked, in the order she used them—toothbrush first, hairbrush last.

As she started to undress, footsteps creaked overhead, and she redid her buttons, deciding to sleep in her clothes.

She carried her things back to her suitcase, retrieved the book she'd been reading on the train, and returned to the housekeeper's room.

Moonlight shone through a gap in the curtains. Kate went to the window and peered up, but the full moon was barely visible through the overgrown trees. Tomorrow, she would find a good place to set up her telescope.

No. Tomorrow she would be on her way back to San Francisco. She would send a telegram to Aunt Lorna on the ship, explaining why she had to return home at once. Not even Mr. Norton could expect her to live in a boarding house with five men. She'd have to stay in a hotel in San Francisco while the house was being remodeled. Aunt Lorna could afford that, now that she was married. She could send a Western Union money order from the ship.

Kate heard movement behind her and whirled to see Hugo silhouetted in the doorway, looking like a killer again with something in each hand. She went rigid, aware they were alone downstairs. "What do you want?"

"Sorry, didn't mean to scare you. Just wanted to tell you I found it." He held up her purse, then leaned into the room just far enough to place it on the wooden chair holding the door. "And I thought you might want this." His other hand held up a flashlight. "I put in new batteries, so it'll run most of the night if you want. Or you can just leave it on the nightstand, in case you need it." He leaned forward and set it on the chair next to the purse.

The toes of his brown shoes had never crossed the threshold, as if to reassure her that they wouldn't.

"Thank you," she said stiffly.

The light from the kitchen cast his face into menacing shadows. "You know . . . I don't really go around stabbing people."

She realized she was squeezing her book against her chest and lowered it. "I am aware of that."

His eyes followed the book. "What are you reading?"

Kate hesitated. Aunt Lorna always warned, *Don't talk about it with boys, darling. They'll think you're as dull as dust.*

She turned the cover and read aloud, "*An Introduction to Differential and Integral Calculus* by Lester W. Hornsby."

Hugo's dark eyebrows lifted. "Well . . . that's an interesting bedtime story. You like math?"

"I thought I did until I started calculus. But I need to figure it out, so I work on a page every night." And, because she was tired of looking like a fool tonight, she added, "I'm going to be an astronomer."

He leaned against the door frame. "You need math for looking at stars?"

"Of course." Why did so few people know that? "Astronomy isn't just looking at stars, it's using math to understand them. It's how theoretical physics is proven. How people like Einstein—" She stopped herself. *As dull as dust.*

Hugo's lips tilted in a half smile. "Ollie never told me you were so smart."

"That's because my grandfather doesn't know me."

"Well, I'm glad you came. For his sake, I mean."

Which reminded her. "Does this house have a telephone?"

He seemed thrown by the question. "Not at the moment, but I'll pay the bill tomorrow."

"I need to send a telegram." Kate glanced at her Rolex and decided it was too late to borrow the neighbor's phone, but every hour she didn't have that money order was another hour she'd have to spend in this house. "Maybe I'll call a taxi and drive to Western Union. Oh—wait." She saw the flaw in her plan. "I can't call a taxi without a phone."

"I'll drive you, if you don't mind sitting on the back of a motorcycle."

Kate stared.

He gave a soft laugh. "Write it out, and I'll drive it down for you. I'm a night owl anyway, and then you can get in bed."

The offer felt too personal for some reason, but she certainly wasn't going to get on a motorcycle with him. "All right." She went to her purse on the wooden chair and pulled out the small notebook and pencil she carried everywhere. The lighting wasn't good, so she went to the kitchen and sat at the table. She flipped pages.

"Wow," Hugo murmured over her shoulder. "That's a lot of lists."

"Do you mind?"

"Sorry." He moved to the side of the room.

Still, she felt his eyes on her as she found a blank page at the back and started writing. *To Mrs. Harvey Wallace on the S.S. Argentina.*

Kate crossed off the name and wrote *Mrs. Donald Norton.*

She wrote several sentences explaining the appalling condition of her grandfather's house and his—she remembered Mrs. Fairchild's description—unsavory boarders, then decided it was too long and drew a line across it. Telegrams charged by the word, and punctuation was extra, so she'd have to use STOP instead of periods. She wrote on the lower half of the page: *Cannot stay here house full of unsavory boarders STOP must return to San Francisco at once STOP situation dire please send money order for one month hotel STOP*

She paused before adding: *Congratulations on your marriage Kate*

She sensed Hugo watching from across the room as she carefully ripped the page from the notebook.

He asked, "You're not going to live here like you said, are you?"

"No." She folded the paper over twice.

"Ollie will be disappointed."

She stood. "I think he'll be relieved."

"Then you don't know him at all." Hugo came toward her, his eyes narrowing. "You're the only family he has."

Kate tightened her hand around the folded paper, realizing he would read what she'd written. "It's not my fault my grandfather and I are strangers."

"It is if you leave." He yanked the paper from her hand and walked away.

CHAPTER 4

Kate woke to sunlight streaming through the window and jazzy piano music in the distance. She sat up, squinting at the drab little room with its dusty dresser and sagging curtain.

Not the least bit frightening.

Every morning, she woke up ashamed of her fear of the dark, vowing to conquer it—or at least do a better job of hiding it. Last night, she'd failed on both counts.

Her slim skirt had crawled up to her waist, and she reached back to unzip it, angry at herself for sleeping in her clothes.

Her hands froze.

Rumbling male voices drifted from the kitchen. Her gaze darted to the open door, but from this angle, all she could see was the wall of the hallway. She stood and quickly tugged down her hemline, then tiptoed to the door and shut it.

Her empty stomach twisted at the smell of pancakes, but that would have to wait.

She sat back on the bed, opened her notebook, and flipped to yesterday's list—*October 9, 1938*. She should have reviewed it last night, but did so now, placing a tidy checkmark next to the tasks she'd completed. Two tasks remained undone: *Unpack* (which was just as well); and *Calculus page 27* (not for lack of trying; she'd spent hours on the train staring at derivatives).

She turned the page and wrote: *October 10, 1938*

1. Calculus page 27. The third day in a row she'd written that page—a small failure.

2. Check newspaper for San Francisco weather. She usually checked the forecast in the evening newspaper, before laying out her clothes for the next day. Another missed step.

3. Check train schedule to San Francisco. Hopefully, there'd be something leaving around noon. She tapped the end of the pencil against her teeth, wondering if she dared board a train before receiving a money order from Aunt Lorna.

Kate pulled out her wallet and counted eighty-three dollars. Plenty to get home—the train ticket here had cost seventeen—but a decent hotel would be about fifteen a night, plus food, plus taxis to get to school. She jotted figures on the reverse page and decided her money would only last three days.

She couldn't leave until she'd heard from Aunt Lorna, which might mean another night in this place, but she could survive that.

In daylight, everything felt possible.

She managed to slip into the laundry room without having to face anyone and opened her suitcase to find everything rumpled and creased. She'd never ironed before. She decided on a dress with striped fabric that hid the wrinkles.

In the bathroom mirror, she looked reassuringly like herself. A lock of reddish-brown, shoulder-length hair had ended up on the wrong side of her part, and she pulled it back. Most of her friends had to sleep in curlers, but her own hair was naturally wavy. She leaned closer and decided her summer freckles were finally fading. Then stood back to see if her figure had developed any curves overnight. Still lean and straight.

Sometimes she longed for the striking beauty of her friend

Susan, but most days she was content with being, as Aunt Lorna put it: *Quite attractive without being showy about it.*

She squared her shoulders and whispered to her reflection two things she knew to be true and two things she wanted to be true. Some days she got creative, but today she stuck to the standard list.

"I am smart. I am sensible. It wasn't my fault. I am not afraid."

Dr. Gimble had reeked of cigar smoke and had cat hair on his sofa, but he'd given her this. As Dr. Gimble had put it, all the soothing words in the world wouldn't help if Kate didn't believe them herself.

Today, she repeated the final want with a little more conviction. "I am not afraid."

She showered and dressed and emerged from the bathroom eager for breakfast.

The kitchen table was cluttered with dirty dishes and orange peels, with two untouched pancakes on a plate in the middle. Kate thought the room was deserted, then noticed a pair of khaki legs sticking out from under the sink, with the mangy dog beside them. Hugo's voice drifted out, muffled and slightly off-key. "*It dooon't meant a thing . . . if it aaain't got that swing. Doo-wah, doo-wah, doo-wah, doo-wah.*"

A smile crept up on her.

Hugo slid out from under the sink but didn't notice her as he dropped a wrench into a toolbox and dug for something else. He looked less like a killer in daylight, but still like trouble. Like the good-looking boy who'd worked at the gas station near her private school, making all the clean-cut girls of Blakely Academy flirt like fools as he'd washed their windshields—until he'd been arrested for stealing car parts and never seen again.

Hugo noticed her and his humming faded. "Morning," he said a bit warily, and she remembered that he'd probably read her telegram.

"I forgot to pay you last night." She went to her room and returned with two dollars.

But when she held them out, he didn't take them. "It was only seventy-eight cents."

She took away one of the bills. "Keep the change."

Hugo frowned but took the dollar.

Reuben entered the kitchen, short and bald, his scowl deepening as he looked at the table. "Those pigs. They didn't leave a single orange. *I'm* the one who got them."

"Stole them, he means," Hugo told Kate. "Neighbor's tree."

Reuben scraped back a chair and sat. "The rich don't own the earth. They let their fruit rot on the ground while the working class starves. That's the problem with this country—sheer greed. And the people in this house are no better. There were *seven* of those oranges."

"See, Figs, that's the problem with being the only communist in the house." Hugo stood and set the toolbox on the counter. "You're morally obligated to share everything you have, while we capitalists get to take anything we can get our hands on."

"Food is shared equally. That's the arrangement." Reuben stabbed a fork into one of the two remaining pancakes and plopped it onto an already-used plate.

"Are you really a communist?" Kate asked, fascinated.

"Well, I don't go to meetings or anything, but I've read stuff, and I'm sick of the rich thinking they're better than everybody else." His eyes narrowed on Kate. "People in fancy clothes who don't do a lick of work, just happened to be born with a silver spoon in their mouth."

Kate felt stung for a second but quickly rallied. "As we've already established, if I *had* a silver spoon, I wouldn't be here right now, I'd be eating breakfast at the Huntington Hotel—*with oranges.*" She saw Reuben reaching for the last pancake and quickly lowered her hand on top of it. "That one is mine. As Marx would say, 'to each according to his needs,' and I *need* that pancake."

Hugo whistled. "Careful, Figs, I think you just found your match."

"Captain of my debate team last year." Kate considered the pancake and decided to eat it straight off the serving plate, which looked relatively clean. She pulled the plate closer and sat. "No hard feelings, Reuben?"

"He doesn't have any feelings," Hugo pointed out.

"Are you kidding?" Reuben hadn't taken his eyes off her. "Finally—someone who can talk about something besides auditions and fourth walls. Do you really know about Marx?"

"Not really. I got an A in my government class, but I get A's in all my classes. I don't suppose there's a clean fork around here?"

Hugo opened a drawer.

"Why do you keep calling him Figs?" Kate asked as she took the fork.

"Reuben Feigenbaum." Hugo leaned back against the counter. "A name no casting director would forget, but he thinks Jim Anderson is more distinctive."

"Charles Kensington," Reuben said, sawing the side of his fork into his pancake. "I changed it last week."

"Right." Hugo's eyebrows lifted. "Because you're a perfect fit for all those yachting, lord-of-the-manor roles."

Kate reached for the syrup, studying Hugo from beneath her eyelashes. Eighteen, she guessed. This morning, his nice shoulders were covered by a short-sleeved shirt, and his almost-black hair had a freshly washed sheen to it. Maybe he'd cleaned up for her.

His gaze shifted to Kate and she looked away.

"So, Reuben, you're an actor too?" She poured syrup. "I thought you were a musician, the way you played the violin."

He speared a wedge of pancake with his fork. "There's no work for musicians anymore. The music is all canned." He looked at her, the fork dangling. "I'm a bookkeeper, really, until this nitwit convinced me to quit my job and go into acting. So now I'm as broke as he is."

"Less deadly than that number-crunching job," Hugo said.

"Unless I starve to death." Reuben shoved the fork into his mouth.

Kate sensed more to the story. "How can a bookkeeping job be deadly?"

Reuben and Hugo exchanged a look. "Go ahead," Reuben said around a mouthful. "Ollie's gonna tell her anyway."

"Reuben used to count money for the wrong people, at this nightclub called the Galaxy. Then his boss got arrested, and Reuben had to go into hiding because he knows where all the bodies are buried."

"Hey," Reuben griped.

"Sorry, figure of speech—where all the money is laundered. So now the feds are parked outside Reuben's apartment with a bunch of questions. But if he talks to them, his boss's thugs will drop him off a dark pier. So he can't go home until the case is dropped."

"Which it will be," Reuben said. "He owns the judge."

"So, Reuben came here to hide out for a while."

It sounded like a gangster movie. Kate looked from Hugo to Reuben. "Are you making this up?"

Reuben swallowed. "Sadly, no. I've been stuck in this asylum for five months with this nitwit dragging me to auditions."

Hugo shrugged. "I told him there's no better place to hide than Hollywood. I've been going to casting calls for two years, and I'm completely invisible."

"Yeah, and it's depressing as hell." Reuben took another bite.

"One phone call, Figs, and your whole life will change. Those studios are made of money." The dog whimpered, and Hugo crouched to scratch its ears. "How'd that audition go yesterday? I forgot to ask."

Reuben talked out of the corner of his mouth. "Said I'm too bald."

"Tell them you'll wear a wig."

"And too short."

"Tell them you can be taller. It's war out there, Figs. You gotta fight for it."

"For what? One line that barely feeds me for a week?" Reuben ran his thumb along the scar on his cheek. "Nobody wants this."

"Sure they do, they just don't know it yet. That scar is your gold mine. I'll bet Peter Lorre got loads of rejection before someone saw dollar signs in those creepy eyes of his, and now he's a big star." Hugo's fingers dug into the mangy fur, making the dog's leg twitch. "That phone call is coming, Figs, and when it does, I'm tagging along for the ride."

"Sure. You can be my chauffeur." Reuben huffed a laugh.

Kate took another bite, her gaze lingering on Hugo as he played with the dog. His khakis were wearing through at the knees and his brown shoes looked ancient, separating from the soles. "So, Hugo . . . you've been acting for two years?"

He glanced up with a wry smile. "If you can call it acting when all I do is stand outside doors hoping to get noticed. This play is my first paying job—besides the Galaxy, I mean. I quit that when I got the play."

The nightclub with a boss in prison and thugs who dropped people off piers. "You worked there too?"

"Scrubbing dishes. I like nighttime work, so I can go on auditions during the day." He laughed. "Not that I go on many of those. Mostly, I just stand outside talent agency doors, hoping someone notices me. And they don't."

It all sounded rather . . . bumbling to Kate. Not a very efficient way of becoming a movie star. "Maybe you could work as an extra until you get a big part. You know—one of those actors who walks around in the background."

Reuben barked a laugh. "Sure, Hugo, why don't you be an extra?"

Hugo stood, giving her a patient smile. "You have to go through Central Casting, and they already have more actors than they can use. Like, ten thousand more. They don't sign anyone new unless you know someone."

"Well . . . you know Oliver Banks."

Reuben barked another laugh.

Kate's face warmed. What did she care? She was leaving today.

Lemmy sauntered into the kitchen, wearing a pinstripe suit, his hat tipped at a jaunty angle. He was a little older than she'd thought the night before—early twenties, maybe. He appraised Kate in return with a sly smile. "You're looking all fresh and pretty this morning. Guess sleeping in the servants' quarters suits you."

Kate stopped chewing, unsure if she'd just been insulted or complimented.

Hugo said with dislike, "What do you want, Lemmy?"

He wiggled an envelope. "Telegram for Miss Katherine Hildebrand."

Kate stood, her chair screeching back. She walked around the table.

"Not so fast. I tipped the delivery boy, so now you gotta tip me. Lucky for you, I accept kisses." Lemmy winked, tapping his cheek.

Kate halted a step away. "I'm afraid my kisses are worth more than that. This will have to do." She held out the extra dollar Hugo hadn't taken.

Lemmy reached for it, but Hugo got there first, snatching the dollar and the telegram. "Don't be an ass, Lemmy." He handed them to Kate.

Lemmy grinned. "Can't blame a boy for trying."

Kate itched to open the telegram, but not in front of them.

"You delivered it, now scram," Reuben said.

"Sure, I'm going." But Lemmy didn't move, pulling a pack of Wrigley's from his jacket pocket. "On my way to visit Moe this morning before visiting hours are over. Thought you might want to tag along, Uncle Reuben, tell Moe what you've been up to lately." He smirked, unwrapping a stick of gum. "Or maybe I should tell him for you."

Reuben glowered. "He's Mr. Kravitz to you."

"Not since he told me I'm like a son to him. You broke his heart when you quit the club, Uncle Reuben, but he's got me now, and I've got my eye on things." Lemmy tapped his temple.

"I am not your uncle," Reuben seethed.

"Sure you are. Your ugly sister married my dad. That makes us family."

Reuben scraped back his chair and stood, his hand tight around his fork. Kate gasped and stepped back, but Lemmy only looked amused, sliding the gum between his teeth.

"Beat it, Lemmy," Hugo said, the dangerous rasp in his voice coming through.

"Sure, I'm going. Don't want to miss visiting hours." He laughed as he left the room.

The air seemed to leave with him, Reuben's anger fizzling into a defeated scowl.

"Ignore him," Hugo said.

Reuben pointed his fork at Hugo. "Fifteen years, I work for Moe Kravitz. We have a certain respect between us—a certain understanding—and that punk comes along—"

"Forget him."

"The only reason he even *got* that job is because I recommended him—on account of my sister—before I knew what a *louse* he was—and now he thinks he can turn Moe against me? He better watch his back."

"Hey," Hugo warned, glancing at Kate.

Her heart raced, but she was also a bit fascinated, following along as best she could. "So . . . this Moe Kravitz is your boss at the nightclub who's in prison? And Lemmy has your old bookkeeping job?"

Reuben's eyes narrowed on her. "Better watch what I say around this one."

"Yeah, she's smart," Hugo said dryly.

"Does my grandfather know he has two gangsters living with him?"

Hugo folded his arms. "Reuben quit that life. He's an actor now."

As if that were so much better. Reuben unemployed. Hugo working in some back-alley horror show. Both of them mooching cheap lodgings off her grandfather. But it was no business of hers. She looked at the envelope in her hand.

"Guess that's your money order," Hugo said. "So you can leave today."

Reuben looked from Hugo to Kate. "Leave? I thought you were going to live here now."

"Changed her mind. Doesn't like the *unsavory boarders*." So he had read her telegram. "You better tell Ollie. He was like a kid on Christmas this morning, talking about you. I had to hold him back from waking you up."

The thought of her grandfather grinning over her bed didn't entice her to stay, but it did prick her conscience. "Well . . . maybe I can leave tomorrow. That gives us one day together. He can show me the sights of Hollywood."

Reuben gave a short laugh. "Slight problem with that."

Hugo shot him a warning look.

"What?" Kate asked. "Doesn't he drive? I can drive if he has a car."

"Ollie doesn't leave the house," Reuben said. "Not a foot out the door in the whole time I've been here—or the two years Hugo's been here. Except the backyard and only if it's dark."

Kate frowned, remembering the striped pajamas worn an hour or two before bedtime. "Why doesn't he leave the house?"

Reuben shrugged. "Doesn't want people to see that he's old, I guess."

She gave a startled laugh. "That's ridiculous. Nobody expects him to stay young forever."

"Actually, they do," Hugo said. "Say the name Oliver Banks, and everyone knows the face. Only problem is, they're picturing Captain Powell, who never ages. As long as Ollie stays inside this house, he's still Captain Powell. Step outside, and those days are over. Step outside, and Ollie loses himself."

Reuben smirked. "Very deep, Dr. Quick."

It all sounded absurd to Kate. "Well, he can't spend the rest of his life in this house. I'll get him outside. I'll tell him we only have one day together, and he has to take me sightseeing. Where is he?"

"In his office looking at your baby pictures," Hugo said.

Kate felt a twist of guilt. She made her way toward the door leading to the rest of the house.

"Say hello to Boots for me," Reuben called after her.

She looked back. "Who is Boots?"

Reuben only laughed.

CHAPTER 5

Kate saw the open door to her grandfather's office, halfway between the kitchen and foyer, but stopped before reaching it to open the telegram in private. She pulled the paper from the envelope and was disappointed to see that it was a message, not a money order.

```
DARLING GIRL HAVING SUCH A MARVELOUS TIME ON
THE SHIP LOVELY WEATHER AND DELIGHTFUL NEW
FRIENDS STOP ANXIOUSLY AWAITING YOUR FIRST
TELEGRAM FROM HOLLYWOOD PLEASE WRITE SOON
AND DO GIVE CLARK GABLE A KISS FROM YOUR MOST
HAPPILY MARRIED AUNT
                              MRS DONALD NORTON
```

Kate reread it. *Anxiously awaiting.* "Too obvious, Aunt Lorna," she muttered.

Aunt Lorna wasn't the sort of aunt who fretted over the details of her niece's life, too busy with her own social calendar. She didn't have any children of her own—by choice—and Kate had been thirteen when she'd moved in, so their relationship had always been more friendly than maternal. Sometimes their paths didn't cross for days, which suited them both.

She'd received Kate's telegram, all right, just didn't want to admit that her new husband wouldn't send the money. *Your most happily married aunt.* Mr. Norton had probably smirked in delight when he'd heard about Kate's dilemma.

She curled her fist around the paper, hating that she needed his money. It made her no better than Aunt Lorna, who'd turned into a flirtatious fool whenever he'd entered the house. *Oh, Donald, I love the way you're so smart.* Kate had rolled her eyes at first; there'd been a series of rich boyfriends since Uncle Harvey's death. Then she'd noticed how often Mr. Norton had scolded her aunt and how quickly Aunt Lorna had apologized. For the soup being too cold and the room too hot. For daring to talk as he read the newspaper. That's when Kate had written her list of *Seven Reasons for Not Marrying Mr. Norton,* hoping it would make her aunt come to her senses. Instead, Mr. Norton had found the list and forced Aunt Lorna to choose between a rich husband and a niece.

She hadn't chosen the niece.

Now, Kate must apologize too. It made her sick, but without his money, she was stuck here. This morning, she'd have to send another telegram, this one addressed to Mr. Norton, begging his forgiveness for her silly list. Knowing him, he'd make her wait, forcing her to send a second, even more groveling apology.

And she would do it. Anything to get out of here.

She had to tell her grandfather she wasn't going to live with him after all. She tucked the telegram back into the envelope and entered his office—and immediately stopped short, taken aback by a stuffed tiger glaring at her, its fangs bared. Her heart settled, and she looked up to see her grandfather sitting behind a desk, wearing a kingly cape with fur trim and a gold crown, gazing down at an open photo album.

"She never told me she was afraid of clowns," he murmured to a stuffed cat on the desk. A black cat with four white paws. Boots, Kate guessed.

Heavy drapes closed out the real world, casting everything into dusty gloom. Her grandfather's office was even more cluttered than the rest of the house, with only a few paths for walking between piles of strange artifacts. Egyptian urns and a golden Buddha. A tattered mummy leaning against the bookcase, its arms crossed. A suit of armor standing guard in the corner.

Old movie props, she guessed.

She made her way toward the desk, stepping over a metal jousting helmet. "Grandfather?"

His face brightened at the sight of her. "Kate! I thought you were still asleep. Come, come, you must look at these. Did you ever see such a precious child?" He held a photograph over the desk.

Kate expected to see herself, but the little girl in the photo was shabbily dressed, with 1906 written in the white border. The child clung to the leg of a young man with dimples—Ollie before his fame and fortune, looking barely older than a teenager. "Is this my mother?"

"That's her—little Evie, always so shy."

"Evie? Was that her nickname?" She'd always been Evelyn.

Ollie handed her another photo. "I love this one."

Kate *was* in this photo, about five or six years old, sitting on a settee next to her mother, both of them in fancy dresses. Every Christmas and Easter, they'd gone to the best photography studio in San Francisco. Sometimes her father had been in the photo too, but not this one. Maybe her grandfather had destroyed all his photos of Johnson Hildebrand, the way Kate had tried one lonely Christmas Day. But she hadn't been able to find any, and Aunt Lorna had tearfully admitted to locking all the photos of her brother in a safe deposit box.

Kate handed back the photo and ignored the next one by looking around the crowded office. "You have quite a collection here."

"Oh, yes, it's a bit of a mess. Reuben's trying to organize me, but I can't find anything in there." He waved a hand at the filing cabinet in the corner. A drawer hung open and documents littered the Persian rug. "He almost threw away my script from *Sea Demon*, if you can believe it. There are collectors who would pay a pretty penny for that. For *all* of this." He swung an arm.

"You're going to sell all these things?"

"Goodness, no! You're as bad as Reuben."

She noticed an enormous painting of Captain Powell on the side wall, on the deck of his ship, his eyes gleaming with heroic bravery. The table below the painting held what must have been movie memorabilia—an old-fashioned flintlock pistol on a wooden stand, a sea captain's hat, and framed photos.

"That sword is real," Ollie said, pointing to a box on the wall beside the painting, displaying a long, thin sword and scabbard. "My friend Frank had it made for my birthday to match the prop I used in the films. It's a beautiful weapon, crafted by a famous swordsmith in Spain—and wicked sharp."

The irony struck her. "A real replica of a fake original?"

"Ha! Never thought of it that way." Her grandfather sank back on the chair, his eyes softening on her. "My darling girl, can you ever forgive me for that appalling welcome last night?"

He looked ridiculous in the gold crown and fur-trimmed cape. "Of course, Grandfather."

"Ollie. I won't pretend to be much of a grandfather. I didn't even recognize you." He lifted a finger. "But in my defense, you did have braces on your teeth in the last photo you sent me."

"Sorry, I know I haven't been very good about writing. Or phone calls." Kate always kept them brief, thinking she had nothing to say to a boring, old man. But now that she faced him, Oliver Banks was anything but boring—and not really that old at fifty-four. Her gaze drifted to the top of his head. "King Arthur?"

He gave an embarrassed laugh and removed the crown. "Henry the Eighth. It's a little game we play. Hats in the wheelbarrow.

Close our eyes, and the first hat we touch, that's our character for the day. Keeps me in practice."

For what? Hugo was right: her grandfather lived in the past. "Grandfather—"

"Ollie, please."

"Ollie. I was hoping you would take me sightseeing today. I've never been to Hollywood."

His face froze for a few seconds before he managed a smile. "Not today, dear. I've promised to help Reuben organize my papers. Maybe next week."

"I won't be here next week; I'll be back in San Francisco."

His eyes widened. "You're leaving?"

Saying it to his face was harder than she'd expected. "I thought Aunt Lorna had arranged for me to live here, but you weren't expecting me, obviously, and you have boarders, and it does seem better if I get back to my own life . . . and you can get back to yours." She glanced at the stuffed cat.

"Oh, I know your bedroom isn't much, but we can fix it up. A little paint. Why don't we try it for a month and see how it goes?"

"I can't take a month off school. I'm already behind in math."

He waved a hand. "Math is easy. I can teach you. Or Reuben can, at any rate."

She resisted an urge to roll her eyes. "I'm in an advanced class at one of the best schools in the country. I'd hoped to find a good school here, but now—" Now, she saw that her grandfather couldn't afford a private school.

"They let you quit at your age," Ollie said, unconcerned. "Hugo dropped out when he was fifteen."

Of course he had. Kate switched to an argument he might understand. "I can't live here with your boarders. It isn't appropriate."

"Oh, they're respectable lads, every one of them."

"Yes, especially Lemmy, who's on his way to visit some gangster in prison as we speak."

"Moe Kravitz?" Ollie looked amused. "Moe isn't a *gangster,* just has a little gambling upstairs at his club. I used to go there myself, back in the day. The police just have to throw him in jail now and then to keep the busybodies happy."

Kate gave up on being tactful. "I can't live here. As soon as I get a money order from Aunt Lorna, I'm going home, probably tomorrow."

His face sagged. There was something childlike about the way he showed every emotion. "Oh, Kate. I thought this was our chance to finally get to know each other."

"Well . . . that's why I thought we should go sightseeing today. Get you out of the house a little before I leave."

His eyes narrowed, suddenly suspicious. "What did they tell you?"

"Nothing, I just think it would be nice to be outside together." An obvious lie. Kate drew a breath. "Ollie, you can't spend the rest of your life inside this house. There's nothing to be afraid of out there."

"Afraid," he scoffed. "I'm not afraid. It's annoying, that's all. Reporters and cameras everywhere I go. Everyone watching my every move."

She wasn't sure if he actually believed he was still a big star or just trying to convince her. Still believed, she suspected. "I don't think it'll be so bad now."

Ollie slumped on the chair, now a petulant child. "It's always bad. Can't even buy a pair of shoes without the salesman asking for an autograph. And *restaurants*! Try eating ribs with a dozen people watching your every bite and dribble." He waved a hand. "You have no idea."

"Actually . . . I do."

It took him a moment to understand, and then his eyes widened in dismay. "Oh, Kate, of course you do. I'm so sorry."

She forced a brief smile. "I guess we have that in common."

"Yes." He hesitated. "I was just reflecting on that, actually . . . how wonderful it is to have you here with me . . . all safe and sound." He slowly moved the photo album aside, revealing an open scrapbook on the desk, filled with newspaper clippings.

Kate didn't understand at first, the headline upside down, then the heavy black type formed words, and her heart lurched.

HUNT FOR HILDEBRAND GIRL CONTINUES

Her head seemed to drain of blood, the bold headline going fuzzy. She pressed her hands against the desktop to keep upright, her thirteen-year-old face smiling up at her—a school photo.

"I'm sorry," Ollie murmured. "I didn't mean to upset you." He started to close the scrapbook.

Her hands shot out to keep it open, her heart thundering. "Wait." She'd never seen the newspapers from that week; Aunt Lorna had seen to that, banning them from the house until the story died down. But here they were—part of her grandfather's treasure trove—front page stories the entire world had read.

So why not Kate? She turned the scrapbook to face her before she lost her nerve.

Her eyes flickered over the opening paragraph several times before her brain settled enough to understand that it was giving a brief recap of the situation.

Kitty Hildebrand, thirteen-year-old daughter of wealthy financier Johnson Hildebrand, granddaughter of movie star Oliver Banks, had been kidnapped from the Hildebrands' Nob Hill home while her parents were at a party. Chloroformed, most likely. Perhaps hidden in the trunk of a car. The kidnapper had left a note demanding a million dollars, claiming that's how much her father had stolen from him, but when he'd shown up to collect the ransom, he'd been ambushed by the police and killed.

Without revealing her location.

At the time of this article, she'd been missing three days. Doctors warned of death by dehydration. Investigators were combing through the kidnapper's papers and property, hoping to find some clue to her whereabouts. Her parents were shown in a grainy photograph, her mother crying, her father kissing her mother's temple. Kate stared at their blurry faces—a day in their life she'd never seen, only imagined.

Her hand trembled as she turned to the next page in the scrapbook.

JOHNSON HILDEBRAND UNDER INVESTIGATION. GIRL STILL MISSING.

While searching the kidnapper's files, suspicious paperwork had been found, prompting a raid of her father's office. The front page photo showed men carrying boxes out of Kate's childhood home, with her father in the doorway, his hands on his hips. He was quoted as welcoming the search if it helped find his daughter, who'd now been missing for five days.

Liar. He would have let her die in that dark hole if it meant keeping his secrets.

Kate turned the scrapbook page, her hand a little steadier now.

HILDEBRAND A MILLION-DOLLAR CROOK. ARREST IMMINENT.

The article explained how smooth-talking Johnson Hildebrand had coaxed millions from investors for new business ventures that didn't exist and used the money to fund his own lavish lifestyle. A Ponzi scheme with profits on paper only, early investors paid back by later investors. The kidnapper had been one of his victims, and now more investors were coming forward, claiming fraud.

Kate prepared herself as she turned the page, knowing the worst was yet to come.

HILDEBRAND KILLS SELF AND WIFE. GIRL STILL MISSING.

According to the housekeeper quoted in the article, her parents' argument had started in the dining room, then moved upstairs. Her father had shouted that he was Johnson Hildebrand for God's sake and had no intention of going to prison. Her mother had screamed that their daughter was probably dead and it was all his fault. Followed by two gunshots. And then silence.

Their daughter, Kitty Hildebrand, had been missing for six days, with no promising leads.

HILDEBRAND GIRL FOUND ALIVE

The kidnapper's cabin in the woods, with its underground bunker, had finally been discovered. Kate didn't remember the moment because she'd been unconscious—hours from death by dehydration, according to the doctor quoted. But the newspaper had a photograph of her limp body being carried out.

Kate stared hard at the photograph, her heart hammering, recognizing the small house in the background, surrounded by tall redwood trees. Remembering the strong hands that had pushed her through a hole in the floor. "I'm sorry," the man had called down, sounding like he meant it, and the square of light had disappeared. When she'd finally stopped screaming and begging, the world had been utterly dark and silent, with no explanation of what was happening or why. Or promise it would end.

She'd explored the dirt floor and found a canteen of water, crackers, and apples. The supply had eventually run out, leaving her hollow with hunger and maddened by thirst. She'd screamed for help in the dark until her voice had given out. Sobbed in despair. Rocked herself to sleep, only to be tormented by nightmares—then jolting awake to the worst nightmare of all: it wasn't a dream.

Kate despised the house in the photograph but couldn't take her eyes off it. Despised herself for not being smart enough to—

"It was a terrible thing that happened to you," Ollie said gently, coming around the desk. "A terrible, terrible thing." He stopped beside her, draping an arm across her shoulders.

Kate stiffened, resisting the urge to turn toward him. She never talked about it with anyone. Never allowed herself to cry.

His hand rubbed her shoulder. "I'd given up all hope of your aunt ever allowing you to visit. But you're here now, and even if it's only for one day, I couldn't be happier."

Aunt Lorna had never said she couldn't visit; it was Kate who'd never asked. Her mother had described her father as a self-centered movie star who'd partied all night and gone on glamorous vacations without her. Aunt Lorna had smirked whenever his name came up, calling him an old fool who'd squandered a fortune. And he *was* an old fool, wearing costumes and talking to a dead cat. Never leaving the house.

But he was the only relative she had besides Aunt Lorna.

Kate closed the scrapbook, making the house of horrors disappear. "Why did you keep these newspapers? They're just a bunch of bad memories."

His hand fell from her shoulder. "Sometimes I like to have a good cry about it. Helps clear the cobwebs."

"It isn't healthy, dwelling on the past." She picked up the loose photograph of her mother clinging to Ollie's leg and returned it to its proper place inside the photo album. "How long has it been since you left the house?"

"Oh . . . I don't know." She heard him take a few aimless steps behind her. "Four years, I guess. I came home from Evie's funeral and just . . . never left."

Kate hadn't left the house either, for a few weeks. Aunt Lorna had finally lured her into the car for a short drive. Then a quiet bookstore.

She closed the photo album and turned to lean against the desk. "Why don't the two of us go for a drive today? You don't have to get out of the car, just point out the interesting sights. Would you like that?"

He avoided her gaze, looking to the side. "Reuben's been hounding me to organize those papers."

"I'll help with that when we get back."

Lively music started somewhere in the house. "Sounds like Aurelio is at it again," Ollie said.

"A short drive, just the two of us."

"Maybe later. Right now, I think you'll find Aurelio much more interesting." Ollie forced a smile. "Run along, you don't want to miss it."

"Miss what?"

"I'm not going to tell you. This is something you must see for yourself."

Kate's curiosity got the better of her, and she left the office.

CHAPTER 6

Kate followed Fred Astaire's singing through the foyer, into the living room, where the song blared at full volume from a record player.

Suddenly, she understood why the dining table had been moved to the foyer.

A teenaged boy with golden-brown skin and dark hair danced across the empty dining room, his black shoes tapping, his body dangling on musical strings. His arms floated gracefully—then swung with power, turning him, one leg trailing. He landed on both feet—heavy—then tapped the other way, weightless again, his feet barely brushing the floor.

The music picked up its pace, and the boy broke free of the dining room, tapping and gliding around the outlying furniture in the living room.

He noticed Kate and stopped short—his arms falling, suddenly human again, his chest heaving for breath. He flashed a handsome smile of white teeth against glistening, overheated skin. "You must be Kate."

She'd been warned, but still gaped at so much virile beauty. "And . . . you must be Aurelio."

The dancer's smile widened, his eyes full of fun. "Aurelio Dios, in need of a dance partner—and here you are!" He took her hand and pulled her toward him in a twirl.

"Oh, no—I don't—"

A new song began—a piano's quick, cheerful high notes.

"Follow me. It's easy." His feet became magical again, tapping with effortless perfection. He moved to her side, still holding her hand, indicating with a grinning nod that she should copy his tapping steps.

Begrudgingly, Kate tried, feeling like a tromping elephant next to a skittering puppy. She liked dancing at parties—had even held her own in a Lindy hop, a few times—but she'd never tapped before. She tried to withdraw, laughing, but Aurelio pulled her into his arms and turned them together in a hopping step, his hand firm on her back. He was lean and lithe, no taller than her, but controlled the dance with ease.

Just a fancy polka, Kate realized, and she started to relax, her feet moving on their own. Aurelio spun her away and then back into his arms, and she managed it with reasonable grace.

Fred Astaire's voice pulled them along, a song Kate recognized from the movie *Swing Time* with Ginger Rogers. "*Pick myself up . . . dust myself off . . . start all ooover again.*"

Aurelio pulled one arm away and slid his other behind her waist, his feet shifting into a lazy tap shuffle. Kate copied the steps and had more success this time, her shoes making a satisfying clicking sound on the terra cotta tiles. Aurelio slowed his feet to match hers, and they went through the exchange a few times in perfect unison, side by side, his arm behind her waist.

The music slid to a conclusion, leaving her breathless and laughing, the record player needle falling into the blank groove at the end.

"You're a natural," Aurelio said.

She gasped for air. "Well—I've never tapped before."

"Oh, that was wonderful!" a girl's voice cried from the doorway, and Kate turned to see Bonnie Fairchild entering, blond and pretty, wearing a sweet yellow dress. Her blue eyes clung to Aurelio as she neared. "That's the routine from the movie, isn't it?"

"That's right." Aurelio stared back, breathing hard, his face a damp, bronzy red. "And you are the fair princess who lives next door."

She laughed. "I'm Bonnie." She dragged her eyes from Aurelio and handed Kate something wrapped in a dishtowel. "I brought a gift to welcome you to the neighborhood. It's banana bread. Our cook made it, but I told her to."

The bundle was warm and smelled divine. "Thank you." Kate wiped a bead of sweat from her temple. "I'm so embarrassed about the way I barged in last night."

"Oh, don't be, it gave me an excuse to visit. Mama said I could, now that you're here. I've always wanted to." Her gaze slid back to Aurelio with a cautious smile. "I know that dance routine from the movie. I had to memorize it for an audition last year."

His face brightened. "You're a dancer?"

"Oh, yes, and I sing too. My voice coach just left the house. She's mad because I'm switching to a coach at the studio, but they don't want me so classical. I'm not an old lady."

"No, indeed," Aurelio said warmly.

Hugo entered the room, his eyebrows arching at the sight of Bonnie. "Thought I heard company." The dog and Reuben followed him.

Bonnie clapped her hands. "Oh, good, now everyone's here! I think I know your names, but I want to hear them from you." She pointed a pink fingernail at Hugo. "You're the killer, aren't you?"

He looked amused. "Most people call me Hugo."

The pink fingernail pointed at Reuben, whose grumpy face had gone splotchy red, the scar remaining white. "Charles Kensington," he said gruffly.

Hugo rolled his eyes.

Bonnie turned back to Aurelio, her smile suddenly shy. "And you, of course. Sometimes I can hear you singing. You should be on the radio."

Aurelio took her hand and bent over it, gazing up with his handsome smile. "Aurelio Dios at your service, princess." His lips caressed the back of her hand.

Honestly. As if none of them had ever seen a pretty girl before. "How old are you, Bonnie?" Kate asked. "Fourteen?"

"I'll be sixteen next week."

"Fifteen, then," Kate said. Aurelio had to be at least seventeen.

But he still held Bonnie's hand, looking enchanted. "Will you give me the honor of a dance, princess?"

Her blue eyes widened. "Of course—oh, but not now! I've got to get to the studio. I just came by—" She forced her attention back to Kate. "Mama sent me over to see if you want to be in my movie. She's friends with the producer, so it's no trouble. It won't be a big part, only a few lines, but it might be fun. Some of the other kids aren't so nice when you're the lead, so Mama thought it would be good to have a friend on set. If you want to." Her voice trailed uncertainly. "It might be fun."

No one moved or spoke.

A part in a Hollywood movie. Without asking or trying—or even wanting.

Kate felt the hungry eyes around her. She'd been invited to a feast in front of starving men. She didn't dare look at Hugo. "Thank you for the offer, but I'm not an actress."

"Oh, it's easy. They just need teenagers in the background while I sing and dance. You can mouth the words. They record all that anyway. Mr. Falcon was excited when Mama told him about you. You know, because you're famous and everything. He wants your name on the posters."

Kate could hear the record turning round and round, the needle stuck in the final groove.

Hugo filled the silence, his voice scraping. "You should do it, Kate. It might be *fun*."

She forced herself to look at him, trying to let him know without words that she knew what he must be feeling. But his eyes were filled with so much simmering envy, she had to look away. "What about them?" she dared to ask. "They're the performers, not me. Can you get parts for them?"

"Oh." Bonnie's blue eyes slid to Aurelio, filled with regret, then back to Kate. "Mr. Falcon only wants you because . . . well, you know . . ." She stopped, seeming to sense she'd said something wrong.

Yes, Kate knew. The same reason Blakely Academy asked her to speak at the fundraising dinner every year. Because morbid curiosity made people spend money. It might have been interesting to be in a movie, but not like this. "I'm sorry, but Mr. Falcon will have to find some other famous girl to help him sell tickets. I'm going back to San Francisco."

"Are you *crazy*?" Hugo took a step, his eyes on fire. "This is *Clive Falcon* we're talking about, one of the biggest producers in Hollywood. You can't turn that down—and why *would* you? Because you can't stand to sleep in some housekeeper's room? Take the pool house, if you want—I don't care—take the whole damn house! We'll all sleep in the backyard if that's what it takes for you to get a part like that!"

The others murmured in agreement.

Kate felt their hungry eyes, but that only made her more eager to flee. "You're performers. I'm not, and I'm not doing it."

"Come talk to Mama," Bonnie begged. "She'll explain it better than me."

If nothing else, it would get her away from Hugo's glare. "All right." She thought of something else. "Can I use your telephone to send a telegram?"

"Oh, sure." Bonnie whirled to see everyone. "Well . . . it's been fun. I've wanted to meet you all for a long time." Her eyes drifted back to Aurelio.

He attempted his handsome smile, but it looked a bit frayed. "I hope we can dance someday, princess."

"Oh, yes, but I'm late for the studio now. A set collapsed yesterday, and the lead boy broke his leg, and I've got to test with a bunch of other boys. Well, goodbye everyone." She wiggled her fingers.

"Goodbye," they rumbled.

Kate had to pass Hugo on her way to the foyer and reluctantly handed over the warm banana bread. "Six equal slices," she told him in a fierce undertone. "And mine better be waiting when I get back."

He took the bread with a mock bow, resentment pouring off him. "Certainly, Miss Hildebrand. I'll put it in your dressing room."

"I am *not* an actress," she hissed. "And what do you care if I'm in some stupid movie?"

He growled back, "The way to break into the business is to know someone, and if you work at Falcon Pictures—we *know* you. *Get it?*"

Kate clenched her jaw. She could have pointed out that Falcon Pictures only wanted her because she'd been kidnapped when she was thirteen and left to starve in a dark hole while her father killed her mother and then himself.

But she bit back the words and followed Bonnie out the door.

CHAPTER 7

"To Mr. Donald Norton on the S.S. *Argentina*," Kate said into the telephone in the Fairchilds' chic living room. "I wish to express my deep regret—" If she said she was sorry for writing the list, he would smell the lie. "—that my list offended you. Stop. Situation is dire here with house full of men boarders. Stop. Must return home at once so I do not get behind in school. Stop. Would very much appreciate money order for one month hotel." She remembered that she would have to reenroll in Blakely Academy. "And tuition. Stop. My best wishes to you and my aunt on the occasion of your marriage."

"Sixty-one words," the Western Union clerk said on the other end of the line.

"Signed Kate, please."

"With tax, that's a dollar eighty-two, charged to Mrs. Fairchild's telephone account."

"Thank you." Kate hung up, already wondering if she should have made the apology more contrite.

"You're not leaving town already?" a feminine voice said, and she turned to see Mrs. Fairchild behind her—even more lovely in the light of day, wearing a soft blue dress that looked nice against her blond hair and porcelain skin.

"I hope you don't mind the telegram. I'll go get my purse."

"Don't be silly, it's on me. But I thought you were going to live here now. I wanted you to be in Bonnie's movie."

"She doesn't want to do it," Bonnie said, perched on the arm of the sofa. "You have to convince her, Mama."

Mrs. Fairchild's gaze lingered on Kate before shifting to her daughter. "Run upstairs and change, Bonnie. Tad wants you in that navy dress with the white collar for the screen tests."

"I don't know why it matters. I already have the part." But Bonnie left the room.

Mrs. Fairchild's red lips flickered a smile. "She's only wearing yellow because she overheard that boy next door say it's his favorite color." She sat on the sofa and patted the cushion. "Come sit by me, dear."

"All right, but I can't do the movie. I'm going back to San Francisco."

"I know. I sent Bonnie away so I could ask about your grandfather."

Kate sat, surprised. "You know Ollie?"

"Of course. We've been neighbors for twenty years. He and my husband were best friends." Mrs. Fairchild reached to the end table and brought back a framed photo showing herself in a skimpy, beaded dress from the 1920s, her platinum hair cut in a short bob, with a handsome man smiling on each side—Ollie with his dimples and a man with a skinny, dark mustache. "The three of us used to do everything together. This was taken at the Galaxy, where I used to sing."

The nightclub where Reuben was a bookkeeper, with illegal gambling upstairs and a boss in prison. Kate looked at the photo more closely and saw a fancy stage in the background. "You were a singer?"

"Until I got married. Goodness, look how young we all

were." The men looked about thirty-five, Mrs. Fairchild quite a bit younger. "Frank was a movie producer when I met him, but he quit the business when he struck oil on Signal Hill."

The name Frank rang a bell. "Did he give Ollie a Captain Powell sword for his birthday?"

Mrs. Fairchild gave a soft laugh. "I forgot about that. They used to have sword fights in the backyard. I was sure one of them would end up impaled." Her smile faded. "I lost Frank to cancer a year ago. He went very quickly."

"I'm sorry."

"It was hard on Bonnie. I hoped . . . I hoped Ollie would come to the funeral, but he never showed up."

Kate wasn't sure how much to say. "He doesn't go out much lately."

"I know." Mrs. Fairchild hesitated. "It was hard on him when you were missing. All the reporters in front of his house, everyone wanting a picture of his grief." She placed a hand on Kate's arm. "We mourned your mother too. She was a lovely girl, always so quiet and well-behaved. She wasn't suited for a life in Hollywood. I was glad when she went to Stanford and married into a respectable family. I didn't know he was . . ."

A thief and a killer.

"Ollie stopped answering the phone after the funeral. Frank and I gave him space for a few weeks, then got worried and followed the housekeeper into the house. But it didn't go very well. We quarreled over something silly, and that was the last time I saw Ollie." Mrs. Fairchild gave the window a wistful glance. "We live yards apart, but it might as well be an ocean."

Kate sensed more to the story. "I'm sorry."

"That's why I was so glad when I realized who you were last night. I can't bring myself to knock on his door, things ended so badly between us, but with you here, it'll seem perfectly natural for me to drop by."

Kate couldn't imagine beautiful Mrs. Fairchild sitting in

Ollie's cluttered living room with its wheelbarrow of hats. "The house isn't really fit for entertaining right now. It's a bit of a mess."

"Then the two of you must come here for dinner. Ollie was always the best dinner guest. He'd have the entire table laughing."

"He's changed since the last time you saw him."

"I know. Time changes all of us, but he's the same Ollie inside, and I'd love to repair our friendship. Please, Kate, don't go rushing back to San Francisco, stay and do Bonnie's movie. It'll only take two weeks, and I'm sure it'll mean so much to Ollie to have you here."

"Only two weeks to make a movie?"

"Preproduction is over. They'd be filming already if a set hadn't collapsed. Oh, please do it, Kate. You'll have so much fun. It's a lovely musical full of teenagers, and I'll make sure you receive a good salary."

"Salary?" Kate's attention sharpened. With money of her own, she could stop apologizing to Mr. Norton.

"It would be such a relief to know you're on set." Mrs. Fairchild glanced at the doorway and lowered her voice. "That's why I called Clive Falcon this morning. I was hoping you could help me keep an eye on Bonnie. I can't be there every second."

"A babysitter?" Kate hadn't expected that.

"An older, wiser friend. Bonnie doesn't have many friends. She had to quit school to keep up with all the dance lessons and auditions. She's worked so hard, Kate, and now—finally—Clive thinks she's ready to be his next young star, like Judy Garland at MGM. It's everything we've hoped for, but all I can do is worry about an entire production counting on my rather silly fifteen-year-old daughter."

"Bonnie will be great," Kate said, with no certainty she would be.

"I know this industry, Kate. I know the *men* in this industry and how they treat pretty young girls. I can't be there every minute, but Bonnie couldn't stop talking about you last night, and it dawned on me that you could be my second pair of eyes."

"I can't miss school for two weeks."

"The studio has a school. Bonnie's tutor is wonderful—a student from Caltech."

"Caltech?" It had the best astronomy program in the country, using the world's largest telescope at Mount Wilson, only a few miles from here. "Could this tutor help me with calculus?"

"I'm sure he could."

Kate wondered if she'd been too hasty, turning down the opportunity. Most people would give anything to be in a Hollywood movie. Like Hugo, working as a dishwasher at night so he could go on auditions. And Aurelio, who belonged in a musical much more than she did. "Is there any way you can get parts for Ollie's boarders?"

"I'm afraid not. I don't work at Falcon Pictures, I'm only friends with the producer."

"But you should see Aurelio dance. And Hugo wants it so much. And Reuben—well, I'm sure he's good at something. They just need a break, that's all, and this could be it."

"I'm sorry, but Clive only agreed to you because—"

"I know why." And suddenly, Kate's three years of debate team training kicked into gear, and she saw her leverage. "Mrs. Fairchild, you want me to do this movie so I'll watch over Bonnie, and Clive Falcon wants me because my name will sell tickets. Well, what I want is for Ollie's boarders to get roles, so I don't have to go home to their envy every night, knowing they deserve it more than I do. That's my condition."

Mrs. Fairchild gave a startled laugh. "I don't have that sort of power."

"Then I won't do it." But as soon as Kate said the words, she knew they were an empty threat, because, all at once, she wanted to be in a Hollywood movie more than anything. Hugo had been right. She'd never have a chance like this again, and only a fool would turn it down.

"You're different from your mother," Mrs. Fairchild mused, studying her more closely.

A subtle way of saying she was more like her father. Kate had heard that a lot when she was younger, when being compared to the brilliant financier Johnson Hildebrand was still a compliment.

Mrs. Fairchild smiled. "Don't look so offended. I like a girl who goes after what she wants. I'll tell you what I can do. Yesterday, half the cast got hurt when a set collapsed. Clive almost canceled the whole thing, but I convinced him to keep going for Bonnie's sake. Today, the studio will be a madhouse of young actors trying out for parts. If your friends can be ready in five minutes, they can go in Bonnie's car, which will get them through the studio gates. After that, they're on their own."

"Thank you!" Kate cried, quickly standing. "I need to tell them."

"I hope you and Ollie can come for dinner soon."

Kate didn't reply, already hurrying out the door.

She expected to find everyone where she'd left them, but the living room was deserted. She returned to the foyer and shouted to the house at large, "I have something to tell everyone—and it's *important*!" She waited a few seconds. *"Do you want to be famous, or don't you?"*

A door opened upstairs and Aurelio appeared, pulling a shirt over his head, his golden-brown chest on full display.

Reuben emerged from another upstairs room, grumbling, "This better be good."

"Is everything all right, my dear?" Kate dragged her eyes from Aurelio's impressive chest to find Ollie standing at the back of the foyer, still wearing the kingly cape. Messy gray hair and whisker stubble. A smear of food on the belly of his pajamas. Hugo emerged around him, wearing a red gingham apron, wiping his hands on a dishrag, the dog trailing behind.

She fought to hold on to her optimism. "Listen carefully, everyone, because we don't have much time. We're leaving for Falcon Pictures in five minutes—*all* of us, in Bonnie's car. I agreed to be in her picture as long as the rest of you get to audition. You're not promised roles, but a chance at least." Her gaze skimmed their startled faces. "Well. Don't just stand there. This is the day you've been waiting for!"

Aurelio reacted first, grabbing the iron banister with both hands. "What do we wear? What are the roles?"

"I . . . I don't know, teenagers, I guess."

"What about me?" Reuben demanded. "I'm not a teenager."

"Everyone gets into the audition. After that, it's up to you." Her heart fluttered with uncertainty as she looked back at her grandfather. "Ollie . . . I think you should come with us too, for that drive you promised me."

He gave a feeble laugh. "Goodness, no, I'm on a break from acting."

"You don't have to audition, just ride in the car and wait in the parking lot. You can wear a hat and sunglasses, if you want, and no one will know who you are."

Ollie took a step back. "No, no, I couldn't possibly."

She struggled to keep the irritation from her voice. "Of course you can. It's just a car ride." He shook his head, and she blurted, "If you don't go, nobody else gets to go."

"That's lousy!" Reuben cried. "Why does the whole thing depend on him?"

"Because he's my grandfather," Kate snapped. "And I don't want him stuck in this house for the rest of his life." She fixed her eyes on Ollie. "You said you don't want me to go back to San Francisco. Well, if you get in that car in five minutes, I'll do this movie and stay for two weeks. If you don't, I'll leave tonight."

Which wasn't true—even without the movie, she didn't have money for a hotel. But Ollie didn't know that.

He paled. "You . . . you said it would be just the two of us. I can't go to a studio."

Hugo grabbed his arm. "Sure you can. I'll be there. Come on, let's get you upstairs and find you something to wear. There must be something that fits." He steered Ollie toward the staircase.

Ollie grabbed the banister. "Not today. Maybe tomorrow."

Reuben growled, "You won't have a tomorrow if you don't do this—because I'll *kill* you!"

Kate's chest tightened with doubt. Ollie looked ready to pass out.

Hugo placed his hand over Ollie's on the banister. "You can do this," he said gently. "One step at a time. Let's get you dressed first." He loosened the older man's grip and forced him up the staircase.

As they climbed, Hugo looked back at Kate with a look on his face that seemed to mean something, she just wasn't sure what. Maybe gratitude for getting them all auditions. Or reassurance that he would get Ollie dressed. Or maybe just sheer amazement that she'd figured out a way to get Ollie out of the house. She was a bit amazed herself.

"Five minutes!" she cried, and they all scurried upstairs, leaving her alone with the reality of what she was doing. Panic quivered inside her, threatening to take over. She hurried to her room, flipped open her notebook, and quickly added two tasks she couldn't have imagined when she'd woken up that morning.

4. Go to Falcon Pictures.
5. Accept a role in a Hollywood musical.

CHAPTER 8

Bonnie honked from the curb, sitting behind the wheel of a shiny yellow car with a chrome angel flying off the hood.

Aurelio whistled as he circled the car. "Spiffy wagon." He looked rather spiffy himself in a pinstripe, double-breasted suit, his dark hair slicked back. He opened the driver's door. "Slide over, princess. You're too young to have a license."

"Oh, no one cares about that. I drive all the time." But Bonnie smiled as she moved over on the wide front seat, making room for Aurelio.

Kate sat on Bonnie's other side, then looked back to watch as Ollie was forced from the house by Hugo on one side, Reuben on the other, his face half hidden by a dark fedora and large sunglasses. He stumbled as he stepped off the front stoop, but Hugo and Reuben kept him upright.

Kate glanced at the Fairchilds' house, hoping Mrs. Fairchild wasn't watching.

Reuben entered the back seat first, sliding to the far side; Ollie was pushed to the center; and then Hugo got in, blocking Ollie's escape. The door slammed shut.

Kate looked over her shoulder to see Ollie breathing through puckered lips, his face pallid beneath the sunglasses. And it occurred to her that, for him, leaving the house was how entering a dark room felt to her. "Are you all right?" she asked, hoping she hadn't made a mistake.

He didn't answer, busy breathing.

"Piece of cake," Hugo said, but he kept his eyes riveted on the older man. "All you have to do is sit here, Ollie, and enjoy the ride."

Ollie blew out a heavy breath, a bead of sweat sliding down his temple. His suit looked well made but too tight, and his shirt buttons strained over his belly. One hand clutched a fuzzy, blue mouse—a child's toy. Hugo caught Kate looking at the mouse and gave a limp shrug.

She said, "You look good, Ollie." But he showed no signs of hearing her.

Aurelio revved the engine and worked the clutch, and the car jolted away from the curb. "Whoa! Powerful engine!" he cried, and Kate wondered how much driving experience he had.

Bonnie clapped her hands. "Oh, this is fun! I can't believe Mama thought of it."

Kate glanced out the back window, but the beautiful gray house had already slipped from view.

"Do you have a script?" Hugo called from the back, and Bonnie handed a bound booklet over her shoulder. Hugo read aloud from the cover, *"Trixie's Big Show."* He flipped pages. "Any idea which lines we should prepare?"

"The best scene is when Trixie dances in the moonlight. But that's only me, I guess. Maybe one of the ice cream parlor scenes. That's where the kids meet and make all their plans. They're putting on a talent show to save the town's old theater."

The car jerked to a stop, and they all swayed forward. "Learn to drive," Reuben griped.

"It's these brakes. You don't have to push them through the

floor like some old jalopy." Aurelio revved the engine, proving the car's power. "Princess, you gotta tell me how to get there."

Bonnie started spouting directions, pointing with a pink fingernail, and the car sped forward.

Hugo raised his voice above the engine. "Okay, I'm going to read a few lines so we can all get a feel for it." He flipped a page. *"That's a swell idea, Trixie. You kids can do a lot of good if you all work together."*

"That's Joe's line," Bonnie said over her shoulder. "He's not one of the kids, he works at the ice cream parlor."

Reuben snatched the script from Hugo's hand. "That's my part."

"Hey," Hugo complained.

The car made a swerving turn, its tires squealing, and they all tumbled to the left, then straightened.

"Read it aloud," Hugo told Reuben. "I want to hear the general tone of the script."

"You think this is Eugene O'Neill? The tone is cornball with a touch of dizzy blond."

"And the songs are terrific," Bonnie said, not seeming to notice the slight. "There's one about ice cream, and we all dance around the tables." She sang in a sweet soprano, *"Chocolate and vanilla . . . eatin' with my fella . . . thaaat's what I call a good time.* Oh—left here!" The car careened, and they all swayed.

Kate felt a bit queasy, and not just from Aurelio's driving. The others knew what they were doing, at least. She hadn't been on a stage since *Doctor Dolittle* in the third grade, when she was Pig Number Three. Her singing was average, at best. Her dancing, just the basics.

She glanced back to see Ollie still holding the blue mouse, his face shining with sweat. The car did feel like an oven. She rolled down her window halfway and was relieved to feel the wind in her hair, but Bonnie squealed and pulled a black-and-white polka-dotted scarf from the glovebox and wrapped it around her blond curls.

The car weaved its way along a twisty highway crowded with cars, then turned down a boulevard, and before Kate felt ready for it, the Falcon Pictures logo loomed in front of them—a medieval-looking shield with a black bird on it. Aurelio stopped at the guard booth and rolled down his window.

"Hi, Wally," Bonnie chirped, leaning over Aurelio. "I brought my friends because Mr. Falcon wants to put them in the picture." An exaggeration, but the guard waved them through.

Aurelio glanced in the rearview mirror and slapped his palm on the steering wheel. "That's it, fellas! We're in!"

Ollie sank lower on the back seat, muttering, "This was a mistake."

"Just stay in the car and take a nap," Hugo said. "If anyone asks, you can say you're Bonnie's chauffeur."

"I used to have one before I learned to drive," Bonnie piped in. She glanced over her shoulder. "Don't you want to audition, Mr. Banks? You could probably have the part of the old theater manager. They already have an actor, but he always smells like liquor." She wrinkled her nose.

Ollie raised a hand and declared in the ringing voice of a sea captain, *"I demand to be taken home!"*

Reuben snapped, "No one's taking you home."

Hugo reached into his pocket and held up a quarter. "Worse case, you can take a bus home."

Ollie snatched the coin.

They drove past a long, two-story office building with palm trees out front, then turned down a road of rambling structures—some office buildings, a lumberyard, and an outdoor area filled with weather-beaten movie props, including a row of Egyptian statues.

"This way," Bonnie said, pointing, and the car turned down a long road flanked by the most enormous warehouses Kate had ever seen, one after another. None of the buildings had windows.

"What do they keep in these huge warehouses?" Kate asked.

"They're the soundstages, silly, where they shoot the pictures." Bonnie pointed to a building on their right with STAGE 5 painted on the wall. "That's where the set collapsed, but I was rehearsing in Six when it happened, and the auditions are in Six today. Park in here."

Aurelio steered the car down the alley between Stages Five and Six and parked next to a white truck. He tried to give the key to Bonnie, but she said, "I don't want to carry it all day, silly. Put it in the glovebox."

Everyone piled out, except Ollie.

Kate shut the door but lingered, looking back at her grandfather through the open window. "This is a nice shady spot. Take a nap, like Hugo said, and I'll check on you soon."

"I do not require *checking on*," Ollie said with dignity.

"He'll be fine," Hugo told her, but he kept glancing over his shoulder as they walked away.

They entered through a side door in the towering wall of Stage Six. Kate expected to enter a colossal space, but the view was blocked by a truck inside the building and a couple of workmen unloading thick power cords. Someone shouted from above, and Kate looked up to see a distant ceiling laced with beams and large metal lights.

They walked around the truck and the wider space came into view—as vast as a football field. Straight ahead, a cluster of round tables and chairs were set up in what Kate guessed was a makeshift ice cream parlor set, with a long line of teenaged boys and girls waiting their turn to audition. A boy and girl stood near the tables, reading lines from a script, watched by three men sitting behind a long table.

"There you are. I expected you hours ago." A thin man with wire-rimmed eyeglasses approached them, carrying a clipboard.

Bonnie leaned toward Kate. "This is Mr. Eckles. He's always in a hurry."

Mr. Eckles's gaze skimmed their group and settled on Kate. "Miss Hildebrand? Mr. Falcon is expecting you."

Aurelio gave a short laugh of amazement. "We're going to meet Clive Falcon?"

"Not you. Just her. This way, Miss Hildebrand. You too, Bonnie." Mr. Eckles walked toward the door they'd just entered.

Bonnie pulled off her polka-dotted scarf and handed it to Aurelio. "Will you put this in the glovebox for me?"

"Of course." He looked honored.

Bonnie hurried after Mr. Eckles, but Kate didn't move, her stomach suddenly full of feathery wings. "Any helpful tips?" she asked, pressing a hand to her stomach.

Hugo's low voice came from behind her. "Find the lie in the dialogue—the lie your character is telling herself, and the lie she's telling everyone else."

Kate turned and stared. "*That's* supposed to be helpful?"

One dark eyebrow arched. "You're Oliver Banks's granddaughter. There must be at least one drop of thespian blood in you. And if there isn't . . . well . . . they want you anyway, don't they?" His eyes gleamed with resentment.

Which made it easier to walk away.

Mr. Eckles drove Kate and Bonnie across the studio in a small, jeep-like vehicle with a canvas awning on top. He parked in front of the two-story office building with the palm trees, and they entered a reception area. One woman typed, and two more sat at a phone switchboard, pulling cords from a panel of blinking lights and plugging them in somewhere else. "Good morning, Falcon Pictures. One moment, please."

Mr. Eckles led them across the reception area at a brisk pace and down a hall lined with movie posters. "They're waiting for you in wardrobe, Bonnie." He glanced back at her without slowing. "I suggest nothing but lettuce today. Mr. Falcon doesn't know about the two pounds." He turned up a staircase. "This way, Miss Hildebrand."

"But—" Kate paused at the crossroads, as Bonnie wiggled her fingers in farewell and continued straight.

"Miss Hildebrand! The entire production team is waiting."

She hurried up the stairs, her stomach now full of swooping bats. They walked down a hall and entered another reception room, fancier than the last one, with wood paneling and only one woman at a desk. Mr. Eckles led Kate through a door, into a long office with an enormous desk at the far end.

A man with a silver mustache leaned against the front of the desk, facing a semicircle of armchairs. "What about the blond kid from Fox?"

"They won't loan him out until November. That's too late for us—unless you want to delay for another few weeks."

"No more delays. This picture is bleeding." The man with the silver mustache noticed Mr. Eckles and Kate, and his expression lifted. "Ah, here she is, boys—Kitty Hildebrand!"

Six heads turned. Kate remained rooted near the door until Mr. Eckles grabbed her elbow and forced her forward, depositing her in front of the semicircle of chairs.

The man with a silver mustache reached out a hand. "Clive Falcon. Thrilled to have you, Kitty. Can I call you Kitty?" He gave her hand a quick pump and released it.

"Kay—" Her voice stuck, and she swallowed. "I go by Kate now."

"Wonderful, wonderful. We're having a quick meeting here to make sure we're all on the same page. You may have heard about our little set collapse yesterday. This is our director, Bert Holiday. Screenwriter, Horace Musgrave. Arthur Ellison—best music man in the business. Wardrobe. Sets. Casting isn't here today because they're a bit busy." He glanced at the open door. "Alice, where's Tad? He should be here for this."

A female voice called back. "I'll find him, sir."

Mr. Falcon clapped his large hands once. "So, Kate, we're just thrilled to have you—a real American hero, the whole country rooting for you. We were thinking you could play Trixie's best friend—that's Bonnie's character. It'll take a little rewrite, but Horace is on board with that, aren't you, Horace?"

"Sure," the screenwriter said blandly, staring at Kate.

"Only a few lines to get your feet wet and your name in the credits. Next time, we'll get you a bigger part. You'd like that, wouldn't you, Kate? To be under contract with Falcon Pictures for future projects?"

"Oh . . . I don't know. I'm not really—"

"We can work out the terms later. Today, let's just see how we feel about things, shall we?" Mr. Falcon's silver mustache lifted in a smile that didn't quite reach his eyes.

The director Bert Holiday spoke up. "Do you have much acting experience, Kate?"

She opened her mouth but was cut off by a heavyset man with a cigar. "She's tall. A lot taller than Bonnie."

Kate relaxed her posture. "Only five-six."

"She only looks tall," a man with a white scarf said. "Legs for days. A figure like that can wear anything. And that hair color is exquisite."

A man murmured to his neighbor, "She's pretty, at least."

"She looks smart," someone else said, as if that were a bad thing.

"A young Katharine Hepburn," the director suggested.

"Sure, but is that what we need in this picture? She's supposed to be an adoring friend to Trixie."

Kate remembered Hugo's advice to Reuben at breakfast. "I can be adoring."

Someone chuckled.

"Can you dance?" a slim, bald man asked.

"Now, boys," Mr. Falcon said, raising a hand. "This is Kitty Hildebrand we have standing here, and we're *thrilled* to have her."

"Sure, Clive, but we need to know what we're working with. Do you know how to dance, darling?"

She swallowed. "A little. Just the usual, I guess. Some foxtrot. I've done the Lindy hop a few times."

The man in the white scarf spoke up. "She doesn't have to dance with a figure like that, just stand there and look good. I'll put her in some tiny shorts for that dance rehearsal scene." He waved a finger at Horace. "Write it that way."

The slim, bald man asked, "What about your voice, darling? Can you sing something for us? Anything. Whatever you auditioned with last."

Kate's throat filled with sawdust. "I'm . . . I'm actually more of a chorus singer, not a soloist."

He flashed a tight smile. "Don't worry, I'm not offering you a solo, just want to hear your tone and register."

Six sets of eyes watched and waited.

And suddenly, Kate had had enough. She stood to her full five feet six inches. "Look—I'm not a singer or a dancer—or even an actress. I never claimed to be. I know perfectly well why you want me in your picture—and that's fine, I'll do it—but I'm not going to stand here and pretend to be something I'm not. Take me as I am—or not at all."

The director Bert Holiday snapped his fingers. "*There's* our interesting girl!"

An excited murmur rose.

"But it's no good," Horace said. "If I write that girl, she'll steal the screen from Bonnie."

"Anyone have a script on them?" Mr. Falcon asked. "Let's have her read a few lines."

No one had a script. Mr. Falcon shuffled through some papers on his desk and came back with a bound booklet. He flipped pages and handed it to Kate. "Different movie, but it'll give us some idea. Read Sylvia's part—smart and feisty but beaten down by tragedy."

Kate stared at the page, black words swimming. She blinked and managed to find Sylvia's name next to a full paragraph of dialogue. She cleared her throat. *"He isn't a wise guy. How wise can he be, letting you guys boss him around?"* Her voice sounded flat to her own ears. She added more emotion. *"You pretend to care about my father, but you're worse than Joey. You're worse than all of them."* Too much, maybe. She toned it down. *"I'm sick of this place and I'm sick of your lies. You shouldn't have come here."* That sounded about right. She kept going, gaining confidence.

Then made the mistake of looking up to see their pained expressions.

CHAPTER 9

All right, so she couldn't act.

Kate walked back slowly across the studio lot, in no hurry to face the others and admit defeat.

Clive Falcon had managed a polite smile beneath his silver mustache. "Wonderful, Kate. The boys and I will discuss things and let you know." He'd raised a hand toward the door, dismissing her. As she'd passed Mr. Eckles, she'd asked about Bonnie and his response had been cool. "She'll be occupied most of the day. Go back to where I found you and wait." No offer to drive her in the little jeep.

The studio was busier now, cars and bicycles passing her on the narrow road that ran between the buildings. A stream of women in glittering dance costumes came through a door, laughing. A young man trotted by, going the other way, carrying an armload of swords. Kate turned the corner and passed a pioneer wagon being draped with canvas, and then a large building full of pounding construction noises and the smell of paint.

It might have been fun for a few weeks.

At least she'd gotten Ollie out of the house. She would reward him with an easier outing this evening, while she waited for Mr. Norton's money order. Maybe a drive to the beach.

Kate entered the road lined by enormous soundstage buildings. The second building had its wide, roll-up door open, and she peeked inside to see a busy hive of activity around a fancy nightclub set.

"You in or out?" a man asked, his hand on a pulley rope.

Kate hesitated, then stepped inside, and the door rolled closed behind her. She moved closer to the set, her heart racing, and found a quiet hideaway between two stacks of chairs where she could watch.

Filming had been paused—or maybe hadn't started yet. On a tiered stage, musicians in white jackets fiddled with their instruments, filling the air with a disjointed whine. On the dance floor, women in sleek gowns and men in bowties wandered or lounged at small tables, smoking and waiting. Off to the side, a cluster of women in short dance costumes rehearsed steps. And everywhere—around the set, and through it, and over it—crew members roamed, pushing costume racks and shouting from ladders.

For a breathless moment, Kate thought she saw Gary Cooper, then the man turned and she breathed again. Still, the fact that he *could* have been Gary Cooper—that in some other soundstage across town it actually *was* Gary Cooper—didn't escape her.

No wonder everybody wanted to be in pictures.

Two actors wandered by eating sandwiches, and Kate looked back to see a buffet table. She hadn't eaten anything since that one pancake. She walked to the buffet table, glanced around, picked up a triangle of roast beef sandwich, and then returned to her hideaway to eat and watch.

"Places, everyone!" a man called through a megaphone.

Suddenly, as if someone had flipped a switch, the messy noise sharpened into orderly quiet. Lights darkened. Other lights brightened. A blond woman in a glittering dress left a makeup chair and joined a man in coattails next to one of the nightclub tables. Above them, a large microphone dangled.

Kate took a bite.

The man and woman tossed lines back and forth—Kate couldn't hear the snappy dialogue but could imagine it—then the woman got angry and left. The man started to follow, but stopped, one arm stretching after her. The band started playing, and the dancers in short costumes shuffled out to perform.

"Cut. Hold your places." The magical tension relaxed as the director looked through one of the cameras. A moment later— *"We'll start after Irene's departure. Music on my count of five. Roll 'em."* The man with the megaphone held up a finger count, and the music started again.

Kate watched and ate her sandwich, mesmerized by how real and glamorous the nightclub looked, even though it was chopped in half, with ugly equipment on one side and chandeliers hanging from industrial beams. Beyond the elegance, wooden poles supported plywood walls. Kate had known movies were shot that way, and yet never noticed while watching them. She thought back on an Andy Hardy movie she'd seen a few weeks ago. The view of the living room had always come from one side—because the other half of the room didn't exist, she realized.

She watched as the dancers went through their number a few times, then, when the director called for a longer break, found a side door and left the building.

As she neared the building with STAGE 6 painted on the side, she remembered Ollie and walked faster, hoping he was all right. But when she turned down the alley where they'd parked, the yellow car wasn't there. She ran her gaze over the parked cars and trucks, confused, wondering if she was in the wrong place, and finally spotted Bonnie's yellow car at the back. She hurried toward it.

And found it empty. She turned, alarmed. "Ollie?" She walked back through the alley, glancing between cars, but he wasn't there.

He must have taken a bus home. But why had Bonnie's car been moved?

Kate entered Stage Six and found the makeshift ice cream parlor gone, replaced by a large square of dance floor with a pianist playing a lively tune. About thirty teenagers sat around the area, watching as six girls performed tap steps in front of the men at the table.

She looked around for the others but only found Hugo, sitting in a row of canvas chairs a safe distance from the dance floor, his feet propped on a wooden box, his slouch indifferent. But he watched the dancers with a sly smile that made her wonder what he was thinking.

Kate felt a quiver of attraction she knew wasn't wise. For one thing, she was probably leaving tomorrow, since she'd failed to impress Clive Falcon. For another, she and Hugo Quick had nothing in common. He wasn't academic or sporty, like most of the boys she knew. Not headed to college. He was an actor who'd dropped out of school when he was fifteen.

He turned his head to look at her, giving her the uneasy feeling he could read her mind. Her face warmed, but when he patted the canvas chair beside him, she had no choice but to walk over.

"Do you know where Ollie is?" she asked as she neared.

"I checked a while ago, and he was gone. Must have taken the bus." Hugo eyed her more closely. "You don't look very cheerful. How'd the audition go?"

She pursed her lips, not wanting to answer. She was used to doing well at things. Winning school awards and tennis trophies.

Hugo gave a soft laugh. "That bad? Better sit down and tell me about it."

Kate hesitated, then sat in the chair between him and a boy with blond hair. "I felt like a cow at the county fair, everyone inspecting and measuring." She lifted her feet onto the box next to Hugo's.

"Welcome to showbiz."

She sank lower, matching her slouch to his, and it felt good. "Would you call me tall? I don't think I'm that tall."

Hugo's gaze slid down her striped dress and outstretched legs. "I'd say you were about the right height." His eyes lingered, and she crossed her ankles.

"How did your audition go?" she asked.

"A quick cut. I knew it was a bad fit as soon as I saw the crowd."

"What do you mean?"

"Who stands out to you?" Hugo nodded toward the dance floor.

Kate looked over the teenagers waiting to dance, all of them attractive in a wholesome sort of way, but not extraordinary. "I'm not sure."

"Exactly. That's what they want in a picture like this—faces that blend in. That's not me."

Kate glanced sideways at his villainous good looks. "No . . . I see what you mean. Not unless the script calls for everybody getting stabbed in the ice cream parlor."

His lips twitched. "I only do that on full moons."

"Lucky me, arriving on the right night."

The piano music stopped and a man called out a name. One girl squealed and ran forward, while the other five walked away looking glum. More names were called and six boys hurried onto the dance floor.

"Why do you put yourself through this torture?" Kate asked.

Hugo gave a wry laugh. "I don't know, but the more they turn me away, the more I want it. Hopeless dreamer, I guess."

"Well, take it from me, fame isn't all it's cracked up to be."

He turned and looked at her, his expression thoughtful. "No, I'm sure it's not," he murmured. "But I don't care about the fame."

The piano music began again, and the six boys started tapping. A boy with freckles tapped the wrong way, then hurried to catch up.

With Hugo's attention on the dance floor, Kate dared to study him more closely. Irish, maybe, with that combination of light skin and almost-black hair. His lips were nicely shaped—a soft contradiction to the rebellious eyes and arched eyebrows. "What *do* you care about?" she asked, genuinely curious.

He thought a moment before answering. "Telling a story, I guess. Making people feel something."

The choreographer shouted at the boy with freckles, waving an impatient arm.

"My mom says I like to read because she named me after Victor Hugo. I used to write these stories I thought were really dark and important, about this ghost named Earl who lived in a department store and scared all the customers." He gave an easy laugh. "I haven't thought about that in a long time."

The low timbre in his voice struck a nice chord inside her. "What else did you write about?"

"Detective stories, when I got older. My mom bought me this second-hand typewriter, and I thought I was Dashiell Hammett." His lips quirked. "And poetry. Lots of bad poetry."

She'd never met a boy who wrote poetry before.

"You smell good, by the way," Hugo said.

It took Kate a moment to catch up to his words, and another moment to decide if she should walk through the tempting door he'd just opened or be sensible and close it. He intrigued her, in a bad-boy sort of way, but if she made two lists, the one against Hugo Quick would be a lot longer than the one in his favor.

She felt him waiting, and his interest piqued her own, making her want to keep that door open a little while longer. "Are you flirting with me, Hugo?" she asked with just a hint of tease. Open, but cautious.

He laughed, and she sensed that she'd struck the right tone. "Just stating a fact. I live with a bunch of men and sleep with a dog. I can't help but notice."

Kate fought a smile, aware that she was flirting back, her

shoulder leaning toward his. "So . . . how did you meet Ollie if he never leaves the house?"

"My dad and I came to fix his plumbing."

She remembered Hugo fixing the kitchen sink that morning. "Your dad is a plumber?" A respectable trade.

"I was sixteen, and all he could talk about was the two of us fixing pipes together for the rest of our lives, and then I saw Ollie's props and costumes, and he started telling me about acting, and I just—I don't know, caught the bug I guess. That night, I told my dad how much I hated plumbing, and he kicked me out."

When he didn't continue, Kate asked, "What did you do then?"

"Got on a bus with everything I owned in a pillowcase and showed up on Ollie's doorstep." Hugo glanced sideways at her. "It was dark and raining, and I was just some runaway kid he didn't know, but he told Mrs. Pace to make me a grilled cheese sandwich and said I could sleep in the pool house. That's Ollie for you."

Kate's heart tugged for that younger Hugo and his pillowcase.

"Now, *he's* the one I'd cast," he said, nodding toward the freckled boy, who'd tripped and fallen.

"Freckles? But he's terrible."

"Exactly. That makes him interesting." Hugo crossed his ankles on the box, mirroring Kate's. His scuffed shoe ended up touching her stylish pump, but neither of them moved away. "You ever see the movie *The Petrified Forest*?" he asked.

"I don't think so."

"It was sort of dark and heavy, but for me, it was like breathing fresh air for the first time. Humphrey Bogart was in it. You ever heard of him?"

"No."

"He's not famous or anything, but that's the kind of actor I want to be. Not some perfect hero, but the kind of guy where you don't know what he'll do next, so you keep watching. He's got another movie coming out next month." Hugo tapped his shoe against Kate's. She thought it was an accident, but then he tapped it again. "If you stick around long enough, maybe I'll take you."

Kate felt his foot leaning against hers and decided to tap it back. "If I stick around long enough, maybe I'll let you."

Hugo turned to smile at her.

And Kate smiled back.

And just like that, she wasn't in such a hurry to go back to San Francisco.

"I swear, the whole world's gone stupid," a voice grumbled, and Kate pulled her eyes from Hugo's to see Reuben shuffling toward them, his bald head glowing with a sheen of sweat. He sank to the canvas chair on the other side of Hugo, holding a newspaper. "People have no idea what's going on over there."

"Over where?" Kate asked.

Hugo groaned. "You had to ask."

"That genius Chamberlain. What a patsy. Signs some paper with Hitler and thinks he's got peace for our time. You want to know who's paying for Chamberlain's precious peace? Jews, that's who, getting sent to Poland right now, by the thousands, and everybody turns a blind eye." Reuben snapped the newspaper open.

"Don't ever ask," Hugo advised in a low voice.

Kate tried to read the headlines from a distance. "It is sort of scary, what's happening over there."

"Right, but nobody wants another war."

The piano music stopped and the choreographer called out a couple of names.

"Where's Aurelio?" Kate asked. "He's going to miss the dance audition."

"He already got cut at the acting," Hugo said. "He doesn't have the right look either."

"But—" Kate sat straighter, pulling her feet off the box. "He'll get to show them his dancing, won't he?"

"Nah, they don't want some Latin lover in a zoot suit."

"But they need to see him dance! He's way better than anyone here. As good as Fred Astaire—only *gorgeous*!"

Hugo raised an eyebrow. "Noticed, did you?"

"Of course I noticed. I have a pulse."

"Well, it doesn't matter. This is a B movie, made quick and cheap for matinees. For moms and kids, everything clean-cut and all-American. They want another Mickey Rooney, blond and freckled, not some boy named Aurelio Dios."

"Mickey Rooney," Kate scoffed. "I don't know a single girl with his picture in her locker. Clive Falcon sits in his office with a bunch of middle-aged men and thinks he knows what people want. If he wanted to make money, he'd put Aurelio Dios in this movie, and every girl in America would buy a ticket—*five times*!"

The blond boy sitting on Kate's other side spoke up. "To see some pachuco? Their mothers wouldn't approve."

Kate didn't know what a pachuco was but could guess from his tone. She turned to him. "Which is why all the girls *would*. They'd hide his picture in their diaries and kiss it when no one was looking."

The blond raised his eyebrows but didn't reply.

She sank back in her chair, annoyed that all her efforts to get them into the audition had come to nothing. "So," she said grumpily. "The only ones who get to show off their dancing are the ones who have the right look?"

"That's right," Hugo said. "And the only ones who get to show off their singing are the ones who have the right look *and* the right dance skills."

She scowled. "It's all wrong, the way they're doing it. The best dancers and singers are getting cut along the way. The three auditions should be completely separate—acting, dancing, and singing. That's the only way to find the best of everything."

"Huh. I never thought of it like that, but you might be right."

"Of course I'm right. Things like that are just obvious to me.

Like school clubs. The most important topics should be discussed first, but the president always spends forever on something stupid and runs out of time. And my aunt's Junior League meetings—the clipboard is always a disaster."

"Clipboard?" Hugo asked.

"For volunteer sign-ups." Kate noticed his amused expression and stopped herself. She hadn't meant to show her fastidious side. A boy like Hugo Quick wasn't interested in girls who joined school clubs and served tea at Junior League meetings.

He said, "Don't stop now, it was just getting good."

"Sorry, didn't mean to rant."

"I'm serious." He waited a few seconds. "Look, I'm not going to sleep tonight if you don't tell me what's wrong with this clipboard."

She smiled. "Fine, then. It never makes it all the way around the room. A hundred women in rows, and no one knows which way to pass it, front or back, and then some dunce passes it across the aisle and an entire section gets missed. I keep telling my aunt they need two clipboards, one for each side, always moving front to back, but they never fix it."

"The world needs people like you to keep it organized."

Kate looked for the tease in his face, but he seemed serious.

The choreographer shouted for a fifteen-minute break, and the room rumbled with movement as everyone went in search of restrooms and food.

Aurelio sauntered toward them, one hand holding his pin-stripe jacket over his shoulder. His pants *were* a little baggy and pegged, Kate noticed, but it wasn't an obvious zoot suit. "You guys ready to scram?" he asked.

"We have to wait for Bonnie," Kate said.

Aurelio glanced at the dance area, which was deserted except for a few young actors sitting around waiting. "Well, I'm going to hoof around on that nice floor while we wait. Catch." He tossed his jacket to Hugo and made his way to the pianist. Kate expected the pianist to shake his head, needing a break, but he laughed at something Aurelio said and sat back down.

The pianist ran his fingers up and down the keys while Aurelio retied a shoelace, then started a peppy melody. Aurelio tapped a few steps with loose limbs, then spun in a circle and started tapping in earnest.

"Wait oh wait oh wait oh wait!" Bonnie cried, hurrying toward them.

Aurelio grinned in delight. "Princess!" He met her at the edge of the dance floor, grabbed her hand, and brought her to the center. The two of them tapped side by side, trying to copy each other's steps, fumbling and laughing, then Aurelio called back to the pianist, and the music changed to the song from that morning, from the movie *Swing Time*. Bonnie's face lit up as Aurelio swung her into his arms, and their feet started hopping in perfect rhythm.

The pianist sang the lyrics. *"Nothing is impossible, I have found . . . for when my chin is on the ground . . . I pick myself up . . ."*

They tapped and turned in the same fancy polka Aurelio had done with Kate at the house, only Bonnie knew the steps and did them with effortless grace, her right hand held by Aurelio's, her left drifting daintily. They looked perfectly paired, both petite, her blond hair glowing next to his gleaming dark. They turned and leaned in easy unison, connected by invisible strings. Even when they missed a step—laughed and found their footing again—they looked enchanting.

The music changed and Aurelio pulled one arm back so they were tapping side by side, his other arm sliding behind Bonnie's small waist—the way he'd tried with Kate, and now she saw how it was supposed to be done. Bonnie and Aurelio turned slowly, side by side, linked by his outstretched arm, their feet tapping in delicate percussion.

The pianist's velvety baritone pulled them along. *"I take a deep breath . . . pick myself up . . . dust myself off . . . start all ooover again."*

"They're good," the blond boy next to Kate said.

"They're amazing," Hugo said. "I had no idea that girl could dance like that."

A magical spotlight seemed to follow Bonnie and Aurelio as they tapped and whirled. Everyone in the room turned to watch, even workmen.

"Can that Latin boy sing too?" the blond asked. "If he can, he's dangerous."

"Oh, he can sing," Hugo said.

As the music slid to a conclusion, Aurelio lifted Bonnie in a playful leap to the side that didn't quite work, and they finished laughing. Their audience laughed with them and clapped.

The blond boy stood and looked down at Kate—taller and older than she'd thought, maybe nineteen or twenty. "You're right. People would pay money to see that." He smiled—handsome enough to make her wish she'd been a little nicer. "You're Kitty Hildebrand, aren't you?"

Which explained the sudden chattiness. She replied coolly, "I am."

He pushed his hands into his pockets, looking amused by the chill. "I'm Tad Falcon, the production manager on this picture. My father just gave me the unwelcome task of finding some way of using you—without really *using* you—and I think I just found the answer."

"Oh?" Kate sat straighter, her face warming as she tried to remember what rude things she'd said about his father. "I know I'm not a good actress."

"No, you're an organizer, and I could use a good organizer around here. How would you like to be my production assistant, Kitty?"

She blinked, unsure what that meant. "Well . . . first of all, I go by Kate now."

"She'll do it," Hugo said.

She glared at Hugo, then returned her attention to Tad—

which meant looking up. He had to be at least six-two or -three. "What does a production assistant do?"

He shrugged. "Help me organize hundreds of people and thousands of dollars. Fetch coffee and get blamed for everything. Work half the night and come back at dawn. I won't lie—it's hard work and no glamour. Oh—and not much money."

Kate stared at him. In a strange way, it sounded fabulous.

"You'll get credit in the publicity, of course. My father will see to that. And—" His lips tilted in a teasing smile. "If you accept the job, I think you'll like your first task." He tipped his head toward the dance floor. "Go tell Bonnie and that Latin friend of yours to meet me in the music department. I want our music director to hear them sing together."

CHAPTER 10

The sun was dipping toward the horizon as they all piled into the yellow car.

"The lead part!" Aurelio cried, sliding behind the steering wheel. "I need to telegram my uncle. Two hundred bucks a week!"

"Oh, I make loads more than that," Bonnie said cheerily. She slid closer to him, leaving plenty of room for Kate on the front seat.

"I won't know what to do with that much money."

"Pay the phone bill," Hugo advised from the back.

"I get to call the Galaxy and tell them I quit their crappy job where they take all my tips." Aurelio laughed as he started the engine. "Nah, I'm just not going to show up tonight."

"Where's Ollie?" Reuben asked, sitting behind Kate.

"Must have taken a bus," Hugo said.

"Six in the morning!" Aurelio looked over his shoulder as he backed up the car. "Why do we have to start so early?"

"So we can rehearse, silly. I know all the songs and dances, but you don't."

"That music guy said he thought I would have a Mexican accent. I said—why would I have an accent? I was born in Fresno."

He and Bonnie laughed together. As the car left the studio, Bonnie turned on the radio, and the two of them sang along to Ella Fitzgerald.

Kate glanced back at Hugo and Reuben, wondering how they felt about Aurelio getting a part when they hadn't. Reuben chewed on a thumbnail, and Hugo stared out the side window, his expression strangely empty. She remembered what a failure she'd felt like after leaving Clive Falcon's office and couldn't imagine feeling that way for two years . . . over and over again.

Hugo's time would come.

Wouldn't it?

Hundreds of cars passed them on the crowded highway, and Kate wondered how many of their drivers had come to Hollywood seeking fame and fortune, only to settle for jobs pumping gasoline or selling vacuum cleaners.

The sky was peachy dusk by the time they turned onto her grandfather's street, lined by lovely mansions. Ollie's property stood out like a dark smudge. Kate hoped he'd made it home all right. The house looked abandoned.

"You have to come inside so we can tell Mama," Bonnie told Aurelio as the car turned into the Fairchilds' driveway. "You too, Kate. The two of you can stay for dinner."

"Thank you, but not tonight," Kate said. As soon as the car stopped moving, she stepped out and hurried down the street.

Hugo caught up. "He's probably in his office."

They went up the long front path and entered the house. Kate found the light switch and flipped it on, illuminating the golden lantern overhead.

A whimpering sound made her look to the staircase.

Ollie sat hunched a few steps up, squinting against the new light, his cheeks damp. At the sight of her, his face crumpled. "I'm sorry, Kate. I tried—I really did—but I couldn't—" His voice cracked. "And now I've ruined everything."

"Nothing is ruined." She took a step and stopped uncertainly.

She rarely cried herself and never knew what to do or say when her friends got upset. She was relieved when Hugo walked by her and sat next to Ollie, putting his arm around his shoulders.

"That's why I gave you the bus fare, so you could leave when you wanted."

"I took the wrong bus. I got lost and walked for hours." Tears streamed from Ollie's eyes. "I was so upset when I got here, I didn't know what I was doing. I couldn't think straight."

Hugo squeezed Ollie's shoulders. "You're home now and everything is fine. Better than fine. Aurelio got a part in the movie, and Kate's going to be a production assistant." His gaze shifted to her. "She's not leaving town for a while."

"I'm not leaving," she echoed.

"But you didn't see. You don't know what I've done." Ollie's voice broke on a sob.

"It's all right. You're home now," Hugo said.

Kate's chest felt hollow. She shouldn't have forced him to go. A person didn't stay inside a house for four years without some powerful feelings holding them back. She should have known that; she had her own irrational fears. If someone forced her into a dark room and locked the door, she would lose her mind. She felt queasy at the thought. "I'm so sorry, Ollie. I shouldn't have made you go."

Reuben and Aurelio entered, stopping short at the sight of Ollie. "What the hell," Reuben said.

Ollie moaned and buried his face against his knees, wrapping his arms over his head. His muffled voice came through. "I don't want to be seen like this."

"You guys go into the living room," Hugo said. "I'll get him settled, then make us some dinner. Food fixes everything." He patted Ollie's shoulder.

"Sure thing," Aurelio said, turning to the living room.

But Reuben didn't move, his eyes narrowing. The lantern overhead cast his face into stark shadows, making the long scar across his cheek stand out. "You think this has something to do with . . . ?" He didn't finish, but the look he shared with Hugo seemed to hold a hidden message.

"I don't know. Give me a minute and I'll find out."

Reuben walked to the living room, looking back over his shoulder with an uneasy scowl.

"What was that about?" Kate asked.

"Nothing." Hugo tipped his head toward the back of the house. "Go on. I'll take him upstairs."

"But—"

"Just go!" Ollie wailed, his head still buried beneath his arms. His gray hair was matted from wearing a hat, and he still wore the too-tight clothes he'd put on for the studio. Not the same jovial man who'd greeted her the night before. And it was her fault. But Hugo could comfort him better than she could, so she obeyed and left.

The back hall was nearly dark this late in the day. She flipped a switch and two sconces flickered into light. She passed Ollie's dark office.

The dog rose to its feet at the end of the hall and whined. The back door was open, like last night, but tonight's breeze had a bite in it. Kate went to close the door but paused, looking up.

The moon was already visible in the sunset sky, hanging at about seventy degrees. It looked full, but she knew it wasn't tonight—a waning gibbous of about 98 percent. She stepped outside and oriented herself, knowing the moon was roughly east right now, which meant north was on her left. She glanced around for a good vantage point for the telescope.

The patio was large but worn by age, with several fat urns filled with barren dirt. A couple of steps led to a swimming pool filled with green water, speckled with dead leaves from the overgrown trees.

No—green, healthy leaves, Kate realized. She walked down the two steps, curious, and saw lily pads and grass growing in the pool. The water rippled and an orange fish skimmed the surface.

She gave a weak laugh. "Why am I surprised?" The pool's pumping equipment had probably stopped working a decade ago.

She wondered if the plants had grown naturally, or if someone in the house—Hugo, maybe—had turned it into a pond on purpose. It was almost pretty.

Kate looked at Hugo's pool house and saw the corner of a bed through the window. She took a step, then stopped herself, glancing back at the house.

The dog watched her, rooted in the doorway.

She returned to the house, hugging herself against the chill. The dog whimpered and backed out of her way. "In or out?" she asked, holding the door. The dog shuffled to the dark kitchen doorway and looked back with lonely eyes. "You'll have to wait for Hugo to feed you." Kate shut the back door and entered the kitchen, flipping the light switch. She took a step—and halted with a gasp.

Lemmy lay sprawled on the kitchen floor, between Kate and the table.

Her alarm quickly hardened into anger, her heart racing. "Very scary, Lemmy, but I never fall for the same trick twice."

He kept up the act, not moving. He'd probably returned from visiting his boss in prison to find an empty house. Ollie had told him they'd gone to Falcon Pictures, and now he wanted to prove his own acting skills, hoping for a chance at Hollywood fame.

But tonight's death pose wasn't as convincing as last night's, his body curled on its side, his face half hidden by his arm. "It can't be comfortable down there." Kate watched for a blink or breath, but there was nothing, and a prickle of unease ran through her. She took a few cautious steps and saw a dark puddle on the checkered floor beneath him, hard to see on the black tiles, but leaking red onto the white.

Her legs turned to jelly. She stumbled back into the wall and screamed.

Hugo arrived in a worried rush. "What's wrong?" He noticed the body on the floor and released an exasperated breath. "Get up, Lemmy. It isn't funny." He looked at Kate. "He's just faking."

She gave a stiff shake of her head, unable to say it.

Hugo's gaze darted back to the floor. "Lemmy?" He walked closer and crouched down.

"Stupid mutt," Reuben muttered, pushing his way around the dog in the doorway. He saw Hugo inspecting Lemmy and his eyes widened. "Jeez, is that for real?"

Aurelio entered behind him, stopping short when he saw.

Hugo took his time, bent low, fingering Lemmy's neck for a pulse, then checking the eyelids. He rolled Lemmy onto his back, and the arm flopped in a strange, stiff way. He pulled back the front of the suit jacket and inspected the bloody shirt underneath.

Kate closed her eyes, but that made her body sway, so she forced them back open.

Hugo rose, shaking his head, holding his bloody hands away from his sides.

"No fooling?" Reuben stepped closer. "What'd he do, slip when he was carrying a knife, or something?"

"Stabbed twice, I think. One of the wounds doesn't look too deep, but the other one is pretty bad." Hugo's eyes met Kate's, his expression grim, and she knew he was remembering what she was remembering.

I was so upset when I got here, I didn't know what I was doing.

She pressed a hand over her mouth, suddenly cold all over. Her father was a killer, and now her grandfather.

Hugo moved toward her and stopped, his own hands covered in blood. He gave a small shake of his head, his eyes tight on hers—a private message she didn't believe. They'd both heard Ollie's tearful confession. *You don't know what I've done.*

"Jeez, I gotta tell my sister that her stepkid is dead." Reuben rubbed a hand over his bald head. "She thinks he walks on water."

Kate said through a dry throat, "We have to call the police."

"Wait," Hugo said. "I need to think a minute." He took a restless step, picking up a rag on the counter.

"What's there to think about?" Kate asked, her voice a little stronger. Lemmy lay dead on the kitchen floor, his blood pooling.

"The sooner the police get here, the sooner they can figure out the truth and arrest his killer."

Hugo wiped his bloody hands on the rag, avoiding her gaze. "The killer is far away by now."

"Or very close," she said tightly.

He rubbed the rag hard around a fingernail.

"You think Ollie did this?" Reuben asked.

Hugo shot him a furious look. "Are you crazy? Why would he kill Lemmy?"

"You saw him blubbering out there. We made him leave the house and he cracked. Maybe Lemmy said something that, you know, got him riled up." He gave Hugo a look that seemed to say more.

Hugo glared back. "Ollie wouldn't kill someone. He won't even kill a spider."

"You don't know what people are capable of," Kate murmured. Her father had been a thief for years, and no one had guessed. Certainly not Kate, lying in a dark hole, waiting for her smart, handsome father to rescue her. She'd imagined him crazed with worry, offering a reward, demanding the police do more. But he'd been too busy hiding his crimes and killing her mother.

Reuben stared down at Lemmy. "Let's not pretend any of us are sad he's dead."

"Show some respect," Hugo snapped.

"For him? He was a louse, and we all know it."

Aurelio hadn't moved past the doorway. "We better call the police."

"Not yet," Reuben said. "I gotta go through my room and make sure nothing has my real name on it. Nothing linking me to the club, or they'll turn me over to the feds."

Aurelio's eyes widened. "Maybe someone at the club did this. None of the upstairs guys like him very much. That's the talk in the kitchen, anyway."

Hugo looked at Reuben. "You think Moe Kravitz ordered a hit?"

Reuben ran a thumb over his scar. "Beats me. I haven't talked to anybody at that place in months. I go near the club, the feds will slap me with a subpoena and make me testify. But there's a way to find out." He crouched next to Lemmy, stuck his fingers inside the shirt collar, and pulled out a string with a key at the end. "Nobody at the club did this. They all know to take the key." He pulled the string over Lemmy's head.

"Why's he so stiff?" Aurelio asked.

Hugo answered, "Rigor mortis." He added gruffly, glancing at Kate, "I studied it for my play."

Reuben searched Lemmy's pockets, not seeming to mind the blood. He pulled out a pack of Wrigley's gum, a handkerchief, a scrap of paper with writing on it, and another key. He stood, shoving the items into his own pockets.

Evidence, Kate realized. "We shouldn't move anything before the police get here."

"Nobody calls the coppers until I say so," Reuben said. "They find out who I am, I'll have to testify, and it doesn't matter if I lie on a stack of Bibles all day long, the minute new evidence turns up, Moe will think I squealed, and that's my death sentence. So I'm Charles Kensington, you got that?" He pointed a bloody finger at Kate.

"Back off," Hugo warned.

"She needs to understand the gravity of the situation."

"I just found a dead body," she said through gritted teeth. "I think I understand the gravity." But her heart beat madly. In the fun of going to Falcon Pictures, she'd forgotten that Reuben used to count money for a mobster now in prison, and Aurelio waited tables at the same shady club, and even Hugo had once washed dishes there.

"What's going on?" a faint voice asked, and they all turned. Ollie stood in the doorway, puffy-eyed but calmer than a moment ago. His gaze shifted to Lemmy and his eyebrows lifted. "Rehearsing without me? I thought you were going to cook something, Hugo."

No one moved for a second, then Hugo gave a gasping laugh. "You don't know."

"Know what?"

"He's dead, you nitwit," Reuben said. "Did *you* do this?"

"Dead?" Ollie's gaze darted back to Lemmy. "No, he's just . . . rehearsing."

His confusion looked real, but Kate had been fooled by a good performance before. "He's been stabbed," she said. "Did you hear anything or see anyone?"

"No, I was . . . I was in my bedroom. I didn't come back here." Ollie looked at Hugo, his brow furrowing in childlike confusion. "Is this some sort of prank? Because I'm really not in the mood for it."

"Not a prank," Hugo said, his voice steadier now that Ollie seemed innocent. He tossed the bloody rag at Reuben. "Clean up, Charles Kensington, get rid of anything with your name on it, then give Aurelio the all clear so he can go next door and call the police. Ollie, you better go upstairs and get in bed. Say you've been there with a headache since you got home and didn't hear anything."

"I *didn't* hear anything." Ollie stared at Lemmy. "He's really dead?"

"Come on," Reuben growled, steering Ollie toward the door. He muttered under his breath, "Jeez, I hate Mondays."

Aurelio left with them, and the room fell silent except for the tick of the clock on the wall. Lemmy looked strangely small and alone on the checkered floor, staring at nothing.

"I'll watch over him," Hugo said quietly. "You go sit in the living room."

"All right."

"Kate."

She turned back in the doorway.

"You won't tell the police about Reuben's real name, will you? He wants to escape that life, and if the feds make him testify against his old boss, he'll end up dead."

She debated for a moment but knew Reuben couldn't have killed Lemmy; he'd been at Falcon Pictures with her. "Reuben who? I thought his name was Charles Kensington."

Hugo's lips curved in a smile of appreciation that made her forget everything else for a moment.

But her mood quickly sobered. "Hugo, you don't think Ollie—"

"No. You saw him. He didn't even know Lemmy was dead. And besides—" Hugo hesitated, glancing at the body. "He's too stiff. That much rigor mortis means he's been dead at least four or five hours. Ollie hasn't been home that long. He took the wrong bus and got lost, so he couldn't have done it."

"We only have his word for that."

Hugo's eyes burned with certainty. "Ollie's word is good enough for me."

He believed in her grandfather more than she did.

"Kate, I don't think we should tell the police about Ollie crying on the staircase. It might give them the wrong idea."

This lie felt heavier than Reuben's. Lying to the police in a murder investigation wasn't smart or sensible. But right now, looking at Hugo, all she wanted was for him to be right. Partly, because she wanted Ollie to be innocent. Partly, because the fire in Hugo's eyes warmed something inside her that had been cold for a very long time.

"Kate." The low rasp in his voice stoked the warm embers. "I can't explain how I know Ollie didn't do it, I just do. He and I understand each other. I know that's not proof, but it is for me."

"All right." For now, at least, she would shield her grandfather— the actor with a thousand faces.

CHAPTER 11

Kate sat alone on the green velvet sofa, her spine straight, her hands squeezed together. Night had fallen, and she'd turned on the lamp beside her—a brass sculpture of a half-naked goddess holding up a glowing world.

Her gaze shifted to the wheelbarrow of hats. Maybe Hugo understood her grandfather, but she didn't, and she couldn't stay in a house where people were murdered.

She heard hushed voices and looked to the foyer to see Hugo, Aurelio, and Reuben huddled at the base of the stairs. Hugo had said he would stay with the body, but she'd seen him carrying a plate upstairs a short time ago—probably food for Ollie—and now he whispered with Reuben and Aurelio. She craned her ears but couldn't hear what they were saying. Aurelio left through the front door, and Hugo walked back toward the kitchen.

Reuben entered the living room, short and stocky, his arms loaded with papers. He crossed to the fireplace, dumped the papers inside, then crouched and struck a match.

"Burning evidence before the police get here?" Kate asked, in no mood to be careful.

Reuben gave her a sideways glance. "This has nothing to do with Lemmy getting stabbed."

"How do *you* know? Unless you know who killed him—and why."

He blew on the embers, then plucked a photograph from the edge of the pile and handed it to Kate. The photo showed a blond girl inside a distant second-floor window, wearing only a bra and panties, stepping into a dress, seemingly unaware of the camera outside. The girl's image was grainy, but it was definitely Bonnie.

"Who took this?" she demanded, horrified. Bonnie had mentioned spying on Ollie's house from her bedroom window; she didn't know they were spying back.

"Not me." Reuben snatched the photo and tossed it back in the fireplace. "I found them under Lemmy's mattress. My guess, he took them in case she got famous. Studios will pay big money to keep photos like that from seeing the light of day." He picked up a different photo and held it toward Kate for her to see—a man with a woman in an evening dress on his lap, both of them laughing. "Most of the photos he took are from the club. Drunk actors misbehaving." He tossed the photo onto the flames. "Some of those movie star marriages aren't as perfect as the studios want you to think."

Kate watched the flames lick around the edges of the pile, her stomach tight with disgust. "Did you know he took pictures like that?"

"No, but it doesn't surprise me." Reuben picked up the poker and jabbed at the smoldering pile. "Lemmy Berman was a snake, through and through, and I'm glad he's dead."

"And Ollie let him live here."

"Your granddad lives in fairy-tale land, in case you haven't noticed." Reuben glanced her way and shrugged. "I didn't know Lemmy was like that either, at first, and by the time I did, it was too late. I couldn't get rid of him."

Kate frowned, remembering Lemmy in the kitchen that morning as they'd eaten pancakes. He'd made a few snide remarks about telling Moe Kravitz what Reuben had been up to lately. Reuben had looked angry, but also a little afraid, biting back his temper. And now it made sense. "Was Lemmy blackmailing you too?"

"None of your business."

Her own temper sparked. "I just found him dead a few feet from my bedroom, and now I'm watching you burn evidence. I think it's my business." She added, feeling reckless, "And I know your real name—Reuben Feigenbaum."

He turned, holding the poker, his eyes narrowing into dangerous slits.

Her heart raced, but Hugo and her grandfather were only a scream away. "Are you in some of those photos?"

His mouth twisted. "Nobody wants to see me in my BVDs." He lifted the poker and pointed to a wide, flat book in the fire, its edges catching fire. "It's that ledger that keeps me up at night, and I'm not burning it to protect myself, I'm burning it to protect your sweet old granddad."

Kate stared at the book—a business ledger, not embarrassing photos—trying to make sense of it. "My grandfather works for Moe Kravitz too?"

Reuben gave a short laugh. "You kidding? Moe eats actors like him for breakfast."

"What do you mean?"

"Big shot movie stars. They come into the club, throwing their money around like it'll never run out. But it always does. And then their good buddy Moe offers to give them a loan. And when their next picture tanks, they borrow more. And when they can't make the interest payments, he takes their mansions and their fancy cars, and then Mr. Big Shot Movie Star is broke and homeless, and Moe Kravitz is richer and laughing."

It sounded like some B-grade gangster movie. "Ollie borrowed money from Moe Kravitz?"

"Plenty, starting five or six years ago, when the studios stopped hiring him."

"Stopped hiring him? He stopped taking roles. He told me about it on the phone once, how he got tired of dealing with the big studios."

Reuben grunted. "Believe that if you want, but that's not what Hugo told me."

Kate hesitated, then asked, "What did Hugo tell you?"

"That movies got sound, and silent film stars went out of style. You know, all the big eyes and dramatic poses. Nobody wants that anymore. He did three talking pictures, and they all tanked. Some critic called him a cloak-and-dagger clown, and then no one would touch him."

Kate felt a bit hollow. She'd imagined a more mutual lack of interest, not Ollie reading humiliating reviews and nobody wanting him.

Reuben fed a couple of loose photographs to the flames. "He was only a name on the books for me. Six months ago, I was getting papers ready to have him kicked out of this house, when Moe got arrested and I needed a place to hide. So I came here." He cast her a sideways look, almost embarrassed. "And a funny thing happened."

"You liked him," Kate guessed.

"I felt sorry for him. He had no clue how much trouble he was in. I organized his bank papers and tried to show him how bad it was. Told him to sell his old movie stuff, and he might make enough to save the house. But he thinks Moe is some nice friend from the good old days who only wants the best for him."

Kate looked at the ledger, which was starting to blacken and curl. "That book shows Ollie's loan?"

"The end of it. July 1938." Reuben touched it with the poker. "After I'd been here a few months, I snuck into the club and brought it back here. Copied the whole thing, fudging numbers so it looked like Ollie paid back the money. Moe doesn't pay attention to details like that. He'd never know. Then I took the fake book back to the club and kept the real one here."

"You erased Ollie's loan." Kate thought it through. "But Lemmy was the new bookkeeper and figured it out."

Reuben snorted. "He was too lazy to dig that deep. But he overheard me talking about it with Hugo, and then I was his patsy and we both knew it. If he told Moe what I'd done, I'd be dead, slow and painful. And Ollie wouldn't smell so sweet either, even though he knew nothing about it."

"Ollie doesn't know? He thinks he still owes the money?"

"I told him I found some old bank account and paid it back. He kept asking me when my unpleasant *friend* was going to move out. But Lemmy was having too much fun to go anywhere. A cat playing with a bunch of half-dead mice."

Kate frowned. "But if Lemmy told Moe Kravitz, wouldn't the fake ledger prove him wrong?"

"Only on the surface. Any decent accountant could figure it out once they knew what to look for. That fake ledger proved I fudged the numbers."

"But—" Kate looked at the fire. "That's the *real* ledger, right? So, you kept it. After Lemmy heard you talking to Hugo, you could have returned it to the club and destroyed the fake. Then Lemmy's story would have looked invented and you would look innocent."

Reuben grunted. "You're too smart for your own good." He turned his back to her and stared into the fire.

It dawned on her. "If you'd done that, Ollie would still owe the money and lose the house. You let Lemmy push you around to protect Ollie."

Reuben stabbed a stray photograph with the poker and pushed it deeper. "I'm no saint. I kept this real ledger just in case. But now Lemmy's dead, and I'm done with it. Ollie's loan is gone for good."

"So . . ." She saw the obvious. "You killed Lemmy for Ollie's sake."

He gave a smirking laugh. "Now you're talking stupid. I was at the studio with you."

Which left only one conclusion. "Then Ollie must have killed him. He and Lemmy were home alone, Lemmy told him you lied about paying back the loan, that he was going to lose the house—gloated about it—and Ollie snapped."

"If he did, I owe him one." Reuben turned slowly to face her. "But I can't see it. It's not so easy, killing a man when you're looking him in the eye. Ollie doesn't have it in him."

Kate didn't want to know how Reuben knew that. "How could you work at a place like that?"

His scarred cheek sagged, making him look sad and sorry. "I didn't know at first. Thought it was just a little crooked gambling. Taking money from folks who had plenty and threw it around. And by the time I knew the whole racket, I was in too deep. That's how Moe operates—makes sure everyone's hands get a little bit dirty, so they can never leave. Like I said, I'm no saint."

The ledger was now fully engulfed in flames, Ollie's loan destroyed. He'd been a fool to borrow money from a man who ran an illegal gambling club, and an even bigger fool not to pay it back.

But Kate had no right to judge. She'd made a horrible mistake of her own once. A mistake that couldn't be erased in a fire. "Thank you, Reuben. My grandfather will never know what you did for him, but I do."

"It's over now," he muttered, sliding the poker back into its holder. "Time to face the coppers, I guess."

Outside, sirens wailed.

Reuben opened the door to two uniformed police officers. They talked in the foyer a moment, glancing at Kate in the living room, then a detective in a suit and hat arrived, and they all walked toward the back of the house.

Kate remained where she was, not wanting to see Lemmy again.

The dog entered the living room, shuffled to the empty wing-back chair, and dropped to the floor with a weary exhalation. "I know just how you feel," Kate muttered.

Outside, tires squealed, a car door slammed, and men's voices called out. Kate expected a knock on the door, but it didn't come, so she stood and peered around the drapes, and saw several reporters setting up camera tripods in the front yard. Two argued over the best location, as more hurried toward the house, carrying equipment.

Her stomach dropped. Of course it would be on the front page—a man murdered in Oliver Banks's kitchen.

A flashbulb popped and flared in front of her, making her squint. "It's the granddaughter!" The other reporters scurried to face the window, more flashbulbs flaring, someone shouting her name.

Kate dropped the drape and stumbled back, her head flooding with a four-year-old memory—her first morning after leaving the hospital, naively opening Aunt Lorna's drapes to find the world staring back, scrambling into motion at the sight of her. The first time she'd really understood that she was famous.

And now it was happening again.

"Kitty! Is your grandfather home?"

"Can you tell us who's been killed, Kitty?"

"Miss Hildebrand?" This voice came from behind her, and she whirled, her heart in her throat, to see a detective in a suit and hat entering the living room. He nodded toward the window. "Sorry about them. Always quick to smell blood, especially at a movie star's house."

She opened her mouth, but her head felt drained of words and blood. Outside, voices still shouted her name.

"Maybe you better sit down. You look kind of pale."

"I'm fine, thank you." But she sat on the green sofa.

"I'm Detective Bassett." He stopped on the other side of the gilded coffee table and pulled out a notebook. "Mr. Kensington says you're the one who found him?"

It took her a moment to realize he meant Charles Kensington—Reuben. "Yes, that's correct." She smoothed her dress over her knees.

"He says you all just got back from Falcon Pictures." He rummaged in his pockets and found a pencil. "That must have been exciting, visiting a real motion picture studio. Are you an actor, like your grandfather?"

"No, I only went because . . ." She wasn't sure how to explain. "The girl next door invited us. Aurelio got a part—he lives here—and I was hired as a production assistant."

Detective Bassett wrote in his notebook. His brown suit didn't fit very well, as if he'd ordered it from a Sears catalog. "And your grandfather? I understand he came home before the rest of you."

"Yes, he . . ." Kate glanced toward the staircase, where they'd found him crying. "He took a bus home earlier. But not much earlier. I mean, he wasn't here very long before we arrived."

The pencil paused, the detective looking up at Kate. "But he didn't find Mr. Berman's body?"

"No, he . . . he didn't go to the kitchen. He was upstairs in bed, I think." Her heart beat faster at the blatant lie.

The last lie she'd told the police had haunted her for four years.

Detective Bassett pushed up the brim of his hat, revealing tufts of gray hair. "Now, that's funny. First thing I always do when I get home is head to the kitchen to see what's good to eat. But that's just me, I guess."

Kate swallowed. "I think he had a headache. That's . . . that's why he left the studio before we did." She hoped her story matched Hugo's and Ollie's.

"One of the officers tells me he was called here last night in a very similar situation, only Mr. Berman wasn't dead, just playing a prank on you."

"Not a prank. They were rehearsing Hugo's play. But I thought it was real." The pencil scratched. It was unnerving to have everything she said written down.

Outside, the rumble of activity had increased. A reporter shouted something and another man laughed.

"You live here with your grandfather?"

She wasn't sure how to answer. She couldn't live in a house where people were murdered, but she didn't live anywhere else either. "I arrived last night to live with him. I didn't know he had boarders, so it surprised me when I found them rehearsing. That's why I thought it was real."

Detective Bassett scratched his forehead. "Seems a funny co-incidence, the way he was lying in the exact same spot. Makes me wonder if the person who killed him was here last night."

"Well . . . he wasn't in the *exact* same spot. But yes, I guess it is a strange coincidence. But we were at the studio when it happened." She added, "So none of us could have killed him."

"Except your grandfather, who came home early."

"But not very early."

The detective puckered his lips. He had a large nose that looked like it had been broken at some point. "I'm sort of wondering—if you all went to the studio together, why didn't Mr. Berman go with you?"

"Lemmy? He wasn't home. He was—" She probably shouldn't mention Moe Kravitz in prison, associating her grandfather's household with a gangster. "I don't know where he went." Another blatant lie. She squeezed her hands on her lap.

"Miss Hildebrand, I know it's not very pleasant, but can you tell me how you came to find him? What you did after entering the house?"

"Well. Hugo and I entered first." Her gaze skittered toward

the staircase. "I walked to the back of the house—because that's where my room is—and saw the back door open. Oh!" Her eyes widened. "Maybe the killer ran out that way."

"Could be." Detective Bassett wrote it down.

"I went to close the door and noticed the moon, so I went outside."

"Yeah, nice full moon tonight."

It was no longer full, but she let it slide. "I returned and found him in the kitchen. I thought he was pretending again, then I saw the blood and screamed." Her thoughts darted over Hugo inspecting the body, and Reuben emptying the pockets, and waiting fifteen minutes while Reuben burned dirty pictures and evidence of his real name and Ollie's crooked loan. But all she said was, "Then we called the police."

Somehow, she'd become part of their scheming.

Detective Bassett closed his notebook. "I think that's it for now, but I might have more questions tomorrow."

Kate watched him leave the room, wondering if she should warn him she might not be here tomorrow. She could probably catch an overnight train to San Francisco. Knock on a friend's door and sleep in a guest room until Mr. Norton sent money for a hotel. No one could expect her to stay here now.

Ironically, Lemmy's death was exactly what she'd needed.

But she'd been excited at the prospect of working at a movie studio. And getting to know her grandfather better. And even getting to know Hugo better. A few weeks of fun while she earned enough money to get back to her real life.

At least her trunks were still packed. She would wait for the police to leave, then go next door and call a taxi. She rose and made her way to the staircase, knowing she needed to tell her grandfather she was leaving.

CHAPTER 12

Three doors were open and one closed. Kate knocked on the closed door.

"Enter if you must," a gloomy voice called out.

She peeked inside. "Am I disturbing you?"

Ollie hurried to sit up on a large, canopied bed fit for a king. "No, no, come in, come in. I thought you were that detective again. Please—sit!" He extended an arm toward a brocade chair near the bed.

The room's disorder was less of a shock than it would have been a few days ago. The space looked like it had been grandly decorated once, with lush fabrics and heavy furniture, but was now crowded with Ollie's hoarded treasures—including a weather-beaten wooden woman over the fireplace—the figurehead from Captain Powell's ship, Kate guessed.

"Dreadful business about Lemmy." Ollie shoved pillows behind his back. "Just dreadful."

"Yes." Several paths led through the mess, and Kate followed one to the chair near the bed.

"Hugo says it must have been a thief after my valuables, and Lemmy came home and surprised him."

"Maybe." She sat cautiously on the shredded upholstery.

"I hope you found something to eat downstairs."

As if she should step over Lemmy's body to reach the refrigerator. "I'm not hungry, thank you."

"Hugo brought me some bread and jam before the police arrived." Ollie waved a hand at some dirty dishes on an ornate nightstand. "He's an excellent cook, by the way. I'll tell him to make his chicken pie for you tomorrow. You'll be quite impressed. Flakey crust and everything."

She needed to tell him she was leaving.

"Ah, Kate," he sighed, leaning back against the pillows. "I *so* wanted to impress you, and instead, I fled the studio like a scared rabbit and wept like a child. What must you think of me?"

"I think . . . I think you were very brave to leave the house with so little notice." She hesitated, realizing this was her chance to ask. "Ollie, when we came home and you were sitting on the stairs . . . when you said we didn't know what you'd done . . . what were you talking about?"

His face crumpled and his head dropped. "I'd give anything to undo it."

Panic spiked inside her. She shouldn't have asked. She didn't want to hear his confession and have to turn her own grandfather over to the police for murder. Lemmy had been a despicable human who'd threatened to take away Ollie's house—his sanctuary. "I understand why you—"

"He'll probably be dead by morning." Ollie lifted his head, his eyes brimming with tears.

Kate stared. "But . . . he's already dead."

Ollie released a breath. "You're probably right. Such a stupid thing to do, but I was so angry when I got home—angry at myself—and I thought, poor Budgie, he shouldn't be trapped in this house with me. So I just . . ." He stretched an arm toward the far side of the room. ". . . set him free."

Kate turned her head and saw a fancy birdcage on a stand near the window, its door open. It took her a moment to understand, then she laughed in relief. "You're talking about a *bird*?"

"Budgie. Best little friend I ever had. Kept me company for nine years, and I released him to the wolves. He won't survive out there."

Kate forced the smile from her face, but the fact that she'd actually suspected her grandfather of murder suddenly seemed ridiculous. If setting a pet bird free made him this upset, he hadn't stabbed Lemmy. "I'm sure Budgie will be fine." She changed the subject. "Aurelio got the lead part today."

Ollie's expression lifted. "Yes, and well deserved! That boy has enormous talent. And *you*! Hugo tells me they offered you a job too—big Hollywood producer!"

She laughed. "More of a coffee fetcher, I think. I'm only seventeen."

"Oh, age doesn't matter in this business. Look at Irving Thalberg. He was only twenty when he took over at Universal Studios. The Boy Wonder, we used to call him. That'll be you, Kate."

She needed to tell him she wasn't taking the job.

"You know," Ollie mused, studying her, "I think you look like Gracie."

"Gracie—your wife?" Kate didn't know anything about her Banks grandmother. Her mother had never talked about her, and Aunt Lorna was from the Hildebrand side of the family.

"Oh, we weren't married, just foolish kids in the same vaudeville troupe. She was an older woman by two years." He laughed. "Not a bad life for a sixteen-year-old boy—a different town every week and a pretty dancer to keep me company." He leaned forward to see around Kate. "There's a photo back there somewhere."

Kate went to a long table against the wall that was covered in

framed photographs. Most were publicity headshots of other actors, with scrawled autographs, but there were a few candid shots
of Ollie: lounging next to a swimming pool with two women in
sunglasses, laughing on a golf course, raising champagne flutes
with Gloria Swanson.

She picked up the golfing picture. The man about to swing
had a slim, dark mustache—Bonnie's father, Frank Fairchild.

"Not that one. Silver frame, back row. Keep going—that's it.
That's Gracie."

Kate brought the frame to the nightstand lamp and saw her
grandmother for the first time—a girl with long curls in a flouncy
dress, posed with one hand holding up her skirt to her knees,
showing off legs in a dance pose. "She looks so young."

"Eighteen and nobody's fool, that girl. She taught me a thing
or two." Ollie leaned closer to see the photo. "She was none too
happy when she found out she was going to have a baby. Had to
leave the troupe and move back with her grandparents. I called
her from the road a few times, but it was too expensive."

The fact that her very proper mother had been illegitimate
was a bit unsettling. "You didn't want to marry Gracie?"

He gave a short laugh. "Turned me down. Wise choice. I was
sixteen without a penny in my pocket. She showed up backstage a
few years later, put a toddler in my arms, and walked out. Said she
was going to Paris to dance. I tried finding her, years later, after
I'd made a success of myself, but never could."

Kate set the frame on the nightstand and returned to the
chair. "What did you do with a toddler?"

"Oh, the women in the troupe helped out. They adored Evie.
One of them said her sister would take her, but by the time we got
to that part of the country, I couldn't give her up. My days were
free. There isn't much rehearsing in vaudeville, same routine every
night, and she played in the dressing room while I was on stage.
Poor thing never had a decent bedtime."

"I had no idea." Kate had imagined her mother growing up

in glamorous Hollywood, with servants and ponies, not traveling with a vaudeville troupe. "When did you come to Hollywood?"

"Let's see . . . Evie was twelve, so that would have been 1913. She needed a real school, and I was itching to do movies. We rented this horrible little room in Culver City. That first year was pretty lean, let me tell you, then I started to get stunt work—driving motorcycles into barns, that sort of thing."

"*Real* motorcycles? Into *real* barns?"

He laughed. "Oh, I loved it. You learn how to use your body doing vaudeville, how to fall and make it funny. That's how I got my first movie role—Billy the bumbling cowboy. We used to make two pictures a week if you can believe it. Just silly nonsense. Nothing like the big productions they have these days."

"When did you start Captain Powell?" Kate leaned back on the chair, stretching out her legs.

"First one was 1917, but nobody paid much attention. Then we did a few more, and, next thing I know, my face is on magazine covers and Chaplin is inviting me to pool parties."

"*Charlie* Chaplin? You knew him?"

"Of course I knew him. I knew all of them. Fairbanks and Mary Pickford. Buster Keaton and Harry Lloyd. Hollywood wasn't so big back then. The best parties were always at Pickfair. I met Thomas Edison there, if you can believe it. And that British writer who wrote about the London detective."

"Sherlock Holmes? You met Arthur Conan Doyle?"

"That's the one. He came to Hollywood."

"But that's amazing. Who else did you meet?"

"Oh, lots of famous writers. They all wanted their books turned into movies."

He talked on, his voice muffled by the pillow below his cheek, telling her about a woman who'd climbed onto the roof of the house and refused to come down, waiting for Captain Powell to rescue her. "So I went up there, of course." He told her about a director he'd hated, and a few women he'd loved, and the two peacocks that had seemed like a fun idea for the backyard until they'd screamed all night.

His voice finally slowed and slid into sleep. Kate took away the magazine he'd been reading and pulled up his blanket.

The house was eerily quiet as she descended the staircase. She found Aurelio and Reuben in the living room, slouched at opposite ends of the fan-shaped sofa, talking in low voices.

"Hey, Kate." Aurelio looked exhausted, the lamp casting shadows across his handsome face. "The Fairchilds sent food. It's in the icebox."

"Are the police gone?" If so, she could go next door and call a taxi.

"Yeah," Aurelio said. "But one of them stayed behind on the porch to keep the reporters away, so you don't have to worry about the killer coming back."

"The killer isn't coming back," Reuben grumbled. "Somebody wanted Lemmy dead, and he's dead, so it's over."

"You want to sleep upstairs in my room?" Aurelio asked her. "It's a mess, but I can clean up fast, and tomorrow I'll move my things out so you can have it permanent."

"Thank you, but I'm fine down here." She didn't want to tell them she was leaving and risk them waking up Ollie so he could say goodbye. Better to sneak out.

"Here, take this." Reuben stood and pulled a gun from his pocket. "You won't need it, but it might make you feel safer." He held the gun toward her on the palm of his hand.

Kate stared at it, shocked. "I'm not touching that thing."

"It doesn't bite. Not unless you cock it and pull the trigger." Reuben waited a few seconds, then slid the gun into his pocket. "Suit yourself."

"Where's Hugo?" she asked, glancing at the empty wingback chair.

"On stage in that gory play of his," Reuben said. "Left a while ago."

The fact that he'd left without telling her stung a little. Now, she wouldn't have a chance to tell him goodbye.

She remembered something else. "I was expecting a telegram today—not the one this morning, something later."

"Didn't see anything," Reuben said. "And if it came while we were gone, the delivery boy would have left a note on the door-step."

Aurelio stood with a groan, stretching his back. "Bonnie says we're leaving for the studio at 5:30. Either of you have an alarm clock I can borrow?"

Reuben said, "Take mine and buy me a new one, now that you're rich."

"I don't get paid until Friday." The two of them walked to-ward the foyer. "Sorry you didn't get a part today, Reuben. Maybe next time."

"You think I want to be in some twinkle-toes movie with a bunch of kids?" They headed up the staircase.

It was time to leave.

Kate made her way to the kitchen, glad the light had been left on. But as soon as she entered, she halted, drawing a sharp breath.

Lemmy was gone, but his blood remained, a smeared puddle with a few stray shoeprints. Aurelio must have seen it when he'd put the Fairchilds' food in the refrigerator but left it for someone else to clean up. Hugo, no doubt.

The dog shuffled into the room and stopped, looking up at Kate with sad marble eyes. He had mottled gray fur and skinny legs. Probably a stray taken in by Hugo.

"I'm leaving," she told the dog, saying it aloud for the first time.

The dog whined and sat on its haunches.

Kate stared at the floor—not fake Hollywood blood—and wondered how long it would take to clean up. She could do that, at least, for Ollie and Hugo.

She entered the laundry room where her luggage was stored—

everything packed and ready to go—and found a mop and pail in a tall cupboard. She carried them back to the sink and filled the pail.

"I've never done this before," she told the dog.

It took her a moment to figure out how the ringer on top of the pail worked, then she pulled the wet mop through and slapped it on the floor. "Here goes nothing," she muttered, pushing it into the blood.

The raggedy strips turned red.

Kate froze, her hands tight on the mop handle. "Why am I doing this?" she asked aloud.

I am smart. I am sensible. Her daily statement to the mirror, two things she knew to be true.

She drew a breath and pushed the mop forward and back, and had the satisfaction of seeing the blood gradually disappear, absorbed by the cloth strips. She dunked the mop in the pail and pulled it through the ringer again, expelling pink water.

"No one can expect me to stay here," she told the dog, who watched from his belly.

She emptied the dirty water and refilled the pail, then mopped with more energy, liking the clean results. It felt good to move, her mind working as hard as her arms.

"I don't care about making movies," she told the dog. She was good at schoolwork and tennis. Good at reminding Aunt Lorna she had a dental appointment at three o'clock.

Ollie was probably long overdue for a dental appointment.

Kate rinsed the mop and refilled the pail, and then expanded her mopping beyond the crime scene, wiping away every speck of grime on the black-and-white checkered floor.

"I am not afraid," she said aloud. The lie she told herself every morning.

Dr. Gimble said she made lists to feel in control of the dark. He suggested baby steps—two seconds in the dark, then three, then four. She'd tried it once and never again.

Dr. Gimble didn't know the deeper reason behind her need to make lists and keep a tight rein on herself. She'd never told him.

Her darkest secret.

No more mistakes.

Living in this house wasn't a baby step, it was a leap off a bridge. Actors and gangsters, her grandfather wearing ridiculous costumes, everyone expecting Kate to drop out of school to work at a movie studio, people murdered feet from where she slept.

"It's absurd," she told the dog, moving a chair so she could mop under the table. When she got closer to the dog, it shifted out of the way—and she thought of a task for tomorrow's list: *Learn the dog's name.*

And that's when she knew she was staying.

A metallic clatter pulled Kate from sleep, the noise gone as soon as she knew it was there. She lay still, trying to decide if she'd dreamed it—

And heard a shuffling step in the laundry room, someone stumbling into her trunks, not turning on the light over the washer.

She sat up with a jerk, her heart filling her throat, her hand grabbing the butcher knife she'd put on the nightstand. Her mind screamed—*Run!*—but as she started to move, the silhouette of a man filled the doorway, blocking her escape.

"You all right?" Hugo's voice whispered.

Kate's heart tumbled out of her throat, allowing her to gasp a breath. "*Hugo.* You scared me to death."

"Oh, wow—I'm sorry." He took a worried step into the room, then seemed to think better of it and stepped back. "I saw you sitting up and wanted to make sure you were all right."

She released a lungful of air, lifting the butcher knife. "You almost got this in your chest." She set it on the nightstand.

He gave a ghost of a smile. "Glad to see you can protect yourself. But you don't need to worry. Whoever did this was after Lemmy, and he got him, so he won't be back."

Almost exactly how Reuben had said it. "You're so sure?"

"Lemmy was the kind of guy who had enemies." Hugo paused, then said in a quieter voice, "I wasn't sure you'd still be here when I got home."

"I almost wasn't." Kate pulled up her knees under the quilt and wrapped her arms around them. "I didn't hear you leave the house."

"I snuck out the back before the police got here, so they wouldn't make me late for work. I can talk to them tomorrow."

Which made sense. "Did you have a good . . . performance?" She wasn't sure how to word it.

"Not really." Hugo leaned against the door frame. He was across the room yet seemed close, somehow. Maybe it was their hushed voices. "It was pretty awful, actually, pretending to stab people after seeing Lemmy like that."

"Oh, right," she said softly. She hadn't thought of that. "Couldn't you just . . . explain and take the night off?"

"It's a job, Kate. I need the money."

She understood that better today than she would have a week ago. "I wish you'd gotten a part in Bonnie's movie." She paused. "Actually . . . I can't really picture you dancing in an ice cream parlor. In a strange way, I think I prefer you in a back-alley horror show."

The corner of his lips lifted. "In a strange way, I'm flattered."

A thrum of attraction ran through her.

"I'm glad you didn't leave, Kate."

"Me too," she murmured.

"Ollie needs you."

"Oh." That's what he meant.

"I've been trying to get him out of the house for two years, and you managed it in one day." Hugo's voice dropped, the rasp coming out. "The house feels different with you in it, as if . . ."

She waited, her heartbeat filling her.

"As if we've been lost at sea, drifting, knowing what we want but not how to get there. And then you showed up and got us into a big audition, and Ollie left the house, and Aurelio got a lead role. And it's like there's a captain at the helm, finally, steering us in the right direction, and we might actually get somewhere."

Kate tightened her arms around her knees, a little frightened by the analogy. She had enough trouble keeping her own life on course, making lists and trying to manage her fears. What she craved was dry land and safety. Friends who behaved as expected and boys she understood at a glance. Not a boy with a dangerous voice luring her into unsafe waters.

She said, "You better go now. I have to be up early."

"Right. Sorry." He took a step backward. "Good night, Kate."

"Good night." She listened as he crossed the kitchen and left through the back door.

Only then, with the spell broken, did she wonder what Hugo had been doing in the laundry room in the middle of the night.

CHAPTER 13

The early morning car ride was quiet, the world dark around them. Kate sat in the back seat, with Aurelio driving and Bonnie too tired to be enamored, her blond head resting against the opposite window.

They drove through the studio gates and parked in front of the two-story office building with palm trees out front.

Bonnie groaned as she left the car. "I'm so *tired*."

They entered the reception room, and Mr. Eckles emerged from a side door, looking impossibly wide awake behind his wire-rimmed glasses. His gaze slid down Aurelio's baggy suit and pegged trousers. "Aurelio Dios? They're waiting for you in wardrobe. Bonnie, show him the way, then both of you go to dance rehearsal. Scene blocking at ten, lunch, voice at one, then back to dance. Are you listening, Bonnie? Can you remember all that?"

Bonnie finished a yawn. "I'm not an idiot. It's the same every day."

"I'll tell your tutor to meet you in the commissary for lunch, then he'll have to follow you around to get in the required hours.

That's all you have time for today." Mr. Eckles's attention shifted to Kate. "I'm told you'll be working with Tad. He's late." The clock on the wall showed 6:10.

"I'll stay with Bonnie for now," Kate said, remembering her promise to keep an eye on her.

"Very well." Mr. Eckles strode away.

Aurelio flashed a grin. "That'll be you, Kate, bossing people around with a clipboard—only prettier."

Bonnie's sleepy eyes opened, shifting from Aurelio to Kate.

"Wardrobe," Kate reminded her.

Bonnie led them down a long hall and out a back door. They crossed a courtyard with two picnic tables—the sky starting to lighten—and entered another building, where costume racks crowded the hall and the noise of sewing machines already filled the air. They walked by a workroom filled with long cutting tables and barrels of rolled fabric.

"*Here* you are." An Asian woman with short black bangs came down the hall toward them. "Felix!" A young man appeared. "Take the boy for measuring. Bonnie, you know the drill." She led Bonnie and Kate away from Aurelio at a brisk pace, glancing back at Kate. "So . . . the rumors are true."

"That war is coming to Europe?" Kate asked blandly.

The woman quirked a smile. "I see why Tad wants you. I'm Mei Chen, but call me Mei. The costume designer is Victor Parish—you met him in Clive's office—but I'm the one who makes it happen."

They passed more costume racks—sailor suits and something covered in blue scales—and entered a large dressing room with a round platform in front of three angled mirrors. Bonnie immediately undressed to her slip and stepped onto a tall scale. Mei slid a weight across the rod and clucked in disapproval. "Another pound."

Bonnie stepped off the scale, scowling. "I barely ate *anything* yesterday. I was starving all day."

"The scale doesn't lie—and the costumes don't fit. Juanita!"

Kate studied Bonnie's petite figure. "There isn't an ounce of fat on her."

An older woman entered, carrying a fluffy blue dress.

"It's her bosom that's the problem." Mei took the blue dress and dropped it over Bonnie's head. "It won't stop growing."

"She's fifteen," Kate said. "They're supposed to grow."

"Not if she wants to keep playing ingenue roles with those big, innocent eyes of hers. At this rate, she'll be the next Mae West."

Bonnie's voice came through the fabric. "I sleep in that Ace bandage you gave me, but it doesn't work." The neckline slipped over her face and the dress settled—too snug on top, showing a line of cleavage.

"Step up," Mei ordered.

Bonnie stepped onto the platform, her gaze finding Kate in the mirror, sliding down her slim pencil skirt. "I'll bet you can eat anything."

"Well . . ." Kate lowered herself to a velvet chair. "I play a lot of tennis."

"I wish I liked sports."

"You're an amazing dancer."

"It's better to be flat chested when you dance."

"Oh, I don't know," Kate mused. "Aurelio seemed to like dancing with you just fine the way you are."

"You think so? Did he say anything?"

He hadn't, specifically, but they'd been a little preoccupied with Lemmy. "I know he's happy to be working with you."

Bonnie's eyes lingered on Kate in the mirror. "So . . . you and Aurelio aren't . . . ?"

"No," Kate said—so automatically she knew it was true. "I mean, it's impossible not to feel *something* when he flashes that smile at you. But no, nothing like that."

"Turn," Mei ordered, pinning the hem.

Bonnie turned. "Mama says he probably has loads of girls. That you can't trust a boy like him."

Kate opened her mouth to defend Aurelio but stopped herself. For all she knew, it was true; she'd only known him a day and a half.

"I'm going to ask Mama if I can invite him to my birthday party on Friday. You'll come, won't you, Kate?"

Kate didn't relish the idea, but said, "Of course."

Knuckles rapped on wood and the door opened a few inches. "Everybody decent?" Tad Falcon entered, looking more like a college student than a movie producer with his blond hair and tall good looks, wearing a V-neck sweater. "How is our pretty little Bonnie rabbit this morning?"

"Bit grumpy," Mei said around a mouthful of pins.

"It's so *early*," Bonnie whined. "I need some candy, Tad."

His eyes darted to Kate, then back to Bonnie. "Not now, bunny rabbit."

"Turn," Mei ordered, and Bonnie obeyed.

Tad held up a folded newspaper. "Looks like your street had some excitement last night."

Bonnie's eyes widened. "Someone was *murdered*!"

Kate glimpsed a photo of herself on the front page, and her stomach dropped. "May I see?" she asked. Aunt Lorna always tried to hide the articles that popped up every month or two—stories of the kidnapped girl rebounding from tragedy to win some debate competition or tennis trophy—but Kate preferred knowing upfront, so she could prepare her mask of indifference.

Tad handed the newspaper over, and she opened it to see a photo of Ollie next to hers—an old headshot from his movie star days, handsome and dimpled.

MURDER AT OLIVER BANKS MANSION

The article mentioned the victim Lemuel Berman briefly before moving on to Oliver Banks—washed-up silent film star, now impoverished, forced to turn his dilapidated Pasadena mansion into a boarding house for aspiring actors. Neighbors complained of loud jazz music and questionable people coming and going at all hours. The body was discovered by Oliver Banks's granddaughter, Kitty Hildebrand. And, in case anyone had forgotten the biggest news story of the summer of 1934, a brief recap was given: chloroformed and taken from her Nob Hill home by a kidnapper, father a crook, murder-suicide. Followed by more recent facts: overdue tuition at prestigious Blakely Academy in San Francisco (the headmaster didn't have the heart to expel her); her aunt Lorna Wallace on the verge of bankruptcy before escaping town with gold-mining tycoon Donald Norton; Kitty now forced to live in her grandfather's questionable household; recently hired as a production assistant at Falcon Pictures. (How could they have known that? Had Detective Bassett spoken to the press?)

Everything true, but slanted to sound scandalous. Even the photo of her was two years younger and more naive, her smile a bit forced, as if happiness remained just out of reach for this ill-fated girl.

The smile *had* been forced; she'd been furious about a science quiz with misleading questions.

Kate folded the newspaper and handed it back, her jaw tight.

"Did you know the man who was killed?" Tad asked in a respectful tone.

"Not really."

"He was murdered *next door*," Bonnie said. "It could have been *me*."

Tad's attention remained on Kate. "If you need a day or two, Kitty—"

"Kate," she said shortly. Kitty was the girl she used to be, carefree and loved, never doubting her safety. She stood, hoping she didn't look as shaky as she felt. "I'm sorry Falcon Pictures got dragged into it."

Tad gave a short laugh. "Father will be thrilled. No such thing as bad publicity if they get your name right." His gaze shifted to the fluffy blue dress. "I think you're right about the shorter length, Mei. Sorry to toss a new lead boy at you at the last minute— Alfonso something. Did he show up this morning?"

"Aurelio Dios," Kate corrected. "And he was here before you."

Tad flashed a smile. "See there—already helpful. Let's get going. I have a lot to show you." He paused in the doorway. "Bonnie, you'll have to work late to help that Mexican boy catch up."

"I don't mind," Bonnie said.

Kate hesitated in the doorway, glancing back at Bonnie, wondering how she could keep her promise to keep an eye on her with her own duties to fulfill. "I'll see you soon," she said, hoping it was true, and then followed Tad.

He led at a brisk pace, back through the wardrobe department and out a door. The morning sun had finally made an appearance, bringing a warm, dry wind that rustled the palm fronds above them. "Santa Anas," Tad called back, two strides ahead.

Kate trotted to catch up, the strong wind pressing her skirt against her legs. "Excuse me?"

"Hot winds that come every fall, full of static. That's why we like the soundstages. Weather doesn't matter—we make our own." He glanced down at her. "Tomorrow, wear lower heels. We cover a lot of ground in this place."

"Can I wear slacks, then?"

"Tomboy, eh?"

"I like a pretty dress as much as the next girl, but I prefer slacks, and my aunt's too far away to do anything about it."

"Slacks, then." He waited for a car to pass, then crossed the road. "In this business, time is money. And people cost money. And people who move quickly save money. And that's *always* the goal, Kate—saving money."

She liked the brisk pace. "I would think making a good movie was the goal."

"That's the director's problem—and the writers, and art department, and music team. The creative people. We're the money *behind* the creative people. They only see their own piece of the puzzle, but we have to keep our eyes on the whole picture at all times. We're the all-knowing eyes from on high." He grinned down at her. "We're the gods, Kate."

"Golly, suddenly I feel inadequate," she joked, but the thought exhilarated her.

Tad laughed. "You'll be a formidable little god by the time I'm done with you."

They walked around an old-fashioned carriage being hitched to the back of a truck. Kate could feel the studio stirring to life around her—cars passing, people entering the buildings that lined the road.

"We producers are the decision makers," Tad said. "For instance—let's say our costume designer insists Bonnie has to wear real silk to the school dance or the scene is ruined. And our director insists he needs a hundred extras at the dance or the scene is ruined. And our writer insists it has to be raining when they leave the dance or the scene is ruined. Well, silk is expensive, and a hundred extras are expensive, and rain is expensive."

"Rain is expensive?" Kate asked.

"Wet costumes. That means *more* costumes, and more wardrobe staff on set, and rain throws off lighting which means more takes, and more takes means time. And what is time, Kate?"

"Time is money."

"Good girl. So—I'm the cruel god who says a high school girl can wear cheap rayon, and the director can use camera angles to make fifty extras look like a hundred, and we'll do fog instead of rain, which gives atmosphere but is a lot less hassle. They all shake their angry fists at God, but eventually get on with it, and the budget is saved." He glanced down. "You keeping up? Figuratively, I mean. Those long legs of yours are doing just fine." His gaze skimmed her pencil skirt.

"It isn't aeronautical physics, Tad."

He laughed. "Thank goodness, or I'd be sunk." He grinned,

looking like a mischievous college boy planning to cheat on an exam. Not a god. And not bad looking.

An open, jeep-like vehicle halted at the edge of the road, the driver jumping out to enter a building. "Good," Tad said, striding toward the vehicle. He sat on the bench behind the steering wheel. "Climb on. This will be faster."

Kate hesitated, glancing at the building.

"He'll be fine. We have these carts everywhere for anyone who needs them. Well, not *anyone,* but they're yours for the taking. And you'll need them; it's a big place."

She sat on the bench and they took off, turning down the road lined by enormous soundstage buildings. They drove past a cluster of women in long hoop skirts, two large cannons, and horses being led off a trailer.

Kate held tightly to the edge of her seat.

Tad parked in the same alley they'd parked in the day before but led her toward Stage Five on the other side. "This is our set," he said, opening a door in the towering wall.

The cavernous space was eerily dark and quiet, only a few lights glowing in the distance. Kate halted for a second, then focused on the dim lights and hurried to catch up, her heels echoing.

They passed the ice cream parlor set first, with small tables in front of a long counter. Everything looked remarkably real. She saw jars of nuts and maraschino cherries. Stacks of ice cream cones. Even a rumpled dishtowel on the counter.

The next set showed the inside of a cozy, middle-class home, with a window overlooking a few fake trees and a painted backdrop.

The biggest set was at the end of the building—a theater stage with velvet drapes, an orchestra pit, and rows of audience seats. Most of the stage floor had collapsed, leaving a dark hole with jagged edges.

Tad walked halfway down the audience aisle and stopped, shoving his hands into his pants pockets, suddenly more serious. "Half the cast was up there when it caved in. Shoddy workmanship—done in a hurry like everything around here."

A man in overalls worked alone at the side of the stage, unloading lumber from a cart. "Doesn't look like they're in much of a hurry to fix it," Kate said.

"Our set builders were already done here and assigned to another picture. I'm told more men will show up later today . . . but that doesn't mean they will." His expression darkened. "I'll be straight with you, Kate. There are a lot of people who'd love to see me fail. I grew up at this studio, but this is the first picture I've managed on my own, and they think I only got the job because I'm Clive Falcon's son."

"Well . . . you did."

He shot her a look.

"But now you get to prove you deserve it."

"How *can* I when something like this happens?" He lifted a frustrated hand toward the broken stage. "Every picture gets behind schedule, but when it's me, they all whisper."

"Let them. Bonnie and Aurelio are going to light up that screen. I think you have a big hit on your hands."

"Maybe. I hope he learns fast. We were supposed to start filming today, so I've got a bunch of expensive crew sitting around waiting, getting paid for nothing. Cameramen and lighting. Makeup. But we can't start filming until the new cast learns the dance numbers, which could take a week. And in eleven days we're booted out of these buildings because another movie is scheduled." He shook his head. "It's a disaster, if I'm honest."

"Well . . ." Kate settled her hands on her hips, intrigued by the problem. "Are there any scenes without the new actors, where everyone is ready to go?"

Tad thought a moment. "The family scenes, I guess. None of them got hurt. But we can't film with construction noise in the background." He nodded his head at the broken stage.

Kate turned to look at the house set in the distance, her mind tugging at the problem—and she saw the answer. "Move the house set. That's faster than waiting for this set to be repaired. What's happening in Stage Six, where we had auditions yesterday?"

"We're rehearsing the new actors in there. The big dance numbers."

"They can rehearse in here. A little construction noise won't matter. When the set builders show up today to fix this stage, first use them to move the house and ice cream parlor to Stage Six, then you can start filming the family scenes right away."

Tad frowned. "That might work, I guess, but that's only a couple of scenes, and then I'm stuck again, waiting for the new actors to catch up."

"Teach them one dance number at a time, starting with the easiest. Film during the day and rehearse the next number at night. Just one scene at a time, but you keep moving forward, nobody sitting around getting paid for nothing." She felt a little surge of victory, knowing it would work. "Are there any scenes with just Aurelio and Bonnie?"

"A quarter of the picture."

"Good. Save those scenes for last, then you can send the other actors home and stop paying them—plus all their wardrobe and makeup staff. Only keep Aurelio and Bonnie around. That saves money, right?"

"Right," he said slowly. "There'll still be gaps in filming, but at least we'll get started." He brought his hands to his head, laughing in amazement. "Why didn't I think of all that? I've got to get those sets moved." He started walking back the way they'd come, calling out, "Keep up, Athena!"

She hurried after him. "Athena?"

"Don't tell me a smart girl like you doesn't know her Greek mythology? We're gods, remember?"

Kate thought back to a class she'd had two years ago and laughed, liking the comparison: Athena, goddess of wisdom and battle strategy.

CHAPTER 14

By the time Kate sat in the commissary to eat dinner, she was exhausted and her feet burned. But the day had been a magnificent whirl of watching voice and dance rehearsals, setting up her own desk area, taking notes on a clipboard, even driving one of the little carts to deliver call sheets. Late in the day, a small construction crew had started moving the house and ice cream parlor sets to Stage Six, and Kate had watched in amazement—thrilled to know that a Hollywood movie set was being moved because of her idea.

Now, Barbara Stanwyck sat across the commissary, eating in a quiet corner with an older man.

"Stop ogling," Tad chided, scooping up the last of his mashed potatoes.

"I can't believe I'm eating dinner with Barbara Stanwyck."

"Well, that's a stretch. Do you want the rest of your roll?"

Kate handed it over. "She was amazing in *Stella Dallas.* I cried at the end."

"Yeah, too bad she's not in our stable. We only have her on loan for one picture."

Her gaze shifted to Tad. "Stable?"

"The stars we have under contract, so they can't work for anyone else." He dragged the roll through his gravy. "But keeping a star is expensive, so if there's a gap in their schedule, we loan them out so they still earn their keep. It's one of the biggest games in Hollywood—swapping stars. Clark Gable is the latest prize." He bit off half the roll.

"What do you mean?" Kate pushed her plate away and leaned her arms on the table.

Tad swallowed. "Took Selznick two years to convince Mayer to give him Gable for *Gone with the Wind,* and it didn't come cheap. But it's perfect casting. They start filming in a month or two." He put the rest of the roll into his mouth.

Kate had devoured the book two years ago, like everyone else, and thought Clark Gable would make the perfect Rhett Butler. "What if an actor doesn't want to do a movie? Do they still have to do it?"

"Pretty much." Tad sipped from his water glass. "If they refuse, we can suspend them for a year without pay. And if they try to work for someone else, we sue them. It's in the contract."

"Sounds terrible."

He laughed, wiping his mouth with a napkin. "Don't feel sorry for them. Most of them are small-town hicks when they get off the train, and we make their dreams come true. Fix their hair and makeup. Teach them how to walk and talk. How to dress. Even give them better names. We turn them into the most glamorous people in the world, and when the fame and fortune goes to their head, we hush up their dirty secrets. So yeah, we expect a little loyalty in return. And if they don't like it, there are ten thousand more begging to take their place."

Kate almost wished she didn't know. "Hollywood doesn't sound so fabulous beneath the surface."

"It's a business. The people who understand that work hard and succeed. The rest go home." Tad set his napkin on the table.

"Speaking of—how about I drive you home? My grandmother lives in Pasadena, and today is her birthday."

"All right." Bonnie and Aurelio would be working late.

They left the commissary, and Tad led her toward a maroon-colored car with a long nose and only one seat. "You drive an Auburn Speedster?" Kate was impressed. A boy she'd known in San Francisco had been obsessed with them.

Tad smiled, opening her door. "And you know cars. Why doesn't that surprise me?"

The night air still held the dry heat of the day, so they drove with the windows down, Kate holding her hair with one hand as Tad whipped the car around other vehicles. He talked over the noise, telling her about the Hays Code that enforced morality in movies. "It wasn't easy to convince hardworking men to spend their money during the depression, so pictures got a little racy to lure them in. Then the studios figured out they could make more money if the whole family bought tickets, so they cleaned things up. My dad likes the Hays Code. Says it's better to police ourselves than have the government step in with censorship laws we can't control. But the creative people hate it because it ties their hands." He glanced at her. "Sorry, I'm talking your ear off."

"I like it. I have a lot to learn."

"And I like teaching you. We make a good team, Kate." He cast her a meaningful smile that made her feel like she was back in San Francisco on a date with an attractive, slightly older college boy.

But, as the Auburn pulled up at Ollie's run-down mansion and several reporters materialized out of the shadows, the reality of her situation came crashing back.

"I'll handle it," Tad said, climbing out of the car.

Which irked Kate. She'd been handling reporters since she was thirteen. But she waited as Tad came around the car and opened her door. He took her hand and helped her out, as flash-bulbs flared, leaving her blinking.

"Kitty! Can you tell us what happened last night?"

"Did you know the young man who was killed, Kitty?"

"Easy, boys," Tad said, still holding her hand. "Miss Hildebrand won't be answering any questions tonight."

As if she were one of his movie stars. Kate started up the long path to the door, and Tad came along, keeping ahold of her hand.

"Tad Falcon, is that you?" Flashbulbs popped. One cameraman ran ahead to catch a front view. "Were you here last night, Tad? How long have you known Kitty Hildebrand? Are the two of you working together?"

"We'll be making a formal announcement tomorrow," Tad said. "But I will confirm that Miss Hildebrand has joined Falcon Pictures, and we couldn't be happier."

Seeking publicity, Kate realized, not avoiding it. She yanked her hand from his and hurried up the path alone, more irritated at herself than at Tad, for being lured by his flirtatious smile in the car. This wasn't a date. Falcon Pictures wanted her for her fame—and now they had the bonus of Lemmy's murder to go with it. She entered the house and quickly shut the door, leaning against it to catch her breath.

She was relieved when she heard Tad's powerful car drive away.

The house seemed unusually dark and deserted, with the haunting whine of Reuben's violin drifting from some place far away, eerily reminiscent of her arrival two nights ago. But tonight, the living room was dark. Kate followed the music toward the back of the house and found the back door propped open again. She cast an uneasy glance into the kitchen, which was empty, and then stepped outside.

A trail of flickering candles led the way to the swimming pool in the distance. Kate followed them, pausing at the top of two patio steps to take in the strange but enchanting scene below.

Beneath the glow of the enormous moon, Reuben stood on the pool's low diving board, playing the violin, suspended over the green water and lily pads. The music was lovely, not jarring like the night she'd arrived, and more candles burned around the pool like twinkling fireflies.

Ollie lay on a long deck chair, staring up at the moon. Closer to Kate, Hugo lay on the ground on a blanket. He turned his head, as if sensing her presence, and for a moment they just stared at each other, then he patted the blanket beside him.

Kate was overly aware of him watching as she walked over, slipped off her shoes, and lowered herself to the blanket. As soon as her head settled on the pillow next to his, she knew she'd landed too close, their arms touching. But neither of them moved away.

The music climbed to a dangerous height and hung there.

"Hello," he whispered, looking up at the moon.

"Hello."

The melody swooped and tumbled for a few breathtaking notes before sliding into gentle order again.

"Ollie thought we should have a ceremony for Lemmy. He wasn't a very nice person, but he lived with us, and no one should die like that."

"No," Kate agreed quietly. "And it's a lovely ceremony."

"We all took a turn on the diving board. Ollie quoted lines from some old Captain Powell movie. At least, I think that's what it was. I was so worried he was going to fall in the pool, I didn't pay much attention."

Kate smiled in the dark. "I'm sorry I missed it."

"And now Reuben's playing a song that doesn't sound like it came out of a madman's head, which is a nice change of pace."

"I blame that violin for my moment of madness the night I arrived."

"So, Reuben gets all the credit? I thought it was my impressive acting."

She remembered Hugo coming at her in the kitchen, his eyes burning with murderous intent, one hand gripping a knife. "Your performance was . . . compelling." She readjusted her position, settling her shoulder more comfortably against his. "Have you taken your turn on the diving board yet?"

"I recited a poem."

She turned her head on the pillow. "That you wrote?"

"Yeah." He kept his eyes on the night sky.

"I want to hear it." He remained quiet. "Just one line."

"Okay, let me think." He paused, and then his voice softened. "And so we see, in the luminosity of stars, the diversity of souls. This one bright, this one fading, this one reflecting the light of another."

Kate stared at his masculine profile. "Hugo . . . that's beautiful."

"Thanks." His lips moved in the barest of smiles. "Is this too dark for you? I can get the flashlight."

The disquiet running through Kate had nothing to do with the dark. She looked back at the moon. "I'm fine as long as there are people close by."

"Well, then." She heard the smile in his voice. "I'll stay close."

Reuben's music flowed easily now, a river of lovely notes.

"I've never seen such a big full moon," Hugo murmured.

"Actually . . . it's a waning gibbous of about ninety-five percent." Kate lifted her arm and pointed. "See how there's a shadow on the right side?"

He leaned his head closer to hers. "Oh, right, I see what you mean."

She tucked her arm back against him, missing the warmth. "It's called a hunter's moon, this time of year, because it rises right after sunset, so hunters can keep tracking animals without stopping for the night."

"I thought it was called a harvest moon in the fall."

"That was in September. The harvest moon is the one closest to the autumnal equinox, and the one after that is the hunter's moon. The dates change every year because lunar phases aren't the same as our—" She stopped herself.

Hide that big brain of yours, darling. Boys might like talking to smart girls, but they don't kiss them.

"Go on," Hugo murmured.

Kate swallowed an urge to tell him more. "I can loan you my copy of *Sky* magazine, if you want."

"I'd rather hear it from you."

He sounded like he meant it, but she kept quiet.

Hugo pointed at the sky. "I know that bright star near the moon is Jupiter. Some kid told me that, once, on a Boy Scout campout."

Kate laughed, turning to look at him. "First of all—you were a *Boy Scout?*"

His lips twitched. "On my honor. But I was kicked out after I used my scoutmaster's sleeping bag to put out a wildfire."

"Sounds like you were a hero."

"Well . . . I sort of started the fire."

"Ah." She smiled, looking back at the stars. "Secondly—Jupiter might have been near the moon on your campout, but tonight, that's Saturn. The planets don't stay in one place, they move in orbit. Tonight, Jupiter is probably . . ." She searched and pointed. "That bright one down there."

"Oh, right, I see it."

"And Venus is . . . already gone, I think. It's only visible at sunset and sunrise."

The violin music grew, swelling around them.

"It's all so big and far away," Hugo mused. "It makes me feel small."

"That's what I like about it," Kate said quietly. "The universe isn't fazed by our world wars and stock market crashes. We think a hundred years is a long time, but even a million years is only a grain of sand in the Sahara."

"How did you get so interested in astronomy?"

A flutter rolled through her. Leave it to Hugo to find the tender spot. As if he sensed the truth.

He waited, gazing upward. And maybe it was the warmth of his arm against hers, or the moonlight, or the violin pulling a yearning note across the night sky, but Kate wanted to tell him. She whispered it. "My father."

One of Hugo's fingers curled around one of hers, a cautious link between their hips.

Her father used to lie next to her like this, pointing out constellations, his voice hushed and eager. Later, she'd realized he had the names all wrong—probably making it up, trying to convince his daughter he knew everything, the way he'd tricked investors.

"I stopped looking at the stars after it happened," she told Hugo in a small voice. "Then I thought . . . it wasn't the stars' fault. They were the one thing I could believe in. The universe only tells the truth. We just have to be smart enough and work hard enough to understand it."

Hugo turned his head on the pillow. "I'm glad you didn't give up on the stars, Kate." His breath warmed her ear. "And I'm glad . . ." His voice faded. Kate looked at him and found him staring at something on the other side of her, in the distance.

He sat up, leaving cold air behind.

Kate turned her head. A girl stood at the edge of the pool area—a pretty girl, a little older than Kate, returning Hugo's stare, her hands clasped at her waist.

"Esther." Hugo shifted away from Kate on the blanket. Only a few inches, but she felt it. "What are you doing here?"

The girl took a step and stopped. "I read there was a murder and got worried." Her hands twisted. "I'm so sorry we argued, Hugo. I can't stop thinking about you."

Kate sat up.

"How did you get here?" Hugo scrambled to his feet and went to her.

"The bus."

"You shouldn't ride it at night."

"I know—but if anything happened to you—and you

thought I was still mad—if you didn't know I love you—" She flung her arms around his shoulders, pressing her face into his neck, and his arms tightened around her with equal fervor. They clung to each other.

Kate felt slapped. And stupid. She was glad Hugo couldn't see her face. She clenched her jaw, trying to school her expression for the polite introduction.

But Hugo didn't look at Kate and the others as he separated himself from Esther's arms. He wiped his eyes, keeping his back to them, then took the girl's hand and led her to the pool house. A light flipped on, the door closed, and Hugo pulled down the window shade.

"Well, well," Reuben drawled, and Kate realized the music had stopped.

She forced her voice into cool indifference. "Who was that?"

"I have no idea," Ollie said, sounding bewildered. "Maybe that actress he mentioned from the play."

Hugo hadn't mentioned an actress to Kate. Did he stab her on stage every night, up close and personal?

"I'm done here," Reuben announced, walking off the diving board. "May Lemmy the snake rest in peace."

"Let's finish our card game," Ollie said, and the two of them made their way toward the house.

Kate stood, her eyes on the pool house. She couldn't hear anything, and no shadows moved behind the window shade. Whatever they were doing didn't involve much talking or movement.

Her heart felt like a stone.

What a fool she'd been, falling for the cozy pillow talk and linked fingers. The thoughtful rasp in his voice. She would have warned a girlfriend against some boy she'd only known two days. An actor who'd dropped out of school when he was fifteen. Of course Hugo had girls in his past. Kate had boys in her past. She'd gone to a movie with Freddie Bayer just last week, and a school dance with Andy Gardner two weeks before that.

She tried to think of a boy whose sudden appearance would bring tears to her eyes, but none came to mind.

Kate returned to the house to find Ollie and Reuben playing cards at the kitchen table, betting with piles of beans that had been painted blue, green, and red—the red being worth the most, she guessed, since there were fewer of them.

As she passed the table, Ollie reached out and took her hand. "He's never talked about a girl, so I don't think he's sweet on her."

"Makes no difference to me," Kate said, but her voice sounded so tight, the lie so obvious, her face warmed.

She got busy unpacking, making numerous trips back and forth between her trunks in the laundry room and the small closet in the housekeeper's room. She hung up her clothes in their usual order—dresses and blouses according to color; jackets, warmest to lightest; party dresses on the left. Sweaters, neatly folded on a shelf.

Every time she walked past the window, she glanced outside, but nothing had changed. She unpacked her telescope, set it up in front of the window, and focused on the pool house. But it only gave her a closer view of the same closed door and drawn shade. She could just make out the vague shape of a person standing behind the shade. The girl, maybe. Hugo would be taller.

A chair scraped in the kitchen, and Kate straightened with a guilty jerk.

She placed her things in the dresser in tidy rows—silk stockings and garters, handkerchiefs and gloves. She folded pajamas with military precision and slid them into the bottom drawer.

Nothing was as it seemed in this town, but she would keep her wits about her. Next time, she wouldn't fall for his little performance.

Tomorrow would be another early morning. She went to the closet to choose a blouse and slacks, but everything was wrinkled. She yanked clothes off hangers, irked at herself for not thinking of it earlier—for not having it on her list.

She entered the kitchen with an armload of clothes. "Is there an overnight laundry in town? Everything I own needs to be pressed."

"Hugo will do it," Ollie said absently, studying his cards. "He presses all my things."

"Your pajamas?" Kate snapped, tired of hearing about the wonders of Hugo. Tonight, Ollie was back in the striped pajamas he'd been wearing when she arrived; she recognized the food stain. "You can't live in pajamas, Ollie. Tomorrow, you have to get dressed."

Reuben pulled a toothpick from his mouth. "His clothes don't fit. He's too fat."

"And that," Ollie declared, laying down a card, "is the pot calling the kettle black."

"You need exercise," Kate said over the top of her armload of clothes. "You agreed to walk around the neighborhood."

"*You* promised to take me."

"I work now, but Reuben can go with you."

"I'm not his babysitter."

"Just a quick—" Kate heard the back door open, and her gaze flew to the hallway.

Hugo entered the kitchen wearing a black leather jacket, his expression tense, his eyes on the floor. The girl stayed back in the hall. "I need to borrow your car, Figs."

Reuben slapped a card on the table. "You gotta pay for the gas."

"No problem." Hugo turned away.

Ollie chirped. "Aren't you going to introduce us to your friend?"

Hugo sighed and turned sideways, lifting an arm to the hall. "This is my sister Esther. She doesn't want to meet you because you're corrupting my soul and she's not supposed to be here." His eyes shifted to Kate. "Except you, I guess. Esther, come meet Kate."

The girl took a tentative step into the kitchen—and the resemblance was suddenly obvious. The same fair skin and dark hair. The same arched eyebrows. Maybe a year or two older than Hugo. She offered Kate a small smile. "How do you do?"

Kate had been raised with impeccable manners but couldn't think of the proper response, her eyes darting to Hugo. "Your *sister*," she breathed, not caring if he could hear the relief in those words.

A muscle in his jaw tightened and released. "One of them. I've got five more, plus a brother."

"Catholic or Mormon?" Reuben asked around the toothpick.

"You shut up," Hugo said, not angry, just an order.

Ollie said cheerily, "You could start a singing group—the Quick Family Singers. Join us, Esther! We want to hear embarrassing stories of Hugo's misspent childhood."

She stepped back. "No, thank you."

"I told you," Hugo snapped. "My dad would belt her if he knew she was here. I'm driving her to Glendale." He cast a final, uneasy look at Kate, and the two of them left.

Reuben worked the toothpick to the other side of his mouth. "Well, well."

Kate stared at the empty doorway, her arms full of clothes, wishing she'd been a little friendlier. She wanted to know more about Esther—and the five other sisters—and one brother—and the father who would belt his daughter.

Reuben and Ollie bickered over their cards and painted beans.

Sister. Kate fought a goofy grin as she dumped the clothes at the end of the table. "Either of you know how to iron?"

Reuben pulled the toothpick from his mouth. "You put the hot thing on the fabric and slide it around."

"Thank you, Reuben."

He eyed her with a knowing smirk. "Someone looks mighty happy after meeting a *sister*."

Kate only smiled as she turned away, humming under her breath as she went to the laundry room to find an iron and ironing board.

Six sisters and one brother, plus Hugo. *Eight* children. He hadn't just run away from a father; he'd left an entire family behind.

Where was Glendale? Not far, she guessed, since Ollie had hired Hugo's father to do his plumbing. And yet, judging from the tearful reunion, Hugo rarely went home. If ever.

She opened the tall cupboard in the laundry room, where she'd found the mop and pail, and saw the ironing board leaning against the side wall. She pulled it out—a bit awkwardly; it was heavier than it looked—and something fell loose behind it, clattering to the ground. She looked down around the ironing board and saw a slim sword on the floor, its long blade smeared by a dull, reddish-brown stain.

Her stomach lurched.

Kate stared, her heart galloping into a faster beat. She recognized the fancy gold handle. It was the same sword she'd seen in a display case on Ollie's office wall, next to the painting of Captain Powell.

It's a beautiful weapon, crafted by a famous swordsmith in Spain—and wicked sharp.

Now, covered in dried blood. Hidden in the laundry room where Hugo had fumbled in the dark last night.

CHAPTER 15

Kate struggled to remain calm as she leaned the heavy ironing board against the wall. She'd thought Hugo was a killer before and had been wrong. Thought Ollie had confessed to murder, when he'd only set a bird free. This time, she wouldn't jump to conclusions.

She drew a steadying breath and turned to look down at the sword.

It looked bigger and more deadly than it had on the wall, the handle a beautiful, burnished gold; the blade, gleaming steel where it wasn't covered in dried blood. A real replica of a fake movie prop.

A murder weapon, hidden by Hugo.

Kate pressed her fingers to her lips, horrified.

Why would Hugo kill Lemmy?

The answer came too fast: because Lemmy knew about the fake ledger that erased Ollie's loan. Just that morning, Lemmy had taunted Reuben about it, threatening to tell their mob boss in prison what Reuben had been up to lately. If Moe Kravitz found out, Reuben would be punished—probably killed—and Ollie would lose his house. Hugo couldn't let that happen.

He'd killed Lemmy to save his friends.

Kate's thoughts darted back to last night.

Hugo had told her to go to the living room while he stayed behind with Lemmy's body. A kindness, she'd thought, but then he'd snuck out the back door before the police arrived, saying he didn't want to be late for work. He must have taken the sword with him, not wanting the police to find it with his fingerprints. Had he carried it on his motorcycle? No, he'd probably hidden it in the backyard—or a neighbor's dark garden—until he returned from his play and found a better hiding place.

Her gaze flickered to the tall cupboard. Why bring it back into the house? Why not leave it in some random dumpster on his way to work?

Because it was a one-of-a-kind Captain Powell heirloom, easily traced back to Ollie—and Hugo—if it were ever found. Kate had read about bullets being matched to a specific gun. Maybe stab wounds could be matched to a specific blade.

She tried to remember if Hugo had looked guilty as he'd stared down at Lemmy's body. What she did remember was him telling her with great certainty that Ollie was innocent, even before seeing the birdcage—because he'd known he was.

But Hugo had been at Falcon Pictures with her when Lemmy was killed. She felt a spark of relief—then remembered that Hugo had been alone much of that time, at least an hour and a half, while she was at Clive Falcon's office and watching the nightclub scene. Was that enough time for Hugo to take a bus home, kill Lemmy, and return? Probably not.

But he hadn't taken a bus; he'd taken Bonnie's yellow car. That's why it was parked in a different place. They'd all heard her tell Aurelio to leave the key in the glovebox.

A telephone rang in the distance, making her jump. She heard Reuben grumble as he got up from the table and realized someone must have paid the phone bill today. She could call Detective Bassett and show him the sword.

But did she want to?

Once the detective arrived, things would move quickly, out of Kate's control. Detective Bassett might suspect Ollie, who owned the sword and was home alone.with Lemmy. And Ollie had the stronger motive—not losing his house. Even if she told Detective Bassett about Hugo hiding the sword in the middle of the night, he might think Hugo hid it to help his friend, the real killer.

It would be in the papers.

Kate groaned and pressed her fingers to her temples. She'd been wrong before. Maybe she should talk to Hugo first and give him a chance to explain. But he was on his way to Glendale and would probably drive to work after that.

"Reuben, who's on the phone?" Ollie called from the kitchen, his chair scraping back.

She couldn't leave the sword here, where Hugo could retrieve it. She had to hide it until she could think straight. But where? Not her own room. She whirled and saw her open trunk, half-full of summer clothes she didn't intend to unpack. Cotton dresses and shorts. A striped beach towel. She grabbed the towel and dropped it over the sword, then knelt and picked it up, being careful to wrap the towel around the edges so her hands didn't touch it. She glanced at the door, then lifted the wrapped sword and lowered it into the trunk, angling it to fit. She carefully worked it to the bottom and rearranged the summer clothes on top.

Kate stood and looked down, her heart racing, hardly believing what she'd done. The clothes looked innocent, showing no signs they hid a murder weapon. The sword could stay there until she'd decided what to do.

She found the kitchen deserted and followed Reuben's voice to the foyer. He stood next to the telephone table at the base of the staircase, Ollie beside him. "Sure, Detective. I'll tell everyone, and we'll let you know if we think of anything." He hung up.

"What's going on?" Ollie asked.

"He says the wound was made by a long, sharp blade—like

a sword." Reuben gave the older man a meaningful look as he strode toward the office.

"I have a sword!" Ollie scurried after him.

"Now you're catching on."

Kate followed them into Ollie's office, wondering if she should tell them what she'd found. But for all she knew, one of them was in on it. She remained back by the armchairs in front of the desk, watching as the two men approached Captain Powell's painting and the sword box on the wall. The glass door on the box hung open by an inch or two. The scabbard was still there, supported by hooks, but the sword was missing.

"My sword!" Ollie cried. "I was in here all day and didn't notice. Where is it?" He touched the empty hooks.

"It could be anywhere in this mess." Reuben turned slowly, scanning the cluttered room. "Did you take it out?"

"No, no—I always keep it in the case. It's very dangerous." Ollie's eyes widened. "You think the killer took it?"

"Very good, Sherlock."

"But it's my favorite thing! We have to tell the police!"

"That Lemmy was killed with your sword? Keep your mouth shut, or you'll end up with a noose around your neck."

Kate leaned a hand on the back of an armchair, drawing a sharp breath.

"But they have to find it! They won't think I killed him. Why would they?"

"Because you look like a loony in those pajamas." Reuben scowled at the messy room, his hands on his hips. "I don't get it. If someone came to kill Lemmy, they'd bring their own gun. Why use your old sword?"

"It's a marvelous weapon," Ollie said, defending it. "Better than a noisy gun."

And Hugo didn't own a gun, Kate guessed. Maybe he'd planned to clean the sword and return it to the case before anyone noticed it was missing, but never got a chance because Ollie was in the office all day.

Reuben grumbled, "Nobody kills with a sword anymore. And stabbing is messy. And none of this makes sense." He headed for the door. "It's probably upstairs in your room somewhere."

"It isn't, I tell you. The killer stole it—and I want it back!" Ollie followed Reuben, leaving Kate alone.

She walked closer to the display case and inspected it. A nice quality box, but no lock, leaving the sword easily accessible to anyone who—

Knew it was real, she realized.

Her gaze dropped to the movie memorabilia on the table below the painting. Captain Powell's dagger looked rubbery, not real. His hat was splotched with paint to give it a weather-beaten appearance. She picked up the flintlock pistol and found it lighter than a real gun would be—a fake prop that didn't shoot bullets. Nothing real except the sword. A random intruder wouldn't know that.

But the people living in this house would.

A small clock chimed ten o'clock. She'd been up since five in the morning, and tomorrow would be another early day. Hugo had probably driven straight to his play after dropping off his sister, so she might as well go to bed.

As she walked through the kitchen, she saw her pile of wrinkled clothes but had no energy left for ironing. She picked up the clothes, carried them to her room, and dumped them in the corner.

Clothes on the floor. She didn't even know who she was anymore.

She lay awake for what felt like hours, listening to every creak in the house, trying to convince herself that hiding the sword had been the right thing to do. When she saw Hugo, she would watch for signs of guilt and be more sure, then give the sword to Detective Bassett.

She didn't want to make another blundering mistake.

Her eyes flickered to her alarm clock and saw 12:05 a.m. She also saw her math textbook, which she'd ignored since arriving.

She heard the distant sound of the front door opening and

closing, and sat up, her heart skittering. Maybe just Aurelio, home from rehearsal. But the footsteps came toward the back of the house, and she knew from the sound, somehow, that it was Hugo. She pushed back the quilt, got out of bed, and hurried through the short hallway to the kitchen. But when she reached the table, she halted, suddenly aware of the stupidity of confronting a killer alone in the middle of the night. She fixed her eyes on the opposite doorway, her heart thundering.

Hugo walked by in the hall, still wearing the black leather jacket, his head bowed, his posture a bit downcast. He glanced at the kitchen and kept going . . . then came back, his head tilting. "You're still up." He looked tired, his eyes shadowed beneath a tumble of dark bangs.

Kate felt a tug of attraction that wasn't very helpful. She kept her voice cool. "We need to talk about Lemmy."

His expression turned cautious. "Did something happen?" He walked closer, his eyes narrowing, and she was grateful for the table between them.

"I found the sword you hid last night."

He didn't move for a moment, then said with deadly calm, "I'm sorry you had to see that."

No denial. Her last flicker of hope went out.

Hugo took a step but stopped when she drew a sharp breath. Their eyes locked across the table, the air throbbing with unspoken fears and accusations. If she screamed, Reuben and Ollie would come running.

"Kate," he said carefully. "I didn't kill him, I swear."

"You hid the murder weapon."

"I never used it." He lifted both hands. "It was on the kitchen floor, behind the dog. I could tell none of you saw it, so I waited until you left the room and then got it out of the house until the police were gone. That's all I did, I swear."

She folded her arms across her racing heart. "Why hide the murder weapon if you didn't kill him?"

"To protect Ollie. That sword is from his old Captain Powell movies. No one else would use it."

"Nice try, but you already convinced me of his innocence."

"He *is* innocent, but I knew the police would suspect him if they saw that sword. He was still upset about leaving the house. I didn't know about the bird yet. But I knew he was crying, and rambling about something he'd done, and looked guilty as hell. I didn't want the police looking too closely at him—and they would if they knew his sword was the murder weapon."

In the distance, the front door opened. They both froze, listening as footsteps ascended the staircase. "Aurelio," Kate murmured. Home from practice at midnight, expected back at six. If she'd learned one thing after a day at Falcon Pictures, it was that making movies was a lot of work.

"Kate," Hugo said in a gentle plea, drawing her attention back. "I didn't want Ollie dragged into some police car with a bunch of reporters taking pictures. I just—I don't know—panicked, I guess. I wanted that sword out of the house until I could think straight. I figured I could give it to the police later and say I found it in the backyard."

Same as Kate. She fought an urge to believe him.

Hugo sighed in frustration, his feet shifting. "Come on, why would I kill Lemmy?"

She had an answer for that. "You didn't want Ollie to lose his house."

The dark eyebrows arched.

"That's right," she said, feeling more in control. "I know about Ollie's loan, and that Reuben created a fake ledger to make it look paid off. And I was standing right here when Lemmy threatened to tell their boss in prison."

"Ollie didn't want you to know about his money troubles."

"It's pretty obvious when the phone bill doesn't get paid."

"Well, I'm glad you know. Reuben really stuck his neck out, doing that, but Ollie can't find out. He thinks Reuben found some old bank account, and it's better that way. I love Ollie, but I don't trust him not to say something to the wrong person without thinking."

"I won't tell him," she said. Hugo's face softened whenever he talked about her grandfather, and she remembered his story about showing up on the doorstep with everything he owned in a pillowcase, and Ollie inviting him in for a grilled cheese sandwich. "Look . . . I know Lemmy was a terrible person, and I know you only killed him out of some . . . some twisted sense of goodness, but Hugo—"

"You *know* I killed him?" He gave a short laugh, looking hurt. "You can look me in the eye and say that?"

Kate tightened her folded arms, trying to hide the quivering doubt inside her. It would be easier if he weren't so attractive in that black leather jacket, looking at her with those wounded eyes. "You said it yourself, how no one would use that sword except Ollie. Only, we both know he didn't. So that leaves you. You knew the sword was real, and you wanted Lemmy dead."

"Half the world wanted Lemmy dead," Hugo snapped.

"But half the world didn't hide the murder weapon."

"I explained all that!" He folded his arms to match hers, his eyes on fire. "All right—if you have this all figured out—tell me why I brought the murder weapon back after I managed to sneak it away from the police."

"Because . . . because you couldn't risk someone finding it. It's a one-of-a-kind heirloom, easily traced back to this house."

"Wrong. I could have driven it to some dark pier and thrown it in the ocean. I brought it back here because the real killer's fingerprints might be on it, and that's evidence, and I actually care about that. But for now, I put it in a safe hiding place."

"Not so safe," she said tersely.

"It would have been if you hadn't gone snooping around. I was going to turn it in today, except that detective came to the house and seems to think one of us did it, so I decided to wait until he focuses somewhere else. And another thing—if I'm such a murdering mastermind, why did I kill him with some old-fashioned sword that points the finger at Ollie?"

Kate's thoughts stilled on that question. If nothing else, she knew Hugo cared about her grandfather.

He continued. "So let's say I grabbed the sword on impulse, not thinking it through. I would have cleaned it and put it back, so no one knew—not left it all bloody on the kitchen floor, then snuck it out of the house, then brought it back to preserve fingerprints. You must think I'm pretty stupid if that's my grand plan."

"I don't think you're stupid," she said automatically.

"Not stupid, just a murderer."

"Hugo—"

"I'm not done. One more pertinent fact." His eyes burned into hers. "In case you forgot, I was sitting next to you at auditions when Lemmy was killed. But maybe that cozy little chat of ours wasn't quite as memorable for you as it was for me. And maybe lying under the stars tonight wasn't either. Maybe you're just playing with me, biding your time until you can get away from this house and its—what did you call us?—*unsavory* boarders."

Kate swallowed. "I didn't know any of you when I wrote that."

"You *still* don't know me—that much is obvious!"

Her head felt crowded. She squeezed her arms across her chest, wanting to believe him—wanting it so much, it scared her.

Hugo glared a moment longer, and then his anger seemed to melt. "I don't blame you for suspecting me. I wondered about Ollie too, for a minute. He was crying, and his sword was covered in blood. But in my gut, I knew he didn't do it, so I hid the sword to protect him. It wasn't the smartest thing I've ever done, but I don't always do the smart thing; I tend to do what feels right. So I trusted Ollie. And I hope you'll trust me, Kate. I hope your heart is telling you I didn't do this."

Kate knew better than to listen to her heart. She'd learned that the hard way. But right now, it was beating so loudly, it was hard to hear anything else.

She had to look away from him to think logically, forcing her emotions down.

All facts pointed to Hugo being the killer. He had motive because of Ollie's loan. Opportunity to sneak away in Bonnie's car. Means to kill Lemmy with the sword. And he'd hidden the murder weapon.

But her heart did murmur something else, a low hum she wanted to trust. The Hugo she'd come to know in the last few days—who calmed an old man with gentle patience, and wrote poetry, and cried when he saw his sister—wasn't a killer. Her head saw all the evidence pointing to his guilt, and yet, somehow, she believed in his innocence.

She took a moment to be sure of her decision, then drew a breath and looked back at him. "Forgive me, Hugo. I didn't know what to think."

He closed his eyes and released a long, sighing breath—and for the first time, she saw how pale and shaky he was. "I didn't kill him, Kate." His eyes lifted to hers, begging her to believe it.

"I know." And she did.

"I'm sorry you found that sword. And I don't mean because it made me look bad. I mean because . . . you shouldn't have to see something like that."

She knew he meant because of what she'd been through four years ago, and she didn't want him thinking of her as that pathetic girl in the newspapers. "I wrapped the sword in a beach towel and hid it in my trunk."

He laughed. "You're serious?"

"Only until I could think straight. Same as you, I guess." She offered a limp smile. "A fine pair we make."

"I'm starting to think so." He let those words hang in the air, with a look on his face that stirred something inside her.

Suddenly, she was aware of her blue silk pajamas. She tightened her arms across her chest. "So . . . I don't think we throw off the investigation too much if we tell Detective Bassett we found the sword in the backyard. The back door was open when we got home, so I think the killer went out that way."

"That's good," Hugo said. He added in a more cautious tone, "It'll be in the papers, I guess, that the murder weapon was Captain Powell's sword. Reporters love that kind of stuff."

"Yes," Kate said slowly, seeing his point. The papers would print an old movie photo of Ollie stabbing someone with the same sword, his eyes wide and dramatic. The reporters would talk to the neighbors and find out he hadn't left the house in years, then slant their articles to make him sound unstable—just as she was trying to convince him to be brave and leave the house.

"Ollie's fingerprints are on the sword," Hugo said. "And mine and Aurelio's. We mess around with it sometimes. And Reuben's too, I'm guessing."

Kate was glad she'd been careful with the towel, not leaving her own fingerprints.

Hugo said, "They'll look at all of us more closely when they know the murder weapon came from this house. They'll figure out Reuben's real name and make him testify against Moe Kravitz—which is pretty much a death sentence. And Aurelio spent a night in jail last summer, after some drunk guy at the club punched him because he didn't like the way his wife was looking at the waiter. So that'll be in the papers."

Just as his career was taking off. And Hugo wouldn't be spared either. Some reporter would take a picture of him on stage, raising a knife with a fiendish sneer.

And Kitty Hildebrand. What would the papers write about her? They'd love that the murder weapon belonged to her grandfather—another killer in the family. They might even throw suspicion her way, hinting that a week in a dark hole would damage anyone's mental stability.

"It's your call, Kate. If you want to call that detective right now, we will. I'll even admit to hiding it, if you think that's important. But . . . ." Hugo waited for her to look at him. "I think it's better if we wait a day or two until his suspicions move away from this house. That sword isn't going to help him find the real killer, only make him waste time on us."

Kate thought about it and nodded. "I think you're right. Let's leave it in my trunk for now. It has a good lock on it, and I'm done unpacking."

"I'll put all your luggage in the attic tomorrow. If they search the house again, I don't think they'll find it there."

"Okay."

Hugo's lips tilted in a slow smile. "Did we just agree to hide a murder weapon together?"

Somehow, that thought was more exciting than horrifying. "You can't tell anyone, Hugo. Not even Reuben."

"I won't." He held his hand across the table. "Our secret."

Kate hesitated, feeling a shiver of uncertainty, then reached out—and the moment Hugo's hand wrapped around hers, the shiver flared into something new. Their hands looked good together: hers, slim and pale with a garnet ring; his, large and masculine. She felt calluses on his palm, but the skin on the back of his hand looked soft. Her thumb slid over it.

Neither of them pulled away.

Her heart thumped madly, warning of danger.

Hugo was the one to separate them. "Good night, Kate." He walked toward the door, looked back over his shoulder with a fleeting smile, and then disappeared.

Kate went to her bedroom window and watched as he crossed the patio and entered the pool house. The light came on and the door shut—the same closed door and drawn shade she'd stared at a few hours ago, but her feelings were much different now.

She touched the windowpane and found it cold.

CHAPTER 16

"He's good," the choreographer told Tad and Kate, as Aurelio tapped and whirled his way around a rehearsal room. "And he looks good with Bonnie."

Tad watched, his arms crossed. "I was worried he didn't have enough formal training."

The choreographer shrugged. "Plenty of stage experience. Says he grew up doing Mexican dance shows with his uncle, then traveled with a hoofer group for a while learning all the modern stuff. He has a unique way of moving. Very loose and natural, but perfect control. It's fun to watch. You can't teach someone to move like that."

At the moment, Aurelio looked exhausted, his arms barely rising as his black shoes tapped and turned. Kate was tired too, after her late night with Hugo, but didn't have to dance all day.

"Okay, let's see if he makes it this time," the choreographer said, and they all watched as Aurelio leaped onto a chair with one foot, then onto a table with the other. His momentum took him past the center of the table, and he whirled, quickly crouching to save himself, as the table wobbled.

The choreographer lifted the record player needle, and the music halted.

"Sorry." Aurelio looked up from his crouch, breathing hard. "I slipped. Table's wet from my sweat."

"You're doing fine," the choreographer said, tossing him a white towel. "Wipe the table and take a few minutes to catch your breath."

Tad leaned toward Kate. "What time is his diction coach today?"

She glanced at her clipboard. "Five o'clock, double-booked with dinner." She frowned. "How is he supposed to eat and learn how to speak at the same time?"

"Aurelio!" Tad called. "We need faster progress on the accent. The diction coach said you struggled yesterday, and you start filming in a few days."

Aurelio came closer, draping the white towel around his neck. Even exhausted and sweaty, he was exquisite, his skin gleaming like light brown silk. He was smaller than most men, but tight with muscle. "Do I have to have an accent? Why can't I just talk like normal? It's hard to learn all that."

"How hard can it be, talking like a Mexican when you're a Mexican?"

Aurelio squinted, wiping sweat above his eyes. "But I don't talk like that."

"Which is why we have diction coaches. All the new actors need them."

"Sure . . . to talk fancy. I get that. But this guy wants me to say things all wrong."

"The Latin angle is one of the reasons we hired you, and we lose all the impact if you sound like you were born in . . ." Tad waved a vague hand.

"Fresno," Aurelio said, starting to look a bit miffed. "I was born in Fresno, California."

"Right, but your ancestors immigrated from Mexico."

"No . . . they lived in California when it *was* Mexico." Aurelio put his hands on his hips. "*Your* ancestors are the ones who immigrated."

Tad looked more amused than annoyed. "It's a role, Aurelio. If you want it, learn the accent." He turned for the door.

Kate cast Aurelio a sympathetic smile and followed. "Is the accent really necessary?" she asked, following Tad down the hall.

He glanced back. "You're the one who convinced me to go with a Latin lover. All those girls kissing his picture."

"They'll be kissing his gorgeous lips, not some fake accent." It was easier to keep up with Tad, now that she was wearing slacks and loafers. The weather was a little warm for the fitted, short-sleeved sweater she wore, tucked in at the waist, but all her blouses were still wrinkled.

Tad turned down the staircase. "The publicity team loves the angle. They're bringing in a Mexican backdrop for the photo shoot and a proud mama to kiss his cheek. They're going to say our music director was on vacation and heard him singing while he drove his donkey cart. Brought him back to Hollywood and was amazed at how quickly he picked up dancing. A complete natural."

"That's ridiculous. No one's going to believe he just learned how to dance."

"People believe what we tell them to believe." They reached the ground floor. "Nobody wants to hear about a boy who's been dancing on stage since he was three. They want rags to riches. Innate talent that springs from nowhere."

"A pack of lies," Kate said.

"More exciting than the truth." They turned down a long hall lined with doors. "It's called *image*, Kate. Every star needs one. You think Shirley Temple's hair grows out of her head that way? She's got a stage mama forcing her to sit still for curlers every night, but nobody wants to hear about that. Movie stars are supposed to be bigger than life. Nobody wants to buy a movie ticket to watch Archibald Leach get the girl."

"Who's Archibald Leach?"

Tad grinned down at her. "Cary Grant. Son of a penniless drunk, expelled from school, called himself Rubber Legs when he started out in showbiz. Hollywood erased all that and turned him into a debonair heartthrob." He opened a door. "Someday, your friend is going to thank me for that accent."

They entered another rehearsal room—larger than the one Aurelio had been in, with a dozen or so teenagers stomping through steps in a line as a man played the piano. Some of the teenagers fumbled with the footwork, but Kate knew that was part of the scene—Trixie's friends learning a dance number for the show they hoped would earn enough money to save the town's old theater.

Sydney—a man Kate had met the day before—called out, "It's right foot over left every time. Step, step, back. Okay, Mikey, give me your line."

A boy with glasses pretended to fall. "Ah, shucks, I'm no good at this! Can't I just do the lighting or something?" The other kids groaned and stopped dancing.

There was a moment of silence before Sydney called with measured patience, "Trixie!"

"Oh!" The girl standing in for Bonnie read from a script. "We need you on stage, Joey. This theater needs *all* of us. But it's getting late, so let's call it a day. Thanks, everyone!" The teenagers fell out of formation, smiling and murmuring as they moved to the side of the room.

Sydney noticed Tad. "Take five, everyone!" He walked toward them.

"Looks like the newbies are catching on," Tad said.

"They're all right. Kids, though—the attention of gnats." Sydney pulled a pack of cigarettes from his shirt pocket. "When do I get to work with the new lead boy? He's gotta know these scenes too."

"Aurelio Dios," Kate supplied.

"He's working on his solo dance right now. Kate, what's his schedule?"

She lifted a page on her clipboard. "This room, one o'clock."

Sydney stuck a cigarette between his lips. "I need a new pianist. This one keeps flubbing up."

"I'll talk to music, but they're short on people right now. Too many musicals going on at the same time." Tad frowned, and Kate knew he thought the music department always sent him their leftovers, as part of the conspiracy to trip up Clive Falcon's privileged boy. "Keep up the good work, Sydney." He opened the door.

"So . . . the music department is short on musicians?" Kate asked as they made their way down the hall. "One of Ollie's boarders is a violinist, and he's looking for work."

"We hire from the unions."

"He could join a union. He's very good." At least, she thought he was, when he wasn't playing the song of the damned. "Can we get him an audition? He acts too."

"Don't waste your time on that this week. We have enough on our plate." Tad glanced down at her, amused. "You're not going to make me hire all your grandfather's boarders, are you?"

She'd been waiting for a good time to mention Hugo. "Actually . . . there is one more actor. He's eighteen, and I think he'd be great in something. Not this movie, something more serious. He has these eyes that draw you in. Sort of dangerous, but thoughtful too. You can't look away." She didn't know how to describe Hugo.

Tad cast her a quizzical look as he opened the outer door. "Sounds like you're getting close to this particular boarder."

Her face warmed as she walked through to the outside. "I just think he's talented and deserves a chance."

"Well, I'm not sure you should be living in that house." They turned down the sidewalk. "I could help you find some place decent to live, if you want. The studio has bungalows at the back where you could stay until you find something better. We keep them for the stars, but they rarely use them."

Two days ago, Kate would have jumped at the chance to sleep

somewhere else, but not now. "My grandfather's house is perfectly decent, thank you."

"A man was murdered there, Kate."

"No one in the house had anything to do with that."

They entered the two-story building with palm trees out front, where Tad had an office in the back corner of the ground floor—purposefully unassuming, he'd told Kate, so people would know he was there to work, not ride his father's coattails. An extra desk had been brought in for Kate, but so far she'd never actually worked there.

They entered the office to find an impressively tall woman leaning against the front of Tad's desk, reading a bound script, wearing a vivid green dress with a gold brooch on the shoulder. "Mindless rubbish," she muttered. Her hair was icy gray, cut in an old-fashioned, chin-length bob.

Tad stopped and put his hands on his hips. "Stella Nixon," he said with distaste. "What are you doing here?"

The woman took her time putting down the script and picking up a cigarette from an ashtray before giving him her attention. The cigarette dangled between two fingers. "Hello, Taddy. Looks like we get the pleasure of working together again."

"What are you talking about? Horace Musgrave is the writer on this picture."

"Not anymore." Her voice had the throatiness of a long-time smoker. "He's been pulled away for more . . . *promising* projects, so your daddy called me in to patch up this sweet little script of yours." She brought the cigarette to her lips.

"No, no, no." Tad walked around his desk and picked up the phone. "He can't take Horace."

The woman seemed unfazed by the rebuff, tipping her chin down to appraise Kate over small, round spectacles. "You must be Kitty."

"Kate," she corrected.

"Yes, that suits you better. I'm Stella Nixon. Your grandfather is an old friend of mine. Not that I'm old, mind you." She smiled, revealing a gap between her two front teeth. The subtle wrinkles around her eyes suggested an age similar to Ollie's, somewhere in her fifties. "I stop by and visit him now and then." The knowing look in her eyes suggested she understood the situation. "I was in three pictures with Ollie, back in the day. Once, he saved me from cannibals, once he shot me, and once he threw me off a bridge. I decided to stop acting and write the scripts."

"Sounds like a wise choice," Kate said.

Tad argued into the phone, "She'll overthink every line. You know how she is. I don't have time for that."

Stella gave Kate a self-satisfied smile as she blew a stream of smoke. "You're certainly the talk of the town, everyone abuzz about you joining Falcon. We need more women in this business. We've gone extinct."

Kate had spent the first hour of the morning watching five teenaged girls sing a song in Trixie's bedroom. "Our picture has more girls in it than boys."

"Pish! I'm not talking about *actresses*." Stella put her hand on her bony hip, the cigarette perilously close to the green dress. "I'm talking about decision makers. Directors and producers. Editors and cinematographers. Have you seen any of *those* of the female variety at Falcon Pictures?"

Kate thought of the men Tad interacted with throughout the day, with manly slaps on the shoulder and the occasional crude joke, and the semicircle of men who'd inspected her in Clive Falcon's office. "No women," she realized aloud.

"Exactly. There used to be plenty of us at the top. I directed fifteen pictures and nobody thought anything of it. Mary Pickford wasn't just some curly-haired sweetheart on the screen, she owned the studio and called all the shots. And Lois Weber was a powerhouse—producing, directing, writing. And Lois's films really said something—like *Where Are My Children?* That movie had the entire country talking about—" Stella caught herself, looking sharply at Kate.

"What?"

"Never you mind. Anyway, *that* was the movie business in the early days—women accepted as equals."

"What changed?" Kate asked.

"Money." Stella flicked the cigarette at the ashtray. "Movies weren't just fun and games anymore, they were big business, which brought in Wall Street investors, and they decided pretty little ladies weren't smart enough for all that complicated money talk." She smiled, showing the gap in her teeth. "Lucky for me, I'm not so pretty. Or so little." She had to be close to six feet tall.

Kate liked her. "So, the women got pushed out of the business?"

"*And* the small men—financially speaking. The studios that got all that nice investment money bought up all the theaters in the country and only showed their own movies, putting the little moviemakers out of business. The big studios got bigger, and the rest disappeared. Now, only a few men run the entire industry, not a woman in sight. And that, my friend, is why all the movies are stereotyped claptrap."

"You're still in the business," Kate said, admiring that.

"Oh, they don't mind us sitting behind a typewriter, but you won't find any women running the show. Dorothy Arzner still directs, but she's the only one. And not a single producer." Stella brought the cigarette to her lips. "Until you."

Kate gave a short laugh. "I'm just an assistant. I run errands for Tad."

"That's not what I hear." Stella blew a stream of smoke. "According to Horace, you talked back to Clive Falcon, saved Tad's movie from a scheduling disaster, and discovered the young Fred Astaire everyone's been searching for."

"That's a complete exaggeration," Kate said, both surprised and a little proud that Horace Musgrave had said nice things about her. "For one thing, Aurelio got that job with his own talent."

"First rule of Hollywood, darling—accept all the credit whether you deserve it or not. That boy has probably been on a hundred auditions and nobody paid any attention—until you. Maybe you should be a casting director." Stella appraised Kate, the cigarette tipped out. "No . . . you look like a girl who wants to run the whole show. I saw you in the newspaper with Tad. Maybe you should marry him and take over Falcon Pictures someday. Clive can't live forever."

Kate glanced at Tad, but he was too busy on the phone to have heard. She lowered her voice. "If I decide to become a producer, I'll get there on my own merits, not with a wedding ring."

Stella's mouth twitched. "Good girl. I was just testing you." She brought the cigarette to her smiling lips.

"Anyway, I'm not really interested in the movie business, long term. I'm going to be an astronomer."

Stella's eyebrows lifted. "The *real* stars, eh?"

"As soon as this movie is over, I'm going back to San Francisco so I can . . ." Kate wasn't sure how to finish the sentence.

Live with my aunt and her new husband who despises me. Attend Blakely Academy, where I'm secretary of the student council and president of the astronomy club. Attend yacht club dances with society boys I don't particularly like but don't mind either.

Stella Nixon wasn't going to be impressed by any of that. And suddenly, Kate wasn't either, wondering why she'd been in such a hurry to leave Hollywood and get back to calculus.

Tad hung up the phone. "I'm stuck with you, Stella, but I don't have time for your funny stuff. Your job is to change the lead boy and leave the rest alone."

Stella twirled a hand in mock obeisance. "Your wish is my command."

"I'm late for a meeting." He pointed at Kate on his way to the door. "Stay here, and don't let her change a word of that script that doesn't need changing. Every word takes time, and—"

"—*time is money!*" Stella declared grandly. "Don't worry, Taddy, I won't waste a dime of your precious budget giving Trixie a brain."

He looked back from the doorway. "And don't fill my assistant's head with your radical ideas!" He disappeared.

Stella murmured, "As if you weren't capable of your own radical thoughts." She stubbed the cigarette and picked up the script. "Have a seat, Kate. We have a lot of work to do."

Kate sat at her desk. "I don't know anything about writing scripts."

"You can do the typing. I've got arthritis lately, which is our little secret. Now—you're a teenaged girl. Tell me if these words would ever come out of your mouth." Stella read from the page in a smoky, dramatic voice. "*You decide for both of us, Juan Pablo. My head is too full of silly thoughts to know what I want.*" She peered at Kate over her spectacles. "Mind you, this is ice cream they're talking about."

Kate smiled as she grabbed a sheet of paper and rolled it into her typewriter. This was going to be a lot more fun than taking notes at a student council meeting.

CHAPTER 17

Tad arranged for Kate to drive a studio car home, since Bonnie and Aurelio had to work late. Only a plain black Buick, but more powerful than her little roadster back in San Francisco. She made a wrong turn in Pasadena and had to pull over to look at a map, but still managed to park at the curb in front of Ollie's house before daylight was gone.

Kate never drove in the dark unless she had someone with her.

No reporters tonight, but as she walked around the hood of the car, Detective Bassett emerged from the house, wearing his rumpled brown suit and hat. He saw her and lifted his notebook. "Miss Hildebrand! I was hoping to catch you tonight! I have a few questions, if you don't mind."

She thought of the sword in her trunk and hoped she wouldn't have to lie outright—and if Ollie were in the room, she'd be lying to him too. "Do you mind if we speak out here? I don't want to distress my grandfather any more than necessary."

Detective Bassett's attention seemed to sharpen at that, but he kept his tone easy as he approached. "Sure, if that's what you want." A woman walked by with a dog on a leash, craning her neck to get a better look at Kitty Hildebrand. "Why don't we sit in your car for some privacy."

"All right." Kate went around to the driver's seat, while the detective settled himself on the passenger side. He shut the door, and a stale aroma filled the car. Kate rolled down her window.

"Not as hot today," the detective observed, keeping his own window closed. "I never like the Santa Anas. All that wind and static makes me jumpy."

"You said you have more questions?"

"A few." He flipped pages in his notebook, his lips pursed. "Can't read my own writing half the time."

Kate tapped a finger on the steering wheel.

"Let's see, here it is. I was hoping you could tell me more about that first night you arrived, when Mr. Berman played that prank on you, pretending to be dead on the floor."

"I told you—it wasn't a prank. They were rehearsing for Hugo's play."

"Sure . . . but still, must have made you angry after a long day of traveling."

She forced a smile. "I didn't kill him over it, if that's what you mean."

He chuckled. "No, no, nothing like that. I'm just trying to understand your relationship with Mr. Berman."

"I didn't have one. I met him once. Twice, I guess, if you include breakfast."

Detective Bassett looked up. "You had breakfast with him?"

"No. He walked into the kitchen briefly." Telling him that Lemmy had been on his way to visit a gangster in prison would help point suspicion somewhere besides Ollie and his boarders, but it also might bring closer scrutiny on Reuben and his fake name, and the fact that both Hugo and Aurelio used to work at the shady nightclub.

The detective wrote in his notebook, the pencil scratching. His ear was round and fleshy, a shade lighter than his ruddy face.

"Is that all?" she asked.

He rubbed the ear, as if feeling her stare. "Maybe you could tell me a bit more about what brought you to Pasadena. You were living with your aunt, I think, but she had some financial difficulties and couldn't pay your private school, so you came here to live with your grandfather. That right?"

Kate struggled to hide her irritation. "You've been reading the newspapers, I see. Nice of them to do your job for you. Only, they didn't get it quite right. My aunt got married, and I wanted to get to know my grandfather better. That's why I came here."

"Oh, sure, that makes sense. Still, I imagine it came as a shock when you showed up to live with your movie star grandfather and realized he wasn't—well, he's not exactly rolling in it anymore, is he? That must have been disappointing."

"Not at all. I was aware of my grandfather's financial situation." A lie. She hadn't known the extent of it. Certainly hadn't known he was in debt to a gangster.

"Well, that's good. He doesn't go out much these days, from what I gather."

She remained quiet.

"Sure has a lot of old stuff in his house. Looks like junk to me, but I imagine some collector would pay good money for it."

"I wouldn't know."

"Wouldn't you?" Detective Bassett turned on the seat to look at her. "Now that's interesting, because he just told me you talked about his things on your first morning here. How he said they were valuable, and you asked if he planned to sell any of it, and he told you no."

Kate frowned, trying to avoid whatever trap he was setting. "We spoke briefly about it. I hardly remember."

"And yet, an hour later, you got everyone out of the house—quite forcefully, I'm told. Even your grandfather, who doesn't go out much. You wanted everyone out of the house pretty bad,

Miss Hildebrand. But then Mr. Berman came home, so the house wasn't as empty as you expected."

Her temper flickered. He was taking Ollie's innocent ramblings and twisting them. "You think I wanted my grandfather out of the house so I could rob him? And Lemmy caught me, so I killed him? You should be writing for Hollywood."

Detective Bassett spread his hands. "I've been doing this job a long time, and if there's one thing I've learned, it's that truth is stranger than fiction. You'd be surprised what people are capable of, Miss Hildebrand." He paused. "Or maybe you wouldn't be. I guess you learned that yourself a few years ago."

Her anger turned to ice. She stared forward, her jaw tight, not wanting to give him the satisfaction of seeing how accurately he'd stabbed. The orange sunset had disappeared, the sky now purple. "You're trying to aggravate me on purpose, hoping I'll lose my temper and confess. The only problem is—I didn't do it. I didn't steal anything, and I didn't kill anyone. I was at Falcon Pictures all day."

"See, now, that's interesting too." Detective Bassett flipped a page in his notebook. "From what the men tell me, there was about an hour and a half, maybe two hours, when nobody knew where you were. I looked at some maps, and that movie studio is about twenty-five minutes away—fifty minutes round trip—which gave you plenty of time to ride here in a taxi and get back with no one the wiser."

It gave her smug satisfaction that he didn't know about the yellow car being moved. "So," she said coolly. "My getaway car was a taxi? And I hid the loot where—my purse?" She lifted the handbag on her lap, barely big enough for a compact and handkerchief.

He scratched his fleshy earlobe. "Maybe you planned to hide things under your bed and sell them later. Or in your empty luggage."

Kate's heart jumped into a panicky beat, but she forced her face to remain neutral. Hopefully, Hugo had put the luggage in the attic today. "That's absurd."

"You've grown up with nice things, Miss Hildebrand. It isn't easy coming down in the world like you have. And he's your grandfather, so it probably didn't feel like stealing. All in the family, as they say."

She hid her fear behind outrage. "I didn't steal anything—and I didn't kill Lemmy. I was the one who found him—and it was horrible—and I would never steal from anyone, let alone my own grandfather! You think you know me because you've seen my picture a hundred times and read a bunch of made-up stories. Well, you don't know a *thing*, because that girl isn't me!" She stopped, grabbing the bottom of the steering wheel.

Detective Bassett watched her closely, unruffled.

She took a moment, then said with forced calm, "I don't think you're stupid enough to think I did it. You're trying to unnerve me. And it worked. But that doesn't change the fact that I didn't do it and the real killer is still out there."

"Not out *there*, Miss Hildebrand—in *there*." Detective Bassett lifted a hand and tapped the car window with its view of Ollie's house. "I think one of you killed him, that's for sure, and I'm going to figure it out."

Her fury collapsed, because a small part of her feared the same thing.

Detective Bassett stepped out of the car, then leaned back to say through the open door, "He was stabbed with something long and sharp, like that sword in the painting on your grandfather's wall. I don't suppose you've seen something like that around the house?"

"No, I haven't," Kate said, and it was the easiest lie she'd ever told.

CHAPTER 18

The house smelled delicious. Kate stood still, breathed in, and decided it was pot roast. Every light seemed to be on, and the high notes of an operatic soprano drifted from the living room, with a scratchy quality that suggested a record player.

She moved to the arched opening.

Hugo sat sideways in the wingback chair, wearing a dark blue beret, his head bent over a *National Geographic* magazine, his legs draped over the arm of the chair. His calves were bare, and for a second, she thought he was wearing green, plaid shorts, then she realized it was a kilt.

"Do ya cool them jumping jacks?" he called over the opera without looking up from the magazine. "Me dog could do better."

"Your dog can't even . . . climb the stairs," Ollie huffed from a few feet away, his outstretched arms rising and falling in lazy jumping jacks, his feet rooted to the floor. Today's hat was a wreath of laurel leaves—which explained the white sheet draped over his shoulder, belted at his waist.

"Aye, but me dog ain't seekin' fame and glory. So move yer legs, ya lazy cur, or I'll be addin' a dozen moor."

Ollie noticed Kate in the doorway and smiled brightly, his arms still pumping. "Kate! You're home!"

Hugo's eyes darted up from the magazine. Their gazes held as she walked closer, full of everything that had passed between them the night before, but all he said was, "Aye, the bonnie lass hay returned." The kilt looked strangely at home on him, with his Celtic pallor and brooding good looks.

She stopped when she reached the dog at the foot of the chair. "I'm guessing you pulled that beret out of the wheelbarrow."

"Tisn't some Frenchie beret, ya daft lassie, tis me Scottish tam." He pulled it off his head, releasing dark, tousled hair. "Only, I'm a fearin' I sound a wee bit Irish."

She laughed. "I wouldn't know." The green kilt had slid up, revealing nice thighs shaped by muscle.

Hugo smiled dangerously, pulling down the hem. "Mind yer wicked eyes."

Kate returned his smile, as the soprano's song peaked in a final high note.

"Twenty," Ollie huffed, lowering his arms. His state of half-dress wasn't nearly as intriguing as Hugo's. "I'm in training, Kate. I decided you were right—I need more exercise. Every hour, Hugo blows the horn, and I walk up and down the staircase twice and do twenty jumping jacks." He patted his belly. "Two weeks and I'll be back in my old clothes."

"Two *months* if you stop sneaking crackers." Hugo spun the dark blue tam on one hand.

"I'm going to act again!" Ollie declared. "I quit because the big studios took over, and I refused to work for the likes of Jack Warner and Clive Falcon. But you've brought me back to life, Kate! I want to *work* again!"

"That's wonderful, Ollie." It was just the fire she'd hoped to ignite in him.

"I always wanted your mother to get into the business, but

she wasn't interested. Now you're here and we can work together. Isn't it marvelous?"

"Marvelous," she agreed, smiling.

"Hugo thinks I should start on the stage, where I can show my full range of expression. You know—move around a little." He spread his arms, and she caught a glimpse of swim shorts underneath the toga, which was a relief. "I always loved stage more than film, connecting with real people, not a camera. I could start at the Pasadena Playhouse, right here in town, then move on to Broadway. What do you think, Kate? Would you like living in New York City for a while? It's glorious in the fall."

She would be at Cal Berkeley in the fall but said, "Sounds fun. I've never been to New York."

"Can you imagine the hoopla when word gets out that I've returned to acting? But I'm going to be very selective. I don't want to work as much as I used to."

Kate glanced at Hugo but couldn't tell what he was thinking.

Reuben's voice shouted from the depths of the house. "Ollie! Get in here and tell me what this is!"

Ollie sighed. "He's had me sorting papers all day like a damn bookkeeper. And *this* one's got me jumping around like a lunatic. I should throw you all out." He patted Kate's shoulder on his way from the room. "Not you, my dear."

She waited until he'd disappeared before asking Hugo in a lowered voice, "Do you think he'll actually go through with it?"

Hugo shrugged, closing his *National Geographic*. "A week ago, I would have said no. But with you here, yeah, I think he actually might."

"But . . . will anyone hire him? What if he gets his hopes up, and nobody wants him?"

"Better to have dashed hopes than no hopes at all, don't you think?"

Kate wasn't so sure.

"He's already famous, at least," Hugo said. "That goes a long way in this town. He just needs to figure out that he won't be playing Romeo anymore, he'll be old Friar Laurence."

She gave a short laugh. "I'll let you tell him."

Hugo's gaze shifted to the ornate coffee table. "He, uh, saw you in the paper this morning."

"This morning?" Kate hadn't seen it. She picked up the newspaper—and drew a quick breath at the sight of her and Tad holding hands, surrounded by reporters and cameras. Kate was a step ahead, glancing back at Tad, who looked at her with concern. The photo had probably been taken as she was yanking her hand from his, eager to get away, but it looked like she was reaching back to make sure they stayed connected. The caption read: *Kitty Hildebrand working hand in hand with studio heir Tad Falcon.*

She read the first few lines of the article—a gossip column.

No grass growing under the feet of Kitty Hildebrand. She only moved in with her movie star grandfather, Oliver Banks, a few days ago but has already become the talk of Tinseltown. First, she discovered her grandfather's accountant murdered in the kitchen. Now, she has snatched the enviable spot of right-hand girl to one of Hollywood's most eligible young producers.

She lifted her eyes to find Hugo watching her. She tossed the paper on the coffee table. "It's rubbish."

"Right," he said carefully. "Because Lemmy wasn't Ollie's accountant."

"Tad was just helping me get through the reporters in front of the house." Which didn't make sense, since she was leading the way.

"Very chivalrous. I didn't know he was here last night."

"He . . . drove me home."

"Ah."

Ollie whooped in the distance, then appeared in the doorway a moment later, his toga drooping off his shoulder. "Come—

come at once! Reuben has found George Washington!" He darted away.

Kate and Hugo exchanged a confused look and followed.

Reuben stood behind Ollie's desk. "I almost threw them out," he said in a dazed voice, looking down at the desk. "Buried under a bunch of fan mail from old ladies."

"What is it?" Kate asked, going around the desk on one side, while Hugo went around on the other. They all stared down at three old letters spread across an open leather portfolio—three papers of various sizes and shades of beige.

"George Washington," Ollie said happily, pressing in behind them. He pushed an arm between Kate and Reuben, pointing to the letter in the middle. "And that's Abraham Lincoln. I forget the other one." He reached for the letter on the right.

Reuben slapped his hand. "Jefferson, and don't touch. They belong in a museum."

Kate stared down, astonished. The writing on the left was hard to read, but the signature was clearly G. Washington; the middle letter was more neatly penned, signed A. Lincoln; and the letter on the right had an impatient scrawl at the bottom—Th. Jefferson. "Are these real?"

"Of course they're real. I bought them at an auction. Well, Frank Fairchild bought them for me, back when I had more money than I knew what to do with. Frank was smart about money. Said I needed to—" Ollie wiggled his fingers. "There's a word for it—when you buy different things—"

"Diversify," Reuben said.

"That's it. Frank had me buying all sorts of strange things—cattle ranches and orange groves, houses I never saw. We bought land together out on Signal Hill when the oil boom happened. Craziest thing you ever saw—hundreds of tall rigs right next to one another. The hill looked like a porcupine."

Reuben turned to look at Ollie. "Are you telling me you own an *oil well*?"

"Oh, mine was a duster. Frank struck black gold and I lost my shirt." Ollie laughed easily. "But you'd be surprised how much money you can make off oranges."

Kate hardly dared to hope. "Do you still own any of these investments?"

"No, no—had to sell it all when the stock market crashed, pennies on the dollar. Those were sad days, everyone dumping their possessions as fast as they could. Made everything worthless overnight. Frank managed to hold on to his oil company, so he rebounded faster than most of us."

"You still have these letters," Hugo said. "Do you think they're worth anything?"

"I should think so. Frank said he had to keep bidding higher and higher. Ended up three or four thousand dollars, I think."

Reuben huffed a breath of disgust. "And you stuck them in a cardboard box." He picked up a business card poking out from behind Abraham Lincoln. The card had a sketch of an auctioneer's gavel on it, with the name Bleeker & Sons and an address in Beverly Hills. "This must be the place where he bought them. I'll drive there tomorrow and see what you can sell them for."

"If Ollie wants you to," Hugo said. "He never sells his stuff."

"Oh, I don't care about these," Ollie said. "No sentimental value. Might as well get some money out of them." He patted Kate's shoulder. "We'll buy you some pretty dresses."

She was touched, but said, "I have plenty of dresses, Ollie, but thank you."

"How about a finder's fee?" Reuben asked. "I could use a new suit."

"Goodness, yes—ten percent!"

"You don't have to pay Reuben," Hugo said. "They're your letters."

"And I'm the one who found them, cleaning up his junky office."

"Fine, but you have to go to the auction house and handle everything."

"No problem." Reuben stacked the letters inside the portfolio. "I'm going to keep this in my room before it gets lost again." He made his way to the door.

Ollie trailed him. "I'm famished. Let's eat."

"Stay away from that roast," Hugo said, following them. "I need to check it."

Kate remained alone behind the desk.

The stuffed black cat watched her with its amber eyes, looking eerily alive. "Hello, Boots," she murmured, understanding why Ollie talked to it. Probably an old pet he couldn't bear to part with.

She looked up at his other old friends around her. The snarling tiger. The mummy and suit of armor. The tables were crowded, the floor a mess, the bookcase crammed with more than books.

Was any of it actually valuable?

Detective Bassett thought she'd snuck home to rob Ollie, which was absurd, but she wondered, suddenly, if that's exactly why the killer had been in the house. They hadn't come to kill Lemmy, but to steal things, and when Lemmy had come home unexpectedly, they'd grabbed the sword on impulse. Kate looked at the sword case on the wall and was startled to see it wasn't there. Two nails remained, but it looked like a couple of pictures had been removed—no indication that it had been a sword case.

"Well done, Hugo," Kate murmured. She didn't mind deceiving Detective Bassett so much, now that he'd accused her of murder.

Captain Powell stared out from the deck of his ship, handsome and brave, his sword raised. He didn't really look like Ollie, other than the dimples, the face too angular, the eyes too fierce. She wondered if the painting was worth anything beyond sentimental value. Probably not.

But the killer had stood right there, close enough to grab the sword.

Kate's heart beat faster as she walked toward the painting. The sword case wasn't near the door. To reach it, the killer had to enter Ollie's office, walk past the snarling tiger, step over piles of magazines and costumes—all with the goal of reaching a murder weapon that looked like a fake Hollywood prop.

It didn't make sense.

Unless the killer was already standing near the sword when Lemmy surprised him.

Her gaze darted over the items on the table below the painting, wondering what was worth stealing. Up close, Captain Powell's pistol and dagger were clearly fake. His captain's hat, just a ratty costume. There were a few framed photos, and some scrapbooks and photo albums stacked at the end of the table—the ones Ollie had been looking at on Monday.

Photos. A thought nudged at the back of her mind, just out of sight. The photo albums felt important, somehow, but she couldn't think why. Out of everything in this room, they were least likely to draw a thief.

"The roast needs ten more minutes," Hugo said from the doorway.

Kate looked up but barely saw him.

"What's wrong?" he asked, coming closer.

"I'm trying to figure out why the killer would be standing right here."

"How do you know they were? Lemmy was killed in the kitchen."

"They used the sword. I don't think someone would do that unless they grabbed it on impulse." She glanced at the empty spot on the wall. "Good job on hiding the display case, by the way."

"I wasn't sure if you'd approve, but Reuben said that detective called, asking about a sword, so I thought we should get it out of sight. We put it in the trunk of Reuben's car, and that detective showed up an hour later."

"I saw him outside, and I'm his new prime suspect. He thinks

I'm greedy enough to steal from my grandfather and I killed Lemmy because he caught me in the act."

"He's just fishing around. He accused Reuben and me too."

"But it made me think," Kate said. "Maybe the killer *was* a thief. Why else would they be in this house when nobody was home? Unless Lemmy brought a friend home with him."

"Lemmy didn't have any friends. He didn't even sleep here, half the time. I think Moe Kravitz told him to live here for a while to spy on Reuben and make sure he didn't plan to squeal, but then Lemmy overheard us talking about Ollie's loan and stuck around, looking for some way to take advantage."

"So," Kate said, her thoughts turning. "The killer wasn't a friendly visitor, and they didn't come here to kill Lemmy."

"How do you know that?"

"They didn't bring a weapon. They used Ollie's sword—nobody's first choice."

"Oh, right."

"They came here to rob Ollie, and Lemmy walked in. Knowing Lemmy, he probably said something nasty that made the killer angry." Kate's eyes narrowed in thought. "Maybe the killer was defending himself."

"Could be. Lemmy was a nasty piece of work."

"The killer was standing in this very spot, close enough to notice the sword and use it. But why? Is something here worth stealing?" Kate looked back at the stack of photo albums, unable to shake the feeling they were important somehow.

"Now, this is interesting." Hugo walked around her, bent, and picked something up.

"What?" Kate turned.

He kept his back to her, studying whatever he held. "So . . . it's your theory that the killer was standing right here at some point?"

"They had to be."

"Then I know who killed Lemmy." Hugo turned slowly, holding up his find. "The person who left this behind."

CHAPTER 19

Kate let out a breath of exasperation. "For a second, I thought you were serious."

"I am. Don't you recognize it?"

It was Bonnie's scarf, black with white polka dots—the one she'd tied around her hair on Monday when Kate had rolled down the car window. "Yes, but Bonnie didn't kill Lemmy."

Hugo's lips curved in a wicked smile. "How do you know?"

"Bonnie" was all she needed to say.

"It's a clue." He opened the scarf between his two hands. "Proof she was here."

"A million women have scarves like that." But it was actually rather unique, Kate realized, with a white chain pattern around the border. She tilted the corner and saw a Chanel label—which meant expensive. She couldn't imagine there'd been many rich, stylish women strolling through Ollie's office recently. "It's probably been here for years."

"I know." Hugo grinned. "But it's kind of fun to picture Bonnie stabbing Lemmy with a sword."

"Not so fun, actually."

"It's just a red herring. Every good mystery needs them."

Kate frowned. "A fish?"

"Misleading clue. But Bonnie doesn't make a good suspect because she didn't have a motive. She never even met Lemmy."

All at once, Kate knew why the photo albums had felt important: they'd reminded her of some other photos, burned by Reuben in the fireplace. Lemmy had taken dirty photos of Bonnie through her bedroom window. Maybe he'd already shown them to her and demanded blackmail money, just as her career was taking off. And now Lemmy was dead. And Bonnie's scarf was here. And her yellow car had been moved during the timeframe when Lemmy was killed.

Kate felt light-headed. She walked to one of the armchairs in front of Ollie's desk, pushed a stack of newspapers to the floor, and sat.

Hugo followed. "You all right? You went pale, all of the sudden."

She rested her elbows on the armrests and pressed her fingers to her temples. "Hugo, I think Bonnie may have done it."

He laughed. "Sorry, I was just joking around. There's no way that girl killed someone." He leaned back against the front of the desk, and the sight of him wearing a kilt calmed her somehow. "It's only a scarf, Kate, probably from some old costume." He dropped it on the desk.

But she wasn't convinced. "Did you notice that her car was moved at the studio? She could have driven here while we were all separated, and nobody would know."

"Why would she? That doesn't even make sense."

"Because there was something in this house she needed to find and destroy, but Lemmy walked in, and she panicked and grabbed the sword." The more Kate thought about it, the more it made sense.

But Hugo only looked amused. "Okay . . . exciting action scene . . . but what in this house would Bonnie need to find and destroy?"

Kate wasn't sure if she should tell him.

"What? I can see that big brain of yours working." He folded his arms, making his biceps stand out. Somehow, wearing a skirt only accentuated his masculinity.

"Lemmy took pictures of Bonnie through her bedroom window. Pictures of her . . . undressing."

One dark eyebrow lifted. "Okay. I didn't expect your imagination to go that direction, but I like the unexpected plot twist."

Her face warmed. "I didn't make it up. I watched Reuben burn the photos. You can ask him yourself."

Hugo's eyes narrowed. "You're serious?"

"Deadly. Reuben didn't think Bonnie knew about the pictures, but what if she did? What if Lemmy had already threatened to sell them to a gossip magazine unless she paid him off? Image is everything in showbiz, and hers is supposed to be sweet and wholesome, not—"

"Slow down. This is Bonnie we're talking about. She wouldn't kill someone over dirty pictures. She would—I don't know—tell her mom or something."

"She didn't plan to kill him. She came to find the photos but doesn't know this house. She saw *those* photo albums"—Kate pointed at the table below Captain Powell—"and came in here. She would have figured out they were Ollie's old photos and moved on, but Lemmy walked in. He probably said something horrible and scared her, and she panicked and grabbed the sword."

Hugo frowned, mulling it over. "It's surprisingly logical. But then, how did Lemmy end up in the kitchen?"

"I don't know. He . . . he staggered in there and died."

"Why not stagger to the telephone and call for help? That's the other direction."

"The phone wasn't working on Monday." Kate tapped her fingers on the armrest. "Is there a first aid kit in the kitchen?"

Hugo laughed. "No, but maybe he thought a dishrag could

save his life, so I'll give you that. But how did the sword end up in the kitchen?"

She tugged at a loose thread on the armrest. "He grabbed it from her."

"After she stabbed him? So . . . Lemmy grabbed the sword and then staggered to the kitchen without dropping any blood along the way? There's no blood trail."

Kate frowned, annoyed that she hadn't thought of that.

"He was stabbed in the kitchen," Hugo said. "So—either Bonnie stalked him there like a cold-blooded killer, sword in hand. Or—he was killed by someone else."

She wrapped the thread around her finger, knowing she should be relieved that Bonnie seemed innocent, but she wasn't convinced. The thread dug into her skin.

"Kate," Hugo said gently. "I was only making up a funny story about the scarf. I don't think Bonnie killed Lemmy and then came back to the studio like nothing was wrong. Remember the way she danced with Aurelio at auditions? She was *singing* in the car on the way home."

"She's an actress."

"Nobody's that good. Not her, that's for sure."

Kate tugged at the loose thread, snapping it free. He was right. Bonnie couldn't kill Lemmy in such a horrific, bloody way, and then return to the studio to dance and laugh. She wasn't the killer—and it wasn't Kate's job to solve this crime. She sighed and stretched out her legs in front of the chair. "Hugo, we shouldn't have hidden that sword. What a stupid thing to do."

He shrugged. "I still think it was brilliant."

Her gaze slid to his kilt and bare legs—rather nice legs, now that she looked at them. He *would* think hiding a murder weapon was brilliant. "It's Detective Bassett's job to solve this crime, and he can't do that without the most important piece of evidence. The killer's fingerprints are probably on that sword."

"I'm not sure that guy could solve it with the sword, finger-prints, and a signed confession."

"I think he's more clever than he lets on." Kate's fingertips rubbed against the rough armrest. She'd been in a spell last night, agreeing to hide a murder weapon while a killer walked free, but it was time to be sensible. "We have to give it to him, Hugo, and we have to tell him it was in the kitchen, because that's part of the puzzle."

Hugo spoke slowly. "I don't think that's such a good idea, Kate."

"We can explain why we hid it—so he wouldn't suspect Ollie."

"He *will* suspect Ollie. He'll suspect *all* of us."

"I'm his biggest suspect right now, but that's his job, and he'll get to the truth eventually. But not without that sword." Her fingers found another loose thread. "I should tell him about Bonnie's scarf too, I guess, and the car being moved. They might be important clues."

"And Bonnie's dirty pictures? Some cop will leak that story to a reporter for fifty bucks, and it'll end up in the papers."

Kate frowned, not liking the thought of Bonnie being taken in for questioning. The movie would be delayed—maybe can-celed altogether, and Aurelio would lose his lead role. All for nothing, if Bonnie didn't do it.

"We'll give him the sword, Kate, but not until he's done sus-pecting the people in this house and focused his attention on the real killer."

She considered that. "Reuben burned more photos besides Bonnie's. He said most of them were movie stars misbehaving at the club. Maybe one of them came to the house to pay off Lemmy, and things got out of hand."

"That makes sense. I'll talk to Reuben tomorrow. He might remember who was in the photos. And I'll search the house for more clues. There might be a blood trail we didn't notice."

Kate looked at the terra cotta floor beyond the Persian rug, the same color as dried blood. "I don't know, Hugo. We should tell the police what we know."

"Let's investigate on our own first. You're smart, and I know a lot about murder."

She flashed a wry smile. "I wouldn't brag about that."

"I'll hide my notebook on how to commit the perfect crime." He was enjoying this.

And so was she, she realized, despite the grisly circumstance.

"Come on," he coaxed. "We'll be like those amateur sleuths in the books. They always outwit the police. You can be Nancy Drew and I'll be Ned Nickerson. You even have the right hair color."

"Nancy Drew is a redhead?"

"Titian. I had to look it up. It's that reddish-brown color, like yours."

Kate raised her eyebrows. "First of all, my aunt's the only person who calls red hair *titian*. For another thing—*you* read Nancy Drew? I thought you were a Dashiell Hammett man."

Hugo shrugged. "Esther may have left a few around the house. Surprisingly hard to put down."

"I have a whole new respect."

"So . . . what do you say, Kate? Want to play detective together?" His eyes locked on hers, daring her to play his game.

She was tempted.

But shook her head. "This is a real murder, Hugo, and if things go wrong, we could both end up in prison for concealing evidence."

The playful light in his eyes dimmed. "You're probably right."

She hated seeing his disappointment—disappointment in *her*, really. She dropped her eyes from his—and saw the green plaid kilt, a reminder of how different they were. He spent his days pulling hats from a wheelbarrow and playacting with an old man in striped pajamas. Last night, he'd pulled her into his spell for a while—a nice spell—but that hadn't been the real her.

Her gaze crossed the rug to her own Italian calfskin loafers. Neatly creased slacks. Cashmere sweater, tucked in. A simple gold chain. Everything expensive but tasteful. A Hildebrand to the core.

She was disappointed in herself too.

I am not afraid.

She lifted her eyes to his. "Hugo."

"Yes, Kate?"

"I want to be Nancy Drew."

He smiled.

Dinner was all wrong.

For one thing, no one was properly dressed. Ollie's toga kept sliding off his shoulder, so he looked naked across the table. Hugo sat at the end, barefoot and bare-legged. Reuben sat next to Kate, his shirt unbuttoned halfway, exposing a dingy undershirt. Even Kate had it wrong, wearing slacks; Aunt Lorna had always insisted on a dress for dinner.

Hugo's pot roast, carrots, and potatoes were delicious but served straight from the pot on the table. Kate asked for a napkin and was handed a dishrag.

Reuben dominated the conversation with rants about politics and religion—something about Stalin and a civil war in Spain. Mentions of Hitler and a few quotes about class consciousness that sounded vaguely Marxist.

Aurelio arrived mid-meal to cheers of welcome. He had large sweat marks under his arms and shoveled food into his mouth, pulling his beef apart with his fingers. Ollie stood and recited a poem in a booming voice—something about dining with friends—and Aurelio sang a little ditty with dirty lyrics.

It was the best dinner party Kate had ever attended.

She was overly aware of Hugo sitting nearby and sensed his matching awareness, their careful glances just missing each other.

He seemed to be making an effort to use good table manners, and she made an effort to relax hers.

"Oh!" Aurelio cried suddenly. "You're all invited to Bonnie's birthday party Friday night. You too, Ollie. I saw Mrs. Fairchild at rehearsal, and she said to invite you special."

Ollie's face froze for a few seconds before he managed a polite smile. "Unfortunately, I have other plans that evening, but you must thank her for me."

Kate remembered how eager Mrs. Fairchild had seemed to repair their friendship. "Maybe you should go, Ollie, just for five minutes. We can go together."

He pretended not to hear, bending to feed the dog.

Aurelio licked gravy from his thumb. "I'm borrowing a suit from the studio." He had a new, stylish haircut, and his face had been groomed to masculine perfection. Kate had seen other men getting worked over in the makeup department: face creams rubbed, nails filed, hairs between eyes plucked.

She said, "Maybe I can borrow suits for the rest of you too."

Reuben barked a laugh. "Thanks, but I'll skip the kiddie party."

"Bonnie said it'll be her mom's friends mostly," Aurelio said. "Directors and producers, so I better look sharp and make a good impression. Guess that's a high bar for you, Reuben."

"Hey," Reuben griped, wiping a greasy finger on his undershirt.

Kate wondered if she should tell Reuben the music department needed musicians but decided against it—not until she knew if she could get him an audition. She looked at Hugo. "You'll go to Bonnie's party, won't you?"

"Can't. Have to work every night except Sunday." He glanced at the clock and pushed back his chair. "I'm late now. Someone else clean up."

"I'll do it," Kate said, earning her a private smile from Hugo. He held her gaze as he walked to the door, nearly running into the wall. He laughed as he disappeared.

Reuben leaned his shoulder toward her. "Careful now," he said in a low voice. "That boy isn't as tough as he looks. You're going to break his heart when you decide to move on."

Kate's gaze darted to the others, but they were too busy dividing up the last of the roast to have heard. She wasn't sure if she should deny any feelings between her and Hugo or insist she would never break his heart. She settled for "I don't know what you're talking about."

Reuben huffed a laugh. "The way you're blushing, maybe you're the one whose heart is in danger."

"Whose heart is in danger?" Ollie asked from across the table.

"Everybody's heart is fine," Kate snapped.

Reuben laughed as he stood. He leaned down to give her a final, quiet warning. "Don't play games with my friend. You and I both know you're way out of his league, but he's a dreamer."

CHAPTER 20

Kate was eager to look in Bonnie's glovebox the next morning. If the scarf was there, the one they'd found in Ollie's office wasn't Bonnie's, which meant she probably had nothing to do with the murder. If the scarf *wasn't* there, Kate would ask Bonnie about it and watch for signs of guilt.

But as Kate and Aurelio stepped out of the house at 5:40 a.m.—ten minutes later than usual—they saw the yellow car disappearing down the road, and Kate remembered she had her own car now.

"She left without us," Aurelio said, surprised.

"She knows I borrowed a car from Falcon. You're stuck with me."

"I'll drive. Give me the key."

"No, I like driving."

Aurelio grumbled but got in the passenger side.

Tad was already behind his desk, bristling with nervous energy, when Kate walked in. He saw Kate and waved a paper. "The recording studio doesn't have Aurelio listed, and that has to happen today."

"It's probably an old schedule. I talked to them late yesterday, and everything is set." Kate put down her purse and picked up her clipboard.

"Nobody answers when I call over there."

"Because the sun isn't up, Tad. I'll stop by on my morning rounds." Kate took the recording schedule and added it to her clipboard.

"That stage set better be done by Saturday. Leo Scully went home with the flu yesterday."

"I'll stop by and talk to his assistant." Kate wrote it on her list, liking that she knew who Leo Scully was and where to find his office. "Take a breath, Tad. I've triple-checked, and everything is on track."

"Bring me a coffee and two donuts before you do anything else."

"Of course, Mr. Falcon. Priorities." Kate batted her eyelashes as she headed out the door.

She didn't stop moving for the next two hours, hurrying from office to office, dropping off papers and picking up other papers, exchanging quick hellos with secretaries who now looked familiar. She spent a half hour in the catering office, straightening out a misunderstanding over how much food would be needed on set the next day, and then detoured to the commissary to pick up a donut for herself, suddenly ravenous.

As she left the commissary, she paused at the side of the road to watch as several flatbed trucks rolled by, carrying caged lions. She'd heard about an African safari movie with Barbara Stanwyck being shot behind the Western town at the back of the studio, but it was too far away for Kate to sneak a peek.

"Wouldn't want to be on that set," a masculine voice said, and she turned to see Bonnie's sandy-haired tutor Glenn Petersen. Kate had met him briefly the day before.

She wiped donut glaze from the corner of her mouth. "Aren't you supposed to be with Bonnie in dance rehearsal right now?"

"Yep, trying to explain the Louisiana Purchase every time she stops for breath, but she's not there."

Kate leaned the clipboard against her hip so she could hold the donut and flip pages at the same time. "Room eight?"

"Room eight," Glenn confirmed. "Aurelio's there, but Bonnie never showed up. I waited as long as I could, but I've got an English exam."

One of the lions roared, drawing their attention. The last truck had stopped as the driver talked to someone through his open window, and the lion paced.

"It's sort of amazing around here, isn't it?" Glenn asked.

"Amazing," Kate agreed, finishing her last bite of donut. It was hard to care about calculus with a lion a few yards away, but she licked her fingers and said, "I've been meaning to talk to you about something, Glenn."

He glanced at his watch. "Can we walk and talk at the same time?"

"That's all I do around here." They turned down the sidewalk together. "You go to Caltech, right?"

"First year, mechanical engineering."

"That's perfect," she said. "Exactly what I want."

Glenn looked at her with a surprised smile. "First time a pretty girl has ever told me that."

She laughed. "I just meant—I need help with calculus."

A stream of women in dance costumes poured out of the hair and makeup building, making them stop. The costumes were tight bodysuits, black on one side, white on the other. Glenn raised his voice above the chatter. "You're learning calculus? I thought you were still in high school."

"I am, but I'm missing school while I do this movie, and I'm getting behind." They followed the dancers down the sidewalk, in the wake of hair spray fumes. "Well . . . I was *already* behind, but this doesn't help. I can't figure out derivatives."

"Everyone struggles with that at first, but it's fun once you get the hang of it."

"I know you're busy with school and might not have the time," Kate said.

"I'll make the time." He looked down at her with a smile that implied interest in more than calculus.

"I mean—it'll be part of your tutoring job, paid by the studio." He was nice looking, in a quiet sort of way, but Kate's only interest was in his math skills.

The dancers stopped to board a bus, clogging the sidewalk. "So—calculus in high school," Glenn said, leading the way around the outer edge of the dancers. "That's advanced stuff for a girl."

Which irked Kate, but she was used to it. "I'm as good at math as the boys in my class. Better than most of them."

"Maybe you are. It's just—" They came out at the other end of the dancers to open sidewalk. "Why bother? You don't need calculus to be a housewife—or secretary or nurse, if that's what you want to do. Or even a movie producer."

"No, but it'll come in very handy when I'm an astronomer."

"*Astronomer?*" He looked amused. "I've never heard of a girl studying astronomy before."

"That's because you settled for Caltech instead of Cal Berkeley."

He hooted. "Fighting words. Caltech is a better school than Berkeley."

"Debatable."

"Einstein taught at Caltech. And if it's stars you're into, our astronomy department is the best in the world. They're building a new observatory with the biggest telescope in the world."

"Palomar," Kate muttered, a bit begrudging. She'd read about the 200-inch mirrored disk and seen pictures of it on its way to Pasadena with a big sign and a lot of hoopla. But it was hard to get excited about the world's largest telescope when she knew she'd never be allowed to use it.

Caltech didn't admit girls.

"How can a school be great," Kate asked, "when it's blocking out half the brain power of the world?"

He laughed. "Yeah, I can see why you'd feel that way. But it's a science school, and science is a man's field—for the most part," he added, glancing her way. He turned down the side of the building toward the parking lot. "So, does that mean you're planning on Berkeley? They have a pretty good telescope too, don't they?"

"Lick Observatory. They discovered Jupiter's fifth moon and . . ." She saw Bonnie's yellow car, and her voice faded.

"Well, this is mine," Glenn said, patting the hood of an old, black Ford. "Nothing fancy, but it gets me around."

Kate forced her eyes back to Glenn, her heart racing. "Okay. Well. I'll bring my math book tomorrow, if you think you can spare a few minutes."

"Absolutely." He opened the door of the Ford, but didn't get in. "And I'll see you at Bonnie's party, right?"

"Yes."

"We can talk about derivatives there." He waited a beat before grinning. "Just kidding, but a dance would be nice."

She kept her smile polite. "Certainly. Goodbye, Glenn."

"Bye, Kate."

She pretended to walk back the way they'd come, waving as his car passed, listening for the rattle of his old engine to fade— then turned and hurried back to Bonnie's car.

The passenger door wasn't locked. Kate glanced both ways in the deserted parking lot, then quickly sat inside and pulled the door closed behind her. She pushed the glovebox latch and it popped open, making her jump.

Two wrinkled maps took up most of the glovebox. Kate pulled them out, looked deeper, and found a man's handkerchief with a lipstick stain, a flashlight, and a green receipt from a car repair shop. At the very bottom, her fingers found Bonnie's car key and a pack of Wrigley's gum that didn't look very fresh.

Kate turned and looked at the back seat, then bent over to search the floor.

No scarf.

She sank back on the seat, unsure how she felt about that. It would have been better to find it, clearing Bonnie's name, proving the scarf in Ollie's office had no connection to Bonnie or the murder. But Kate couldn't help but be intrigued that the missing scarf matched her theory. Bonnie must have worn it to hide her blond hair when she snuck into Ollie's house and dropped it by accident. She had a reason to kill Lemmy, a car to get there, and had left evidence behind.

All the clues fit.

But Bonnie *didn't* fit; Hugo was right about that. How could she stab Lemmy, and then dance and laugh with Aurelio an hour later as if nothing had happened? Kate's common sense balked at the idea. It seemed impossible.

But she'd accepted the impossible before.

People weren't always what they seemed, even more so in Hollywood.

The car was too warm and stuffy suddenly, sweat beading on her forehead. She couldn't get enough air. She reached for the door handle, her fingers fumbling, her lungs tight, and finally yanked the lever and pushed the door open.

She inhaled fresh air, her heart thumping.

Kate's fear of enclosed spaces wasn't as obvious as her fear of the dark, but it was just as strong, taking control at inconvenient moments, like in small bathroom stalls and dressing rooms.

She kept the door open as she folded the two maps with trembling hands, trying to restore some sense of order.

But her mind drifted back to where it shouldn't go: Aunt Lorna standing next to Kate's hospital bed, telling her in a tear-choked voice that her parents were both dead. Explaining, in sobbing bits and pieces, how her father had been the one who pulled the trigger.

The impossible suddenly possible.

Kate returned the folded maps to the glovebox and got out of the car.

"Kate!" She whirled, her heart in her throat, and saw Tad at the far end of the parking lot, his hand raised.

She hurried toward him, trying to think of an excuse for being in Bonnie's car.

But he didn't seem to have noticed, turning toward the building with palm trees. "Is Leo still out sick? And did you talk to Mei Chen?"

"Leo Scully still has the flu, but the theater set is on schedule, and Mei agrees about toning down the white." Kate flipped through her clipboard as they walked, quickly recapping everything she'd accomplished in the last two hours. She ended with, "And I talked to Bonnie's tutor about helping me with calculus. I told him the studio would pay for it. I hope that's okay."

Tad shot her a look as they entered the building. "You're past the age requirement for schoolwork. You don't have time for that."

"I'm only seventeen, and missing school to be here, and I need to keep up because next fall—"

"All right, all right, but do it on your lunch break."

They entered Tad's office and found Bonnie asleep in Tad's chair, her head nestled in the crook of her arms on the desk.

"Looks like we have a stray bunny rabbit," Tad said, amused. He approached with a sly smile, lifted a blond curl, and tickled Bonnie's cheek with it. She sat up with a gasp, and he laughed. "Aren't you supposed to be at dance rehearsal right now?"

Bonnie groaned, slumping in the chair. "I tried, but my feet won't move. I need some red candy."

Tad's smile fell, but he kept his voice light. "What you need is a cup of coffee."

Bonnie scowled at the beverage cart beside the desk. "I hate coffee."

"Coca-Cola, then. Stand up, bunny rabbit. I need my chair."

She complied with exaggerated weariness, turning to lean her hips against the desk. "Really, Tad, can't I have one? Pretty please."

"One Coca-Cola, coming up." Tad picked up a fat stack of papers tied with string and held it toward Kate. "Run this upstairs to my dad's office, will you? He wants to approve Stella's changes."

Kate took the papers, not relishing the thought of entering Clive Falcon's office again. As she walked through the doorway, she glanced back and found Tad watching her, waiting for her to be gone.

She made it all the way down the hall and halfway up the staircase before the uneasy feeling creeping through her reached her feet. She'd made a promise to Mrs. Fairchild. She quickly retraced her steps, slowing as she neared the office. Carefully . . . quietly . . . she peered around the door frame.

Bonnie still leaned against the desk, and Tad now stood in front of her, his hand on her waist, watching with a bemused expression as she drank from a glass. He murmured something in a soothing tone, then noticed Kate and moved back, his hand dropping. "What is it?" he asked too sharply. Then, with false indifference, "It's the big office at the top of the stairs. You can't miss it."

"I've been there before. I just wondered if Bonnie wanted to come with me. The walk will wake her up, and then she can go to rehearsal."

"Excellent idea. Off you go, bunny rabbit."

Bonnie set down the glass with a happy sigh. "I feel better already. I *love* a good nap." She winked at Tad as she walked away— and it struck Kate that Bonnie wasn't quite as naive as she seemed.

She was a performer.

Kate waited until they were out of view from Tad's office, halfway up the staircase, before tugging Bonnie's arm to a stop. "What is that red candy Tad gives you?" she hissed.

Bonnie's lips pouted. "He just got mad at me for talking about it, but I thought you knew. He doesn't want people to find out or everyone will want it, and it's only for stars."

"I don't want it. I'm just curious, that's all." Kate added in a conspiratorial tone, "He expects me to know everything, but then doesn't tell me, and I can't read his mind."

"He *does* do that. But you can't tell Mama or she'll think I'm working too hard and make me slow down. Tad says he sees it all the time—a girl about to make it big, but her mother holds her back, and her career is over before it even begins. Stars have to make sacrifices. So you can't tell Mama, promise?"

Kate hesitated. "I promise."

"It's just pills that help you wake up. It's from a doctor and everything."

Kate waited for a man to pass at the bottom of the stairs before whispering, "It's a drug, Bonnie. He's giving you some sort of stimulant."

"*Medicine.* It's good for you, honest. I can dance all night and not even get tired. Except if I take it too late, I can't sleep and need a sleeping pill."

"Jiminy Cricket, Bonnie, you can't be popping pills to wake up and then more to go to sleep."

Bonnie scowled. "It's not *bad* for you. I feel swell when I take it."

"I'll bet. It's not medicine, it's the studio's way of working you to death." Kate wondered how many other stars in the Falcon stable were popping pills to keep up with their grueling schedule of five or six pictures a year, which she knew was standard.

"You won't tell Mama?"

Kate regretted that promise but said, "I won't tell her."

"She invited all these boring old movie business people to my birthday party. You're coming, aren't you?"

"Yes." Kate wasn't sure how to bring up the scarf and decided to just dive in. "Bonnie, I wanted to borrow the scarf in your glovebox, but it's not there."

"I know, Aurelio lost it. Mama's going to be so mad when she finds out. She bought it for me in Paris."

"Aurelio?" Kate remembered Bonnie handing him the scarf at auditions, asking him to put it in the glovebox for her. Was he the one who'd driven home and dropped it in a scuffle with Lemmy? It might have fallen out of his pocket.

"He says he'll buy me a new one, but it's from Paris and everything. He feels terrible."

Why would Aurelio kill Lemmy? He didn't know about Ollie's loan, as far as she knew. Had Lemmy threatened him with blackmail photos?

"I better go," Bonnie said. She wiggled her fingers and turned away.

"Bonnie, wait." Kate descended two steps to the girl's level. "Someone moved your car during the auditions. Do you know who that was?"

Bonnie opened her pretty mouth but seemed incapable of speech for a few seconds, before snapping, "How should I know? I'm very busy around here, in case you haven't noticed." She hurried away.

Kate stared after her, stunned—and confused. Clearly, Bonnie knew something about the yellow car being moved. But unless Bonnie was a much better liar than she seemed, Aurelio was the one who'd dropped the scarf and murdered Lemmy.

CHAPTER 21

Kate spent the rest of the day trying to find Bonnie or Aurelio alone, but they were both constantly surrounded by people, hurried from voice recordings to wardrobe fittings to manicures. She wouldn't even see Aurelio in the car later, since he was scheduled to work late.

The end of her day was spent delivering copies of the new scripts around the studio, and by the time she got back to Tad's office, she was so exhausted, she didn't care who'd killed Lemmy. She saw the sun starting to sink through the window and snuck out while Tad was on the phone, so she could get home before dark.

As she got out of the car in front of Ollie's house, she didn't see any signs of Detective Bassett or reporters, but a feminine voice called her name, and she turned to see Mrs. Fairchild coming down her front walkway, looking like a beautiful ghost in a pale gray dress that fluttered as she walked. Kate hesitated, thinking of Bonnie's red pills and the scarf and the fact that Bonnie might actually be involved in murder, then walked to meet Mrs. Fairchild where the two properties met at the road.

Mrs. Fairchild reached out to briefly squeeze Kate's hands. "I've been watching for you out the window. It's so horrible about that man getting killed. I heard you were the one who found him. How are you doing?"

I've been suspecting your daughter of murder, Kate thought, but all she said was, "Work is a good distraction." Something occurred to her. "I never thanked you for my job. You're the reason I have it."

"Well, I'm glad it all worked out. Clive tells me you're doing a wonderful job and the movie is finally coming together." Mrs. Fairchild glanced at Ollie's house. "That boy is a surprising choice for the lead role, but I watched them at rehearsal today, and they do have a sort of . . . nice energy together."

She must have seen them after Bonnie took the pill. Kate felt torn between her two promises—one made to Mrs. Fairchild, one to Bonnie. She said cautiously, "You asked me to keep an eye on her."

Mrs. Fairchild immediately picked up on the cue, her attention sharpening. "What have you seen?"

Kate wasn't sure how much to say.

"Is it Clive? Have you seen him and Bonnie together? He has a reputation, but he promised me—"

"No!" Kate cried, appalled, thinking of the middle-aged man with the silver mustache. "He never comes near our rehearsals. We send him a daily report, but he leaves the details to Tad."

Mrs. Fairchild relaxed. "That's good. Tad is a nice young man."

Who supplied her daughter with stimulants and sleeping pills. "He makes Bonnie work long hours. She seemed exhausted today."

"That's how it is in Hollywood—too much work or none at all."

"But she's dancing until one in the morning and expected back at six."

"She's young. I endured it myself before I married Frank.

Even parties felt like work, scrambling to meet the right people." Mrs. Fairchild gave a tired smile. "I'm still scrambling for Bonnie's sake."

"Is it worth it?" Kate asked. "I mean . . . is that really the life you want for Bonnie?"

"If you were a performer, you wouldn't ask. It's a driving need, and Bonnie thrives on it."

"She *is* good," Kate said. She'd watched Bonnie rehearse a musical number with several other girls that afternoon, and Bonnie had been noticeably better than the rest, drawing all the attention.

"Being good isn't enough. There are a thousand girls just as talented and pretty as Bonnie, but only a lucky few will get to work in the best productions, doing work they can be proud of. The rest will end up in low-quality pictures that make them look ridiculous. Bonnie wants more than that, so she doesn't mind missing a few hours of sleep."

"I helped revise her script yesterday." Kate smiled, thinking of Stella. "We gave her some great lines."

"That's nice." Mrs. Fairchild's gaze drifted to Ollie's house. "I've been wondering how Ollie is doing with all the police and reporters. I've wanted to call or knock but haven't had the nerve. Do you think he'd accept a visit from me?"

Kate thought of Ollie in his toga the night before. "Not yet, but soon, I hope."

"Please, Kate—please find a way for me to see him again. It would mean so much to me to repair our friendship. He probably thinks I've forgotten all about him, but I haven't. Not for a moment."

Kate looked into the lovely blue eyes and understood, suddenly, that Mrs. Fairchild hoped for more than neighborly friendship. But the man she remembered had been a handsome movie star. "He's changed a lot in the last few years."

"I know, and I've changed too. I don't care about that. I just want to sit next to him and hear his voice again—to help him return to acting, if I can. I know everyone in the business. Your grandfather was born to perform, Kate. He lost his confidence when talking pictures came out, but the world will welcome him back if he gives them a chance."

Whatever Mrs. Fairchild felt for Ollie seemed deep and genuine. Kate wondered how her grandfather felt in return. If there'd been looks of longing on both parts. Maybe even—Kate didn't like to think of it—an affair with his best friend's wife. Maybe that was why the three of them had argued, four years ago.

"He's been talking about returning to acting," Kate said.

"Oh, that's wonderful! Do you think he'll come to Bonnie's birthday party? I've invited everyone who matters, all the important producers and directors, nearly a hundred guests."

"I doubt he'll go, but I'll try." Kate wished Hugo didn't have to work, so he could be at the party and meet people. She realized something else. "Does Tad know Bonnie's having a big party on the first day of filming?"

Mrs. Fairchild released an annoyed breath. "That movie was supposed to have wrapped by now. Tad wanted me to cancel, but I convinced him it was a good excuse to talk about the movie all night. I really just want everyone to see that Bonnie's now old enough to be taken seriously. And it would be perfect if Ollie could be there."

"I'll try."

"Oh, Kate, I'm so glad you've come to live here. You're just what Ollie needs." Mrs. Fairchild gave Kate's hands a final squeeze and turned back to her house.

Kate watched her for a moment, then turned up the path to Ollie's house. It *would* be nice if her grandfather could reconnect with Mrs. Fairchild—not only for his career, but to give him a reason to get dressed and walk out the door every day. An exciting new start to his life.

As she opened the door, she wondered what hats had been

pulled from the wheelbarrow today, but the house was quiet and nearly dark in twilight, only a shaft of light coming from Ollie's office. Kate heard the clunk of typing and walked that way.

She was surprised to see Stella Nixon strolling in front of Ollie's desk. "But *why* does he care enough to stay?" Stella asked in her throaty voice. She wore another green dress, this one even brighter, with a black and white scarf instead of a brooch.

Hugo sat behind the desk, his fingers working the keys of a black typewriter with impressive speed. "He hates his father." He pushed the carriage return lever and kept typing.

"But how does the audience *know* that?" Stella noticed Kate and turned with her gap-toothed smile. "Kate, my darling protégée!"

Hugo's eyes darted up, his fingers halting.

Stella leaned against the front corner of the desk, the cigarette tilted out. "I hope Taddy threw a nice big tantrum when he read our script changes."

"Only a small one." Kate smiled as she walked closer. "But you were right about Mr. Falcon liking the line about Ursa Major, so it stayed. I distributed copies this afternoon."

"Clive always appreciates a little sass in his characters." Stella brought the cigarette to her lips.

"Ursa Major?" Hugo queried.

"Oh, it was fabulous, darling." Stella blew a ribbon of smoke out of the corner of her mouth. "We turned Taddy's little Trixie into a budding astronomer. Kate knew all these clever things to add about stars, and supernovas, and these . . ." She twirled the cigarette. "Kettle rules."

"Kepler's laws," Kate corrected.

"She's a gem. I want her to take over Hollywood, but alas, she's determined to leave our vital work of entertainment and explore the scientific meaning behind the universe. To each their own."

Hugo's attention lingered on Kate. "Yeah, she's just biding her time until she can get back to San Francisco."

"Actually . . ." Kate held his gaze, her heart beating faster. "I'm not so sure about leaving anymore."

His eyes caught fire in the way she was getting used to and liked. "Oh?"

And suddenly she *was* sure. "I'm going to stay here until college."

"I knew it!" Stella declared. "You've caught the moviemaking bug, and there's no cure."

"You like working at the studio?" Hugo asked, still a bit cautious.

"I do, and I think I'm good at it. I don't get as flustered as Tad, and the work is exciting. I saw lions today, and Bonnie's tutor is going to help me with calculus so I can keep up with math. I already have a pretty impressive record at Blakely, so I think I can still get into Berkeley without any trouble." She added, a bit breathlessly, "Plus, I like living here with Ollie . . . and everyone."

"Well." Hugo's lips curved in a slow smile. "*Everyone* is happy about that."

Kate smiled back.

"Mm," Stella hummed from the sidelines. "Getting a bit warm in here."

"Feels good to me," Hugo said.

Kate pulled her eyes from his, her face on fire. "So—what are the two of you working on?"

"My new play." Stella tapped the cigarette over an ashtray. "I've been stuck for weeks, every line sounding false. I was ready to scrap the entire thing. Then I met you yesterday, which made me think of Ollie. So I came by to make sure he was all right after that *ghastly* murder, and as soon as I saw Hugo, I knew he was the solution to all my problems."

"Well, not all of them," Hugo said, leaning back in the chair. "You've still got that cat."

"Oh, and she's worse than ever, darling. A *monster* of a pet. We *despise* each other."

The desk was cluttered with dozens of wadded-up papers—evidence of creative attempts and failures. "How did Hugo solve all your problems?"

"Voice. It's the story of three teenaged boys—completely outside my purview. I was *mad* for attempting it. *Doomed* for failure. And then Hugo started talking, and suddenly there stood my expert. A window into the soul of the adolescent boy."

He shrugged. "It comes naturally."

"And he's a damn good typist too."

"What's the story about?" Kate asked.

"Death." Stella brought the cigarette to her mouth.

Kate waited.

Stella blew a stream of smoke. "Three boys at a boarding school, and their favorite teacher keeps trying to kill himself. *Ridiculous* attempts. Dark humor. *Very* dark. The boys save him, one by one, forcing them to face their own private demons. They finally convince the teacher that life is worth living, but then he dies saving one of them. And that's the irony—you see?"

"I see," Kate murmured, a bit horrified.

Hugo grinned. "I think it's brilliant. It's going to open at the Pasadena Playhouse next summer."

Kate tried to remember where she'd heard that name before—and remembered Ollie in his toga. Her interest sharpened. "Is there a part for Ollie in your play? He wants to get back into acting."

"Ollie?" Stella huffed a laugh. "I adore him, of course, but this isn't his sort of thing at all. Just three boys in a boarding school, their teacher, and a couple of bit parts."

"What about the teacher?"

"He isn't a heroic teacher, he's troubled and confused and . . . well, about as different from Captain Powell as you can get."

"But that's what Ollie needs—something different, so people don't think he's trying to re-create the past. A fresh start."

Stella pursed her lips, squinting over her round spectacles. "I see your point, and it would be lovely to see Ollie on stage, but he can't play my teacher. I can't picture that at all."

"I can," Hugo said. "The way the teacher performs in front of the class, and the students all laugh and think he's great, and then he goes back to his room and tries to kill himself. Ollie could play those two extremes and make it believable."

Stella frowned. "But I pictured the teacher younger and more, I don't know, *complicated*. Not Oliver Banks, bigger than life."

"Well, think it over," Kate said. She snuck a glance at Hugo, unsure if he would appreciate her meddling in his career. "What about Hugo playing one of the boys?"

He smiled wryly. "I already asked. She said no."

"I didn't say *no*, darling—I said if I had *my* say, you'd play Alfred, but the director has his own favorites. But I'll try to get you an audition, at least, and he might remember you for something else. Now, I've got to run, but I'll be back in the morning." Stella stubbed her cigarette in the ashtray and picked up a stack of papers from the desk.

"How early?" Hugo asked. "I work late."

"Well, I don't breathe before eleven, so when I say morning, I mean noon, and noon is evening, and evening is night. Everybody knows that about me."

"Think about Ollie for that teacher role," Kate said.

"Of course," Stella said without much weight. She strode across the office in her green dress, as tall as a man, and they heard her footsteps clicking toward the front of the house.

"And that's Stella," Hugo said. "She knows everybody in this town but still drops by to see Ollie now and then, one of his few friends who still does."

"It would be nice if she got him that part."

He shrugged. "Oliver Banks is a risk. Even if she decides she wants him and somehow convinces the director and producer, I'm not sure he would get up on that stage."

"How did he do today? Is he still climbing the stairs and doing jumping jacks?"

"Every hour, complaining like it's Mount Everest." Hugo's smile turned sly. "I took him to the hardware store."

Her eyes widened. "He left the house?"

"With a cowboy hat and a bandana covering half his face. I thought the store manager was going to call the town sheriff. But we bought something for you. Come on, I'll show you." Hugo stood and led the way to the kitchen.

The room was deserted, but smelled good, and Kate saw a pan on the stove. "What's for dinner?"

"Spaghetti and meatballs." Hugo entered the short hallway to Kate's room and stopped, pointing down. "I told him you needed that."

An electrical cord ran from the laundry room, along the edge of the hallway. Kate followed it into her room and found a small, blue lamp shaped like a mermaid on the wooden chair holding the door open.

"That's as far as the cord reaches, so you have to keep the lamp near the door, and the door won't shut with the cord in the way, and if someone wants to use the washer, they have to unplug the lamp. But you have light now." He leaned forward and flipped the switch on the lamp, and soft light danced through the beaded shade. "All of Ollie's lamps are too big and heavy, so we stopped at Goodwill on the way home and bought this."

Kate stared at the blue mermaid, her throat tightening with unexpected emotion. The mermaid had a chip in her tail, showing white ceramic. But it was the prettiest lamp she'd ever seen. "Thank you," she managed.

Hugo leaned against the door frame. "I'm going to drill a hole in the wall and install a proper light, but I need to read up on it first so I don't electrocute myself."

"Yes, please don't die on my account." Which reminded her of

Lemmy. "I searched Bonnie's car today, and the scarf wasn't there, so the one we found is probably hers. But when I talked to her, she said Aurelio was the last one to have it. She gave it to him right after we arrived at the studio."

Hugo gave an easy laugh. "So, now you think Aurelio killed him?"

"Someone dropped that scarf in Ollie's office. Maybe Lemmy took blackmail photos of Aurelio too."

"Why would he? Aurelio didn't have a movie career to protect when Lemmy was killed. He didn't have that part yet. And no money to pay off a blackmailer. He was just a waiter."

She hadn't thought of that. "Both Aurelio and Lemmy worked at the Galaxy. Maybe they argued about something there."

"Aurelio never had anything to do with the shady business upstairs. I'm sure of that."

Kate wasn't so sure but didn't want to argue about it.

"I looked for a blood trail today," Hugo said. "Didn't find one, so he must have been stabbed in the kitchen. And—speaking of stabbing—I better go. Flynn wants me there early tonight because he's adding new stuff to the show. Attendance hasn't been that great."

She wished he didn't always have to leave for work so soon after she got home. "Break a leg."

"See there—you really are in showbiz now. Spaghetti is on the stove if you're hungry. Ollie and Reuben already ate and went upstairs." He took a step back, but didn't leave. "So . . . you like your mermaid?"

She gave him a look. "You know I love it."

He laughed as he turned away.

A short time later, Kate heard his motorcycle start up outside, rev with power, and then fade away.

Then she decided to search Aurelio's bedroom.

CHAPTER 22

Kate removed her loafers at the bottom of the staircase and crept up slowly, not wanting to alert Reuben and Ollie, who seemed to be in their individual rooms, their doors closed. A step creaked near the top, and she froze, ready to pretend she'd come upstairs to say hello, ready to explain that the flashlight in her hand was because she was afraid of the dark.

But neither door opened.

She entered Aurelio's room, held still for a moment to listen, then turned on the flashlight and carefully closed the door behind her.

She had to hurry. Aurelio could come home at any moment.

She swung the flashlight beam across the room and found it larger and grander than she'd expected, decorated in Ollie's days of wealth, everything a bit tattered and old fashioned. The large bed wasn't made, and there were a few bits of clothing on the floor, but it was much tidier than most of the house, and Aurelio's possessions seemed sparse.

Kate went to the nightstand first, not really sure what she was looking for. Some proof that he was involved in Moe Kravitz's shady business dealings. Or some clue from Lemmy's killing, like blood on a shirt.

The flashlight illuminated an alarm clock on the nightstand, a folded handkerchief, wooden rosary beads with a cross, and a few coins. Kate picked up a framed photo of Aurelio at a younger age, standing next to a man who looked enough like him to be his father—or maybe the uncle she'd heard him talk about.

She sat at the edge of the bed, opened the nightstand drawer, and found a small Bible with worn edges, a key, and three blue envelopes. She pulled out the envelopes and saw that they were all letters from someone named Carla Dios. A mother or sister, maybe. Or grandmother. She reached her hand into the back of the drawer and found two cough drops.

Nothing to implicate Aurelio with Moe Kravitz's business or Lemmy's murder.

And she knew, suddenly, that it was wrong for her to be here invading Aurelio's privacy. She would be furious if someone went through her nightstand drawer and found the small notebook where she wrote her most personal lists and thoughts. She slid the blue envelopes back into the drawer.

Behind her, the door handle turned.

Kate jumped up from the bed, and the flashlight fell, sending a wild beam of light. She snatched it up and straightened, her heart hammering in her chest.

Aurelio stood silhouetted in the doorway, his handsome face lost in shadow. His shirt was tucked under his arm, his chest bare, his shoulders carved with tight muscle. "What's going on?" he asked, sounding tired, not angry. "Is something wrong?"

She clutched the flashlight at her waist, wishing she had a story ready. "No, I was only—" Aurelio flipped the light switch, and she squinted in the sudden glow from the ceiling.

"You want my room after all?" he asked. "I don't mind. You should be up here with Ollie."

She exhaled in relief at the easy excuse. "Yes! I was looking at the room. But I can see you're all settled here. And I like the privacy downstairs, so I'll go. I'm sorry." She took a step.

But Aurelio still blocked the doorway, his attention shifting to the nightstand, his eyes narrowing. "Were you . . . looking in my drawer?"

Kate squeezed the flashlight, her pulse racing. "No, it was already open when I—" The lie stuck in her throat. She'd come for answers, not to tell fibs and run away. She turned off the flashlight and lowered it to her side. "I was searching your room, Aurelio, because you were the last person to have Bonnie's scarf."

For a few seconds, he didn't react. Kate held her breath, hoping for a confused denial. Hoping for a reasonable explanation that proved his innocence.

"So that's it," he said in a low voice. He tossed his shirt on the ground and walked toward her, his muscled chest drawing closer, his eyes locked on hers. Too late, Kate managed to move her feet, but he grabbed her wrist, his face only inches from hers. "Wait." She opened her mouth to scream, but something in his eyes stopped her: he looked more miserable than dangerous. "I'm not a thief," he said.

Thief? So it hadn't been about blackmail photos. He'd come to steal from Ollie, and Lemmy had caught him in the act. Kate forced her voice to remain neutral. "I'm sure it was an accident, Aurelio."

"It was."

"I understand. Please let go of my arm."

"Sorry." He released her at once, looking surprised that he'd even held her. He turned and sat at the edge of the bed. "I'd give it back if I knew where it was. I apologized and promised to buy her a new one, but her mom cracked some joke about me stealing it."

Kate glanced at the door, knowing she should run, but she also needed answers. "You're talking about the scarf?"

"I know it was stupid to take it, but I just wanted something of hers. I've seen her next door but never thought I'd meet her. Then she handed me that scarf, and it was like one of those princesses giving a kerchief to a knight, and I wanted to keep it." He sighed and leaned his elbows on his knees, tilting his head to look up at her. "I lied and told her I lost it, and she got upset. I didn't know it was some special thing from Paris. I was going to give it back and say I found it in my jacket at home, but when I looked in the pocket, it wasn't there. So I really did lose it."

"You . . . you don't know where you dropped it?"

"No, I looked everywhere. I said I'd buy her a new one, but I don't get paid until Friday." He looked up with worried eyes. "How much do you think a scarf like that costs?"

"Aurelio . . ." She spoke carefully. "I found the scarf."

He sat straighter. "You did? Where is it?"

"You dropped it near Captain Powell's sword case, the day Lemmy was killed."

He frowned, confused. "You sure it's the right scarf? I haven't been in there. I thought maybe I dropped it in wardrobe, but I looked all over and can't find it."

Kate watched him closely. "I think the scarf I found was dropped by the person who killed Lemmy."

"Oh," he said glumly. "That's not it, then." He looked dejected, not guilty. "I only wanted something of hers. I didn't think it was stealing."

Not a killer hiding his tracks, just a boy who liked a girl.

Aurelio didn't kill Lemmy. But he was the last person to have Bonnie's scarf, and since he'd never been in Ollie's office—he'd barely even been home since getting the part—the scarf they'd found probably wasn't hers, just part of the mess of that room. A red herring after all.

"I'm not a thief, Kate."

"I know. I'm sure Bonnie's scarf will turn up. You better get some sleep." She made her way to the door, grateful he hadn't picked up on her real reason for searching his room.

"Kate."

She looked back.

"They aren't going to fire me at Falcon Pictures, are they?"

"Fire you? Over a missing scarf?"

"Because I messed up on the voice recording today. We had to do it a million times, but I've never done a recording before. I'll do better next time."

"Aurelio, you're doing great. Really. Everyone's calling you a young Fred Astaire."

He didn't look convinced. "Being in a movie is a lot harder than I thought it would be. I've been on stage all my life, but this is different. More money and everyone telling me what to do. And that fake accent. I don't mind doing it for the movie, but they want me to do it in interviews and say the studio taught me how to dance. My uncle isn't going to like that. He taught me everything I know."

"I'll talk to Tad about it, but he seems pretty set on that being your image." Kate hesitated. "From what I've seen, actors don't have a lot of control over their careers once they're under contract with a studio. But you do have one power over them, Aurelio."

"I do?"

"Your talent. Just keep dancing the way you do."

She'd meant it as encouragement, but he only looked more exhausted. "I'm trying."

"You're doing great, Aurelio. You really are." She looked at his tired face and felt guilty for ever suspecting him of murder.

Tonight, for the first time, Kate closed her bedroom door—most of the way, still cracked an inch for the electrical cord.

She pulled out the small, private notebook she kept in her nightstand drawer and wrote a new list:

Ollie—crying because of bird, not murder—innocent
Reuben—would have used his gun—innocent
Hugo—only hid sword to protect Ollie—innocent
Aurelio—different scarf, no motive—innocent
Bonnie—dancing and laughing right after—innocent

She closed the notebook with a sigh of satisfaction and returned it to the drawer. No one in the house had killed Lemmy, and as soon as Detective Bassett reached the same conclusion, she and Hugo would give him the sword and her days as Nancy Drew would be over.

Although, she wasn't quite ready for it to be over. Now that she was safe in her own room, she could see that it had been rather exciting, searching the glovebox and sneaking into Aurelio's room. Tomorrow, she would tell Hugo what she'd learned.

Kate pulled up the covers, but then lay awake, more interested in staring at the mermaid lamp than sleep. It seemed too bright for sleeping, even though it was dimmer than her bedside lamp in San Francisco. She'd gotten used to the distant glow from the kitchen and missed the hum of the refrigerator.

She heard someone entering the house, followed by two deep voices. The deeper voice was Reuben's, she decided. And, as the voices moved toward the back of the house, she recognized the other voice as Hugo's.

Kate sat up, glancing at the alarm clock. Only 10:20 p.m.—too early for him to be home. She remembered what he'd said about low attendance and wondered if the play had closed.

Their voices entered the kitchen, hushed and anxious. Kate slipped out of bed and stood next to the cracked door.

"It's on page three," Reuben murmured, followed by the crackle of the newspaper she'd seen on the table. "His arrest got a first page headline, and his release barely gets a mention. There it is, bottom right."

Had Moe Kravitz, the owner of the Galaxy, been released

from prison? Kate tried to remember page three but wasn't sure if she'd gotten that far; she'd skipped ahead to the entertainment section—a first for her.

Hugo whispered, "I thought they had lots of evidence this time."

"They did. That's why he had to stay in for so long, waiting for the story to die down, so no one would notice when some crooked judge dropped the charges."

"Well, don't worry about it. You quit the Galaxy months ago, and he's been fine with that."

"I gave him Lemmy, and a lot of good that did me." A pause, then a muttered, "He probably left the books a mess. It's going to take months to straighten out."

"You're not going back there. Moe will hire another book-keeper."

"He doesn't want just anybody looking at his books, learning his dirty secrets."

"What's he going to do?" Hugo asked. "Drag you back by your hair? You don't have any."

"Very funny. He owns me, so why hire somebody new when he can just order me back? I've got no choice."

"You've got a choice. This is America."

"Jeez, you don't know how naive you sound." Kate heard a few shuffling steps, and then Reuben said in a voice so low she had to press her ear to the door's cracked opening, "I told you how I picked up that guy at his house and drove him to the meeting."

"I know, but you were just doing as you were told. You didn't know they were going to kill him when he got there."

Kate covered her mouth with one hand.

"I knew I wasn't taking him to a birthday party. His wife got a good look at me in the car, and this scar isn't so easy to forget. If I don't go back to work, Moe will snap his fingers, and I'll be arrested for murder. And there won't be some nice, crooked judge letting me out. He'll be obeying orders to make sure I hang, silencing all those secrets."

"Come on . . . you're not that important to Moe Kravitz. He isn't going to waste his leverage with some judge because his bookkeeper wants to quit and be in pictures."

"He's got two people who know all the details of his racket, and I'm one of them. He's going to order me back, and the only way I can refuse is to get on a steamer ship and disappear in Brazil."

"You gave up that idea," Hugo said. "You don't want to spend the rest of your life in some foreign country where everybody speaks Portuguese."

"Look at the map, you dope. It's in South America—*Spanish*."

A breathy laugh from Hugo. "See, you can't go there because you don't even know what language they speak. Stay here with us. You've been happy since you moved in, right?"

"I've been *poor* since I moved in. I had money for Brazil, and you convinced me to stay, and now I've spent it all and have to work for Moe to save up again." More shuffling steps. "Jeez, he's going to be on a warpath, making sure everybody knows he's back in charge. This town is going to rain blood, and he's going to make sure my hands get dirty."

"Reuben . . ." Hugo's voice stretched in a low plea. "You can't go back to that life. When you started there, you didn't know what you were getting into. But now you do, so if you go back, you're making that choice. That makes you . . . responsible."

"Don't give me your Catholic guilt."

"Then go to Brazil. I'll get you the money somehow."

A snorting laugh. "With all those acting jobs? And that's another thing—one phone call from Moe, and no studio will hire me."

"Now you're being paranoid. Why would a movie studio take orders from a mobster?"

"Again, you show your ignorance. Half the producers in this town owe him money, and the other half have big shot movie stars on their payroll who owe him money. Plus, Moe has his thumb on their unions. A word from Moe, and the whole industry shuts down."

"That's twisted."

"You don't know the half of it."

"Well, you can't go back to that life. I'll get you the money for Brazil. Ollie can give you all the money from the George Washington letters, not just a finder's fee. He owes you that much for all the time you've spent organizing his stuff."

A grunt from Reuben. "Yeah, I'll have sweet dreams tonight thinking about all the money I'm going to get out of Oliver Banks. I'm going to bed." Their footsteps retreated, and Kate heard Hugo leave through the back door.

She went to the window and watched him enter the pool house. But he left the door open, spilling golden light, and emerged a moment later. He walked to the pool area and disappeared into the shadows.

Kate pulled on her silky robe, tied it around her waist, and made her way outside.

CHAPTER 23

The soft crooning of Fred Astaire drifted from the pool house. It was another warm night, the air still.

Hugo sat on a lounge chair, his legs stretched out, his head tilted back to look up at the moon. Kate approached cautiously, hugging her waist, wondering if she should mention what she'd overheard. She decided against it, not wanting to admit that she'd eavesdropped.

He must have heard her coming but didn't turn to look. The light from the pool house cast his face into sinister angles, making him look like the dangerous boy she'd seen that first night, stabbing Lemmy in the kitchen.

"What happened with your play?" she asked quietly, stopping next to the lounge.

His eyes shifted to look at her. "I was fired. Or I quit. I'm not really sure which happened first. Turns out there is a limit to what I'm willing to do for a buck."

Kate turned and sat at the side of the lounge, her lower back pressing against his thigh. There wasn't quite enough room, but he didn't move over. "What do you mean?" she asked.

His eyes reflected silver moonlight. "I told you how Flynn wants to add things to the play to bring in bigger crowds. I thought he meant more blood and fiendish laughs. Turns out it was more . . . carnal delights. More kissing girls after I kill them and ripping out their hearts. More of everything. Except clothing. Less clothing."

She tried to hide her shock. She'd known it wasn't the best of shows but hadn't considered the details.

"He never paid me, and now he never will. He keeps a goon at the door who throws out anybody he doesn't want to see. I've seen him break a man's leg and throw him in the gutter. I had to call an ambulance."

"Then I'm glad you quit. You don't belong at a place like that."

"It was only a stepping-stone." Hugo released a long, worn-out breath. "I wanted to go home with presents for everyone, so they'd know I haven't been wasting my life for two years. But as it turns out . . . I have."

"No, you haven't. You've taken the road less traveled, and it wanders a little, but that doesn't mean you're not getting somewhere. It just takes time." Kate squeezed one of his hands, only meaning to comfort, but he turned his hand and wrapped it around hers. And they were immediately back in that place they'd been two nights ago—warm skin that felt good together. Neither of them spoke for a moment, watching Hugo's thumb slide slowly over the back of her hand.

Soft music serenaded them. Something about moonlight and longing.

"Tell me about your family," she said.

"They're just normal, nothing fancy." His thumb explored one of her knuckles. "My mom is quiet and likes to read. She bakes bread every day, so the house always smelled good when we got home from school. We'd all sit around the table, and she'd cut these thick slices, and the butter would melt in, and that was always the best part of the day."

Kate couldn't imagine running away from that. "What's your dad like?"

His thumb paused. "He's all right but notices anything wrong and has to complain about it. He thinks movies are depraved and books are lazy. But he's a hard worker." Hugo's hand looked like it knew how to work, and his forearm had a nice ridge of lean muscle.

"Esther seems nice."

"Yeah, she's the oldest. Always good at school and doing the right thing. She works at an insurance company now and gives most of her money to my mom. She said things are pretty tight right now because Dad hurt his back."

It was Kate's turn to caress Hugo's hand, her finger finding the soft skin inside his wrist. "Are you the second oldest?"

"Yeah. Then there's Rose. She's really pretty and has a million friends. Brendan is fifteen. He just dropped out of school to work with my dad, but he never liked school anyway. Maureen is quiet and reads a lot. Shanny is nine." He smiled. "Shanny is great. Always joking around. My mom was sick after she was born, so I used to give her bottles and rock her to sleep. Then, when she started kindergarten, I walked her to school every day." He stopped abruptly, looking to the side.

A few days ago, his angular face had looked fiendish to Kate; now, she saw brooding sensitivity. A lock of his dark hair crossed his forehead, and she resisted the urge to brush it back. "Sounds like you and Shanny are close."

"We used to be. She hasn't seen me much in the last two years. And I barely even know Clare. She was only four when I left."

"Your family sounds nice, Hugo."

He looked at her. "I didn't leave home because I have a horrible family. *I* was the one who was horrible."

"I doubt that."

"There's just something inside me that hates following rules. Even when I was little, the teacher would say draw a circle, and

I'd start drawing a square. I'd see all the other kids getting stars on their papers, doing what they were told, but I didn't want to be one of those mindless sheep. So I ditched a lot of school."

Kate had been one of those kids collecting stars. "You're a creative thinker."

"That's what my mom says. So I dropped out of school to work with my dad, but then it was nothing but pipes and listening to him complain all day, so I started ditching him too. I'd jump on a freight train and ride around with the hobos, just for the fun of it. Be gone for a day or two. Then my mom would cry, and I'd feel bad, and try to be a plumber again."

She could see why Ollie's unconventional house had attracted him. "And then you came here."

"Yeah." But his frown deepened. "I had all these grand visions, about how I was going to be in movies, and my family would all go to the theater to see me, and my parents would be so proud." He released her hand, his fingers slipping from hers. "But it's been two years, and I'm starting to think I'm just fooling myself."

"A new job will turn up, Hugo."

"Washing dishes? It took me months to get that job, and I gave it up for the play."

"A better acting job, more worthy of you." But the words sounded hollow, even to Kate. She'd seen the dozens of headshots Tad received in the mail every day, and he tossed them in the trash. She couldn't even promise Hugo an audition at Falcon Pictures, let alone a part. But something else occurred to her. "Now you can go to Bonnie's party tomorrow, since you don't have to work."

He flashed a wry smile. "I thought I got out of that. It's not really my crowd."

"But that's the point. I can introduce you to people." She wanted to take his hand again, but it looked content resting against his waist. "I *might* even dance with you."

"I've seen the Fairchilds' parties. I don't have the right clothes."

"I'll get you a suit from the wardrobe department. What size do you wear?"

"I don't know. I don't shop for clothes, Kate. I glue cardboard inside my shoes." He looked to the side.

A new song drifted over them, a lonely horn stretching out low notes.

"You'll get a new job, Hugo."

He looked back at her. "People like you get jobs. One day in Hollywood, and you're a production assistant." He didn't sound bitter, just stating a simple truth.

"Only because I'm famous."

"No, because you're the kind of person people want to hire. It's written all over you."

"You mean . . . one of those mindless sheep collecting stars?"

Hugo sat straighter. "Don't ever apologize for deserving stars, Kate. It's what I like about you. Being around you makes me feel like . . ." He shook his head slowly, searching her face. "I don't know the right word for it." He put a hand on the curve of her neck, as if touching her might help him find it.

Kate held her breath.

"Steadier," he said softly. "Being with you makes me feel steadier, Kate, like I have a trail of stars to follow, mapping the way."

"A constellation," she murmured.

"That's it. You're my constellation, Kate." He seemed to notice her silky robe for the first time, his hand sliding down the soft sleeve, his gaze following. He picked up the silky tie around her waist. "Reuben thinks you're going to break my heart, and I'm a fool for walking into it."

"Reuben doesn't know everything."

"He says I take things too seriously." He kept his eyes lowered, wrapping the silky tie around one of his fingers. "Like . . . the way I've only kissed one girl. He says I need to kiss a different girl every night for a week just to get it out of my system, so I don't fall so hard." His eyes lifted to meet hers. "Do you think I should do that, Kate?"

"I'd rather you didn't," she said, her voice little more than a whisper.

"That's good, because I can't do it that way. For me, a kiss has to mean something."

Kate's attention had stilled on one point. "Who was the girl you kissed?"

He shrugged limply. "I took her dancing a few times on the Santa Monica pier. Aurelio set it up. He took a girl from work, and I took her cousin."

"So . . . it must have meant something if you kissed her. That's what you said."

"It was just her name that meant something. *Rosalina*." He caressed the syllables. "I mean . . . how could I not kiss a girl named Rosalina? The way it rolls off the tongue."

He was teasing her. "Like *Kate*?" she asked, a name of hard edges.

He laughed. "I like Kate just fine." He touched the faint scar at the edge of her eyebrow. "What happened here?"

"I fell off my bike and got stitches."

His fingertip moved back and forth over the scar, making her eyelid feel heavy. The finger moved down her temple, brushed hair behind her ear, and then found her earlobe. "Does it hurt when you get your ears pierced?" He rubbed the tiny hole.

"Only for a moment, then it heals."

The lonely horn was joined by a cautious piano. A song for the middle of the night, when slow dancers barely moved.

"So . . . you're going to stay," Hugo said. "That gives me a little more time before you break my heart."

"I don't plan on breaking your heart, Hugo." Her own heart floated in her throat, making it hard to breathe.

"Reuben says you probably date lots of different boys, and it's just casual for you."

"You need to stop listening to Reuben." But her heart sank a little, because the arrow had hit true. She had dated lots of boys over the last year or two, and it had always been casual—including three kisses that hadn't lasted long or meant much, and one kiss that had lasted long but still hadn't meant much. Four names written in the special notebook in her nightstand drawer.

"I don't mind," Hugo said quietly. "For you it can be casual." He slid his legs off the other side of the lounge and walked around. "I want to dance with you, Kate, but not at a fancy party." He held out his hand and helped her rise.

They settled into proper dance position, her left hand on his shoulder, her right resting in his, their feet gently shifting to the music. Kate had danced this way a hundred times.

And yet, never like this.

Never alone in the moonlight with someone who pulled at every string inside her. Never so aware of the shoulder beneath her left hand—because she'd never danced with a boy wearing only a shirt, she realized. Always suits with shoulders pads and the whiff of expensive cologne. Hugo smelled like himself. She leaned in, liking the scent, and he pulled her closer, tucking their hands against his warm chest.

His other hand rubbed her spine. "This thing you're wearing is soft," he murmured.

She nestled into him. Dancing in a silky robe wasn't on her list of things to do before she died—also in the nightstand notebook—but should have been. So much better than a stiff satin gown with a corsage in the way.

Their bodies conformed nicely, keeping up the pretense of dancing.

"I'm on the edge of a cliff, Kate."

She tightened her arm around his shoulder, breathing in the scent of his neck. "I won't let you fall."

"Maybe I want to fall. Maybe I want to kiss you and never feel solid ground again."

As he spoke of falling, something rose inside her. "That's a lot to expect of one kiss."

"After that, you can break my heart."

"I won't break your heart, Hugo."

"That's disappointing." His breath warmed her temple. "Every good actor needs to be crossed in love at least once, and I was hoping you'd do that for me, Kate. Hoping it very much, actually."

"Well . . ." She turned her head. "If it means that much to you."

Their lips met.

They kissed slowly, washed in moonlight and lonely music. Warm lips and soft breaths. A tender exploration, barely touching the surface of something much deeper. A kiss in no hurry.

Hugo's hand slid across her shoulder and cupped her cheek. "Not disappointed," he murmured.

She silenced him with more kissing, her hand sliding up the back of his neck, making sure it didn't go anywhere. The kiss deepened, the music disappearing. Only breathing and longing and Hugo's hands sliding along the silky back of her robe. He pulled at her waist, bringing them closer, and she wished it were closer still. Her mouth reached for more.

After some time, Hugo separated enough to murmur, "Is it still one kiss if we pause to breathe now and then?"

"I think so." Her lips moved to his cheek, and then his jawline. "I mean . . . if you're going to pine over one kiss for the rest of your life . . ." She kissed the soft skin below his ear. "We might as well do it properly." Her lips found his neck.

His head tilted. "Break my heart, Kate."

She did her best to oblige.

CHAPTER 24

Somehow, even with Tad barking orders and the director furious about bad lighting and Bonnie crying because her shoes were too tight, Kate managed to sneak away from filming the family scenes in Stage Six.

She walked quickly toward the wardrobe building, a secret smile on her face. Hugo needed a suit for the party.

Hugo.

Every step, Hugo. Every breath, Hugo.

Only now did she realize how tiring it had been, holding her spine so rigid for the last four years, afraid to relax for a moment in case she made a mistake.

Last night, Hugo had softened that spine nicely.

She bit her lower lip as she walked, fighting a goofy grin. He'd walked her back to the house, kissed her briefly, then watched with a contented smile as she'd gone inside and shut the door. She'd expected to lie awake for hours, gazing at the blue mermaid, but had fallen asleep quickly, jolting awake when the alarm went off.

Hugo Quick. Never on a list of what she wanted, but exactly what she needed.

A man came out of Stage Three with two enormous blood-hounds on leashes, and she wondered what Hugo had named his dog. Something creative and unexpected, like everything about him. One of a thousand things to ask and learn.

Last summer, she'd had a crush on her friend's cousin who'd come to visit for a month. She'd been excited when he'd asked her to go sailing in the bay, but he'd talked nonstop about boxing on the drive over, and then been more interested in working the sail than anything she had to say, and they'd both been silent as they'd eaten hamburgers. One day had drained them of conversation.

She couldn't imagine ever running out of things to say to Hugo. Private jokes to smile over. Tonight, they would smile secretively as they danced at Bonnie's party, knowing last night's dance had been so much better.

"Someone looks happy," a woman's voice drawled, and she looked up to see the wardrobe manager, Mei Chen, coming out of Stage One.

"Mei! I was on my way to find you. I was wondering if I could borrow a few suits for a party tonight. I know Aurelio is borrowing one, and I need"—Kate counted quickly in her head: Hugo, Reuben, Ollie—"three more. Although there's a good chance only one of them will get used."

"It's against the rules to take costumes home. I only made an exception for Aurelio because Tad signed an order."

"Oh." Kate's hopes dropped. Without a suit, Hugo couldn't go to the party.

Mei cracked a smile. "So glum, all of a sudden. Don't worry, I'm a rule breaker. I just put twenty-four dinner suits in storage, and no one will notice if a few disappear for a while. They're in the storage building behind Stage Five—and if you get caught, keep my name out of it."

"I will—thank you!" Kate started to leave, then turned back. "What size does Aurelio wear, so I can guess the others?"

"Thirty-eight jacket. Pants . . . probably thirty-two waist, thirty length."

Kate jotted the measurements on her clipboard. "Thank you!" She hurried to one of the motorized carts and drove back the way she'd come, slowing as she turned between Stage Five and Stage Six, not wanting Tad to see her. But the alley was deserted. She drove past parked cars and trucks—including her own borrowed Buick—to the back end of the enormous soundstages.

She'd never noticed the long, narrow storage building before. It didn't have any windows, just a door at one end. She entered, flipped a light switch, and looked down a long hall lined by numbered doors with metal latches instead of doorknobs.

The first couple of doors had padlocks on them, but the third padlock dangled open. Kate pulled it off and the door swung inward, assaulting her with a musty odor. She couldn't find a light switch, but the hall light illuminated enough for her to see a space about the size of a small bedroom crowded with boxes and rolling costume racks. The costumes looked Civil War era. Dark blue soldiers' uniforms with gold trim. A rack of full-skirted dresses. Barrels filled with rifles.

The next storage room didn't have a padlock but was empty.

Tad had probably noticed her absence by now. Kate hurriedly opened the next few doors to find garish circus costumes, cowboy clothes, and brown and gray business suits for daytime.

Finally, near the end of the hall, she pushed open a door and saw a rack of glimmering evening gowns and—she gave a little cry of delight—two racks of black suits at the back. She entered eagerly, pushing the gowns out of the way, but as soon as her hand touched the first rack of suits, the door swung shut behind her—

Casting her into darkness.

Kate whirled, her eyes wide but seeing nothing, her heart exploding. She stumbled in the direction of the hall—banged her shin, pushed the gowns—and fell against the door. Her hand clawed at the smooth wood, seeking a doorknob she knew wasn't there—only a latch on the other side. She dug her fingertips around the edge of the door, trying to get a grip and pull it open, but the gap was too narrow. She yelped a scream.

A scream no one would hear.

Days of screaming into a black void with no reply. As if she'd stopped existing.

Her fingertip finally caught the edge of the door, and it swung open with remarkable ease, flooding her with wonderful light. She stumbled through the opening into the hall—turned to keep an eye on the sinister trap—and pressed her back against the far wall. She slid to the cement floor and pulled her knees into her chest, holding in her thundering heart.

She watched as the door drifted slowly shut. Just a door eager to swing on a hinge. No kidnapper. No danger. She pressed her palms against her temples, trying to push that truth into her brain.

You're safe.

A whimper of frustration escaped her.

She'd made no progress at all. Years of therapy with Dr. Gimble. Sleeping with the light on and lying to herself in the mirror every morning. *I am not afraid.* Lists—and more lists—so she felt prepared. Four years of gritted teeth, forcing the terror into submission, visualizing it locked inside a fortress like Dr. Gimble had taught her. And in one second of darkness, the fear had crushed her fortress and roared to full strength, filling every inch of her.

Don't cry. Don't cry.

She pressed her hands against her cheeks, holding her jaw steady. No quivering allowed. No weakness.

I am safe. It wasn't my fault. I am not afraid.

She drew a deep breath and released it slowly through her lips. A few more deep, deliberate breaths, and the fear shrank back into its dark, quiet place.

For now.

Kate forced herself to stand on wobbly legs.

She looked down the long hall to the exit, then back at the closed door. Hugo needed that suit. Not just to dance with her at a party but to meet the right people and find his big break. So he would know he could be successful.

She lifted a trembling hand, steeled herself, and pushed the door open. Her gaze skimmed the semi-dark and saw the crate that had given her shin a bruise, filled with women's fancy evening shoes. Holding the door open with her hand, she stretched one leg toward the crate, caught the corner with her foot and dragged it back, propping the door. It seemed heavy enough to hold, but she used the same technique to drag a second crate and stacked them, creating a sturdy doorstop.

Slowly, she advanced into the room, one arm extended, glancing back every few seconds to make sure the door hadn't budged. As soon as her hand touched a rack of suits, she yanked it back to the doorway. Then, before her courage faltered, she retrieved the second rack of suits.

She leaned her forehead against the door frame, light-headed. "You're fine," she whispered.

Her nerves settled a little as she inspected the suits and slid hangers. The suits were all identical—probably from a large dance number—with handwritten labels giving measurements. She found what she guessed would be Hugo's size rather quickly. Reuben was so short, his pants would have to be taped up no matter what, so she ignored length and grabbed a waist and jacket measurement that seemed right. Ollie was probably thicker in the middle than any of the professional dancers who'd worn these suits, but she kept sliding hangers and found a larger size at the end of the rack.

She gathered the suits in her arms—surprisingly heavy—and backed out of the room, then pushed the two crates out of the way with her foot. She watched as the door swung shut, closing in the dark, then turned and hurried down the hall.

*   *   *

Kate entered the house in a rush, her arms full, knowing the party started in fifteen minutes. "Hello?" she hollered. "Anyone home?"

"In here," Ollie called from the living room, and Kate walked that way to find him sitting on the green velvet sofa, leaning forward over a round fishbowl on the coffee table. "Hugo and I went to a pet store today." A goldfish darted about in the water.

Clever Hugo, knowing how to lure Ollie out of the house. "He looks happy. What's his name?"

"Gwendolyn the Gold."

"*She,* then. I've got suits for the party." Kate deposited them on the fan-shaped sofa, glanced at the measurements, and pulled out Ollie's jacket and pants. "These are for you."

"That's nice of you, dear, but I don't think I'm going."

"Well, if you change your mind." She tossed them onto the sofa beside him. "Where is Hugo?" she asked as casually as she could manage, glancing over her shoulder.

"He and Reuben went to find someone to appraise George Washington. They drove to that auction house on the business card yesterday, but it's a dentist's office now, so they need to find someplace new."

Kate glanced at her watch. "I better go get dressed. Show them these suits when they come in."

"I will but don't get your hopes up. I'm not sure any of us are going, except Aurelio."

"Hugo is," she said a little too fiercely, and Ollie's face took on a knowing look that made her blush and hurry away.

Her excitement grew as she looked over her long party dresses, wondering which one Hugo would like best. He'd never seen her in anything pretty—and a silk robe. Her hand skimmed rough ivory lace and scratchy blue netting . . . and paused on soft satin. She didn't usually wear pink, but it was a pale, creamy shade, and the smooth fabric would feel nice under Hugo's hands when they danced. The dress had sheer sleeves and a delicate layer of chiffon over the skirt.

She changed in the bathroom, then stood on tiptoe to inspect herself in the mirror over the sink. The satin bodice fit with snug perfection.

The band started playing next door as she touched up her makeup. She hummed as she fastened a necklace and slipped earrings through her pierced ears. A dab of perfume—only a touch since Hugo would hold her close.

Kate looked out her bedroom window and was disappointed to see that the pool house was dark. She walked to the living room and found Ollie and his suit gone, but the other two suits still where she'd left them. She glanced at her watch. Bonnie had begged her to arrive early, but another ten minutes wouldn't matter. If Hugo hadn't come home by then, she would leave a note on the suits and go ahead without him.

She climbed the staircase, hoping Ollie had changed his mind.

"Come in," he called when she knocked.

The room was dark. Kate hesitated, trying to see the bed.

"Goodness!" Ollie exclaimed from the direction of the moonlit window. "What a vision of loveliness!" He sat on a deep window seat, his feet on the cushion, nearly invisible in the shadows.

"It's fun to dress up now and then." Kate stopped next to the window seat and realized he was watching the party, one floor below. A gap in the trees gave a good view into the Fairchilds' living room, and he'd opened the window a few inches, allowing him to hear the jazzy dance music and indiscernible chatter. Mrs. Fairchild stood near her own window, wearing a sleek blue gown, her platinum blond hair curled tightly around the bottom half of her head, holding a wine glass as she conversed with two men.

"Dorothy always did throw the best parties," Ollie mused quietly. "Part Hollywood, part business, part nightclub crowd. Very selective. It's an honor to be invited, so everybody shows up."

"You're invited. We can go together."

He gave her a rueful smile. "You have admirable skills of persuasion, Kate, but a Dorothy Fairchild party is a bit much for me at this point in my life. I can admit that." Tonight, he wore green plaid pajamas and his feet were bare. A little boy spying on a grown-up party.

Kate sat at the opposite end of the window seat, slipped off her shoes, and pulled up her legs inside the billowing chiffon skirt.

They watched as Mrs. Fairchild exchanged air kisses with a pretty, younger woman.

"I miss the people," Ollie said quietly. "I never cared much about the fame and fortune. Oh, it was fun to buy whatever I wanted, and the fame was exciting before it got tiresome. But mostly, I loved the people I worked with. Moviemakers are a fabulous bunch. We'd work ourselves to the bone, and then stay up all night talking about our next great idea, everyone dreaming big. I miss all that."

"You'll be back on stage soon and return to the parties." Kate hoped that was true.

Mrs. Fairchild turned slightly, her gaze drifting out her window toward Ollie's house. Kate doubted she could see into the dark bedroom, but pushed down the pouf of her pale pink skirt so it wouldn't catch the moonlight. Mrs. Fairchild's eyes shifted up to look at Ollie's window—and it occurred to Kate that she wasn't standing within his view by accident.

"You'd better hurry along, or you'll be late," Ollie told her.

"I'm waiting for Hugo." She added a second too late, "And Reuben."

Ollie looked amused, his dimples deepening. "I have a feeling Hugo will appreciate that pretty dress you're wearing."

Kate opened her mouth, unsure if she should admit to the relationship or keep it quiet for now. Ollie didn't look likely to believe a denial. "It's a little frightening how much I like him, to be honest."

"Why should that be frightening? Falling in love should be exhilarating."

Her eyes darted to his. "I didn't say anything about love."

"Come now, it only happens a few times in our lives—once if we're lucky. You don't want to pretend it's not happening and miss the whole thing."

Which made a strange sort of sense, but she wasn't the sort of girl who fell in love with a boy she'd only known a few days. She pulled her knees tighter against her chest, tucking her skirt around them. "You can't be in love with someone you barely know."

"Of course you can. It's called love at first sight."

"I don't believe in all that. It takes years to fully know someone, and even then, you find out you never really—that they weren't actually—" Her voice caught, surprising her. She turned to look out the window, fighting a sudden tightening in her throat.

"Kate," Ollie said gently. "Hugo is nothing like your father."

"I didn't mean that." A silly lie.

"You can trust your heart with that boy. He's as true as they come."

She pressed her forehead against the cool glass, wanting to ignore all the lessons of the past and believe her grandfather. "I haven't felt like myself since coming here."

"Is that a bad thing?"

She wasn't sure.

Mrs. Fairchild had moved out of view, and an elegant couple now stood in front of the window. The man said something with a sly smile and the woman laughed. Kate didn't have to hear them to know the dry, flirtatious tone of their banter. She'd grown up spying on social events like this one, full of expensive clothes and superficial smiles, everyone too sophisticated to feel anything.

"Hugo and I come from very different places," she murmured.

"That's why he's so perfect for you. And you're perfect for him. He's a good lad, but his head is in the clouds half the time. You'll help him stay grounded."

Kate lifted her gaze to the night sky. She wasn't sure she wanted Hugo grounded. Last night, it had been nice to float in the stars with him.

The night air coming through the window felt good.

She cast a sideways look at her grandfather. "Now . . . let's pry into *your* love life."

He gave an easy laugh. "I reached the end of that bumpy road a long time ago."

"What about Mrs. Fairchild?"

Ollie looked startled, then uncomfortable. "There's nothing like that between us. We've known each other a long time."

"Was there ever more than friendship between you?"

"Of course not, she was my friend's wife." His eyes met hers, then skittered away. "I do have *some* principles."

A car pulled up at the curb and two women emerged. They made their way up the Fairchilds' front walkway, their voices cheerful.

"Frank wasn't the most attentive of husbands. Dorothy was lonely, and we were good friends, but that's all it was."

"But she wanted more," Kate guessed.

Ollie rubbed a finger against a smudge on the window. "The three of us used to go to Catalina Island on the weekends. One trip, Frank stayed out all night, and I came perilously close to comforting Dorothy. But I didn't, and it only made things awkward between us. I started making up excuses not to see them so often. And then I stopped seeing anyone."

"She's been a widow for a year."

"Yes." Ollie rubbed at the glass. "I did try to go to the funeral. I got dressed for it. Stood at the living room window and watched as Dorothy and Bonnie left the house in their black dresses. But I couldn't make myself walk out the door." He released a long sigh. "It's one of my deepest regrets."

"She still cares for you, Ollie. I see it when she talks about you."

"I'm a different man now. Too many years have passed."

"She was hoping you would come to the party." Kate stopped his protest. "I know you're not ready for that, but keep her in mind, that's all I'm saying." She nudged his leg with hers. "There are worse things than having a beautiful woman next door carrying a torch for you."

He laughed gruffly. "Go on and have a good time. I'll send Hugo when he gets home."

Kate slid her feet into her shoes and took a few steps, then came back and hugged her grandfather's shoulders. "Thank you for the advice about love," she said, her cheek pressing his bristles.

"You darling girl, I'm so glad you came to live with me."

"Me too," she whispered.

CHAPTER 25

The Fairchilds' chic living room was already packed with people, the air filled with the rumble of voices and soft laughter, women in long gowns leaning closer to hear the latest scandal, men plucking appetizers off trays as they talked business. The long room stretched toward French doors that opened to the backyard, where the band played.

To Kate, the scene was reassuringly familiar.

But this crowd looked a little flashier than Aunt Lorna's circle, as one would expect in Hollywood, the dresses more glamorous, the voices more animated. Kate spotted a few faces that looked familiar from the studio—and two actresses she recognized from her favorite movie last year, *Stage Door,* but she didn't know their names.

Clive Falcon stood out in the crowd with his tall stature and distinctive silver mustache, wearing a white dinner jacket over black pants. He stood with a cluster of men, but had his head turned to watch Mrs. Fairchild across the room as he sipped his cocktail.

Kate didn't see Bonnie anywhere, and no signs that this was the birthday celebration of a sixteen-year-old girl.

Heads started to turn as people recognized her, and she stood a little straighter, suddenly aware that she was alone, breaking Aunt Lorna's number-one rule of party survival: *Always have a sidekick.*

"Kate!" a woman's voice called, and she turned to see Stella Nixon's hand lifted at the deep end of the room—the only woman with a straight bob haircut in a sea of fashionable curls. The hand turned into a summons, and Kate weaved her way through the crowd. "Where is Hugo? I must tell him he was correct about the coatroom scene—one *hundred* percent correct." Stella flicked her cigarette over a potted plant. Her beaded gown was long and lean and very green.

"He'll be here soon, I hope." Kate glanced over her shoulder at the front door.

"I've been trapped in that coatroom scene for *weeks,* wrangling with those *bickering* school boys, and Hugo saw the problem at once. They shouldn't argue until they get down to the lake, or the emotional timing is all off. Hugo is a godsend, truly." She brought the cigarette to her lips.

Kate liked hearing Hugo praised. "He'll get credit for his contribution, I hope."

"Oh, I should love nothing more, believe me, but that's not how it works in this business. It's the name on a project that brings in investors, and in this case, that's me. All those shiny awards on my shelf. I can't have two or three names on my scripts or it dilutes all the impact. You understand?"

"I do, but Hugo deserves some compensation."

"So—you're an agent now?" Stella looked amused. "I better be careful, or I'll be giving a cut to both of you."

"I don't want a cut, but Hugo—"

"Stand down, darling. You're completely right. I'll pay him fifty cents an hour for the time he gave me. How does that sound?"

"*Fifty cents?* You just called him a godsend."

"Sixty cents, but not a penny more. I'm a starving artist."

"Well, you'll have to negotiate with Hugo, obviously." Although Kate suspected he'd been quite happy to do it for free.

Stella tilted her cigarette in Kate's direction, looking amused.

"You're a girl after my own heart, Kate—and that boy's heart, I'd say, judging by the way he couldn't stop talking about you today."

Kate froze. "What did he say?"

Stella laughed, blowing a stream of smoke. "Nothing that isn't written all over your face."

"Kate!" Tad's voice called, and she turned to see him entering from the backyard, his jacket unbuttoned, his bowtie crooked, his blond hair disheveled. His gaze moved down her party dress with appreciation. "You clean up nice."

"And you look like you're enjoying the party."

He laughed, smelling of alcohol, his cheeks too red. "Been up since four in the morning and never felt better. Come meet my old schoolmates. Nothing but old fogeys in here."

"No offense taken," Stella drawled.

"Oh. Hello, Stella. We made a few changes, but your script is going to stand for the most part, so you can go back to your own projects now. Still working on that old script of yours about the Trojan horse?"

"Forever, darling. I'll be typing in my casket." She brought the cigarette to her lips, her eyes narrowed with dislike.

"Come on," Tad told Kate, tugging her hand toward the French doors.

Kate resisted, looking back. But Stella waved her on, calling out, "I'll tell your great American author where to find you!"

The backyard looked magical, lit only by the large moon and strings of lights. A small orchestra of men in white jackets played off to the side, while couples danced on the patio.

Kate spotted what must have been Tad's crowd standing near a bar—five college-aged boys and two girls being a little more boisterous than anyone else. Bonnie stood at their fringes, wearing a sweet party dress with puffed sleeves, but she looked a bit lost, her smile strained. She saw Kate and brightened, hurrying toward her. "You're here! Where's Aurelio?"

"He had to rehearse late, but he'll be here soon."

Bonnie whirled to face Tad. "You promised he could leave early tonight!"

Tad smirked, and it occurred to Kate that he'd made Aurelio work late on purpose. "Don't fret, bunny rabbit. Plenty of dance partners to keep you happy. I think Charlie's got his eye on you, eh, Charlie?"

A lanky boy lifted a glass. Kate was surprised to see Bonnie's tutor Glenn Petersen standing next to him and exchanged a small wave.

"My old gang from Marlowe Prep," Tad said. "That's Goose, Charlie, you know Glenn, Mike, and—sorry, I forget your name." The last boy threw an olive. "Oh, yeah, that's Beezie. Avoid him."

"Don't the girls have names?" Kate asked.

"Sure—that's Goose's skirt, and that's Mike's skirt."

Everyone laughed, including the girls. One of them called out, "I'm Norma, and that's Betty."

"And this is Kitty Hildebrand," Tad said. "But you all knew that."

They shouted friendly hellos. At a glance, they reminded Kate of her friends back home, just a year or two older. "Do any of you go to Caltech, like Glenn?" she asked, which drew a chorus of jeers. She gathered from the overlapping voices that Beezie went to Caltech, three of them went to USC, and Betty went to Cal's LA campus.

Tad said, "I have to drag them off the school playground now and then, so they can see how the real world works."

"We can't all have movie moguls for fathers!" Goose called out. "Some of us actually need an education before someone will pay us!"

Tad laughed, but Kate could see the jab stung.

Charlie held a drink toward her. "Your hands look empty."

She didn't take it. "No, thanks." Having her faculties dulled, leaving her unprepared, was Kate's idea of a nightmare.

"Birthday girl, then." Goose handed the drink to Bonnie with a wink.

Bonnie stared at the amber liquid, her eyes wide.

"Probably good to keep a clear head tonight," Kate advised, putting a tentative hand around the glass. Bonnie nodded, and Kate set the drink on the bar.

"What did I tell you, boys?" Tad swung an arm around Kate's shoulders, bringing his boozy breath too close. "She keeps me in line. We make a good team."

"At work." Kate extracted herself.

Bonnie's tutor came forward, not looking happy about Tad's behavior. "How about a dance?" She gave him a grateful smile and took his arm.

"I didn't realize you and Tad were old school friends," she said.

"That's how I got the tutoring job." They started foxtrotting, Glenn leading with small, precise steps, keeping a respectful distance between them. He said, "I looked for you on set today to talk about calculus, but you looked pretty busy."

"Sorry, it was a hectic day." Kate turned her head to keep an eye on the French doors, hoping Hugo would appear.

"If you don't work on Sunday, I thought we could drive to the beach. Might as well sit somewhere nice while we talk about derivatives."

"Oh . . ." She spotted someone inside the house who looked like Hugo, but wasn't. "Actually, I think doing it at the studio is better."

"I told my uncle about you. He belongs to an astronomy club."

Bonnie danced past them, struggling to follow Charlie's rather loose interpretation of a foxtrot. "Keep up, Bonnie rabbit!" he called out, and Kate wished he could see what Bonnie was capable of with a decent partner.

"One-dimensional tubes," Glenn said, and Kate realized she'd missed part of what he was saying. "He knows it's all nonsense, but it's fun to think about. Anyway, he said his friend could probably give us a tour."

"Tour?"

"Of Mount Wilson. His friend works there."

Kate stopped dancing. *"Mount Wilson Observatory?* That would be amazing!" She forced her feet to move again. "That's the first thing I thought of when I found out I was moving here, but I heard it's only open to the public in the summer."

Glenn's hand tightened on her back. "I'll call my uncle in the morning."

She bit her lower lip, aware that taking advantage of Glenn's romantic interest to see an observatory wasn't a very nice thing to do. Also aware that she would probably do it anyway.

He started talking about a lecture on gravitational forces he'd attended a few days ago, but she barely heard, wondering if Edwin Hubble would be at the observatory. The prospect of meeting Edwin Hubble in the very place where he did his work made her feel giddy.

"Now, there's a funny sight," Glenn said, looking over her shoulder at the house. Kate craned her neck but couldn't see that far. She noticed a couple of women at the edge of the dance floor also looking toward the house, laughing behind their hands. Glenn's careful dance steps finally turned her enough to see what amused them—

And her heart dropped.

Reuben, Hugo, and Aurelio stood just outside the house, side by side, their heads turned to look at the band, giving her a moment to observe them unnoticed.

The suits were a disaster. Too baggy, too tight, too long, too short. She'd forgotten about taping up Reuben's pants, so they puddled at his ankles, and his jacket was too snug, pulling at the buttons. Hugo's jacket was huge, hanging past his wrists, while his pants were too short, revealing white socks. Aurelio had a bowtie, but Hugo and Reuben wore long daytime ties, brightly colored and striped. Completely wrong. And the shoes—brown, scuffed, cracked and dirty. Kate kicked herself for not borrowing black evening shoes—for not remembering one of Aunt Lorna's favorite sayings: *The shoes—that's how you spot a society imposter.*

The suits and shoes were Kate's fault, but even if they'd been perfect, the three of them looked like a comedy sketch—obvious misfits at a posh party: Reuben, short and grumpy, his scarred cheek drooping; Hugo, a dangerous street thug who might pocket the silverware; Aurelio, too eager and grinning, literally bouncing on his toes.

Kate flushed with embarrassment for them—and anger at herself. Hugo had known he wouldn't fit in, but she'd insisted, filled with grand visions of introducing him to producers and directors. But she couldn't introduce him wearing that ridiculous suit and loud tie, looking like—

Hugo saw her.

His mouth curved in a slow, personal smile that made her heart turn over, but the smile hesitated before fully forming, and she knew he'd seen her own doubts.

"Aurelio!" Bonnie squealed, abandoning her dance partner to run to him. She gave him a quick embrace, then pulled back to greet them all with a happy laugh, her excited voice rising above the music, welcoming them to her party—despite how they looked. As if she hadn't noticed.

Kate was ashamed of herself.

The song ended. "Excuse me," she said to Glenn. "Some friends of mine have just arrived."

"I'd like to meet them." He came with her, his hand settling on her shoulder as they walked.

Hugo's gaze settled on her shoulder too, his eyes tightening.

"—and I got mad at Tad for making you work late, but now you're here, and we can dance for everyone, and everything is *perfect*!"

Kate met Hugo's puzzled eyes. "Hello," she said, unsure how everything could feel so tense between them after last night.

"Hello. You look beautiful." His voice had that low rasp in it that she loved, but it only made him seem more out of place—a rebel with dark, tousled hair. "I like your dress."

"Thank you." Her own voice sounded too proper.

Glenn held out his hand to Hugo. "Glenn Petersen. I work with Kate."

Hugo shook his hand, his eyes narrowing with a wicked glint. "Hugo Quick. I live with her."

"Glenn is *very* smart," Bonnie said. "He goes to college, and has the *fattest* books, and talks about Einstein."

"Engineering student," Glenn told Hugo, seeming to sense the competition. "Caltech. How about you?"

"Actor, currently out of work." He was enjoying this.

"Where's the food?" Reuben asked. "I didn't put on this penguin suit for nothing."

"Oh—this way!" Bonnie grabbed Aurelio's hand and led them all through the French doors.

Kate did her best to walk with Hugo as they entered the house. "Sorry about the suits," she murmured.

He cast her a confused look. "What do you mean?"

She didn't know what to say to that, only seeing the differences in their lives.

Bonnie weaved them through the crowd to a long table pressed against the side of the living room, covered in trays and tureens and a showy display of flowers. Bonnie's three-tiered birthday cake was at one end of the table, with several slices already carved out of it.

"Mm, I always like those scallops with bacon," Glenn said to Kate. "And the ham looks good. Shall I fix you a plate?"

Kate was overly aware of Hugo on her other side. "No, thank you. I'm not hungry." She added, "And if I were, I'd fix my own plate."

Hugo huffed a quiet laugh that made her feel understood. She kept close to him as he picked up a plate and moved down the table, dishing up food.

"So, Kate." Glenn kept up on her other side. "If I can arrange Mount Wilson on Sunday, does that work for you? I can bring a picnic basket, and we can stop along the way."

Hugo slapped a spoonful of mashed potatoes onto his plate.

Kate felt the pull of two opposing gravitational forces—Hugo on one side, Mount Wilson Observatory on the other. "I, uh, don't think this Sunday is good for me."

"All right. We'll find another date."

She wished he hadn't used that word, but hearing it generated a quiet growl from Hugo that suddenly made everything clear. "Glenn . . . I left my wrap in the backyard. Would you mind fetching it for me?"

"Of course." Glenn put down his plate and hurried away.

Hugo cast her a quizzical look.

"I didn't bring a wrap." He still frowned, so she added, "You can't blame me for being tempted by the world's largest aperture telescope."

"Is that what he is?"

She laughed at that, and Hugo smiled in return—and finally, they were back in last night.

"This is disgusting," Reuben said, crowding in beside them, taking a bite from a chicken leg.

Kate dragged her eyes from Hugo's. "Doesn't it taste good?"

"Sure. The extravagant waste tastes fine." Reuben wiped his mouth on the back of his hand. "Enough to feed a hundred starving people, and nobody's touching it."

"Nobody eats at parties like this," Kate said. Even though every hostess put out a lavish spread, eager to impress.

"Kings and queens of the capitalist system, bored by a feast. They don't know the taste of real hunger."

"Pipe down," Hugo said, reaching for a roll. "I'd like to enjoy some of this extravagant waste before you get us thrown out."

The three of them moved to the back corner of the room, while Bonnie and Aurelio remained near the birthday cake, giggling.

Reuben lifted a forkful of mashed potatoes. "The farmer who grew these probably lost his life savings to a bunch of Wall Street crooks."

"He's just miffed because the letters were fake," Hugo said. He took a bite of his roll.

It took Kate a second to understand, then her eyes widened. "George Washington is fake?"

Hugo spoke out of the side of his mouth. "And Lincoln and Jefferson. All forgeries, according to the expert we saw today. Good quality though, so it's not surprising Ollie got scammed."

"Frank Fairchild is the one who got scammed," Kate said. "He bought them on Ollie's behalf."

"Worthless paper," Reuben muttered. "I'll bet that auction house was in on it. That's why they disappeared. Laughing all the way to—" His voice halted, his gaze riveted on the front of the living room.

Kate turned to look.

A handsome man with wavy, gray hair entered the room, followed by two large men. He wasn't dressed for an evening party—a pinstripe, double-breasted suit with a red flower in the lapel and a flashy red tie—but his eyes raked the room as if he owned the place. His gaze lingered on beautiful Mrs. Fairchild.

"Jeez, I got to get out of here." Reuben shoved his plate into the hands of a passing caterer. He turned, but the French doors were clogged by laughing people. He started toward a side hall that probably led to the kitchen, but only got two steps before the man in pinstripes noticed him.

Reuben froze.

The crowd seemed to part as the man crossed the room, trailed by one of the large men. As he neared, he stretched out his arms, but the hands he clasped on Reuben's upper arms seemed more like an iron cage than a greeting. "Reuben Feigenbaum." His smile didn't reach his eyes. "You've been on my mind all day, and now here you are, where I least expected, the very man I'm most eager to see."

Reuben's bulldog face paled.

"That's Moe Kravitz," Hugo whispered near Kate's ear. "The most dangerous man in Los Angeles."

CHAPTER 26

Reuben and Moe Kravitz stood a couple of feet away, close enough for Kate and Hugo to hear.

"All day, friends have stopped by to welcome me home," Moe said. "And I noticed your absence, Reuben. We had a little celebration dinner at the club, and your seat was empty."

"I didn't want to impose," Reuben said stiffly.

"Impose. You hear that, Boris?" Moe looked amused, glancing over his shoulder. "All day, I'm asking—where's Reuben? I need a rundown of the books, so I know how things stand, and nobody can find you. I have Boris call the house where you're staying, and nobody picks up the phone. So I tell Boris we should drive over, and nobody answers the door."

Reuben's bald head shone with sweat. "I've been out of the house all day."

"Then I see Dorothy is having a party next door. We're old friends, Dorothy and me—she used to sing at the club—so I drop in to say hello. And who should I find at that party, but the very person I'm most eager to see." He patted Reuben's scarred cheek. "I'm a free man again, Reuben, and it's time to get back to work."

Reuben's throat rose and fell in a swallow. "I'm working in pictures now, like I told you a while ago."

Moe spread his hands. "There's no need for that now. I appreciate you hiding here on my behalf, but the investigation is over, and we can all go back to business as usual."

Hugo made a low sound, drawing the attention of the man named Boris. Kate grabbed Hugo's hand and squeezed.

"But I want to work in pictures," Reuben said.

"I understand. It's an exciting business. But I need you, Reuben. I glanced over the books today and can't make heads or tails of it. I have to say—I wasn't so impressed by that nephew of yours. I would have fired him if he hadn't gotten himself killed."

"He wasn't my nephew," Reuben said, his acid tone returning.

"You recommended him. Which is interesting, because I sensed no friendship between the two of you when he visited me in my temporary situation. And then somebody killed him at the house where you're living." Moe watched Reuben closely. "What can you tell me about that?"

"Nothing," Reuben said gruffly. "We just came home and found him. I don't think it had anything to do with your business, if that's what you're worried about."

"That's reassuring, but now I don't have a bookkeeper, and I'm eager for you to come back, Reuben. Never any trouble with you, nose in the books, everything nice and tidy." Moe placed a hand on Reuben's upper arm, squeezed, and released it. "You're an important person to me, Reuben. That's why I had Boris keep an eye on Ollie's house these last few months, to make sure you stayed safe."

Boris leaned forward to whisper in Moe's ear. Moe listened, then turned his head to look at Kate, two steps away.

A chill ran through her. She fought an urge to flee as Moe walked toward her, while Reuben watched in alarm.

"Miss Hildebrand." Moe flashed a brief smile, taking her hand between both of his in a warm bundle. "I hope you'll forgive my impertinence in introducing myself, but I'm an old friend of your grandfather's, and it is my pleasure to meet the remarkable young woman I have read so much about. My name is Moe Kravitz."

"How do you do?" Kate murmured, her hand trapped, her heart racing.

"I read in the papers what happened a few days ago, and it distresses me that you had to find this young man who worked for me in such an unpleasant situation. I'd like to assure you I'm giving the police my full cooperation in finding his killer, so you can feel safe in our city."

He released her hand, and she resisted the urge to wipe it against her party dress.

His gaze turned to Hugo. "And you must be the young man who waits tables at my club. Forgive me, but I have so many employees."

Hugo had paled but held Moe's gaze. "You're thinking of Aurelio."

The large man behind Moe whispered in his ear. "Boris says you used to wash dishes at the club. Do you mind if I ask your name, young man?"

"Hugo Quick."

"*Hugo Quick.*" Moe seemed to absorb it. "I suspect we didn't fully utilize your talents, Mr. Quick. You have the look of someone who might appreciate more interesting work than washing dishes. You must come by the club if you're ever in need of employment, and I'll tell my people to keep an eye out for you."

Hugo didn't blink. "I'm set for now, but thank you."

Moe turned back to Reuben. "I know the investigation made you lose the lease on your old apartment, Reuben. I appreciate the sacrifice. I'd like you to stay in one of the rooms at the club until you find a new place, and then you'll be close while we get the business back in order. Go pack your bags while I catch up with a few people here, and we'll drive back together."

Reuben's eyes shifted. "I have my own car. I'll pack tomorrow and drive over the day after that. That gives me time to settle things here."

Moe considered it and nodded. "Sunday, then." He put a hand on Reuben's shoulder. "I was disappointed you didn't welcome me home today, Reuben, but you know me, I'm not the sort of person who holds grudges. I take care of business and move on." He lifted the hand to Reuben's scarred cheek and patted. "I'll see you Sunday." He walked toward Mrs. Fairchild, trailed by Boris.

Reuben watched him go, then released a sagging breath.

"Come on," Hugo said. He took Reuben's arm and led him toward the side hall.

Kate started to follow, but Glenn stepped in front of her. "I can't find your wrap. What does it look like?"

"I must have left it at home. Excuse me." She tried to go around him.

"There you are!" Tad grabbed her arm. "I talked to the band, and they're going to play so Bonnie and Aurelio can dance for everyone. Where are they?"

Kate cast a distracted glance over the crowd and saw Bonnie and Aurelio still standing near the table. "Over there, by the cake."

"Bonnie!" Tad called, pulling Kate's arm that way.

She unpeeled his fingers and hurried toward the side entrance where Hugo and Reuben had disappeared, pausing to let a caterer pass with a stack of clean plates. Finally, she entered the dim hall, but no one was there. She passed a bathroom and glanced into a small study with a white desk. The opening straight ahead led to the kitchen, and just before that, another hall turned toward the front of the house.

Hugo's voice came from around the corner. "What he said about Lemmy—I swear he knows what we did."

She stopped.

"He doesn't know anything," Reuben's growling voice said. "How could he?"

"That Boris guy has been watching the house."

"Watching *me*. You were just some dishwasher they never noticed. That's why we had you do it, and you handled it like a pro. Quick in and out, planted the fake evidence, and now Lemmy is dead and everything is good."

The blood seemed to leave Kate's head. She pressed a hand against the wall to steady herself.

"I didn't like the way that Boris guy was looking at me in there," Hugo said. "Real suspicious, like he saw me that day but can't quite place it."

"Boris looks at everyone like that. Stupid people panic and give themselves away. You're not stupid, so stop panicking."

Dishes crashed in the kitchen, drowning out Hugo's reply.

Kate's thoughts crashed with them, wild and confused, trying to find some innocent meaning behind the words. But all she found was a confession of murder. A few hours before Lemmy had died, he'd threatened to tell Moe Kravitz that Reuben had erased Ollie's loan. If he'd done that, Reuben would have been punished—probably killed—and Ollie would have lost his house. A motive for Reuben and a motive for Hugo. A reason for them to work together to get rid of Lemmy.

"Let's get out of here," Reuben said. "I need to start packing."

"You're not going back to that club. I'll get you the money for Brazil."

"Not before Sunday you won't."

"I've got some ideas." A pause, then Hugo said, "You think I need to disappear too?"

Kate's heart dropped. She didn't want Hugo to disappear—and she didn't want him to have done something that required it.

"You disappear, you only draw attention to yourself. Just lay low. Nobody knows what you did unless you give them a reason to look twice." Shuffling movement. "You coming?"

"I should let Kate know I'm leaving the party."

She stiffened, not wanting to be found around the corner.

"You're fooling yourself with that girl."

"I know . . . but it's fun while it lasts." She heard the smile in Hugo's voice—this boy she barely knew. Last night, he'd kissed her in the moonlight, and now he talked about fake evidence and disappearing. Had he snuck Bonnie's scarf from Aurelio's pocket and planted it, knowing the blackmail photos gave her a motive, then pretended to find the scarf when Kate didn't notice it herself? Part of her wanted him to come around the corner so she could ask.

But how could she believe his answers?

Her father had fooled her for thirteen years. Even now, looking back, her brain knew the facts, but her heart still had a hard time believing the truth about Johnson Hildebrand.

Her heart—so easily duped by a charming deceiver.

Panic bubbled inside her. She had to get away where she could think straight—away from Hugo's spell. Two caterers walked from the kitchen, and she used their noise to camouflage her own, following them back to the party. She dared to glance back as she reentered the living room, but the hall was empty.

The party seemed more crowded suddenly, the laughter louder. Kate longed to leave, but Hugo and Reuben were leaving the house right now, and she didn't want to run into them. She threaded her way through the crowd, her thoughts reeling around everything Hugo had said and done since Lemmy's death.

First, he and Reuben had tampered with the murder scene, emptying Lemmy's pockets and removing evidence. Hugo had hidden the bloody sword, and when she'd confronted him, he'd talked her into not telling the police and offered to hide her trunk in the attic. The next day, he and Reuben had taken the display case off the wall so Detective Bassett wouldn't know a sword was missing. That night, he'd pretended to find the scarf and challenged her to play detective with him—again, not telling the police. When she'd suspected Aurelio, he'd insisted Aurelio was innocent—because he knew he was. And last night in the moonlight—

Kate's heart squeezed. He'd told her about losing his job and a mother who made homemade bread, making her want to comfort and kiss him—not suspect him.

Had it all been an act?

He is an actor.

She pressed a hand to her stomach—and felt the smooth, satin bodice of her party dress, chosen to feel nice when she danced with Hugo.

She hadn't been smart. She hadn't been sensible.

Tad's angry voice cut through the chaos in her mind, slurred and superior, and she looked up to see him near the birthday cake, a few feet away. "You better watch yourself," he said, pointing a finger at Aurelio.

Aurelio glowered, several inches shorter than Tad, but his fists were clenched. "If you ever try something like that with her again, I'll—"

"Aurelio," Bonnie wailed, clinging to his arm.

Tad smirked. "Don't tell me you believe in that sweet little girl act of hers? Trust me, she's not as innocent as—"

Aurelio's fist stopped the words. Bonnie screamed as Tad toppled back into a large man, who shoved him away. Tad righted himself and swung, but Aurelio dodged easily, as Bonnie squealed and fell sideways into the three-tiered cake. Absurdly, she whirled and tried to save the cake, grabbing it as it smashed into her chest.

Kate pushed through the crowd and grabbed Tad's arm as he lifted it to swing again. *"The movie,"* she reminded him in a sharp undertone. "We have filming tomorrow, and you'll bruise him."

Tad tried to shove her off, then saw who it was and calmed. "That worthless little—"

"—is the star of your picture," she hissed, keeping a tight grip on his arm. "You've had too much to drink. Go outside and cool off."

Tad pointed an angry finger at Aurelio with his free hand. "You'll go nowhere in this town, I'll see to that!"

"Tad." Kate squeezed his arm. "Everyone is looking."

Mrs. Fairchild appeared at the edge of their circle, her horrified gaze landing on Bonnie, who was covered in cake. She released a furious breath. "You *silly* girl!"

Bonnie's bottom lip quivered, her smeared arms held out to her sides.

"It's my fault," Aurelio said, futilely brushing at the clumps of cake and frosting.

Mrs. Fairchild snapped, "Get away from her."

"Tad started it!" Bonnie wailed.

"Hardly." Tad rubbed his jaw.

The party had gone unusually quiet. Mrs. Fairchild shot a quick glance over the room and straightened her posture. "I think it's best if you and your friends leave," she told Aurelio with rigid composure.

"Mama—that's not fair!" Bonnie's blue eyes welled with tears.

"It's all right," Aurelio murmured.

Kate stepped forward. "Let's go upstairs, Bonnie, and I'll help you clean up."

But Bonnie burst into tears and fled, pushing people aside.

Kate hurried after her, weaving her way around guests and side tables. She entered the front foyer as Bonnie was nearing the top of the staircase. "Bonnie, wait." She started up after her.

"Kate!" Hugo called.

She stopped halfway up—took a second to inhale, preparing herself to see him with new eyes—and then turned. She gripped the banister.

Hugo gazed up, his brow furrowed. "What happened?"

He didn't look like a killer; he looked like the boy who'd offered her his heart last night, knowing she might break it. Doubt squeezed her chest.

"Kate?" His concern deepened.

He looked so wrong at this party in his oversize suit—not a suave performer putting on an act, but raw and real. And honest. "We need to talk," she told him. "But I need to help Bonnie first."

Aurelio came from the living room, his expression stormy. "We've been kicked out." He left through the front door.

But Hugo didn't move, his eyes on Kate. "I'll wait for you. There's a little office by the kitchen."

"All right." She would demand answers soon, but for now, she followed Bonnie upstairs.

CHAPTER 27

Kate found Bonnie standing in the middle of her bedroom, sobbing, her cake-smeared arms extended.

"Let's clean you up." She led Bonnie across the hall to a bathroom, washed her arms in the sink, then handed her a towel and brought her back to the bedroom. She unzipped Bonnie's dress and helped her out of it. "Your slip is clean. You just need a new dress."

Bonnie drew a shuddering breath. "Did Aurelio leave?"

"Yes."

"Then I'm not going back down there."

"Yes, you are," Mrs. Fairchild said, entering the room. "Thank you, Kate," she said in polite dismissal.

Kate picked up the dirty dress and crossed the hall to the bathroom.

"Stop crying. You'll ruin your makeup. All those people are here to see you."

"No, they're not. They don't even know I exist."

Kate tossed the dress in the tub.

"And whose fault is that? You've been giggling with that boy all night, when you should be working on Tad. He's the one who can get you somewhere."

Kate paused in the dark bathroom, behind the half-closed door.

"I don't care about Tad. I love Aurelio."

"No, you don't. You're just smitten by a handsome face."

"He's sweet and funny and makes me laugh." Through the crack near the hinges, Kate could see Bonnie sitting at the edge of the bed in her slip. "He works harder than anyone, but Tad's always mean to him and tells him to work harder. It isn't fair." Bonnie sniffed. "Tad's just jealous because I'm not hanging on his every word anymore, telling him how great he is."

"Well, you should be. He's one of the most powerful people in Hollywood—or will be someday." Mrs. Fairchild handed her a handkerchief. "We've talked about this."

"I tried." Bonnie wiped her nose. "But he doesn't like me like that. He did at first, but now he's tired of me."

"You're a pretty girl. You can make him interested again."

"I don't want to. I love Aurelio."

Mrs. Fairchild moved out of view. "A silly crush that will end in a week. Meanwhile, Tad will find some other girl to put in his movies." Her voice became distant, as if she'd entered a closet. "That's the problem with growing up as you have. You don't appreciate what you have—this house, the private singing lessons, the social connections. I would have given anything for that when I was your age."

Bonnie looked toward the voice. "I *do* appreciate it."

"I was hungry every day as a child. Horrible basement apartment with screams outside my window. I slept with a knife under my pillow. I came to Hollywood with nothing but ten dollars and a pretty face. I spent the money on a nice dress, which meant I didn't eat for two days, but that dress got me a job singing in a bar, and a year later, I was headlining at the best nightclub in town, where I met your father." Mrs. Fairchild reappeared with a lavender dress in her arms. "I didn't accomplish that by chasing every handsome face that walked by. Learning which men are worth your time is an important skill for a woman, and you're old enough to learn it."

"You told me you worked hard so I don't have to."

"Well, I can't hold the interest of men like Clive Falcon forever. You'll have to fend for yourself soon." She looked down at Bonnie's upturned face, and her tone softened. "Life is a series of choices, and I want you to make the right ones."

Bonnie sniffed. "Aurelio is a good choice."

"I know it seems that way now." Mrs. Fairchild paused, holding the lavender dress against her waist. "There's a man downstairs, right now, that I almost married."

Bonnie blinked, surprised.

"Not a very nice man, but he owned the club where I sang, and I was terribly impressed. Then your father started coming into the club and sent me flowers every day, and I realized there were better men in the world. Whenever I see that man, I shudder to think how close I came to settling for him." She wiped a finger over Bonnie's damp cheek. "Don't settle, darling. A woman is only as important as her husband."

"I'm only sixteen."

Her mother laughed softly. "Yes, darling, but it's time to practice." She laid out the dress on the bed. "Freshen up your makeup, and then find Tad downstairs and remind him how irresistible you are." She kissed Bonnie's forehead and left the room.

Kate waited for her to descend the staircase before leaving the bathroom. She took a few steps toward the stairs . . . then stopped and returned to Bonnie's room.

Bonnie didn't seem surprised when she entered. "You heard all that, didn't you?"

"Yes. I'm sorry."

"I'm glad. She talks that way all the time, and I hate it."

Kate sat beside her at the side of the bed. "It isn't true what she said about only being as important as your husband. Maybe that's the kind of importance she wants, but not me."

Bonnie seemed to relax. "That's why I like you, Kate. You don't care about stuff like that. You say what you want, and Tad respects you."

"You deserve respect too, Bonnie. Don't let him call you bunny rabbit. You're not his pet. You're *extremely* talented. That's why producers will want you in their movies, not because you flirt with them."

"I hope so. I want to be a big star."

"I think you will be. But even if you're not, that doesn't determine your worth."

"You make a lot more money when you're a star."

Kate smiled. "I know . . . I mean your *real* worth. The fame won't be *you*. It's only the world watching you. They take pictures and write stories but get it wrong half the time. Don't believe their version of you."

"I like talking like this."

"Me too." Kate hesitated, not wanting to bring up the car, but she needed answers before seeing Hugo again. "Bonnie . . . do you remember the day of auditions when your car was moved? You didn't want to tell me about it, but I need to know. It's important."

Bonnie looked at her lap. "I was embarrassed, but I don't care anymore."

"So . . . you *did* drive your car that day?"

"Not me, Tad. We were watching the auditions, and he got bored and said he wanted to show me the star bungalow he's trying to get for me so I don't have to drive home when I work late. So we drove across the studio in my car, but as soon as we walked in the bungalow, he started kissing me, and I wanted to leave. We'd kissed before, but I'd just met Aurelio, and I didn't want to kiss Tad anymore. So I pushed him away and went back to the car. He was really mad, but I didn't care. As soon as we parked, I got out and left."

Kate bit back her anger at Tad, not wanting to upset Bonnie further. "You did the right thing. That's what I meant about holding on to who you really are." Bonnie was the one who'd moved the yellow car, which meant it had nothing to do with Lemmy's murder.

Which meant Hugo couldn't have done it because he'd been at the studio when Lemmy was killed. Without the car, he had no way of getting home and back that quickly. Kate pressed a hand to her mouth, a laugh bubbling out.

"What?" Bonnie asked.

"I've been so stupid, Bonnie. I imagined all these reasons for the car being in a different place. *Crazy* reasons."

Bonnie wiped her nose on a handkerchief. "It already *was* in a different place. Tad just parked where we found it. Someone else moved it first."

Kate's heart dropped. But if Bonnie and Tad had used the car in the middle of auditions, it still gave Hugo an alibi. "Bonnie, *when* did you and Tad use the car? Was it right after we arrived, or had we been there a long time?"

"A long time. I went to wardrobe first, and then they tested makeup on me, and then Tad and I watched auditions, and *then* we drove to the bungalow. After we got back, I walked around for a few minutes because I was upset, then I came in and danced with Aurelio."

Which left an hour, maybe, before Bonnie and Tad took the car. Barely enough time for Hugo to drive home, kill Lemmy, and park the car in a different place. Possible, but almost an alibi. She had to talk to him.

Kate stood. "You better get dressed, Bonnie, and go back to your party."

"It isn't *my* party. I don't have any friends here if Aurelio is gone."

"Don't I count?"

"Oh!" Bonnie looked up, appalled. "I just meant—"

"I know." Kate smiled. She walked to the door, then paused to look back at the window. "Close your drapes whenever you change your clothes, Bonnie. That man who got murdered in our house used to take pictures of you through your window. The pictures have been destroyed, but you should know that."

Bonnie's mouth fell open.

Kate descended the staircase, steeling herself to face Hugo, armed with more facts than she'd had ten minutes ago.

"There you are," Glenn said, rising from a chair in the foyer. "Is Bonnie all right?"

"Actually . . . I think she's going to be fine."

"I thought we could go back to dancing."

"Glenn . . . I need some time to myself right now."

"Oh. Sure. I'll just—"

"Go somewhere else," she suggested.

She entered the hall that led to the kitchen, where Hugo and Reuben had stood talking in secret. It dead-ended at the side hall where she'd listened. As she came around the corner, she saw Hugo in the study, standing behind the white desk, quickly opening and closing drawers.

Kate froze in the doorway.

He closed the last drawer and straightened, not noticing her, giving his full attention to three items clustered on top of the desk. He picked up an overstuffed envelope, folded it over, and tucked it into his jacket pocket. Then he picked up a loose photograph, looked at it briefly, and added it to the pocket. He paused on the third item, turning it for inspection, giving Kate a glimpse of a gold frog about the size of an egg. He slid the expensive-looking frog into his pocket.

"Hey, put that back!" Glenn ordered from behind Kate.

Hugo's head jerked up.

"I saw you take that. Hand it over." Glenn walked to the desk.

Hugo's eyes didn't leave Kate's. "I'm not stealing," he said evenly.

"Empty your pockets," Glenn said.

Kate warmed with embarrassment for him—and disappointment. He probably thought the Fairchilds had more than they needed, so he might as well take a few things—not for himself, but so Reuben could escape to Brazil. He probably felt cheated by the world after being fired without pay. But she hadn't known he was the sort of person who turned into a thief when it suited his needs.

Because she didn't really know him.

"Put it back, and no one needs to know," she said quietly. "Right, Glenn?"

Hugo's eyes shifted to Glenn and then back to Kate. "Well," he said in a dangerous voice. "Looks like Nancy Drew has a new partner."

Her throat tightened. She wanted to scream that Glenn meant nothing to her, that all she wanted was to return to last night and stay there forever, but Hugo had made that impossible. *He* was the one whispering about planted evidence and stealing things. *He* was the one who wasn't the person he'd pretended to be.

But all she said was a steely, "Put it back."

Hugo put his hand in his pocket and pulled out the frog, holding it with two fingers so they could see it clearly as he set it on the desk. Kate thought about the overstuffed envelope, maybe filled with money, and the photograph, but didn't have the heart to mention them in front of Glenn. She would ask Hugo about them later, along with everything else.

"You better leave," she said.

His eyes burned into her with unspoken words. "I don't suppose you want to walk back with me."

She was tempted but also terrified; she didn't trust herself with him. "I should stay for Bonnie."

Glenn turned to her. "I'll walk you home later."

Behind his back, Hugo picked up the gold frog and slipped it into his pocket. Kate looked away quickly, not wanting him to know she'd seen and was going to let him get away with it.

He seemed in a hurry to leave now, walking around the desk. As he passed her in the doorway, he said in a low voice, "Well done on the breaking-my-heart thing. It just happened a little sooner than I expected."

She opened her mouth but couldn't think what to say as she watched him walk away.

"I'm glad he's gone," Glenn said. "Do you want to return to the backyard?"

Kate stared at the place where Hugo had been. "Yes." She needed fresh air.

Thirty minutes later, as she stood in a quiet corner of the backyard watching Bonnie dance with Glenn, she was surprised to see Aurelio sneaking his way around the outer edge of the crowd, coming toward her.

He leaned close enough to be heard over the band. "You better come home, Kate. Your aunt is here."

CHAPTER 28

Kate's head churned with questions as she and Aurelio walked up the path to Ollie's house. Aunt Lorna was supposed to be on her honeymoon right now.

Everyone stood in the foyer, surrounding the oversized dining table, scowling at one another, watched over by the tall bear in the corner wearing a Three Musketeers hat.

Aunt Lorna stood closest to the door, in the pose Kate knew so well: one hand on her hip, chin elevated. Ollie stood on the left side of the table, looking like an angry child in his green plaid pajamas, his hair sticking up. Reuben stood on the far side, his arms crossed, his scarred face cast into evil shadows by the lantern overhead. Aurelio moved to the remaining side of the table, his eyes wide and curious.

Hugo wasn't there.

Aunt Lorna turned, her expression softening at the sight of Kate, her arms opening. "*Darling!* I came as soon as we reached port and saw the newspapers. I can't imagine what you've been going through." She squeezed Kate's shoulders, touching their cheeks together with the scent of face powder and perfume.

"What about your honeymoon?" Kate asked.

"Well, I couldn't leave you here with people getting murdered in the kitchen. How are you holding up?" She leaned back and took in the pink dress. "Why—you look lovely! I'm always saying you should wear more pink." Ironically, Aunt Lorna's ivory-and-green plaid jacket—the latest fashion with its pleated shoulders—matched Ollie's rumpled pajamas. Her hat was stiff and oddly shaped, topped by two large poufs of black and green.

Kate looked at Reuben across the table. "Where's Hugo?"

"Borrowed my car," he said gruffly. "Didn't say where he was going, but he seemed upset. You two have a fight or something?"

She didn't reply, wondering where Hugo had gone so late. And why borrow Reuben's car when he had his motorcycle? Was he out thieving for Reuben and needed a place to stash his loot? She hated thinking that way, but she'd just seen him stealing with her own eyes.

"I've got us a suite at the Huntington Hotel," Aunt Lorna said. "Such a relief after the horrible place I had to stay last night. I've had a grueling journey, Kate, in the most terrifying little planes. But I'm here now, and we'll go home tomorrow."

Home. Away from all the mistakes she'd made here. "What about Mr. Norton?"

"Oh, he's in complete agreement. We can't have you on the front page, finding murder victims. The two of you can manage to get along until you leave for college. We both just want you safe and sound."

On the other side of Aunt Lorna, Ollie scowled. "She's perfectly safe here."

"Oh, yes," Aunt Lorna clipped, turning to face him. "*Perfectly* safe. Your accountant stabbed in the kitchen. Living with boarders. It's a wonder she wasn't murdered in her bed."

"Lemmy wasn't Ollie's accountant," Kate said, as if that mattered. "Really, Aunt Lorna, I've been fine here."

"You don't have to be brave for me, darling. If I'd known it was this bad, I would never have sent you here. We'll catch the first train in the morning."

"She's old enough to make her own decisions now," Ollie said. "So you can stop keeping us apart and filling her head with lies about me."

"Ollie, she didn't," Kate said.

His voice rose. "Did she tell you I tried to see you after the funeral? Came to the house three times, and she wouldn't let me inside. Called me a flashy embarrassment!"

Kate looked at her aunt, appalled. "You did?"

Aunt Lorna pursed her lips. "You weren't ready for visitors, and he kept banging on the front door. His career was over, and he wanted the attention of the reporters. It was pathetic."

"I *wanted* to see my granddaughter!" he thundered. "For four years, you've kept me away from her! Told that housekeeper to say she wasn't home if I called—oh, yes, I figured out *that* little trick! Probably hid my letters too! Thought you could turn her into a high society snob like the rest of you Hildebrands, but she's got my blood in her too!"

"*Really!*" Aunt Lorna fumed.

"Ollie—" Kate began, but she didn't want to admit she'd been the one who'd told Hattie to say she wasn't home, not wanting to talk to an old man she didn't know.

"I'll tell you why she kept us apart, Kate. Because I called her a hoity-toity bitch with her nose in the air—said it to her face! And her brother, putting on his posh airs when he was nothing but a common—"

"Ollie, stop!" Kate cried. Aunt Lorna's face had paled. "It's not Aunt Lorna's fault I never visited. I never . . ." She drew a breath. "I never wanted to come. I'm sorry, but I didn't know you back then, and I didn't know it would be this . . . nice," she finished lamely.

He still glared at Aunt Lorna. "She poisoned your mind against me, the way they poisoned Evie's mind. Made her think

I wasn't classy enough for their lifestyle. I wasn't even invited to the wedding!"

Aunt Lorna said loftily, "You told Evelyn you were shooting a movie in Hawaii."

"I *told* her what day I'd be back! And next thing I know, I'm reading about her wedding in the newspaper—with a picture of *your* father in his fancy top hat!"

Aunt Lorna settled both hands on her hips. "Evelyn didn't want you turning her wedding into a Hollywood spectacle, like you did her birthday parties."

"Her birthday parties?" Ollie looked taken aback.

"Ponies and magicians and a hundred guests. Everyone knew Evelyn preferred small gatherings. I mean, *really.* And that childhood you gave her—dragged from town to town as you made a fool of yourself on stage, and then leaving her alone in this big house while you played with your movie star friends. She couldn't *wait* to escape."

Ollie's face reddened. "Well—I did my best," he sputtered. "And it wasn't until your brother—"

"Stop!" Kate cried, spreading her arms between them. "Ollie, I'm sorry I didn't visit sooner. I should have. And Aunt Lorna, I do like living here. It's been wonderful, actually." *Until tonight.*

"Don't be absurd, Kate. This is no place for a well-bred girl." Aunt Lorna's gaze shifted to Reuben, who looked dangerous with his scowling, scarred face. "We'll take the morning train and stay at the Fairmont until the house is done with the remodel."

The anger in Ollie's face collapsed. "But she likes it here. She's working in the movie business now."

Aunt Lorna raised a skeptical brow. "Sounds like I arrived just in time. Go pack a few things, darling, and we'll return for the rest in the morning."

"Kate," Ollie said in a hollow voice.

She didn't know what to do, her stomach knotting. Last night, the decision would have been easy—a hundred reasons to stay. Tonight, a hundred reasons to escape.

Reuben said darkly, "Go ahead and leave, then. I warned him you would."

She might never see Hugo again if she left right now. Never have a chance to ask her questions and hear his reasonable explanations.

Or his lies.

Maybe it was better this way. She could hold on to that one lovely kiss in the moonlight, without tarnishing it with an argument. Without having to call the police and see Hugo arrested for robbery and murder.

She forced herself to look into her grandfather's pleading eyes. "I'm sorry, Ollie, but I'm going to spend the night at the hotel."

He still looked hopeful. "And tomorrow?"

"I think it's best—" Her voice caught. "If I go back to my school. But I'll return for visits."

Aurelio asked, "What about the movie? What should I tell Tad?"

Somehow, she'd forgotten about that. Tomorrow was the first big day of filming with the entire cast, including two musical numbers. Kate looked at her aunt. "I have to go to work tomorrow."

Aunt Lorna gave a short laugh of surprise. "You really do work at a movie studio? I thought he made that up."

Ollie made an indignant sound. "She's a producer."

"Assistant," Kate corrected. "But tomorrow's a big day, and I need to show up. I'll get things in order there, and we can leave the next day. Aurelio, I'll pick you up at five thirty in the morning." She walked around the table, feeling Ollie's wounded eyes on her as she made her way through the back archway.

She pulled out the small suitcase she'd stored under the bed and filled it with essentials while Aunt Lorna lamented the butcher knife on the nightstand and criticized the ridiculous mermaid lamp. "Honestly, Kate, I had no idea his house would be in such a state."

Kate gathered her alarm clock and math textbook. "I sent you a telegram the first night I arrived, and you pretended you didn't receive it."

"I thought it was just a little homesickness and you needed to adjust. I didn't know about the murder."

"I'm sorry you had to leave in the middle of your honeymoon."

Aunt Lorna waved a hand. "Oh, the ship was fun, but once we landed, it was nothing but talk about gold mines and dinners with the roughest people. I was relieved to flee."

The house felt empty as they walked to the front door, everyone gone to bed. Kate glanced up the staircase but knew nothing she could say to Ollie would make it any better. Tomorrow night, she would give him a proper goodbye and make plans to visit over her Christmas holiday.

In a few days, she would be back at Blakely Academy, sitting at a desk.

Aunt Lorna prattled in the taxi about turning the downstairs study into a bedroom for Kate. "It's small, but Donald insists on having your old room upstairs with its view of the street. Would you mind terribly if we decorated in mauve, so it matches the rest of the downstairs rooms?"

"Mauve is fine."

The Huntington was the grandest hotel Kate had ever seen, but Aunt Lorna still complained about the slow elevator and color of the carpet. They entered a lavish, two-bedroom suite. "I don't feel a bit tired," Aunt Lorna said, trailing Kate into her room. "Shall I order room service? I want to hear all about this movie thing you've gotten yourself involved with. You're not *acting,* I hope."

Kate dropped her suitcase on the large bed. "I'm exhausted." The room looked like her old room in San Francisco, done in pale blue.

"Well, you can't leave me on my own *all* day. Do your movie thing in the morning, and we'll go sightseeing in the afternoon. Have you found any good food in the area?"

Hugo's cooking.

"I can't leave work midday," Kate said. "But you can come to Falcon Pictures and watch the movie being filmed. I'll leave your name at the front gate."

"Oh! Now that might be interesting."

"Good night, Aunt Lorna." Kate gave her aunt a gentle nudge out the door and closed it.

The tears, suddenly, felt perilously close.

Kate got ready for bed in a sumptuous bathroom, and then stood at the window to look down at an enormous swimming pool several floors below.

This was her real life. Not swimming pools with green water and a violinist on the diving board. Not hunting a killer on her own and dropping out of school to work at a movie studio. Not falling for a penniless actor with a head full of dreams.

She looked up at the moon, wondering if Hugo had come home yet and noticed her empty room.

What a fool she'd been. Lists and more lists, but they couldn't protect her from herself.

The world thought Kitty Hildebrand was so smart and sensible. A brave survivor. All those awards at school. Even Stella Nixon seemed impressed.

The moon knew the truth.

The kidnapping had been Kate's fault. She'd lied to the police, so they wouldn't know her part in it. But Kate knew, and the moon knew.

And her mother was dead because of it.

CHAPTER 29

Work was a welcome distraction the next morning.

The last small family scene was shot, a short break was taken, and then a crowd of cast and crew poured into Stage Six. Everyone's nerves seemed on edge as they rushed around, preparing for the first big scene in the ice cream parlor.

Tad avoided Kate, remaining close to the director and cameraman, which was fine with her. She had enough on her mind, and as long as she didn't have to talk to Tad, she didn't have to tell him she was leaving town.

Aunt Lorna arrived in the middle of the chaos, delivered by a taxi, looking out of place in a chic, plum-colored suit and rigid, cone-shaped hat that was the peak of fashion. She linked her arm with Kate's for a tour of the enormous building, pausing every few steps to ask questions, fascinated by the frenzied activity around her.

"Such darling little dressing rooms on wheels," she said, peering through the door of Bonnie's wardrobe trailer. "So clever, the way they can roll them right into this huge building. This one doesn't have many costumes in it, but the other one was crowded. Why don't they spread it out a little?"

"This is Bonnie's wardrobe trailer," Kate said distractedly, glancing over her clipboard. "She and Aurelio have their own trailers, and the supporting cast has to share the other two."

Men shouted overhead, adjusting lights, and Aunt Lorna tipped her head back. "I hope one of those lights doesn't fall on us." She took a step, still looking up, and nearly ran into a man carrying a ladder. "I beg your pardon!" she cried, pressing a hand to her chest, but the man didn't hear, already several strides away. "I'm afraid I'm in the way. Would they mind if I took one of those chairs?"

Kate glanced at the four chairs where actors were having their noses powdered. "Those are for hair and makeup. You can sit on the step of Bonnie's wardrobe trailer, if you want."

Aunt Lorna looked at the step with a dubious frown. "I don't understand why they don't have more places for people to sit."

"Because we don't sit. Everyone has a job to do."

"I see." But Kate doubted she did. Aunt Lorna had never worked a day in her life—raised in wealth and then married to a wealthy man. When Uncle Harvey had died, her income had stopped, but she hadn't gone to work; she'd spent her way into bankruptcy and then found another rich husband. "If I'd known there wouldn't be chairs, I would have worn lower heels." A subtle hint that Kate had failed in her duties as hostess. "I suppose comfortable feet are the reason you're dressed that way. But really, Kate—slacks and loafers? This isn't a sporting event."

Kate bit back a response, knowing it was pointless. Aunt Lorna considered herself the foremost authority on appropriate dress. "Make yourself as comfortable as you can, and I'll be back later."

"Is there some sort of food service? I wouldn't mind a—"

Kate hurried away.

Bonnie stood on the far side of the sound truck, her chin

raised as the wardrobe manager, Mei Chen, reached down her neckline to insert a discreet safety pin between two buttons.

"Stop chewing your fingernails," Mei scolded, her face close to Bonnie's chest.

Bonnie lowered her hand. "I hope I don't flub the second verse like I always do."

"That's why the songs are prerecorded," Kate said, stopping beside them. "So you can focus on your performance." She added, "So you and Aurelio can focus on each other while you're singing."

Bonnie's gaze shifted to Aurelio, who had his back turned as he talked to the choreographer. "Does he know I didn't want him to leave the party last night, it was only Mama?"

"He knows."

"Then why won't he even look at me?"

"Because he doesn't want to cause trouble with Tad, I'm guessing." Kate glanced over her shoulder and saw Mrs. Fairchild at the coffee cart. "Plus, your mother is here." Mrs. Fairchild had driven in with Bonnie and remained close all morning, keeping an eye on her daughter's career.

"Hello, everyone!" Glenn called cheerfully, coming around the sound truck.

Kate muttered, "You have *got* to be kidding me," which earned a short laugh from Mei as she worked on the safety pin.

"Glenn, what are you doing here?" Bonnie asked. "I don't have tutoring on Saturdays."

"Didn't want to miss all the fun." He smiled at Kate. "I brought my books and found a quiet place to study in Stage Five. No one in there today. Maybe you can join me on your lunch break and we can go over calculus."

"I doubt it, Glenn, it's a pretty busy day, but thank you."

"Well, I'll be in Stage Five if you change your mind. I'll check back with you later."

"Places, everyone!" the assistant director called through a megaphone, and the noisy chaos immediately settled down, actors hurrying toward the ice cream parlor. Some sat at the tables, two moved behind the counter, and one picked up a tray of fake ice cream sundaes.

"Almost done," Mei said, her face close to the safety pin.

Mrs. Fairchild returned with her cup of coffee. "Kate, who was that woman I saw you with?" She took a sip, leaving a stain of red lipstick.

"My aunt Lorna. She arrived last night."

Mrs. Fairchild's lovely eyes widened. "Your father's sister? What's she doing here?"

Kate hesitated, knowing she should tell Tad first. "She found out about the murder and wants to take me home."

"You're not leaving?" Bonnie cried.

"Oh, Kate." Mrs. Fairchild placed a hand on her arm. "I thought you were going to live with Ollie now. I wanted the two of you to come to dinner next week."

"Done," Mei declared, giving the front of Bonnie's blouse a final smoothing.

"Bunny rabbit!" Tad shouted from twenty feet away. "Bert's ready! You're holding things up!"

Bonnie looked at Kate, a bold question in her eyes.

Kate shrugged. "Now or never, I guess."

Bonnie inhaled with a shaky smile and turned to face him. "Don't call me bunny rabbit!"

He didn't seem to hear, talking to the director.

"Don't be difficult, darling," Mrs. Fairchild said, giving her daughter a nudge. "Go on."

But Bonnie didn't move, her fists clenched at her sides, her cheeks flushing a splotchy red. She lifted her chin. "I said . . . *don't call me bunny rabbit!* I am not an animal! Call me by my name!"

Heads turned.

"Bonnie," Mrs. Fairchild scolded, appalled.

Tad turned slowly, glanced at the watching crowd, then said

with strained patience, *"Miss Fairchild . . .* would you be so good as to grace us with your presence so we can begin filming?"

Bonnie smiled pertly. "Yes, I'd be happy to." She strode over, with her mother beside her, hissing in her ear.

As the director walked Bonnie and Aurelio through the scene, Tad sidled up to Kate. "I take it you're the one who put her up to that."

Kate kept her eyes on the ice cream parlor. "You demean her when you call her fluffy little names."

"The nickname fits. Hopping around like she doesn't know where she is half the time. Nothing but fluff between the ears."

She kept her voice low. "Smart enough not to stay in a bungalow alone with you."

His head turned sharply. "What did she tell you?"

"Enough to know you're the animal here, preying on a fifteen-year-old girl."

"How dare you judge me."

"Not judging, Tad, just good advice. That's what you pay me for. And here's some more: Treat people with respect and they'll give you the same. *That's* how you convince them you're not just riding your father's coattails."

"Lights!" the assistant director called, and the room darkened, except for those on the ice cream parlor.

Tad glared at her a moment longer, then walked away to stand near the camera.

"Camera rolling!" the assistant director called. "Action!"

Immediately, the actors turned into characters, smiling over banana splits, a man wiping a glass behind the counter. Bonnie sat at a table with friends, swapping lines. Kate couldn't hear the words but had watched enough rehearsals to spot the mistakes: Bonnie forgetting to sip from her soda, causing an awkward pause before her next line; not taking the theater ticket her friend handed her.

As Bonnie left the table, looking glum because the town's theater was closing, Aurelio entered the ice cream parlor. She dropped her sweater, and when Aurelio bent to pick it up, they bumped heads. They both straightened with a laugh, in what was supposed to be a cute first meeting, but Bonnie looked nervous, her face still flushed from confronting Tad.

"Cut," the director called. He approached and gave her a little pep talk, patted her shoulder, and returned to sit next to the camera.

"Come on, girl," Mei muttered, watching beside Kate. "Shake off the nerves."

Aurelio said something close to Bonnie's ear and squeezed her hand, and it was like a light turned on inside her. They exchanged a warm, personal smile, their gazes holding, then returned to their starting places.

"Action!"

This time, Bonnie moved through the scene with ease, interacting naturally with the other teenagers. She left the table, dropped her sweater, and laughed sweetly after bumping heads with Aurelio. The moment felt real, their smiles shy but hopeful. They left the ice cream parlor together and strolled along the sidewalk, into the soft lighting of streetlamps.

Bonnie started singing, and the sound team started the voice recording on cue, her voice filling the building, surprisingly rich and heartfelt for such a young, petite girl. Aurelio joined in on the chorus. His voice wasn't as exceptional as his dancing but provided a nice background to Bonnie's. He looked comfortable and happy with the camera rolling—like himself—and Kate was glad he hadn't learned the fake accent well enough to use after all.

Pretended not to learn it, she suspected, forcing publicity to quickly scratch the exotic backstory of him being discovered in Mexico as he drove a donkey cart.

"Now *that's* electricity," Mei murmured near Kate's ear. "They're going to light up those movie screens."

But Kate wouldn't be here helping it happen, only watching in theaters like everyone else.

"Cut!" The voice recording stopped abruptly. Bonnie listened to the director, and then trotted toward Kate and Mei. "The close-up shows red lipstick on my collar."

"No doubt your mother's shade," Mei muttered. "Come into the trailer. We've got the backup dress."

As they approached the wardrobe trailer, Kate spotted Aunt Lorna talking to someone near the coffee cart, probably complaining that her favorite brand of tea wasn't there.

"How did it look?" Bonnie asked breathlessly.

"Amazing," Kate said. She followed them into the trailer and shut the door behind her.

"It's so much fun when it's for real and—" Bonnie's blue eyes widened, staring behind Kate. "My scarf! What's it doing here? I thought Aurelio lost it."

Kate spun to see the black-and-white polka-dotted scarf hanging from a hook by the door. She frowned, knowing that was impossible. Hugo had taken the scarf to the pool house for safekeeping. Even if everything he'd said was a lie, he had no way of getting the scarf into Bonnie's trailer—and why would he?

"We found it in the wardrobe department a few days ago," Mei said, pulling a dress off a hanger. "I kept forgetting to give it to you."

"I'm so glad," Bonnie said. "Aurelio felt terrible."

Kate took the scarf off the hook and stared at it, thinking back to where it had been: Bonnie wearing it, Aurelio putting it in his pocket, Hugo sneaking it from Aurelio to plant as false evidence, Hugo pretending to find it in the office to divert suspicion from himself.

And yet, here it was.

Or was it? Kate ran her hands over the silk fabric and realized the polka dots were bigger, and it didn't have a chain design around the border. The same Chanel label, but not the same scarf

Hugo had picked up in Ollie's office. "Bonnie, this isn't yours. The polka dots are too big."

Bonnie glanced up as she stepped into the new dress. "That's mine. It's my favorite."

"It's hers," Mei said. "I've seen her wearing it enough times. Felix found it in one of the men's dressing rooms."

"Aurelio must have lost it there," Bonnie said, sliding her arms into the sleeves. "Kate, will you put it in my car before I lose it again?"

"Sure," Kate said faintly.

She left the trailer and walked toward the outer door, looking down at the scarf, trying to make sense of it. If this was Bonnie's scarf—put in Aurelio's pocket and dropped in the wardrobe department—the one they'd found in Ollie's office *wasn't*.

"Weather finally cooling down," the man stationed at the door observed. He had the job of bolting and unbolting the door whenever filming stopped and started to prevent disruptions.

"Yes," Kate murmured. The fresh air felt good. She spotted Bonnie's yellow car at the deep end of the alley and walked that way, circling the back end of a car that was parking.

The only reason she'd thought the scarf had something to do with Lemmy's murder was because she'd thought it was Bonnie's. But it had probably been in Ollie's office for years, unrelated to the murder, just part of an old costume. Or maybe dropped by Stella Nixon on one of her visits.

Hugo didn't plant it.

She gave a little laugh of relief, wondering what else she'd gotten wrong. She'd overheard one conversation and jumped to conclusions, without giving Hugo a chance to explain. He'd stolen from Mrs. Fairchild, yes, but to help his friend. Stealing was wrong but a far cry from murder.

She walked faster toward the yellow car, overcome by a desperate need to talk to him. Hating how things had ended last night. She could call him on the phone. Or better still, sneak away from the studio and drive home. She hastily returned the scarf to the glovebox, shut the door, and looked up—

To see Hugo getting out of the car that had just parked.

Kate stared in amazement. He'd come to see her, as eager to set things right as she was. "Hugo!" she called, hurrying toward him.

His head snapped around, his eyes widening in alarm at the sight of Kate—not glad to see her.

Her heart slipped a little. "What are you doing here?"

Hugo cast an anxious glance at the otherwise deserted alley. "I can't talk right now." He walked around the back of his car to the passenger side, and she realized he was wearing a white jacket for some reason. Up to something, obviously.

Her heart tumbled the rest of the way. "How did you get past the guard at the gate?"

Hugo opened the front passenger door and pointed to a tray of sandwiches on the seat. "Catering costume. I gave him a sandwich."

A lot of effort to sneak into Falcon Pictures. Her voice chilled. "I overheard you talking to Reuben last night. Did the two of you—"

"Kate—I can't talk right now, but I'll find you later. Pretend you didn't see me. Pretend you didn't see this." Hugo leaned into the car, reached into the glovebox, and straightened with a gun in his hand. He stuck it into his back waistband and pulled the white jacket over it.

"Hugo! What are you doing?"

"Just a precaution. Keep your distance, and I'll explain later." His eyes met hers, burning with their usual fire, lighting a matching flame inside her—despite everything. "Kate, I know who killed Lemmy."

"What?" She'd thought Hugo was the killer—until she'd seen Bonnie's scarf—and now he had a gun. "Hugo, please—whatever you're doing—whatever you've done—"

He placed a hand on her cheek. "Wait here so I can find you. Trust me, Kate." He kissed her, his lips warm and already familiar, then pulled back with a fleeting smile. He lifted the tray of sandwiches and hurried toward Stage Six.

Kate stood frozen, still feeling his kiss, watching as the man at the door allowed Hugo to enter with his white catering coat and tray of sandwiches.

And gun.

Kate groaned and hurried after him.

She halted inside the door, momentarily blinded by the darker interior. Her eyes adjusted, and she saw Hugo's tray of sandwiches on a nearby table—no longer needed to trick the guard, his hands now free to hold a gun. She whirled, searching, and found him skulking along the outer edge of the interior, his eyes scanning the cast and crew, seeming to look for someone.

She started after him.

"There you are!" Mei grabbed her arm. "Drive over to the wardrobe building and tell Felix we need those extra shoes after all. I called, but no one picks up."

"I can't—I'm sorry." Kate pulled free and hurried after Hugo, halting a few steps later when she saw Aunt Lorna ahead. Kate veered to avoid her, hurried around a cluster of actors, and spotted Hugo disappearing behind the sound truck. She broke into a trot, but by the time she'd rounded the truck, he wasn't there.

She turned, her eyes darting.

Why did he come here? If he knew who killed Lemmy, why not call the police? Why sneak into Falcon Pictures with a gun? To seek his own justice? He hadn't even liked Lemmy.

Whatever he planned couldn't be good.

"Places!" the assistant director called through the megaphone, and Bonnie and Aurelio returned to their marks near a lamppost, ready to sing again with Bonnie wearing her new backup dress.

The building was about to darken. Kate turned, her heart

thumping, and saw a telephone on the wall. She should call the police. Or at least shout a warning.

Trust me, Kate.

Her fingers touched her lips. She didn't want to call the police on Hugo. She wanted to talk to him and hear a reasonable explanation.

She wished he hadn't kissed her.

A white jacket caught her attention near the outer wall, and she hurried toward it, only to find the actor who worked behind the ice cream counter—and it occurred to her that Hugo might have removed his jacket to blend in.

"Lights!" The room darkened, except for the soft glow of streetlights around Bonnie and Aurelio, which meant the door had just locked for filming. Which meant Hugo couldn't leave the building. "Camera rolling!"

Kate moved as quickly as she dared, sticking close to the outer wall so she didn't disrupt the filming now underway, her gaze skimming. She stepped carefully over cables and detoured to look around large equipment. At this rate, it would take ten minutes to walk the perimeter of the enormous building. She circled behind the set, where it was darker, her heart racing.

Bonnie's singing filled the air, soon joined by Aurelio's, and the romantic lyrics heightened Kate's resolve to find Hugo. He deserved a chance to explain himself, and she deserved an explanation.

She heard footsteps and spun around, but it was only two cast members—a boy and a girl, stifling giggles as they disappeared behind a truck.

The music stopped for a moment, then started up again at the beginning.

She passed the halfway point and walked faster. Hugo wouldn't be here behind the set; he was looking for someone. But who?

As she reached the populated end of the building again, the lights flared on, making her squint. "One hour lunch!" The building erupted in noise and movement, everyone flowing toward the now-open doors. Kate ran to a ladder and quickly climbed, turn-ing her head to search the moving throng, but Hugo wasn't there. Maybe he'd been the first person out the door. Or maybe he'd left before the doors were locked. He may have even driven away.

She descended the ladder and made her way out to the alley. Hugo's car was still there—Reuben's car, she guessed. She hurried to it and looked in the windows, then turned and scanned the al-ley, sighing in frustration. "Hugo, where are you?" she muttered.

She forced herself to think logically.

He'd come here with a purpose, because he knew who killed Lemmy. The gun was a precaution, he'd said—probably Reuben's gun. He wouldn't want to confront a killer in crowded Stage Six, where the lights went out at a moment's notice, and he had to be silent, and the doors were locked. He would find the killer and suggest they go somewhere private.

Her gaze landed on the door to Stage Five, across the al-ley, where the theater set had been rebuilt. She hurried to it and stepped inside, then paused to let her eyes adjust.

The vast space seemed deserted, only a single light at the far end, casting ominous shadows over the old theater set. Kate walked tentatively closer, her heart racing, her footsteps the only sound.

"Hugo?" Her voice echoed.

Someone sat in the front row of the audience seats—the sil-houette of a man or older boy. "Hugo?" He didn't move, and a new dread filled her. She walked faster, hurrying down the center aisle of audience seats, her eyes riveted on the dark silhouette. "Hugo, is that you?" She rounded the front corner in front of the orchestra pit.

And halted with a yelp.

It wasn't Hugo.

Bonnie's tutor, Glenn Petersen, sat in the middle of the front row, his head tilted slightly, his eyes staring at nothing, with a bullet hole in his temple leaking a stream of red.

CHAPTER 30

The cast and crew stood in a hushed semicircle at the opening to the alley, kept back from the crime scene by the police. One by one, they were being questioned by a couple of young officers and told they could leave. But no one did. The crowd only grew.

Kate, on the other hand, had been ordered to stay until the police were done with her.

She stood against the outside wall of Stage Six, along with the other key members of the production team, including Tad, the director, the cameraman, and Mei. They watched from a distance as the police searched the cars in the alley and roamed in and out of the surrounding soundstages.

Searching for a boy named Hugo Quick.

Kate had told the police everything. How Hugo had snuck through the studio gates in a white catering jacket. How he'd tucked a gun into his waistband and disappeared in Stage Six. What he'd said about knowing the identity of Lemmy's killer.

When she'd mentioned Lemmy Berman's murder, the Pasadena Police Department had been contacted, and Detective Bassett had arrived a half hour later. Kate had been worried he would arrest her on the spot—he already suspected her, and now she'd found a second murder victim—but he'd acted sympathetic as he'd interviewed her, even patting her arm. "Don't worry, we'll catch him. They make our job easier when they kill twice." He'd left her and entered Stage Five to inspect Glenn's body.

"I don't see why you've been ordered to stay," Aunt Lorna complained, standing next to Kate. "You had nothing to do with it."

"I found the body, Aunt Lorna, and I saw Hugo with the gun."

"Who is this Hugo?"

There were too many ways to answer that question. "One of Ollie's boarders" was all she said.

"Of course," Aunt Lorna said dryly.

"It's all so strange," Mrs. Fairchild murmured, standing on Kate's other side. She looked pale and horrified, her fingers pressed to her red lips. "Why would that boy kill Bonnie's tutor? Did they even know each other?"

"They met last night," Kate said. She didn't answer the first question about motive. Glenn had caught Hugo stealing at the party, but she didn't think that's why he'd been killed. More likely, Glenn had stumbled across Hugo with the gun. Whatever Hugo had been doing here—stealing something or stalking someone— Glenn had seen and been silenced.

And it was her fault. If she'd sounded a warning about the gun, Glenn would still be alive. But Hugo had known exactly what to say to make her stay quiet, turning himself into a hero instead of a villain: *I know who killed Lemmy.* And then he'd kissed her.

She hated that part of her still hoped he was innocent, somehow.

A few yards away, Tad argued with a police officer over how long it would take before they could resume filming in Stage Six. "Nothing happened in there. You've searched the place. Why can't we go back to work?"

"The investigation has barely started."

"Barely started? How long is this going to take? You see all these people standing around here—they cost money! Every minute we're not filming is more than you make in a month!"

"Glenn was his friend," Bonnie said in a whimpering voice, standing on Mrs. Fairchild's other side, "and he doesn't even care." She'd finally stopped crying. She held a cluster of handkerchiefs, since practically everyone had given her one. Aurelio had comforted her for a while until her mother had taken his place, ordering him away with a pointed look.

Now, Aurelio paced like a caged tiger as he watched the police, his arms folded, his expression fierce. He caught Kate's eye and summoned her closer with a jerk of his head.

"Are you sure it was Hugo you saw?" he asked her in a low voice.

"Of course I'm sure. We spoke to each other." *He kissed me.*

"And he said he knows who killed Lemmy? Did he say who it was?"

"No." She hesitated. "Because he made it up. Hugo is the one who killed Lemmy. I overheard him talking to Reuben last night."

Aurelio shot her a look. "That's crazy. Why would Hugo kill Lemmy?"

She couldn't tell him about Ollie's loan. "I can't say, but there was a reason."

"I don't believe it. Hugo wouldn't do that—and he wouldn't do *that*!" He pointed an angry finger at Stage Five. Aurelio had seen Glenn's body before the police had arrived and closed off the building.

"Then where is Hugo now?" Kate asked, hoping for a good answer. "Why hasn't he shown up, wondering what's going on? Or shown up to explain to the police who did this? Why is he hiding right now if he didn't kill Glenn?"

He scowled. "I don't know. Maybe he got shot too. Maybe he's lying somewhere, bleeding."

"Aurelio . . ." Kate swallowed, trying not to picture Hugo lying dead somewhere. "Hugo was the one with the gun."

"If he came here with a gun, he had a good reason, and it wasn't to shoot Bonnie's tutor."

Kate looked down the alley to the car Hugo had driven—still here, which meant *he* was still here. But where?

The crowd at the opening to the alley shifted and separated, allowing one of the motorized carts through, driven by Mr. Eckles with Clive Falcon at his side. Mr. Falcon stepped off the vehicle before it had even stopped moving and strode toward Tad.

"Goodness," Aunt Lorna murmured, looking impressed. "Who is that?"

"Dad." Tad didn't look happy to see him.

"They catch the loony who did this?"

"They're looking for him now. Everything is under control. We'll resume filming soon."

The police officer standing next to Tad said, "Not until we've completed our search. These are big buildings."

"How many men have you got down here?" Mr. Falcon demanded. "Do I need to call the police commissioner? The mayor?"

A sudden flurry of activity erupted from Stage Six, and an officer trotted across the alley. A moment later, Detective Bassett emerged from Stage Five and hurried to Six.

The officer who'd run across the alley called out, "Which of you knows about the wardrobe trailers?" Mei raised a hand and was led away, and a moment later, the same police officer returned and approached Kate. "Excuse me, Miss Hildebrand, can you come with me, please?"

"This has gone on long enough," Aunt Lorna protested, taking ahold of Kate's hand. "My niece has suffered a terrible shock. I'm taking her to our hotel now, and if you have any more questions, you can find us there."

"I'm fine, Aunt Lorna."

Her aunt whispered near her ear. "There will be reporters here soon, taking pictures of you at a murder scene. Our family name on the front page again."

Kate yanked her hand free. "You think I care about that right now?"

The police officer said with strained politeness, "I'm afraid I must insist that Miss Hildebrand come with me."

"Take a taxi to the hotel, Aunt Lorna." Kate followed the police officer into Stage Six.

He led her across the dim interior toward Aurelio's wardrobe trailer, passing Mei along the way. "He's the only one who uses that trailer," she overheard Mei tell another police officer.

As they neared Aurelio's trailer, Kate heard the pop of a camera flashbulb inside. "Go on in," the officer who'd escorted her said. "Not room for all of us."

She stepped up into the small trailer and found Detective Bassett and a police photographer staring down at a row of open shoeboxes on the floor. The camera took another photo, and the flash spotlighted a black handgun inside one of the boxes.

"Is this the kind of gun you saw Mr. Quick carrying?" Detective Bassett asked her. "We'll match the bullet, but it's helpful to know at the moment."

Kate stared down, trying to make sense of it. "I . . . I think so. I only got a glimpse. But what's it doing in Aurelio's wardrobe trailer?"

"Looks like someone didn't want it to be found. Smells like it was fired recently."

Hugo must have hidden it here. There'd been a lot of confusion after she'd found Glenn and called for help, the entire cast and crew in a stir. Hugo could have slipped in here easily, hidden the gun, and then disappeared. But why hide it in Aurelio's trailer? To make him look guilty? Kate couldn't imagine Hugo doing that. He'd probably hoped to retrieve it later.

The other detective called through the trailer door, "The Mexican boy says he doesn't know anything about it."

"Of course he doesn't," Kate snapped. "Aurelio had a camera on him when it happened. He had nothing to do with this."

"That's all for now, Miss Hildebrand," Detective Bassett said. "But don't go far."

She left the building and found Aurelio being questioned by another detective in a suit. He looked startled and pale, talking fast, his hands moving. Kate glanced around and was relieved to see Aunt Lorna was gone, not witnessing another one of Ollie's boarders in trouble with the police.

Bonnie pulled free of her mother's hold and ran to him. "Aurelio, what's happening?"

Aurelio told the detective in a frantic voice, "I was only in jail for one night, and it wasn't even my fault. That guy hit me first."

"Come away, dear," Mrs. Fairchild urged, pulling at Bonnie's shoulders.

Clive Falcon put his hands on his hips. "Tad, I thought that boy was the star of your show."

"He is." Tad tried to approach Aurelio but was blocked by a uniformed officer. He called out, "He couldn't have done it! He was on set!"

"Do you know how much this delay is costing me?" his father demanded.

"Let's take him down to the station," the detective standing next to Aurelio said to the uniformed officer. "Away from this circus."

Aurelio stepped back with raised hands, looking panicked. "I didn't do anything!"

"We can do this nice, or we can put you in handcuffs," the officer said.

Bonnie squealed, reaching out, as her mother held her back.

"You can't take him *now*!" Tad cried. "We're in the middle of a shoot!"

"Oh, I think you can stop worrying about that," Clive Falcon barked. "This picture is shut down for good."

Tad whirled to face his father. "They're just questioning him! We'll be filming again in a few hours!"

"You weren't ready for this, Tad. I should have stopped it last week. I gave you a second chance and a third, but that's it—I'm pulling the plug on this disaster of a movie." He strode back toward the cart, where Mr. Eckles waited.

"Dad!" Tad hurried after him.

Kate felt ill, watching it all. None of this would have happened if she'd turned in the bloody sword the night she'd found it and told the police about Hugo hiding it. He would have been taken in for questioning. His fingerprints found on the murder weapon. He would have been behind bars, and Glenn Petersen would still be alive.

She saw Detective Bassett emerging from Stage Six and walked toward him.

He saw her face and gave her his full attention. "What is it?"

Kate spoke in a low voice, for him only, but clearly enough that there could be no misunderstanding. "Lemmy Berman was killed by Captain Powell's sword. Hugo Quick hid it in the laundry room, and I found it the next day. I should have given it to you, but I didn't. And right now, it's hidden in my trunk in my grandfather's attic."

CHAPTER 31

Kate drove home alone in her borrowed Buick. Her job at Falcon Pictures had ended, which meant she probably shouldn't have taken the car, but she was halfway home before that dawned on her. She would have to return it later with Aunt Lorna, on their way to the train station.

She drove slowly, in no hurry to tell Ollie what was happening.

She'd overheard Detective Bassett as he'd radioed the Pasadena Police Department and told them to search Oliver Banks's attic for a sword. He'd been furious at her for hiding it but hadn't seemed to suspect her of murder. The fact that she'd volunteered the information was in her favor, and when she'd explained her reason—to avoid bad press for her grandfather—Detective Bassett had seemed to believe her. She'd added, for good measure, "I know a thing or two about bad press," which had earned her another sympathetic pat on the arm.

Sometimes being Kitty Hildebrand had its benefits.

As she drove up to Ollie's house, she saw a police car leaving—probably with the sword.

She found Ollie alone in the living room, pacing, muttering

to himself. He stopped when he saw her, looking like a frightened child. "Kate, what is happening? The police said they found my sword in your trunk, and it's covered in blood."

All the tension inside her softened at the sight of him. "I can explain."

"Did you kill Lemmy? Did he attack you or something? I don't blame you if he—"

"No! I hid it to protect you, so the press wouldn't know he was killed with your sword. I never used it. I found it in the laundry room."

"Laundry room?" He shook his head, befuddled. "What was it doing there?"

"Hugo hid it. To protect you, he said, but I think he was protecting himself. Let's sit down and I'll explain." She moved to the green velvet sofa.

Ollie followed but didn't sit, standing over her. "The police said a boy was killed at the studio today, and everyone thinks Hugo did it. Why would they think that?"

"Because he was there with a gun. I think it had something to do with—" There was no easy way to say it. "Ollie . . . Hugo killed Lemmy."

"No." Ollie sank to the sofa beside her. "That's ridiculous. Why would Hugo kill Lemmy?"

She debated telling him about Reuben erasing his loan. Maybe he deserved to know, but if he ever returned to the outside world, he might run into Moe Kravitz and say the wrong thing. Forget the details and thank his old friend for forgiving his debt. And the one thing Kate knew for sure, in all this madness, was that she didn't want Ollie to lose his home to that mobster.

Which meant she couldn't explain Hugo's motive. "I overheard him talking to Reuben last night." She glanced at the foyer. "Where is Reuben?" She could ask him about it.

"Out looking for Hugo. The police said he's missing, so Reuben took a taxi to Hugo's parents' house to see if he's there. I wanted to go with him. I did try." Ollie was dressed, she realized, wearing a shirt and pants that were too tight. "But I couldn't force myself—" His voice broke. He leaned forward, grabbing his head with his hands. "Where is Hugo?"

Emotion swelled inside her, bringing an unwelcome need to cry. She resisted, placing a hand on her grandfather's back. "I don't know. I feel like I don't know anything."

He asked in a hollow voice, "Are the police going to arrest him?"

She hesitated. "I think so."

"Hugo wouldn't kill anyone."

"I heard him talking about it last night, and I saw him holding a gun at Falcon Pictures."

"He didn't do it!" Ollie abruptly stood and stalked away. "If he had a gun, he had a good reason." He turned to face her, his arms spread. "I know my boy!"

Kate shot to her feet, something snapping inside her. "And I knew my father, but it was all a lie! You never know what people are really like! You only see the side they show you!"

"Hugo is nothing like your father!" Ollie walked around the wingback chair, his hands on his hips. "*Johnson Hildebrand.* Never just John—oh, no, he wanted the whole fancy name. So smug and superior as he robbed people blind."

"I know my father was a bad person! That's what I'm trying to tell you! People put on an act, and I can't see through it! That's why I like science—facts I can trust! But then Hugo—and this place—and I was fooled all over again! I can't live here, Ollie!"

He whirled to face her. "Hugo wasn't fooling you!"

"He *murdered* two people!"

Ollie paced again, growling under his breath. "I should have paid better attention this morning. He was upset, but I thought it was because you're leaving. He kept asking about the frog and the photo, and I should have asked why."

The fire inside Kate instantly cooled, like a hot stove turned off. "He told you about the gold frog?"

"No—I told him. He asked if I gave it to Mrs. Fairchild, and I said yes, a long time ago, and he said no, I mean recently, and I said of course not, I haven't seen her in ages. I didn't understand why he was so interested."

Kate stood perfectly still, her heart suddenly racing. "Ollie, tell me about that gold frog."

"It was just a silly gift."

"A long time ago?"

"Catalina Island." He sighed and turned to face her. "Frank slept in because he'd been out all night, so Dorothy and I spent the day together. She was upset about Frank, and I wanted to lift her spirits. When she took a fancy to this little gold frog with red eyes in a jewelry store, I snuck back later and bought it. I gave it to her for her birthday a few weeks later. She cried when she opened it, which made Frank suspicious, and everything was awkward after that. One of the ruby eyes had fallen out somehow, so I brought it home so I could get it fixed. But I stopped leaving the house and never got around to it."

A gold frog missing one eye, making it easy to recognize. "Ollie . . . where has that frog been for the last few years?"

"On my desk. I use it as a paperweight. I forgot it was hers, to be honest, I'm so used to seeing it there. But Hugo and I looked this morning, and it's gone."

Because Hugo had put it in his pocket. He'd been waiting for Kate in the study, seen the frog on Mrs. Fairchild's desk, and known at once it should be on Ollie's desk. He'd taken it because it was a clue—*I'm not stealing*—but hadn't told her because she'd so clearly sided with Glenn.

"Ollie, can you think of a reason—any reason at all—for that frog to be in the Fairchilds' house last night?"

"No. That's what Hugo asked. And he wanted to know about the photo."

"Photo?" The one Hugo had put in his pocket.

Ollie waved a vague hand. "This old picture of Frank and me

at our oil wells. It belongs in my office, beneath the sword he gave me, but Hugo and I looked for it this morning, and the frame is empty." His forehead creased. "Kate, what's going on?"

She wasn't sure, but she was going to find out. "Ollie, we're going to the pool house." She hurried through the house and out the back door. Halfway across the patio, she glanced back.

Ollie stood frozen in the doorway. "I don't usually go outside during the day."

Kate continued without him—then sighed and walked back. She passed him, entered his office, grabbed Captain Powell's hat, and returned to place it on his head. "Let's go, Captain. Hugo needs us." She strode away, not daring to look back.

She stopped inside the pool house door, her gaze skimming the small, tidy room with an attached bathroom. A bed, a desk with a black typewriter, a bookcase, more books stacked on the floor, more books on the nightstand.

Also on the nightstand: the gold frog, photograph, and over-stuffed envelope.

Kate picked up the frog first and found it surprisingly heavy. Carved gold, with one ruby eye and an empty dip where one eye was missing. A fancy paperweight to most people, but not Mrs. Fairchild, who'd cried when she'd opened it. To her, it was a sym-bol of Ollie's friendship and love. Dorothy Fairchild was the only person who would pick it out, amongst all the other knickknacks in Ollie's office, as the one treasure to take home.

Kate put down the frog and picked up the photo. A younger Ollie and Frank Fairchild stood at the side of a road with land be-hind them, both grinning, their thumbs pointing over their out-side shoulders—Ollie pointing to the left side of the photo, Frank the right. The shrubby land behind them was divided down the middle by a fence, with several tall, wooden oil derricks on both sides, some of the pointed tops out of view. The ground was lit-tered with heavy pipes and equipment.

Ollie entered, wearing Captain Powell's hat.

"Tell me about this photo," Kate said.

He peered over her shoulder. "That's our land on Signal Hill. The whole area was sprouting oil, everyone buying up lots as fast as they could, tearing down houses so they could drill. It was terribly exciting."

Hugo had found the photo on Mrs. Fairchild's desk, out of its frame—another item he knew didn't belong there.

Kate picked up the overstuffed envelope and pulled out folded papers. The top page was a typed letter from Jensen Julander & Veit, Attorneys at Law. She read aloud, "Enclosed you will find your revised will with the change you requested, leaving the property known as 1640 Rowland Drive, Long Beach, California, to Mr. Oliver Banks. As we discussed on the telephone on Monday, I will arrange for a notary—"

Kate's gaze darted up to the date, October 12, 1938, which had been Wednesday. On Monday, the day Lemmy was murdered, Dorothy Fairchild had called her attorney to change her will, leaving a house to Ollie.

"Ollie, what is this house in Long Beach she's leaving you?"

He shook his head. "I have no idea. I doubt I'll outlive her—I'm nine years older—but I'm touched she would do such a thing."

Kate snatched up the photograph again, focusing on a small house in the far distance on Frank's side of the photo, behind the oil derricks. "Do you think that's it?"

Ollie considered it and shook his head. "No, that land didn't belong to Frank. The man who owned it wouldn't sell. Kept living there with derricks all around. I bought several lots in a row, but Frank's property had to jog around that man's. Drove him crazy."

Kate put down the will and picked up the frog and photo, one in each hand. "Mrs. Fairchild took these things from your office, Ollie, and the only day she could have been there was when Lemmy died. She saw us get in Bonnie's car and knew the house was empty."

"Why in the world would she come to my house?"

"I'm not sure," Kate said slowly. "Maybe to get the frog, which was rightfully hers. Or maybe . . romantic nostalgia, being in your house again. But Lemmy came home and caught her."

Ollie gave a startled laugh. "You're not thinking Dorothy killed him? She would have been embarrassed if he caught her snooping, but she wouldn't kill him over it."

"No," Kate agreed, frowning. "But she *was* in your office that day—these items prove it—and she changed her will right after, leaving you a house in Long Beach."

"That must be why Hugo drove to Long Beach after the party last night. He told me this morning. I should have asked why."

Kate's heart beat faster. Hugo had driven to Long Beach in the middle of the night to find answers—by himself, because Kate had turned against him. He'd learned something there and then snuck into Falcon Pictures with a gun. He'd told Kate he knew who the killer was—probably Mrs. Fairchild, although Kate had a hard time believing that.

Somehow, Glenn had ended up dead, and the police thought Hugo was the killer—because Kate had told them he was.

"Ollie, we have to find Hugo. We have to—" Panic gripped her. "I don't know what to do."

"Maybe we should call that detective."

"He isn't going to believe me. I told him Hugo hid the sword, and he isn't going to understand about some stupid frog. Mrs. Fairchild didn't even steal it—it belongs to her."

"Let's go to the studio and search for him."

"That place is enormous and swarming with police. If Hugo is there, they'll find him. No, what we need is proof of his innocence when they arrest him. Come on." Kate gathered the frog, photo, and lawyer's paperwork and left the pool house, crossing the patio.

Ollie trotted after her. "Where are we going?"

"Long Beach. We have to follow Hugo's trail."

"But it's nearly an hour away."

Kate's mind raced as she entered the house. She could go next door and confront Mrs. Fairchild, but that would only alert her to their suspicions. What they needed was information—the same information Hugo had acquired last night.

She should have trusted him.

Kate grabbed her purse off the foyer table and hurried out the front door.

"Wait!" Ollie cried behind her.

She turned, exasperated. She would have to leave him behind.

But he'd only paused to take off the sea captain's hat and toss it on the foyer table. He hurried out, pulling the front door closed behind him, and passed Kate on the walkway. "I am not Captain Powell! I am Ollie Banks, and I am off to save my boy!"

CHAPTER 32

"That used to be a Chinese restaurant," Ollie observed, watching the town roll by from the passenger seat. He cracked a peanut shell, tossed the peanut in his mouth, and dropped the shell in an empty shopping bag.

Kate had stopped for gas. While the attendant had filled the tank and washed the windows of the borrowed Buick, she'd run into a neighboring grocery store for car snacks, sodas, and a couple of maps. On one map, she'd seen that State Route 15 was the best way to get to Long Beach; on the other, she'd seen a closer view of the street address in Long Beach. Ollie had been right; it would take close to an hour to get there.

Kate glanced at her watch as she drove and saw 2:40. Hugo had been missing for close to three hours.

As she drove, her mind sifted through everything she knew, trying to fit the pieces together.

The scarf had probably been dropped by Mrs. Fairchild. She'd bought Bonnie's scarf in Paris, and a similar scarf for herself, with smaller polka dots and a chain border. She'd used the scarf to cover up her distinctive platinum blond hair, in case a

neighbor glanced out their window, and left it behind by accident.

They'd been too preoccupied getting Ollie out of the house
that morning to lock the front door.

"Ollie, when we went to auditions, how long did you stay in
Bonnie's car before you left for the bus? Bonnie and Tad took the
car for a short drive, but someone else moved the car before that.
I don't suppose you know who that was?"

"It was me."

Kate jerked her head to look at him. "*You?*"

He cracked a peanut shell. "I was a bit grumpy after you all
left. I decided to drive home and got the key out of the glovebox.
But driving terrified me, and I never made it off the studio lot. I
never drove much in the old days, and all the pedals felt different.
I came back and parked at the back, so I didn't hit any cars."

Kate laughed dryly. "I thought someone in our group drove
home, murdered Lemmy, and came back."

"You thought *Hugo* did that," Ollie said in a tone of chastise-
ment.

"I overheard a few things and thought the worst." She
squeezed the steering wheel. "I didn't trust him."

*Well done on the breaking-my-heart thing. It just happened a
little sooner than I expected.*

She wondered what Hugo and Reuben had been talking
about at the party, if it wasn't Lemmy's murder. Probably Ollie's
erased loan.

Suddenly that seemed obvious. The fake evidence had been
the fake ledger, planted at the Galaxy. Reuben couldn't go there,
with the feds watching, so Hugo had done it—snuck into a gangster's office so Ollie wouldn't lose his house, probably during the
day when the nightclub was quiet.

That's why we had you do it, Reuben had said, *and you handled
it like a pro. Quick in and out, planted the fake evidence, and now
Lemmy is dead and everything is good.*

They were glad Lemmy was dead because he couldn't tell Moe Kravitz, but they didn't kill him.

"Cars move faster than I remember," Ollie mused.

"Sorry, I can slow down if you want."

"No, go faster. We're on a rescue mission."

Kate pressed harder on the accelerator and passed an old Model T, eager to find answers—and Hugo.

"Here," Ollie said. "I shelled some peanuts for you."

"Thank you." She held out her hand. "I'm glad we're doing this together."

"Me too."

She finally turned off State Route 15 onto Willow Street. They passed shops and houses, and then a strange sight appeared ahead of them, a few miles away.

A low, rounded hill was covered in tall oil derricks—hundreds of them, close together, towers of wooden scaffolding spiking upward, making the hill look like it was covered in sharp fur.

"Signal Hill," Ollie said. "But they call it Porcupine Hill."

"I see why. I thought we were in Long Beach."

"We are. Long Beach surrounds Signal Hill. There's oil all around here. You can smell it."

"Yes," Kate agreed. A thick, oily, sulfur smell.

They passed a few towering derricks along the road, intermingled with houses, schools, and billboards.

Ollie held the map. "Turn right at this corner. And then the second left."

Kate turned, and then turned again onto Rowland Drive. She pulled the car up at the curb in front of 1640 Rowland Drive and turned off the engine. She stared out the window in amazement.

"Well, I wasn't expecting that," Ollie said.

They both got out and stood side by side, exactly where Ollie and Frank Fairchild had posed for a photo, many years ago. The fence was still there, dividing the land, but the two properties had changed significantly, in different ways.

The property on the right looked abandoned. The wooden oil derricks, weather beaten. The pumps, silent.

The property on the left had newer derricks, and Kate could hear the pumps at work, filling the air with the heavy smell of fossil fuel long buried beneath the earth. There was a small office building with a sign: FAIRCHILD OIL COMPANY, 1640 ROWLAND DRIVE, LONG BEACH.

"Ollie, she isn't leaving you a house. It's her oil wells."

"Why would she do that? Frank had lots of investments, but the oil was always one of his best incomes. She should leave it to her daughter."

"It does seem strange." Kate hugged herself, feeling the damp chill of ocean air. "Why go to the effort of changing her will on the same day she snuck into your house and took the frog and photo? It's all connected, Ollie."

"I don't see how."

Kate tipped her head, studying the two properties in front of her. "Ollie . . . you and Frank were standing on the wrong sides." She went to the car, retrieved the photo, and held it up. Ollie stood on the left, Frank on the right.

"The photo must be reversed," Ollie said. "Like when you put a slide in the projector the wrong way."

"No . . . look at the house." Kate pointed to the house far behind Frank in the photo—the neighbor who wouldn't sell his land. Then she pointed to the real house in front of them, still on the right, behind the barren, unproductive property.

She understood, all at once, but didn't want to tell Ollie.

He figured it out on his own, pointing to the productive side, with its working pumps. "That's my land. Those are my oil wells."

Kate waited for that to sink in before adding more weight. "I think he cheated you, Ollie."

"No," he said in low disbelief. "It must have been some sort of mix up."

"The old letters he bought for you at auction were forgeries. I thought the auction house cheated him, but I think Frank must have been in on it. Or maybe the auction house never existed, and Frank hired someone to forge the letters. Did you ever see the auction house?"

"No," Ollie said quietly. "I never saw any of it. The orange orchards. The houses he bought and rented out for me. I wrote checks to his investment company, and he gave me paperwork showing what I owned. Investing in the future, he said."

Kate could picture it easily—Ollie, suddenly rich and famous, accepting the advice of a friend who had a good head for business.

"I had to sell everything when the stock market crashed," Ollie said. "Frank handled that too. I got very little back, but that wasn't surprising. The entire country was in a depression, everyone losing everything." He gave a hollow laugh. "Only, I didn't have anything to lose. I'd already given it to Frank."

"He stole it," Kate said. "Used you as his personal piggy bank, and when your land struck oil, he pretended it was his. Probably forged some documents, in case you ever noticed, knowing he could fast talk you into believing you were wrong."

Ollie huffed a bitter laugh. "That was Frank—a fast talker."

Kate looked at the photo in her hand, trying to understand what it had to do with Lemmy's murder. "This photograph proves that he switched the properties—that you own all that oil. Did Mrs. Fairchild know about this photo?"

"She's the one who took the picture that day. Put it in a frame and brought it over. Helped me find a place to put it, beneath the sword Frank gave me." Ollie paused. "She used to make up little excuses like that to come over. I knew what she was up to but never let it go anywhere. We were just good friends."

"I think she loved you, Ollie. If she knew her husband was cheating you, she would have told you."

"But she changed her will, so she *did* know."

Kate frowned, seeing that it didn't add up. "She must have found out recently."

"Frank died last year," Ollie said. "Maybe he told her on his deathbed."

Not out of guilt, Kate suspected, but fear of a lawsuit. "He warned her, Ollie. He knew how she felt about you, and that the two of you might get together someday and talk about finances. If you ever saw these oil wells and figured it out, you could sue his widow and child for millions of dollars for past profits. You could take everything they have."

"I wouldn't do that."

"Well, you should," Kate said fiercely. "All that money they've been spending is yours. Frank probably cheated other people too, and your lawsuit could lead to dozens more." She shivered in the damp air. It was all too familiar.

"He warned her," Ollie said faintly.

"It's just a guess, but it makes sense. She probably consoled herself that she could marry you, and then you'd have what was rightfully yours—and she'd have you. But she knew this photograph would give it all away. Ever since I arrived, she's been asking me to help her get back into your house on a social visit. When you left the house on Monday, she saw her chance."

"She took the frog too. I didn't even notice it was gone."

"And then Lemmy came home. She wasn't just embarrassed; her entire fortune was at stake—and her relationship with you." Kate imagined how horrified Mrs. Fairchild must have been, whirling to see Lemmy with his knowing smirk. "He didn't know why she was there but must have sensed her fear. Knowing him, he blackmailed her—said he would keep quiet if she paid him."

"I never liked him much," Ollie muttered.

"She killed him in the kitchen. My guess, she pretended to go home for his blackmail money, and then snuck back inside, got the sword, and . . ." Kate couldn't say it.

Ollie made a small sound of disbelief. "Dorothy wouldn't kill someone."

But Kate had overheard another side of Dorothy Fairchild—growing up rough with a knife under her pillow, coming to Hollywood with nothing but ten dollars and a pretty face, almost marrying a mobster until a better deal came along.

She remembered something else too. "She killed Glenn today. I don't know why. Maybe Glenn overheard when Hugo confronted her and—" Kate was gripped by sudden panic. "*Ollie!* We have to go! We have to go *now!*" She ran around the car and had the engine running before Ollie had even opened his door.

"Where are we going?"

"Falcon Pictures! We have to find Hugo! He had the gun, but he wouldn't shoot Glenn or hide it in Aurelio's trailer. Mrs. Fairchild must have grabbed it from him. But Hugo wouldn't run away and hide—he would warn people—he would warn me!—unless he was too hurt to move! Ollie—hurry!"

Ollie pulled his door closed, and she pressed the gas pedal.

Kate kept the car moving at top speed along the highway, crossing lanes to pass slower vehicles.

Ollie asked, "If Hugo figured this out last night, why didn't he go to the police?"

"Probably the same reason he wanted to hide your sword—so your name wouldn't be caught up in a big scandal, just as you're starting to rebuild your life. The papers would love it—a beautiful killer and a stolen oil well fortune. He probably hoped she would give the oil back quietly, without reporters hearing about it." She glanced at her grandfather. "It was the reporters during my kidnapping that drove you inside."

"Not the reporters," he said somberly. "The realization that I wasn't a hero after all, just an ordinary fifty-year-old man."

"You've never been ordinary, Ollie."

"My granddaughter was missing, and then my daughter was dead, and I didn't save either of you."

Kate tightened her grip on the steering wheel. "We're saving Hugo now. That makes us both heroes." She had to believe that.

The traffic was heavier than it had been earlier. She weaved her way through the cars and trucks as quickly as she dared.

"That was brave of Hugo," Ollie said, "confronting her when he knew she killed Lemmy."

And foolhardy, Kate thought, especially taking the gun. A *precaution,* he'd called it. "He knew she wouldn't want a scandal hurting Bonnie's career. That's what he banked on, anyway—you getting your oil wells back without any fuss. And in return, he wouldn't tell the police about Lemmy."

"But then she would get away with murder."

Kate mulled that over. "I think he was more concerned about you getting your oil wells and rebuilding your life without a scandal. He doesn't care so much about Lemmy."

The guard at the gate of Falcon Pictures recognized Kate and waved her through, but she paused the car in front of him. "Do you know if the police have found the boy they were searching for? The one they think killed the tutor?"

"I know they took away the one who's an actor. They never found his friend. The two boys were working as a team, I guess. Probably stealing something, and the tutor got in the way. That's what I heard."

Kate resisted an urge to set him straight.

She drove as quickly as she dared through the narrow studio roads, weaving the car around the usual chaos. As they neared buildings five and six, she was glad to see the crowd and the police cars were gone. But her doubts rose. "Ollie . . . if the police couldn't find Hugo, how can we?"

"We'll find him, Kate," he said, with such hardy conviction she almost believed it.

The alley between Stages Five and Six was deserted. Kate

parked and was relieved when Ollie stepped out of the car without seeming overly anxious about being back at a studio. Whatever transformation he'd undergone taking off Captain Powell's hat seemed to have stuck. "Let's start in Stage Five," she said, hurrying that way. "That's where Glenn was killed." But the door wouldn't open. She yanked in frustration.

"Let's try the back," Ollie said.

"Yes!" Kate ran in that direction, glancing back to see Ollie huffing behind her. She tried the other door on that side of the building—locked—then ran around the back corner, near the storage building where she'd gotten the suits. The wide roll-up door along the backside of Stage Five was open a few inches. "This way, Ollie!" She grabbed the rope on the wall and pulled, and the door rolled up. When it was several feet off the ground, she wrapped the rope and ducked inside.

Kate halted, her chest tightening at the endless darkness in front of her.

Ollie entered beside her, gasping for breath. "Must be . . . a switch somewhere." He moved away from her along the outer wall, not seeming to mind the dark. Kate heard his echoing footsteps—a grunt as he ran into something—and then the sound of a large lever being pulled.

In the distance, a few lights flickered to life. Kate heard another lever, and more lights flickered on.

They'd entered the building behind the theater set, most of the enormous space out of view. Kate broke into a run, darting around equipment and plywood walls. "Hugo!"

Ollie's voice joined hers, moving the other direction.

She ducked under wooden beams. Peered into rolling carts. Ran around a supply truck and opened the back. "Hugo!" She trotted up the stairs onto the theater stage, searched it quickly, and then returned to the ground floor. She dropped to her belly to look under the stage—forced herself to crawl into the ominous shadows—but only found empty space. She crawled out, relieved to be back in open air.

Ollie's voice echoed in the distance. "We're coming, my boy!"

Kate halted when she reached the front of the stage and saw the front row of audience seats where Glenn had died. She forced herself to walk down the center aisle, looking carefully between each row of seats. "Hugo!" Now that she was in the wide, open space, her voice sounded small and frightened.

Much of the enormous building was open and visible, and they ran out of places to look.

"He isn't here!" Ollie called out.

"Let's go to Stage Six!" Kate ran toward the back of the building, waited for Ollie, and they ducked under the rolling door together.

Across the pavement, Mrs. Fairchild emerged from the storage building where Kate had gotten the suits. She saw them and halted, looking harried, her eyes widening. "Ollie! What are you doing here?" The blood seemed to drain from her face.

"You!" Ollie cried with furious venom. He stalked toward her.

"I . . . I just found that boy in here. He's been shot. I think he's dead." Mrs. Fairchild opened the door to the storage building behind her.

CHAPTER 33

Kate felt strangely numb as she hurried into the long hall lined with numbered doors. Hugo couldn't be dead. She would have felt the new black hole in the universe. The sudden emptiness in her heart.

She hadn't felt it when her parents had died.

"I just found him and was running to call the police." Mrs. Fairchild reached for the latch on the third door, her hands shaking.

Kate rushed past her into the storage room and then halted, her gaze flying, only seeing Civil War uniforms and full-skirted dresses. Barrels of rifles and piles of hats. She spun, searching.

"There he is!" Ollie ran past her and crouched on the floor in the back corner. Kate hurried after him and saw Hugo curled on his side, his eyes closed, unresponsive as Ollie patted his cheek and tried to rouse him. "I don't think he's breathing."

Kate dropped beside Hugo's legs with a terrified whimper. The white catering jacket was covered in blood. She picked up his hand, and it was cold and lifeless. "Hugo" was all she could say. His fingers moved slightly against hers, and she nearly sobbed in relief. "He's alive, Ollie! His hand moved!"

"Thank God."

"Aurelio must have done it," Mrs. Fairchild said in a quavering voice, still back in the doorway. "I'm so glad they arrested him."

Ollie shot a furious look over his shoulder. "*You* did this! Over some *stupid* oil wells! You think I care about that?"

"You . . . you know about the oil?"

"Kate looked at the photo and figured it out. She's smart that way." He added bitterly, "Smarter than her grandfather." He shifted out of the way, allowing Kate to move closer to Hugo.

"It's Kate. Can you hear me?" She touched Hugo's cheek, but he showed no signs of awareness, his eyes closed. "I'm . . . I'm going to call an ambulance." Her arm brushed something wet, and she forced her attention from his pallid face to the blood-soaked jacket. He could bleed to death before the ambulance arrived. "I'm going to try to bandage you first." Her fingers fumbled with the jacket buttons, which were slick with blood.

Ollie seethed, "What a fool I was, thinking you and Frank were my friends."

"I didn't know." Mrs. Fairchild's voice broke with tears. "Frank never involved me in his business—you know that. He didn't tell me until he was dying. I was horrified."

It was hard to open the small shirt buttons with him lying on his side. "Hugo, I'm going to move you." He didn't show any signs of having heard. Carefully, she rotated him onto his back. She didn't want to hurt him, but the fact that he showed no pain at all didn't seem good. Her fingers trembled on the last few buttons, then she opened his shirt to find his chest covered in blood.

She felt light-headed and had to drop her head, breathing through her mouth.

"I wanted to give the oil wells back," Mrs. Fairchild said, still in the doorway. "But how could I? You didn't come to the funeral. I wrote a letter, begging you to call me, but you didn't."

Kate inhaled and forced herself to inspect Hugo's chest,

searching for the wound. She found a small bullet entry—not as horrible as she'd feared—and then a worse opening around his side, perhaps the exit wound.

"You broke into my house and killed Lemmy over a stupid photo!"

"I didn't mean for that to happen. He walked in as I was picking up the photo. Oh, Ollie, he was a horrible man! Said he had photos of Bonnie that would ruin her career unless I paid him off. I went home for the money, but when I came back—I don't know—I can't explain it. He said vile things, and I panicked."

The wounds weren't bleeding much now, which seemed like a positive sign. Or maybe a bad sign that his heart had slowed. Kate moaned and pressed her bloodied fingers to Hugo's throat, feeling for a pulse.

"You'll hang for this," Ollie said.

Mrs. Fairchild sobbed weakly. "I know. I've been in hell, waiting for the police to show up. I knew my fingerprints were on the sword, but by the time I calmed down enough to go back, you were home. I called my attorney to change my will, sure I would hang. I wanted to prove to you that I wanted to give the oil back. That I wasn't part of it."

Kate felt a feeble pulse in Hugo's neck and whimpered in relief. She wrapped her hands around his pale face. "I'm sorry I doubted you, Hugo." She kissed his forehead, then his icy lips.

"Frank is gone now, Ollie, and we can be together."

"You think I want to be with you after you've shot Hugo?"

"It was an accident. He forced me to come into this building. Said he would tell the police about the man I killed unless I gave you the oil. I wanted that too, Ollie, but he frightened me. I tried to take the gun—to protect myself—and it went off. I didn't mean to shoot him. I ran to call an ambulance."

"But you didn't," Ollie snapped. "You left him to die."

"I ran into Stage Five to find a phone, and Bonnie's tutor saw me with the gun. I tried to explain, and he insisted I sit down. I felt so faint. I don't know what happened next."

"You shot him in the temple," Kate snapped over her shoulder. "Then hid the gun in Aurelio's trailer. I don't think you were quite as frazzled as you pretend. Ollie—we have to call an ambulance."

"Yes, of course." He started to rise.

Hugo moaned.

Kate and Ollie both cried out and bent over him. His eyes fluttered open, met Kate's briefly, and then closed again. "We're here," she said. "We're going to get you help."

The shadows deepened, the light dimming.

The door closing.

Kate screamed and scrambled to her feet, lunging toward the opening, watching in horror as the door swung shut, taking the light with it.

The world went dark.

Her hands hit the door a second too late. She banged with her fists, her heart exploding in panic. "No, please, you can't!" She ran her hands over the smooth surface, feeling for a knob she knew wasn't there. "We won't tell anyone!" Her fingers found the side edge and managed to get a grip. The door opened a crack, bringing a line of light.

A strong hand yanked it closed, and Kate heard a padlock slide into the latch.

"No, please," Kate cried, her hands clawing at the edge. "You have to let me out—*you have to let me out!*"

"Dorothy, open that door!" Ollie shouted.

Mrs. Fairchild wailed back, "I went to your house so we could be together, so that photo wouldn't come between us!"

"I'll make sure you hang for this!"

There was a moment of silence before Mrs. Fairchild said in a leaden voice, "You don't mean that, Ollie. I know you love me."

"I never loved you! I felt *sorry* for you, and I felt sorry for Frank for having to deal with your constant moods!"

"Please," Kate begged, struggling to hold back the terror. "Please let us out."

Mrs. Fairchild said more calmly, "Tell me where that photo is, and I will. That's why I came back after the police left, but the boy doesn't have it on him."

"It's in the car!" Kate cried. "I'll give you the photo if you open the door! Please—just let us out!"

Mrs. Fairchild's footsteps clicked away.

"No," Kate wailed, pressing her forehead against the door.

"She'll be back," Ollie said with false bravado, still at the back of the room with Hugo.

But Kate knew she wouldn't. Her voice had been too calm. Ollie didn't love her. If she came back, the truth would come out, and she would be arrested. Her only hope was to take that photo and leave them to die. The movie was canceled, and Stages Five and Six would be deserted for the next week or two until the next picture was scheduled. No one would find them until it was too late.

Kate heard the outside door opening. She pressed her fingers to the faint glow at the edge of the door, holding on to it as long as she could.

The hall light snapped out.

Kate's eyes widened, straining but seeing nothing.

She screamed—a scream pulled from her lungs, filling the black void. Her legs buckled, and she sank to the ground. She curled her knees into her chest.

"Kate." Vaguely, through the scream that wouldn't stop, she heard Ollie calling her name, and then he was behind her, his arms around her. "I'm here. You're not alone this time."

The scream ran out of air. Kate needed air. Her lungs tightened in panic. She grabbed at Ollie's arms around her chest.

His arms squeezed, holding her together, his cheek pressed against hers. "I'm here."

She stretched up her chin. "Can't . . . breathe."

"Plenty of air in here. Let's breathe together." He made an exaggerated sound of inhaling.

She gulped a mouthful of darkness.

"Now let it out slowly." He exhaled loudly, the warmth hitting the side of her face. She managed a weak puff. "Good girl. Now in again, deep into your lungs." He made another noisy inhalation.

Kate drew a ragged breath and released it. Then another, pulling a little deeper, her lungs stretching.

"I'm here with you, Kate. I'm not going anywhere."

Not going anywhere. Trapped forever in endless darkness. A tidal wave of panic rose inside her, the scream rising. Ollie seemed to sense it, pulling her against him. "Hang on, Kate. I'm here." His arms squeezed, holding back the panic.

Slowly, breath by breath, heartbeat by heartbeat, her body relaxed and her lungs loosened, allowing more air.

"All my fault," she croaked. "If I'd given the sword to the police—her fingerprints—"

"Wouldn't have proved anything. She would have said they were from years ago."

"I should have trusted Hugo." Tears slid down her face. "I thought he killed Lemmy and Glenn. He would never think that of me."

"We found him, and he's going to be fine. Take a moment to catch your breath, and we'll find a way out of here."

"People are dead because of me. I write lists, but I keep making mistakes."

"Hush, now. You're the most capable person I've ever met."

"It's an act. People think my father was the fraud, but I'm the biggest fraud of all. I'm not smart. I'm not sensible." She inhaled a shuddering breath. "Mommy died because of me."

She sat perfectly still, listening to the dark silence.

She said it again with more force. "Mommy died because of

me!" It felt good to finally say it aloud. She shouted it into the dark. *"Your Evie is dead because of me!"*

Ollie squeezed her arm. "Don't say that," he ordered, a new chill in his voice.

Kate liked that chill. Wanted to be punished. "I lied to the police! I lied to everyone, so no one would know it was my fault!"

His arms slackened around her. "What are you talking about?"

"There wasn't any chloroform! He didn't hide in the house and grab me! The newspapers wrote that, and Aunt Lorna talked about it, and the police asked me if he put a funny-smelling rag over my nose—so I went along with it. I made up a big fat lie about chloroform and the trunk of his car, but he never forced me to go with him."

"Of course he did." Ollie's voice was as heavy as the dark. "You were kidnapped."

Kate said it aloud for the first time, shouting it into the black void. "I went willingly! I packed an overnight bag!"

The confession echoed and slowly settled.

"That's not true," Ollie murmured, his arms loose around her.

She spoke more calmly, her throat raw. "It is true. He knocked on the door, and I walked to his car."

"Why would you?"

Kate remembered it clearly. The evening sunset behind the quiet-looking man on the doorstep. Her parents gone to a cocktail party, as they so often were.

"Kate?"

"He said he'd been at the party with my parents, and they'd all decided to spend the weekend at his house in Woodside. To see his new horses. My parents were in the roadster, so they'd asked him to swing by and pick me up. He waited downstairs while I packed my bag."

"You were thirteen. He told a convincing lie."

"But it wasn't convincing. I knew Mommy would have called and told me, but he was shy and awkward, and I didn't want him to think I didn't trust him. We drove out of the city on this dark road with big trees, and every time we stopped at an intersection, I knew I should get out and run, but I didn't want to make him feel bad."

Kate had thought about that car ride a million times in the last four years, wishing—so much futile wishing—that she'd jumped out and fled.

"He kidnapped you, Kate."

"He didn't trap me in that car; I trapped myself. I sat there making polite conversation while he told me about his niece in the hospital. And when I saw the house in the woods, I knew Mommy and Daddy would never stay at a place like that, but I didn't want to embarrass him by saying his house wasn't good enough. So I walked inside, but there wasn't any furniture." A sob escaped her. "I tried to run, and he grabbed me."

Ollie's arms tightened around her. "I'm so sorry, Kate."

She wanted to tell him everything and never say it again. "There was a hole in the closet floor, and he threw me in. I fell on a mattress and looked up to see the latch closing. I heard it lock. He said there was food and water and he would be back. But he never came back. And it was all my fault."

"It wasn't your fault. He was a horrible man."

Kate sniffed back tears. "He just wanted his money back. Daddy stole from him—over a million dollars."

"That wasn't your fault either. Your father fooled a lot of people."

"He fooled me." Kate worked her hands out of Ollie's hug and wiped her face. "He's still fooling me. My head knows he was a bad person, but sometimes I still feel like I love him."

"Of course you do. He was your father." Ollie patted her gently.

"I don't feel like I'm allowed to love him. Or remember the good things, like decorating the Christmas tree, and the way he used to sing in this loud, silly voice. If I remember those things, it's like he's fooling me all over again."

"His love for you was real, Kate."

A low moan came from the back corner.

"Hugo!" Kate scrambled up, appalled she'd left him—and then froze, facing darkness. She carefully felt her way around a barrel of rifles, her heart racing, then used a rack of costumes as her guide, her hands moving along the wool sleeves. She sank to the floor and crawled the rest of the way. "Hugo, I'm here." Her hands fumbled over his bloody jacket before finding his shoulders, and then the sides of his face. She kissed his lips, which were tight and cold. "You're freezing."

Ollie said behind her, "I'll find something to warm him up."

"I'm so sorry about last night, Hugo. Ollie and I drove to Long Beach. We figured it out and came to find you."

"Mm" was all he managed.

Ollie dropped heavy wool soldiers' uniforms over Hugo's legs. "Bundle him up."

Kate tucked the coats around Hugo. "I thought you were dead."

"Acting," he said in a thin voice. "Didn't want her to shoot me again."

"Kate, come help me with this door," Ollie called. "Maybe we can pull off the hinges."

She didn't want to leave Hugo. She ran her fingers over his face to orient herself and kissed his lips again. "I'll be back."

"Counting on that," he rasped.

Kate made her way carefully in the dark, her arms outstretched. She stumbled into the barrel of rifles, then touched Ollie's back.

"Hinges are on the inside," he said. "There's a bolt we need to slide up, but my fingers are too big. You try."

They switched places, Kate moving close to the door. Her fingers found the metal hinge just over her head. It felt rusted and immovable. "I wish my hands would stop shaking."

"I'll get something to warm you up." Ollie shuffled behind her and returned to drape heavy fabric over her shoulders. She tried to put her arms into sleeves, but only found slits—a cloak, she realized. She slid her arms through the slits and did the top button, and the warmth felt good.

She kept working on the hinge. "Are you all right, Hugo?"

"Still breathing," he said weakly.

Ollie murmured near her ear. "How long do you figure we've been in here? A half hour?"

"Maybe." She hesitated. "Why?"

He kept his voice low. "I expect she'll be back with a gun soon."

Kate drew a sharp breath. "She wouldn't shoot *you*, Ollie."

"I think we left her no choice. She can't take the chance of someone finding us or us escaping."

He was right. "I'll try the lower hinge." Kate crouched on the ground.

"I think we better prepare for battle. You keep working on that, and I'll get us some weapons. At least we have plenty of options in here."

"Ollie—they're all fake."

"A fake sword still strikes a hard blow—I should know. And we'll have the element of surprise." She heard him searching behind her. "What do you fancy? A rifle with bayonet? Dagger? Pistol? The Civil War had everything." Something toppled over. "Aha! I found the swords, my weapon of choice. Good reach with a sword."

"Ollie, we can't fight her with movie props!" Kate's fingernail was in shreds, digging into the hinge.

"What you need is a hat. That'll help you get into character."

Kate growled in frustration. "I don't need a hat!" She stood to work on the top hinge again. "Hugo, say something so I know you're all right."

"You need a hat," he said in the ghost of a voice.

She laughed weakly.

A moment later, Ollie placed something on her head, and she reached up to feel a straw bonnet. "Hold still while I tie the ribbons. It'll help you stay warm."

She lifted her chin, her fingers tugging at the rusty metal.

Ollie asked quietly, "Any chance with the hinges?"

She lowered her hands, her fingertips burning. "I don't think so."

"Here, I brought you a sword." He pressed the handle into her palm. "Are you right-handed?"

"Yes, but—"

"We'll go over a few basic moves. It all starts with good feet. En garde position."

"Ollie—"

"Spread your feet a little, right foot pointed forward, left pointed out. I wish I could see you. Are your feet about a foot apart?"

"Yes," she said to appease him. Then, so it wasn't a lie, she positioned her feet as he'd said.

"Hold out your sword to touch mine. Where is it?" Their swords tapped. "There! Bend your knees a little. Advance on your right foot, retreat on your left—but we don't have enough room for that, so we'll just tap the swords a few times. Ready?"

His sword banged into hers, nearly knocking it from her hand. She stiffened her hold.

"Now hit my sword back," he said.

Kate complied, tightening her grip so her sword met his with equal force. They repeated the move a few times, the swords striking each other a little differently each time, her body moving with the hits. The metal made a satisfying clanging sound.

"How is this going to help us fight off a gun?" she asked.

"It isn't. Just warming our blood and calming our nerves." His sword knocked hers out of her hand. "Sorry. Good job, though. Better than Hugo."

"Hey," he protested weakly.

"We better get into position. We need the advantage of height. I always leaped on my enemies from higher ground. Help me stack boxes near the door."

Kate didn't argue, knowing it was pointless, and it felt good to move. She and Ollie fumbled about in the dark, finding crates and stacking them on either side of the door. She asked, "Shouldn't we be stacking them in front of the door, so she can't open it?"

"We're not trying to barricade ourselves in, we're fighting our way out. Here." He pressed a sword back into Kate's hand. "We'll each take a side." He nudged her toward the side of the door with hinges, and she heard him move to the side that would open.

She climbed onto the crates, a foot or two off the ground, and then cautiously straightened, her legs shaking. She gripped the fake sword, knowing it was completely useless against a gun. "Are you there, Hugo?" Her voice trembled.

"I'm here, Kate." His voice sounded stronger.

She heard the outside door open, and a bright light appeared around the edge of their door. Kate squeezed her sweaty palms around the fake sword, listening as the click of Mrs. Fairchild's footsteps drew closer. They could attack, but all Mrs. Fairchild had to do was pull a trigger. They couldn't outrun a bullet.

Ollie declared fiercely, "We fight for our lives, our liberty, and the people we love!" In the glow from around the door, Kate could just make out his shadowy form. He had his sword raised above his head, and she copied his stance.

The padlock rattled as Mrs. Fairchild removed it. She must have left it unlocked, only looped through the latch, knowing she would come back. Knowing she had to kill them. The door cracked open and the barrel of a handgun appeared. Ollie swung down, and a deafening shot rang out. The gun flew from Mrs. Fairchild's hand, skittering across the floor.

Kate jumped down and yanked the door open, filling the storage room with glorious light. "Are you shot?" she cried.

"Not a scratch." Ollie grabbed Mrs. Fairchild's arm and shoved her into the wall, then stood back with the tip of his sword pressed against her back, looking completely legitimate in his Civil War uniform and general's hat.

"Ollie," Mrs. Fairchild whimpered. She tried to turn to see him, but Ollie tightened his grip on her shoulder, the sword touching her spine.

Kate picked up the handgun and tried to give it to Ollie, but he didn't flinch. "Put it in my pocket," he ordered, and she complied. "Now, run for reinforcements."

An ambulance. Kate glanced at Hugo, who lifted a feeble hand in approval, then darted into the hall. The long cloak got in her way, so she lifted it with both hands. The straw bonnet slid off the back of her head, held on by the ribbons beneath her chin. She ran out the door, into a beautiful October sunset.

There would be a phone in Stage Five. Kate ducked under the roll-up door and ran around the theater set, trying to guess where the phone would be, glad they'd left the lights on. She rounded the front corner of the stage set—and pulled up short.

Clive Falcon and two men with cameras stood near the front row where Glenn had been shot. "That's the seat, boys. You can see the red stain." A flashbulb popped. "Are you sure we can't make the evening edition?"

"Hey!" Kate shouted, her blood boiling.

The men turned.

"Kitty Hildebrand!" Clive Falcon cried, delighted. "She's the one who found him. Kitty, can we get a photo of you standing next to the chair?"

"I'll give you something better than that," she shot back. "You want the publicity photo of your life? It's in the storage building behind us. The killer has just been captured by a true hero—my grandfather, Oliver Banks. Put *that* on your front page!"

Kate saw a phone on the wall, lifted the cloak, and ran.

EPILOGUE

A cool November breeze came through the Quicks' kitchen window, but sweat rolled down Kate's temple as she stood at the counter, peeling potatoes over a big bowl. Esther had made it look easy when she'd demonstrated, but the potato peeler seemed to have a mind of its own, sticking when Kate wanted it to slide over curves, sliding when she wanted it to stop.

She used her wrist to push back a strand of damp hair on her forehead.

"Try to not cut off so much," Esther said, glancing over Kate's shoulder. "Just get the skin and eyes, so you don't waste the potato."

"Eyes?" Kate stared at the half-bald potato in her hand.

Esther smiled, reaching for the peeler. "I'll do it."

"Peeling potatoes is the easiest job there is," twelve-year-old Maureen said, looking up from the puzzle she was doing on the kitchen table. "If she can't do that, what can she do?"

"More than you," sixteen-year-old Rose said, crimping the crust of an apple pie. "You're hopeless in the kitchen. Besides, Kate doesn't have to cook. She's our guest."

"But I want to help," Kate said. She'd been excited about

cooking a Thanksgiving dinner with Hugo's mother and sisters, but so far, she'd only felt in the way in the cramped kitchen. Her first task had been taking the rolls out of the oven, and she'd dropped the hot pan on the floor. Mrs. Quick had hastily picked them up with a reassuring, "Don't worry, Kate, I mopped yesterday."

"I don't know why you started that puzzle in here, Maureen," Esther said, peeling a potato with remarkable speed. "We need the table space."

"She wants to be by Kate," Rose said with a knowing look.

"Me?" Maureen scoffed, placing a puzzle piece. "You're the one always talking about her clothes."

Rose flashed an apologetic smile at Kate. "You do have nice clothes. I like that dress you're wearing. I read in a magazine that teal is the color of the season, but I don't look good in it."

"I think you'd look good in any color, Rose," Kate said, and she meant it. Rose was beautiful, with a flock of boys after her that kept her father angry and Rose sneaking out of her bedroom window.

Mrs. Quick opened the oven door, releasing the warm, savory aroma of a turkey roasting. She stuck a baster in the pan, drew up liquid, and dribbled it over the pale turkey. "Such a big bird this year, it's going to take forever to cook. We'll be eating late."

"We can put out more hors d'oeuvres," Esther said, dropping another potato into the bowl of cold water. Kate had noticed that she often took charge, while Mrs. Quick was more soft-spoken. "Kate, you can make the pimento dip. That's easy."

Kate wasn't sure what pimento dip was but said, "All right."

She went to the sink to wash the potato dirt off her hands and saw Ollie through the window, teaching nine-year-old Shanny how to fight with stick swords in the backyard. Shanny advanced, her stick whacking with solid hits, her body in proper fighting stance, as Ollie stepped back, losing ground. But he hooted in delight.

Kate had gotten him into a clothing store recently, and he had a fresh haircut.

Six weeks ago, while Hugo had been in surgery, they'd all eyed one another suspiciously from opposite ends of the waiting room: Hugo's parents and Esther on one side; Kate, Ollie, Reuben, and Aurelio on the other. But after the doctor had entered to say surgery had gone well and a full recovery was expected, they'd all hugged and shaken hands and introduced themselves. Since then—with Hugo recuperating at home with his mother's nursing, and Ollie's household making frequent visits—they'd all become comfortable together.

"I guess Kate could do the olives," Maureen said, looking up from the puzzle. "You do know how to use a can opener, don't you?"

"Don't be sarcastic, Maureen," Mrs. Quick chided. "Everyone knows how to use a can opener." She touched Kate's shoulder. "Why don't you go keep Hugo company."

"But—"

"There isn't much left to do. You can help Shanny set the table later."

Kate didn't argue twice.

She walked into the adjoining living room and found Hugo where he'd spent much of his time in the last few weeks, reclined across the sofa. He shifted straighter when he saw her, bending his knees to make room for her at the far end—where Kate should remain, it had been made clear by Mrs. Quick.

After a week in the hospital, he'd spent his first days home in bed. Kate had liked sitting in his small boyhood room, teasing him about the Flash Gordon poster on the wall, reading his favorite books aloud. But she'd been relegated to a stiff chair by the door, and Maureen had always remained in the room, reading on fifteen-year-old Brendan's bed—not conducive to a romantic visit, or even a long one.

When Hugo had recovered enough to recline on the sofa,

Kate had been offered an armchair a safe distance away, with Mrs. Quick catching up on her mending near the window. Or sometimes, Maureen with her book.

A few weeks ago, Hugo had relapsed suddenly and been rushed in for a second, more complicated surgery and five days in the hospital. After that, Mrs. Quick had seem relieved whenever Kate showed up to distract him from his pain and boredom, even suggesting Kate sit at the far end of the sofa so Hugo didn't have to shout across the room.

But still, no privacy in the crowded house. And still, after all this time, just that one real kiss between them.

Today, Hugo had more color in his cheeks, and she could tell from the way he sat—only slightly reclined—that he wasn't in much pain. She dared to hold his hand briefly, glancing at Mr. Quick and Reuben playing gin rummy across the room, before sitting at the opposite end of the sofa.

"So," he said, his eyes drinking her in. "We've discovered something you're not so good at."

"You heard all that?"

"More entertaining than the radio." The corner of his mouth lifted. "I'm guessing you've never used a can opener."

She pushed against his leg, unable to deny it. "How did *you* learn to cook? Your brother never helps in the kitchen."

Hugo shrugged. "I like to cook. Brendan doesn't. How's the dinner situation at Ollie's place these days?"

Kate lifted her voice to be heard across the room. "The only thing Reuben knows how to cook is stew."

"Hey," Reuben griped, staring at his cards. "I made roast chicken on Sunday, and everybody liked it."

Kate grimaced at Hugo, making him laugh.

He dared to stretch out one of his legs, tucking his toes under her hip—a little trick they'd learned. "Aurelio called and told me about his new movie role. Sounds like a big deal and a lot of money. How come he didn't come today?"

"He's having Thanksgiving with Bonnie in San Diego." Bonnie had moved in with her uncle's family. "I talked to her on the phone yesterday."

"How is she doing?" Hugo asked.

"She needs to be closer to Hollywood. The studio is trying to figure out a living situation." Mrs. Fairchild had been denied bail while she awaited trial, and the beautiful house next door to Ollie's sat empty. "She starts rehearsing for her new movie next week. The publicity team has done a great job spinning the story, making her out to be a sympathetic, innocent victim of her mother's crime."

"She *is* an innocent victim," Hugo said.

"She is," Kate agreed. "And I'm glad her career wasn't ruined because of it. In fact, it's probably helped. Everyone knows her name now, and that's half the battle of stardom."

"Such a pro," Hugo teased, his toes prodding her hip. Then, more seriously, "Do you miss all the excitement?"

Kate hesitated before admitting, "Yes. And I wish I'd gotten a movie role for you before it all ended. And I wanted Reuben to audition for the music department."

Hugo glanced at Reuben and lowered his voice. "He said he likes his new bookkeeping job. Not much money, though."

"That's one good thing that came out of you getting shot, Hugo. Reuben was so upset, he stood up to Moe Kravitz and refused to go back."

Six-year-old Clare pranced into the room and deposited a fuzzy toy dog on Kate's lap. "This is Mr. Puppy. Pretend I don't know where he is." She pranced out.

Kate laughed. "She's adorable."

"Spoiled rotten." But Hugo smiled.

"Speaking of furry pets," Kate said. "Your dog misses you and still needs a name."

"I told you . . . his name is *the dog*."

"I thought you were supposed to be some sort of brilliant writer or something. Rover, at least."

Hugo perked up. "Hey, speaking of writing, guess who came by to visit, wanting help with her script?"

Kate's eyes widened. "Stella Nixon—*here*?" Kate liked the Quicks' small, cramped house, but it felt very far away from Hollywood.

He grinned. "My mom didn't like her much. Opened all the windows to air out the cigarettes. And Stella used the nice candy dish as an ashtray. But she offered me a job when I'm ready. Typing mostly, I think, but some story development too."

Kate squealed and grabbed Hugo's calves. "Hugo!"

"What's going on?" Mr. Quick asked sharply, looking up from his cards, and Kate hastily let go.

Hugo fought a smile. "Oh, she's just excited about derivatives."

"Right," Reuben drawled. Surprisingly, he and Mr. Quick got along quite well. Reuben said it was because he let Mr. Quick win at gin rummy, but Kate had heard them talking about politics, and they seemed to have similar views.

Hugo whispered to her, "I haven't told my family about the job yet, in case it doesn't happen."

She whispered back, "It will happen, Hugo, and it's just the start." She wrapped a reassuring hand around his ankle, and for a moment their eyes held, making her remember what it had felt like to dance in his arms.

He smiled slowly. "So . . . how *are* those derivatives lately?"

She laughed, releasing his ankle. "Very well, thank you for asking. The teacher is good. Better than my teacher at Blakely." Kate had enrolled at Pasadena Junior College, which taught grades eleven, twelve, thirteen, and fourteen, but she only planned to stay one year before leaving for a full university. "And . . . speaking of school . . ." A coy smile played at her lips.

"You look very mysterious, all of a sudden."

She'd imagined what this moment would be like, telling him.

"As you know, I've always planned on attending Cal Berkeley, up in the Bay Area."

"Very far away," Hugo murmured.

"Not *very* far, but a day on a train, yes. Well, I'm not sure if you're aware, but Cal Berkeley has an extension here in Los Angeles. It's a newer campus, but growing fast, and not *very* far away. In fact, it's *very* close, so . . ." She felt breathless, seeing the look on his face. "I visited the campus a few days ago and decided to attend there next fall and keep living with Ollie."

"Kate" was all he said, but she saw the rest in his eyes.

Mr. Quick and Reuben stood, talking about automobile parts, and walked out the front door.

Leaving them alone for the first time in six weeks.

Kate felt shy suddenly, unsure what to do.

But Hugo's smile turned roguish. "You're not going to stay all the way over there, are you?" He crooked his finger, beckoning her closer.

She gave a small, relieved laugh and moved to sit at the edge of the sofa beside him—and as soon as his hand touched her waist, everything melted inside her. Their lips met in a soft kiss that quickly warmed, lingering. Hugo separated long enough to give her a private smile, and then their mouths found each other again, arms sliding around backs, heads leaning in to one another. Her hand roamed his warm shirt and felt the bandage along his side, but she was too preoccupied to understand what that meant for a moment.

Then he flinched.

"Sorry," she murmured, pulling back. "I don't want to hurt you."

"This is the best I've felt in a long time." His hand slid behind her neck, drawing her back for another kiss, this one hungrier, and the room disappeared, leaving only Hugo and his arms around her, and their lips wanting more.

"They're kissing!" Shanny's voice cried from the doorway. "You owe me a nickel, Rose!"

They separated with a breathy laugh. "I always knew you were dangerous," Kate said, starting to rise.

But Hugo caught her hand. "Just stay and talk. I want to hear about this fancy new school of yours."

"University of California at Los Angeles," she said, sitting back beside him.

"So . . . ?" His fingers wrapped around hers between their hips, out of view if someone walked in. "What have you decided? Are you going to be a big-time movie producer or a big-time astronomer?"

Kate had pondered that question a lot in the last few weeks. She'd loved working at the studio and missed it. But whenever she looked through her telescope, jotting notes in her astronomy notebook, her pulse quickened and she lost track of time. And when her *Sky* magazine had arrived in the mail two days ago, she'd lain on the green velvet sofa for hours, turning pages.

"I made a list for each career, analyzing the pros and cons."

"And what did you conclude?" Hugo asked.

"I threw the lists away." She smiled, remembering the moment. "I'm going to step into the dark and see where life takes me. It's a little scary, not having my course mapped out, but it's a big world out there, and I don't want to be afraid of it." She'd never looked into Hugo's eyes this closely before—another universe she wanted to explore. "I've learned something since coming here." She leaned forward, brushed her lips against his, and then whispered in his ear, "The sky is the limit."

ACKNOWLEDGMENTS

Thank you to my agent, Barbara Poelle, for responding with ALL-CAPS ENTHUSIASM when I pitched the idea of a YA murder mystery set in Old Hollywood. Thank you to my editor, Ali Fisher, for your spot-on insights and expertise in shepherding my story through the publication process. Thank you to the entire team at Tor Teen for turning my words into a book, especially Lesley Worrell for such a sensational cover. Thanks also to Amy Stapp for that initial "Yes, please!" when I first started writing *Chasing Starlight*.

My heart overflows with love and gratitude for my talented wordsmithing friends: Jen White, Tiffany Odekirk, Brittany Larsen, Melanie Jacobson, and Aubrey Hartman. We meet once a week for friendship, good eats, and critiquing, in that order. They nudged this story in the right direction countless times. I don't know how anyone writes a book without them.

Love and appreciation for my supportive husband, Mark; our four remarkable children, who make parenting look easy; and wonderful Sabrina and Rosie.

I'm so grateful for Turner Classic Movies. I set out to watch a few old films to learn about moviemaking in the 1930s and quickly became an avid (obsessive) fan, my TV airing a nonstop stream of black-and-white singing, dancing, and snappy dialogue. Special thanks to the TCM hosts who've taught and entertained me so well: Ben Mankiewicz, Alicia Malone, Dave Karger, Eddie Muller, and Jacqueline Stewart. Your work is important. I especially loved learning about the role of women in moviemaking in Alicia Malone's book *Backwards and in Heels,* which helped form my main character, Kate, and the ever-fabulous Stella Nixon.

I won't try to list all the movies I treasure from this era, but do yourself a favor and watch *Stage Door, The Big Sleep, The More the Merrier, To Have and Have Not, You Can't Take It with You,* and *His Girl Friday.* Amazing dialogue in all of them. If you want to see the inspiration for Aurelio and Bonnie's dance audition, go online and watch Ginger Rogers and Fred Astaire in a short video called *Dance Class Swing Time 1936.* I've watched it a hundred times and still need more.

I'll add a warning: Vintage films are often sexist and racist. In a strange way, it's so blatant, it actually showcases how ignorant and abhorrent those attitudes are. One example from the pre-Code era of 1933 is a movie called *She Had to Say Yes,* which shows the standard practice of sexual harassment of working women during the Great Depression. It made my blood boil. Old movies are history lessons as well as entertainment, and sometimes that history shows its ugly side.

As I wrote this book, I often thought of my grandfather James Anderson, who was grateful to get a job as a propmaker at the MGM movie studio during the Great Depression and ended up staying thirty years. He always worked the graveyard shift, and then spent his days studying advanced mathematics for fun—a brilliant, deep-thinking man who never had a chance to attend college. His craftsmanship was part of the magic at MGM and gives me a personal connection to the Golden Age of Hollywood.